# POKÉMON™
## ADVENTURES
## RUBY & SAPPHIRE

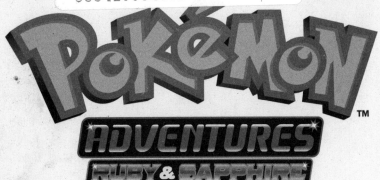

**Pokémon ADVENTURES
Ruby and Sapphire**
Volume 21
Perfect Square Edition

Story by **HIDENORI KUSAKA**
Art by **SATOSHI YAMAMOTO**

© 2014 Pokémon.
© 1995–2014 Nintendo/Creatures Inc./GAME FREAK inc.
TM, ®, and character names are trademarks of Nintendo.
POCKET MONSTERS SPECIAL Vol. 21
by Hidenori KUSAKA, Satoshi YAMAMOTO
© 1997 Hidenori KUSAKA, Satoshi YAMAMOTO
All rights reserved.
Original Japanese edition published by SHOGAKUKAN.
English translation rights in the United States of America, Canada,
the United Kingdom and Ireland arranged with SHOGAKUKAN.

English Adaptation/Bryant Turnage
Translation/Tetsuichiro Miyaki
Touch-up & Lettering/Annaliese Christman
Design/Shawn Carrico
Editor/Annette Roman

Printed in the U.S.A.

Published by VIZ Media, LLC
P.O. Box 77010
San Francisco, CA 94107

10 9 8 7 6 5 4 3 2 1
First printing, March 2014

www.perfectsquare.com     www.viz.com

# Pokémon™ Adventures
## Ruby & Sapphire

21
VOLUME TWENTY-ONE

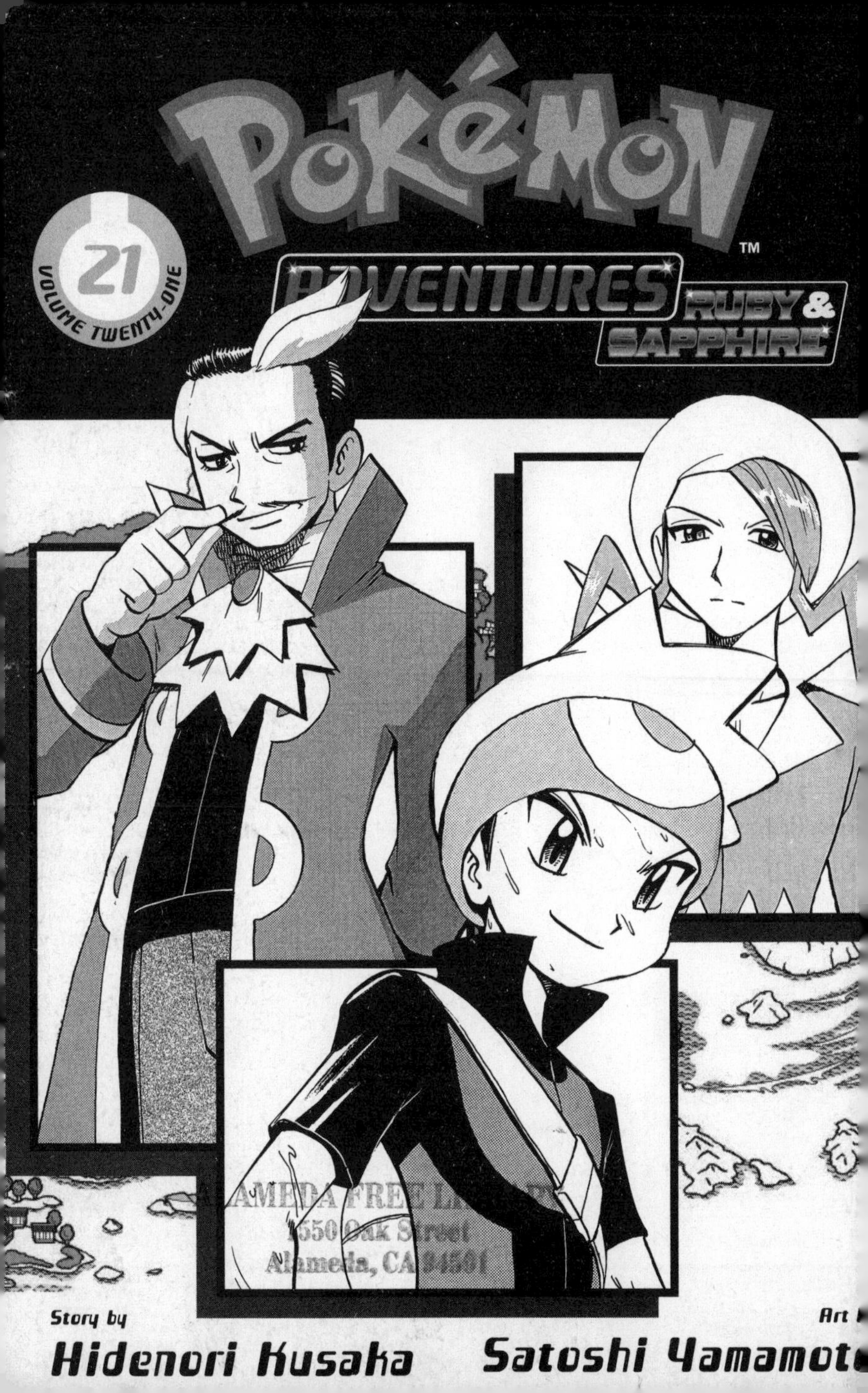



Story by
**Hidenori Kusaka**

Art b
**Satoshi Yamamoto**

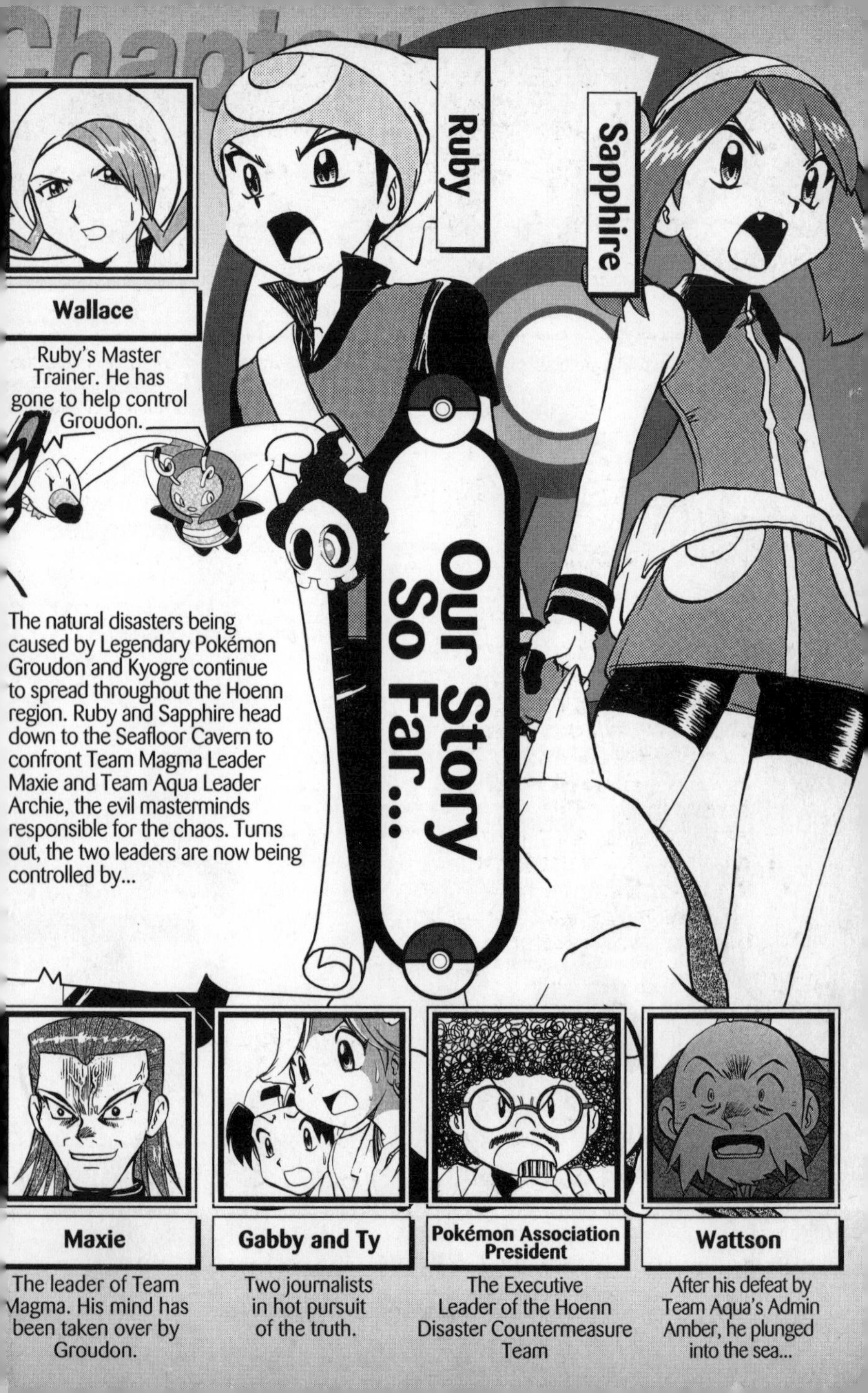
Our Story So Far...
Sapphire
Ruby
Wallace
Ruby's Master Trainer. He has gone to help control Groudon.
The natural disasters being caused by Legendary Pokémon Groudon and Kyogre continue to spread throughout the Hoenn region. Ruby and Sapphire head down to the Seafloor Cavern to confront Team Magma Leader Maxie and Team Aqua Leader Archie, the evil masterminds responsible for the chaos. Turns out, the two leaders are now being controlled by...
Wattson
After his defeat by Team Aqua's Admin Amber, he plunged into the sea...
Pokémon Association President
The Executive Leader of the Hoenn Disaster Countermeasure Team
Gabby and Ty
Two journalists in hot pursuit of the truth.
Maxie
The leader of Team Magma. His mind has been taken over by Groudon.

**Flannery**

Currently facing a difficult battle against Team Aqua's Shelly to gain control of Kyogre.

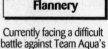

**Winona**

Sapphire's Master Trainer. She has rushed to aid Flannery and Wattson.

**Brawly**

Together with Wallace and Roxanne, currently fighting the members of the Three Fires.

**Roxanne**

Currently fighting the Team Magma member who want Groudon to triumph.

Meanwhile, the Gym Leaders gather their strength to stop the Legendary Pokémon—but the situation gets worse when Team Aqua and Team Magma show up! Finally it becomes clear where the two Pokémon are headed—to Sootopolis City, the mystical place where history slumbers and the two are said to have fought in ancient times! Once there, the battle between the two Legendary Pokémon begins again, and everyone begins to converge on them...

..the Red Orb and the Blue Orb they were using to control the Legendaries. A fierce battle breaks out between the four of them. They are engulfed in two bursts of energy and pulled towards Groudon and Kyogre before the battle is decided...

**Steven**

The strongest Pokémon League Champion.

**Wally**

Ruby's friend. Currently at the Sky Pillar being trained by Norman.

**Norman**

Ruby's father. Currently at the Sky Pillar training Wally.

**Archie**

The leader of Team Aqua whose mind has been taken over by Kyogre.

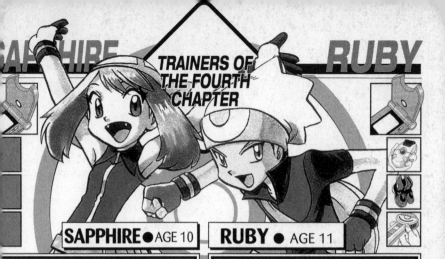

# TRAINERS OF THE FOURTH CHAPTER

## SAPPHIRE ● AGE 10

A wild Trainer whose dream is to challenge and defeat every single Gym Leader in the Hoenn region!!

**CHIC** BLAZIKEN ♀
Introverted. Uses fire-type moves.

**RONO** LAIRON ♂
Mischievous. Proud of his toughness. Its favorite move is Take Down.

**LORRY** WAILORD ♂
Bold. Sapphire rides the waves on Lorry's back.

**PHADO** DONPHAN ♂
Befriended by Sapphire at Mauville City. Hasty nature.

**TROPPY** TROPIUS ♂
Sapphire flies through the air on Troppy's back. This calm Pokémon usually stays outside its Poké Ball.

**RELLY** RELICANTH ♂
Has the power to take people with it to the very depths of the ocean. Hardy natured.

## RUBY ● AGE 11

A Trainer who wants to be the champion of all the Pokémon Contests. Visual beauty is a priority for Ruby. He has zero interest in Pokémon Battling. But does he secretly have a talent for it...?

**MUMU** SWAMPERT ♂
A Pokémon given to Ruby by Professor Birch. Easygoing. Represents Toughness.

**NANA** MIGHTYENA ♀
Intense. Represents Coolness.

**KIKI** DELCATTY ♀
Naive. Represents Cuteness.

**FOFO** CASTFORM ♀
Changes form in response to weather changes. Cautious.

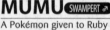

# Pokémon Adventures

## Ruby & Sapphire

Volume 21 — Volume Twenty-One

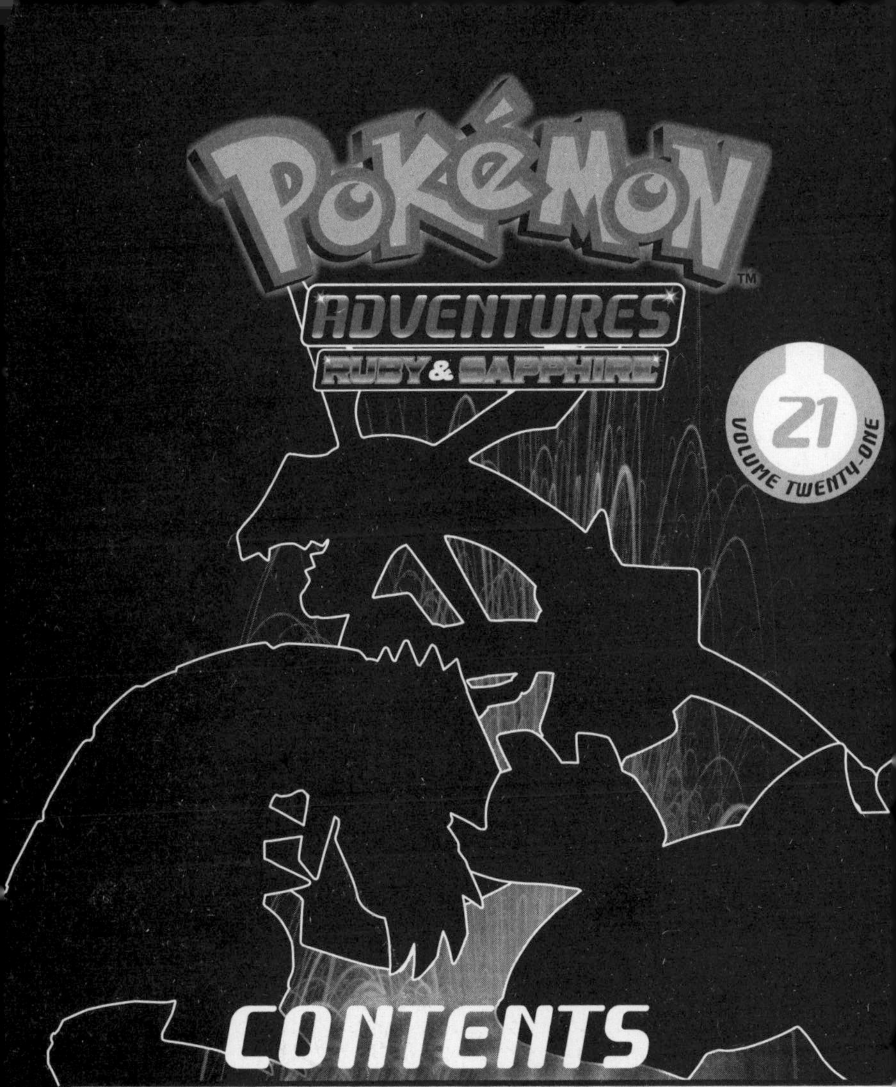

# CONTENTS

# ● Chapter 250 ●
# The Beginning of the End with Kyogre & Groudon XII

Pokémon™ Adventures Ruby & Sapphire

The Fourth Chapter

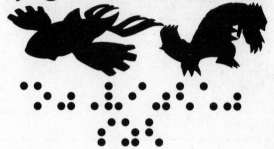

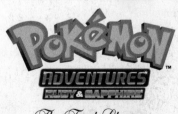

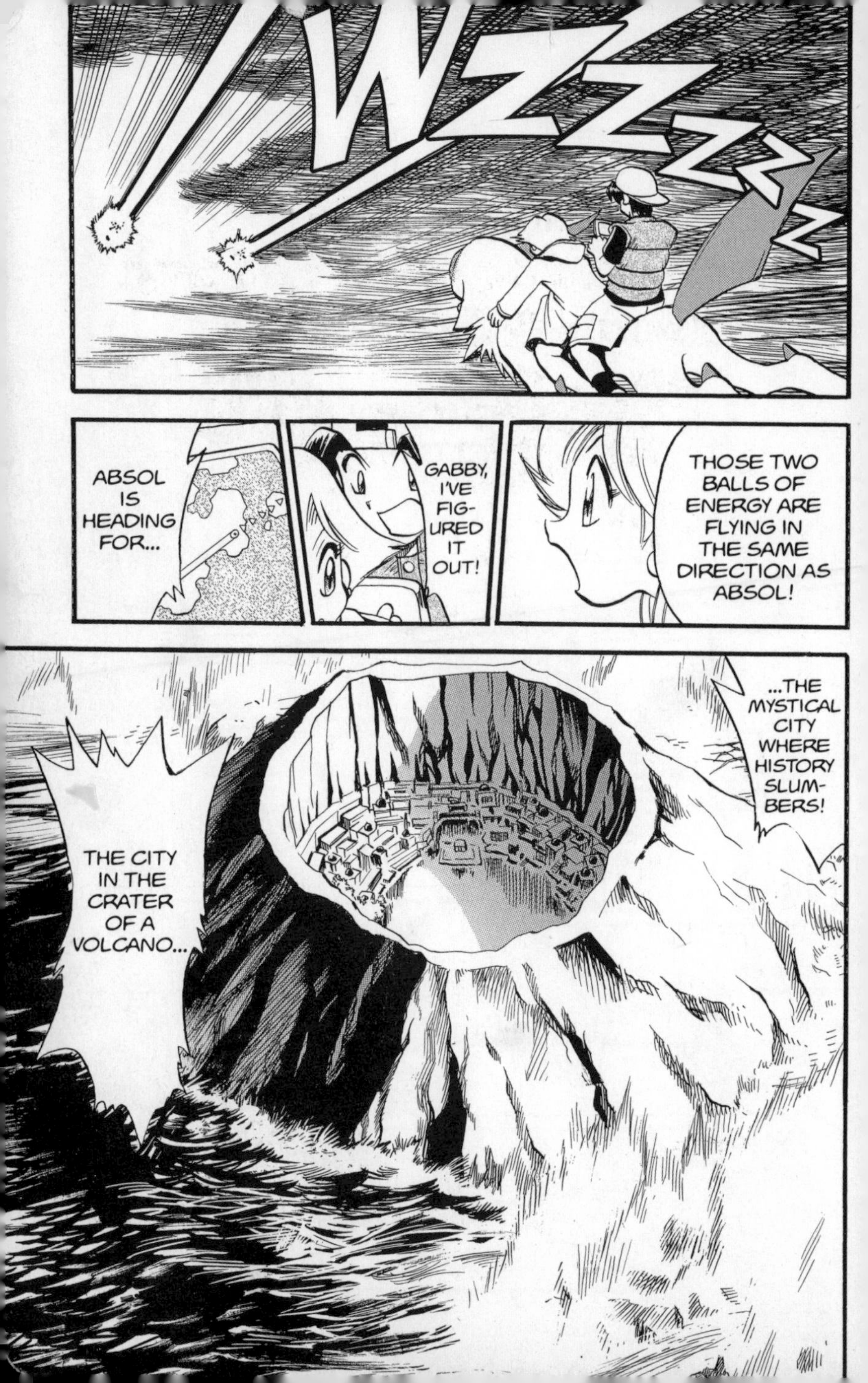
WZZZZZ
THOSE TWO BALLS OF ENERGY ARE FLYING IN THE SAME DIRECTION AS ABSOL!
GABBY, I'VE FIG-URED IT OUT!
ABSOL IS HEADING FOR...
...THE MYSTICAL CITY WHERE HISTORY SLUM-BERS!
THE CITY IN THE CRATER OF A VOLCANO...

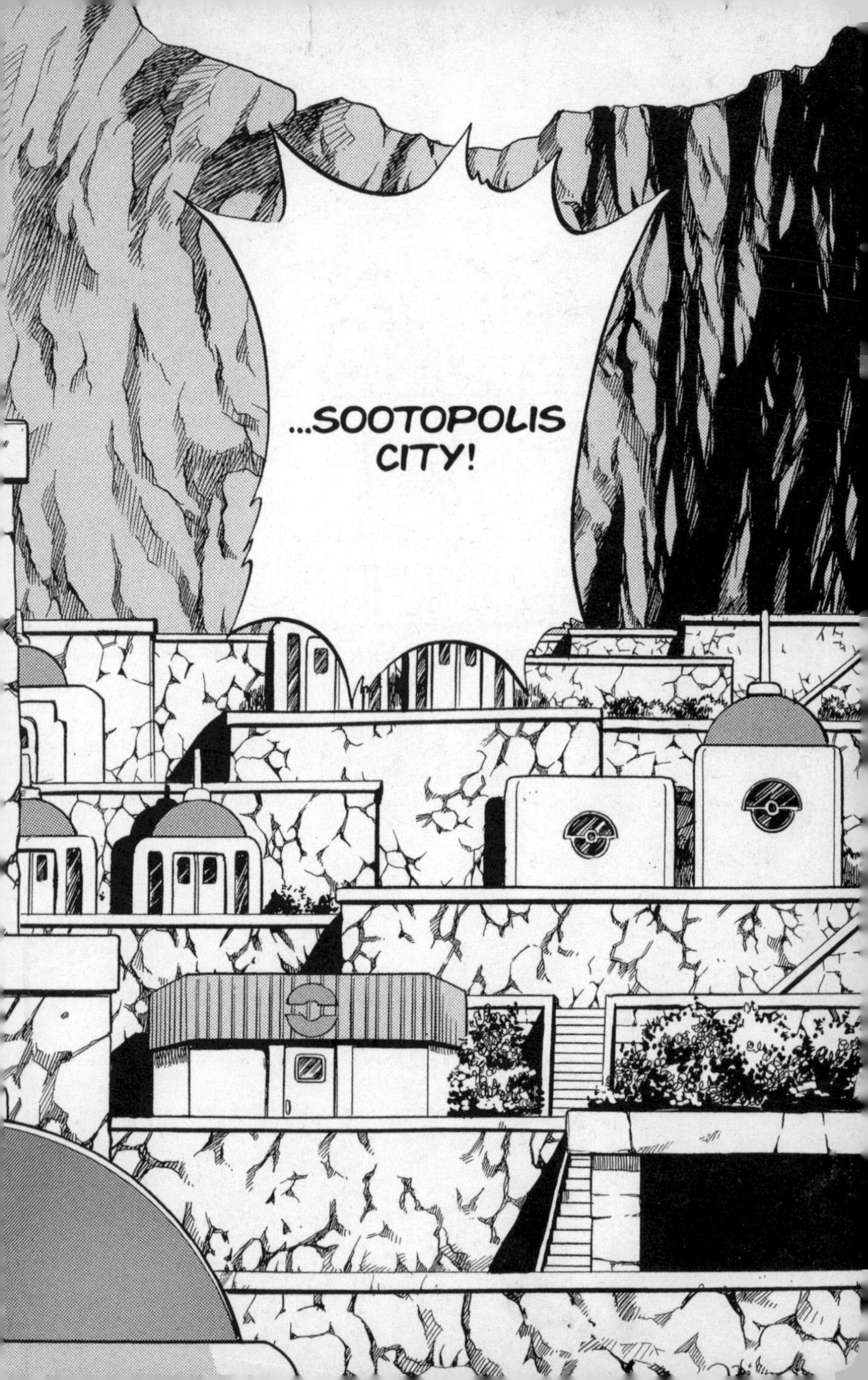
...SOOTOPOLIS CITY!

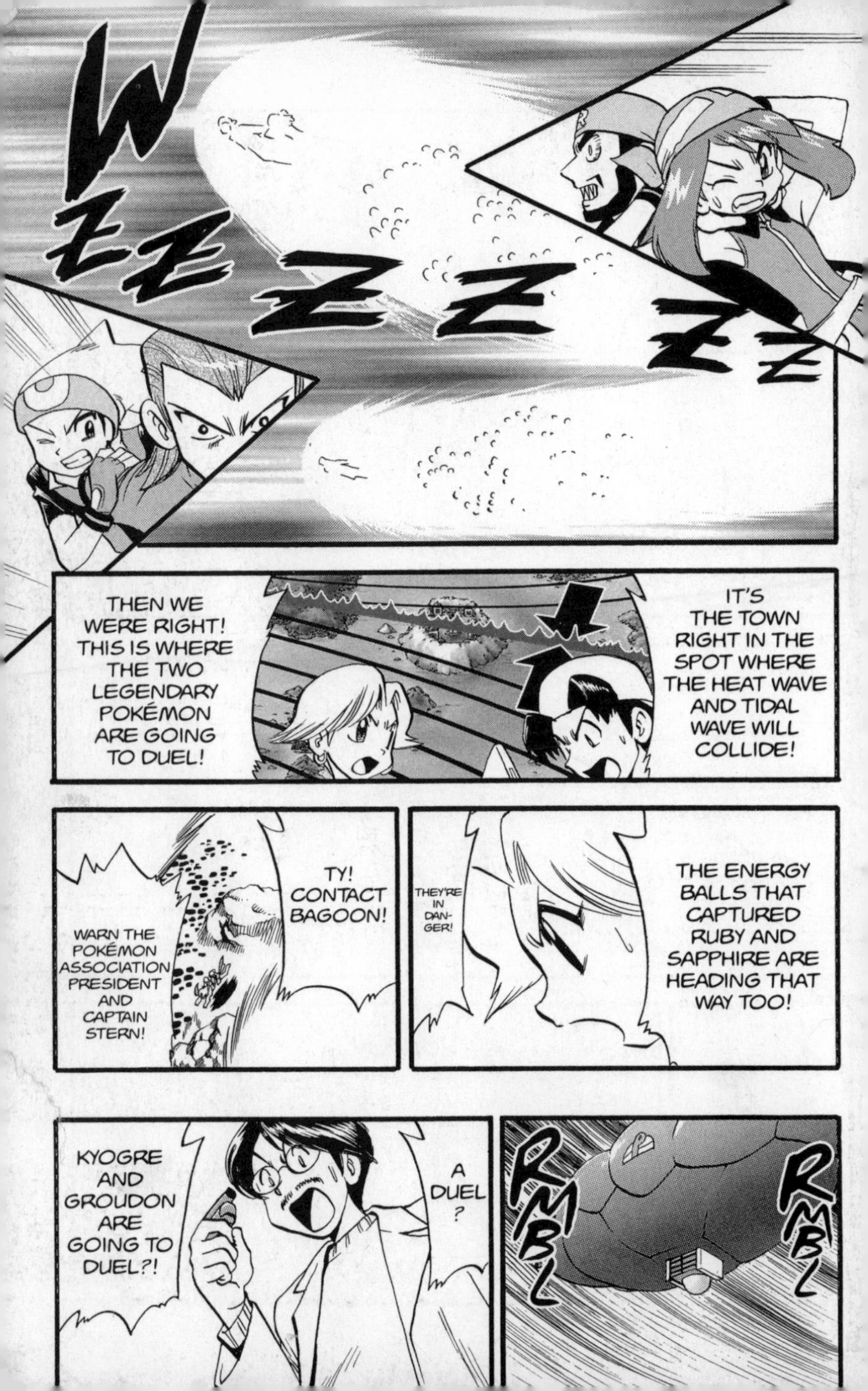
WZZZZZZ
IT'S THE TOWN RIGHT IN THE SPOT WHERE THE HEAT WAVE AND TIDAL WAVE WILL COLLIDE!
THEN WE WERE RIGHT! THIS IS WHERE THE TWO LEGENDARY POKÉMON ARE GOING TO DUEL!
THE ENERGY BALLS THAT CAPTURED RUBY AND SAPPHIRE ARE HEADING THAT WAY TOO!
THEY'RE IN DAN-GER!
TY! CONTACT BAGOON!
WARN THE POKÉMON ASSOCIATION PRESIDENT AND CAPTAIN STERN!
RMBL
RMBL
A DUEL?
KYOGRE AND GROUDON ARE GOING TO DUEL?!

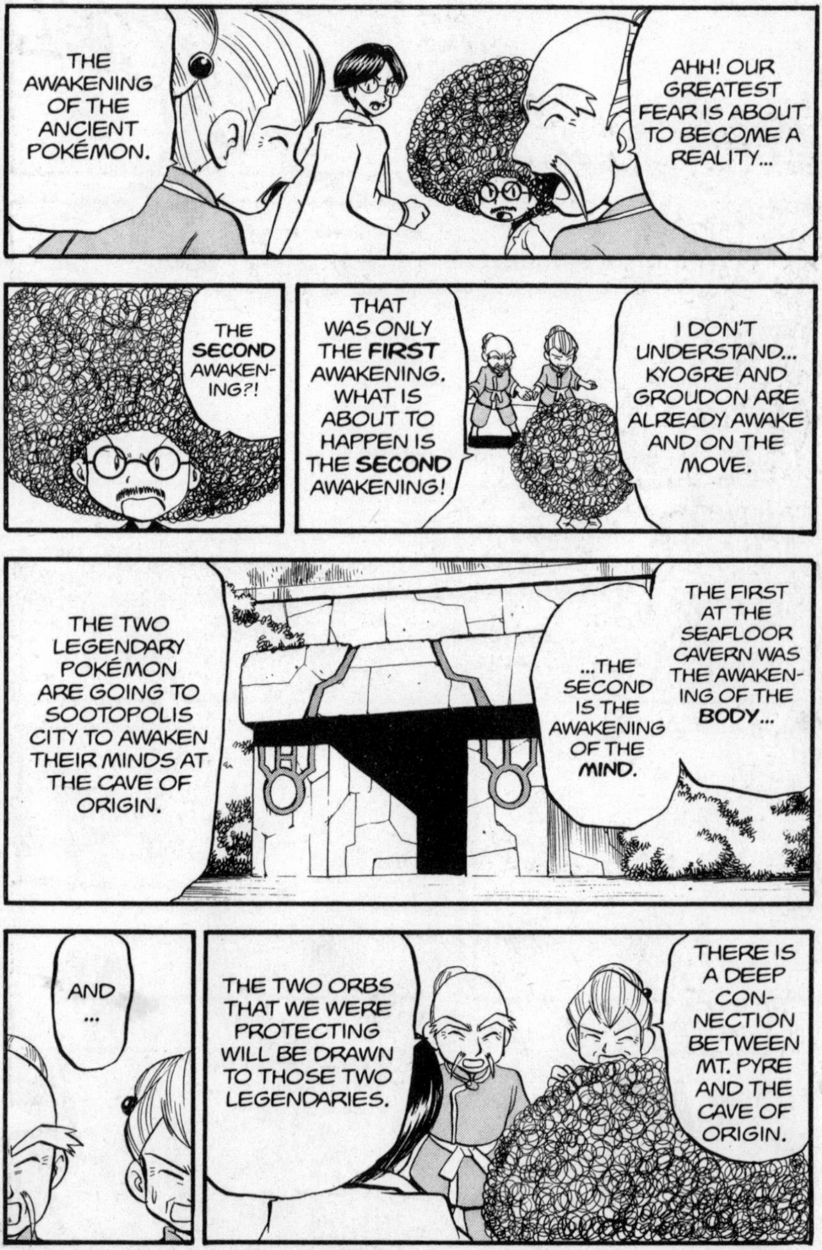
AHH! OUR GREATEST FEAR IS ABOUT TO BECOME A REALITY...
THE AWAKENING OF THE ANCIENT POKÉMON.
I DON'T UNDERSTAND... KYOGRE AND GROUDON ARE ALREADY AWAKE AND ON THE MOVE.
THAT WAS ONLY THE **FIRST** AWAKENING. WHAT IS ABOUT TO HAPPEN IS THE **SECOND** AWAKENING!
THE **SECOND** AWAKENING?!
THE FIRST AT THE SEAFLOOR CAVERN WAS THE AWAKENING OF THE **BODY**...
...THE SECOND IS THE AWAKENING OF THE **MIND**.
THE TWO LEGENDARY POKÉMON ARE GOING TO SOOTOPOLIS CITY TO AWAKEN THEIR MINDS AT THE CAVE OF ORIGIN.
THERE IS A DEEP CONNECTION BETWEEN MT. PYRE AND THE CAVE OF ORIGIN.
THE TWO ORBS THAT WE WERE PROTECTING WILL BE DRAWN TO THOSE TWO LEGENDARIES.
AND ...

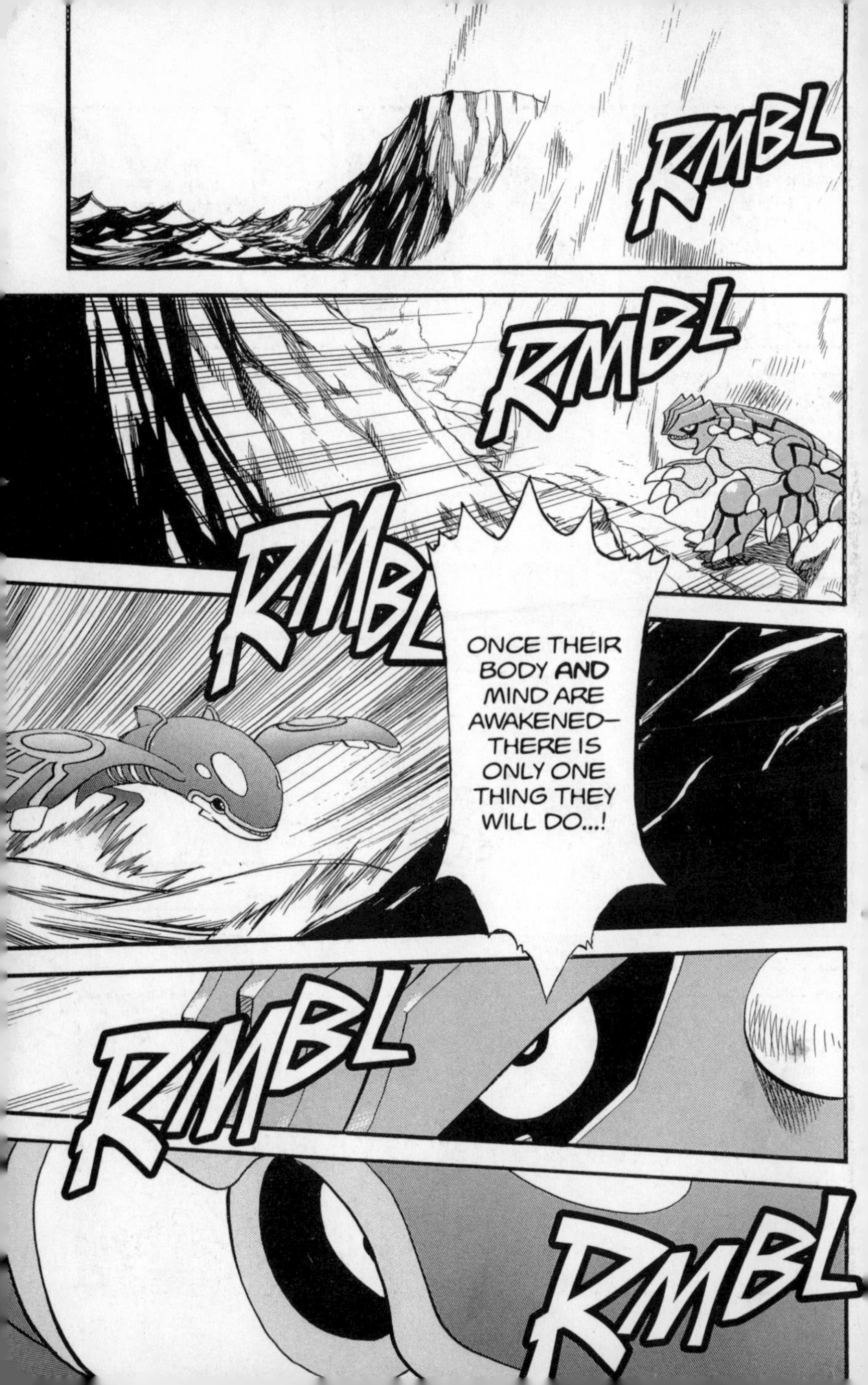
RMBL
RMBL
RMBL
ONCE THEIR BODY AND MIND ARE AWAKENED— THERE IS ONLY ONE THING THEY WILL DO...!
RMBL
RMBL

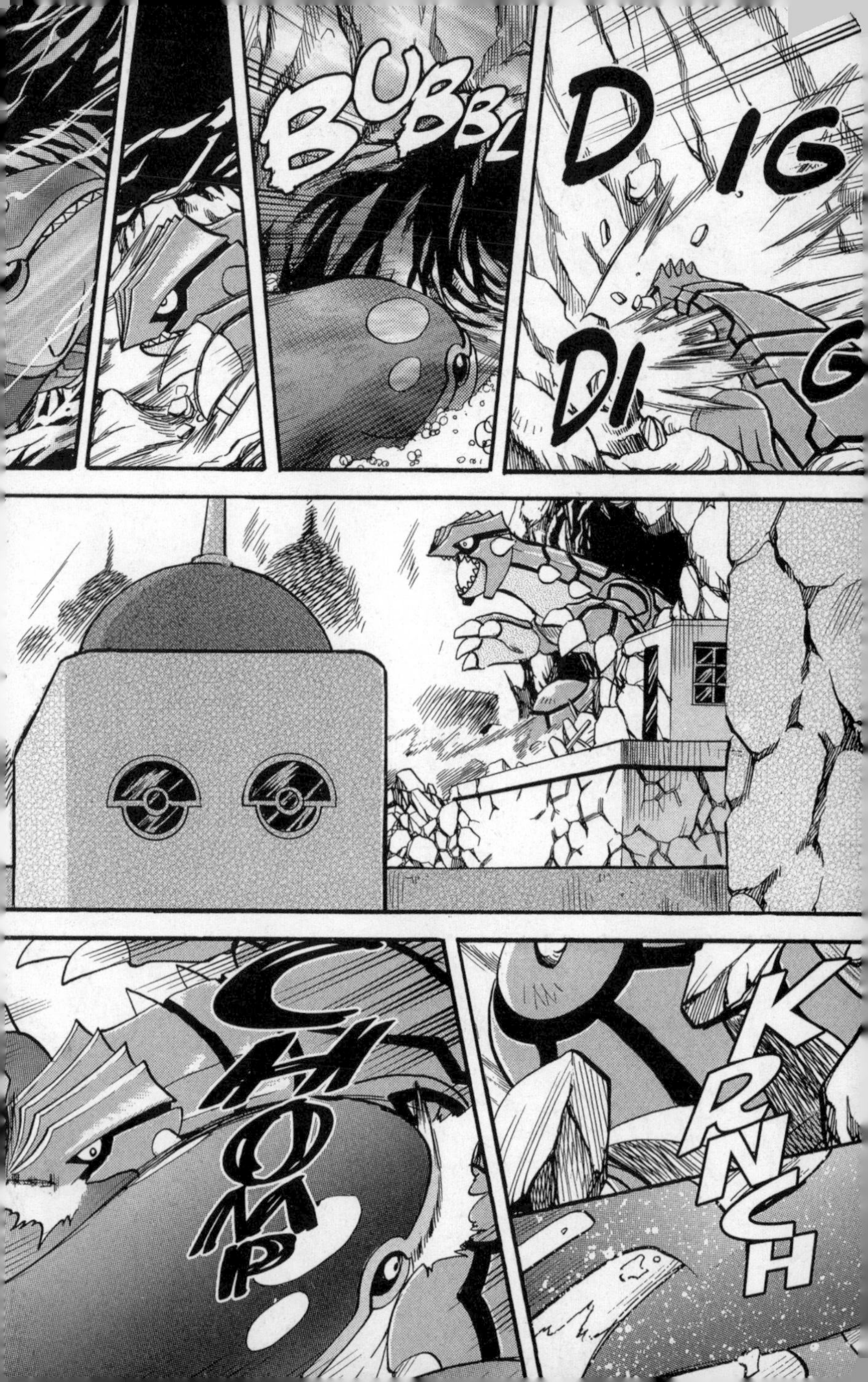
DIG
DIG
BUBBL
KRNCH
CHOMP

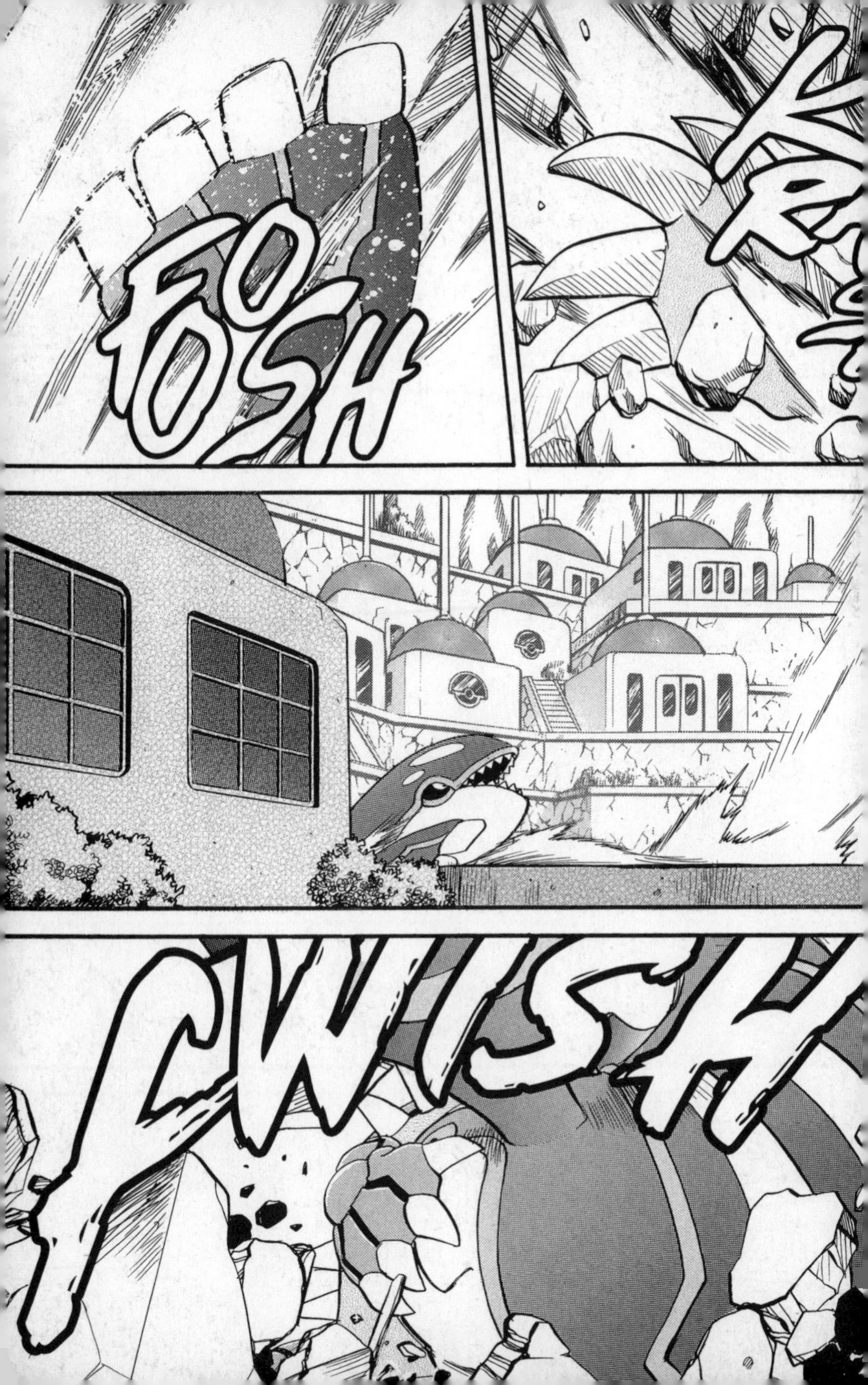
FOOSH
CWISH

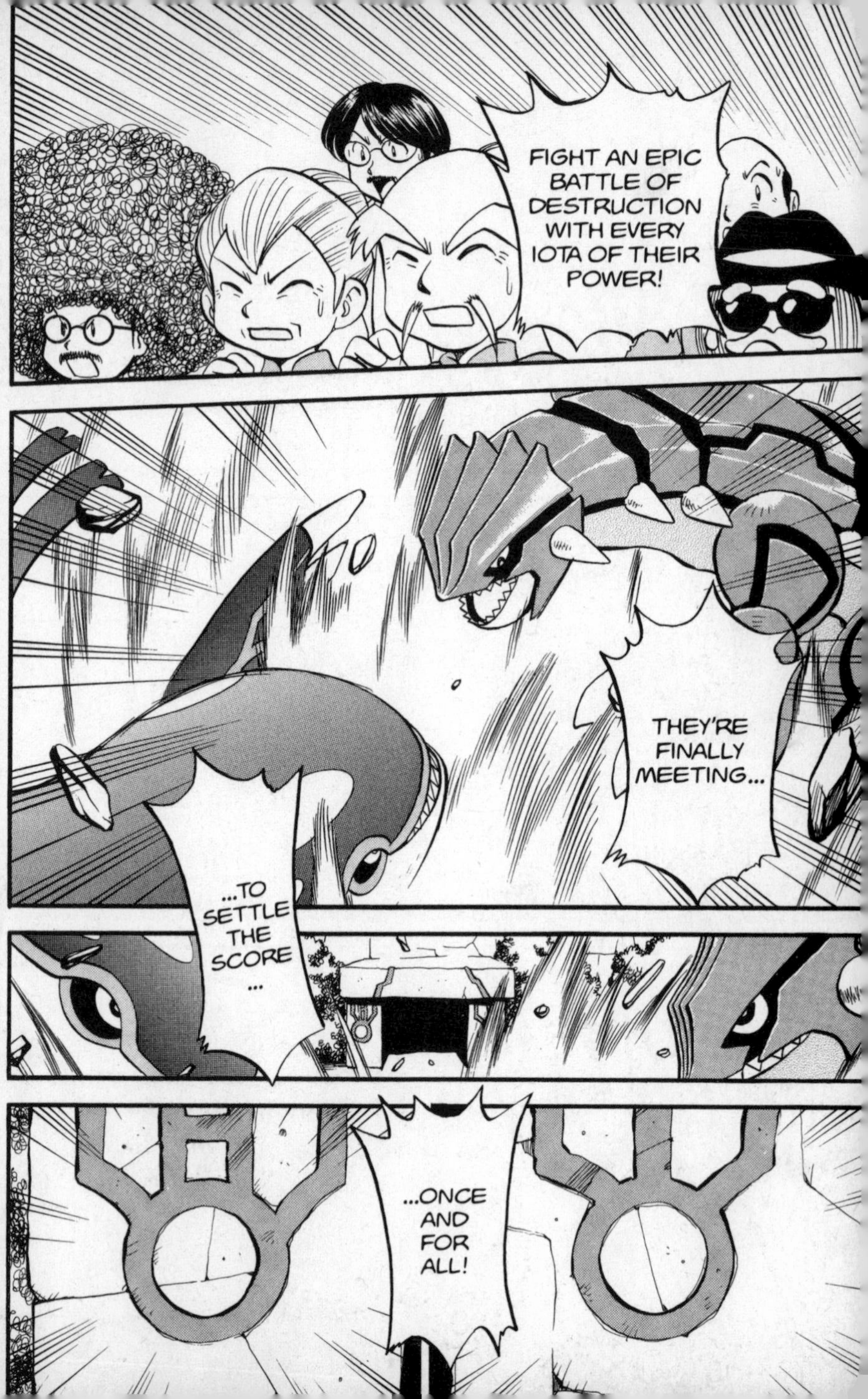
FIGHT AN EPIC BATTLE OF DESTRUCTION WITH EVERY IOTA OF THEIR POWER!
THEY'RE FINALLY MEETING...
...TO SETTLE THE SCORE...
...ONCE AND FOR ALL!

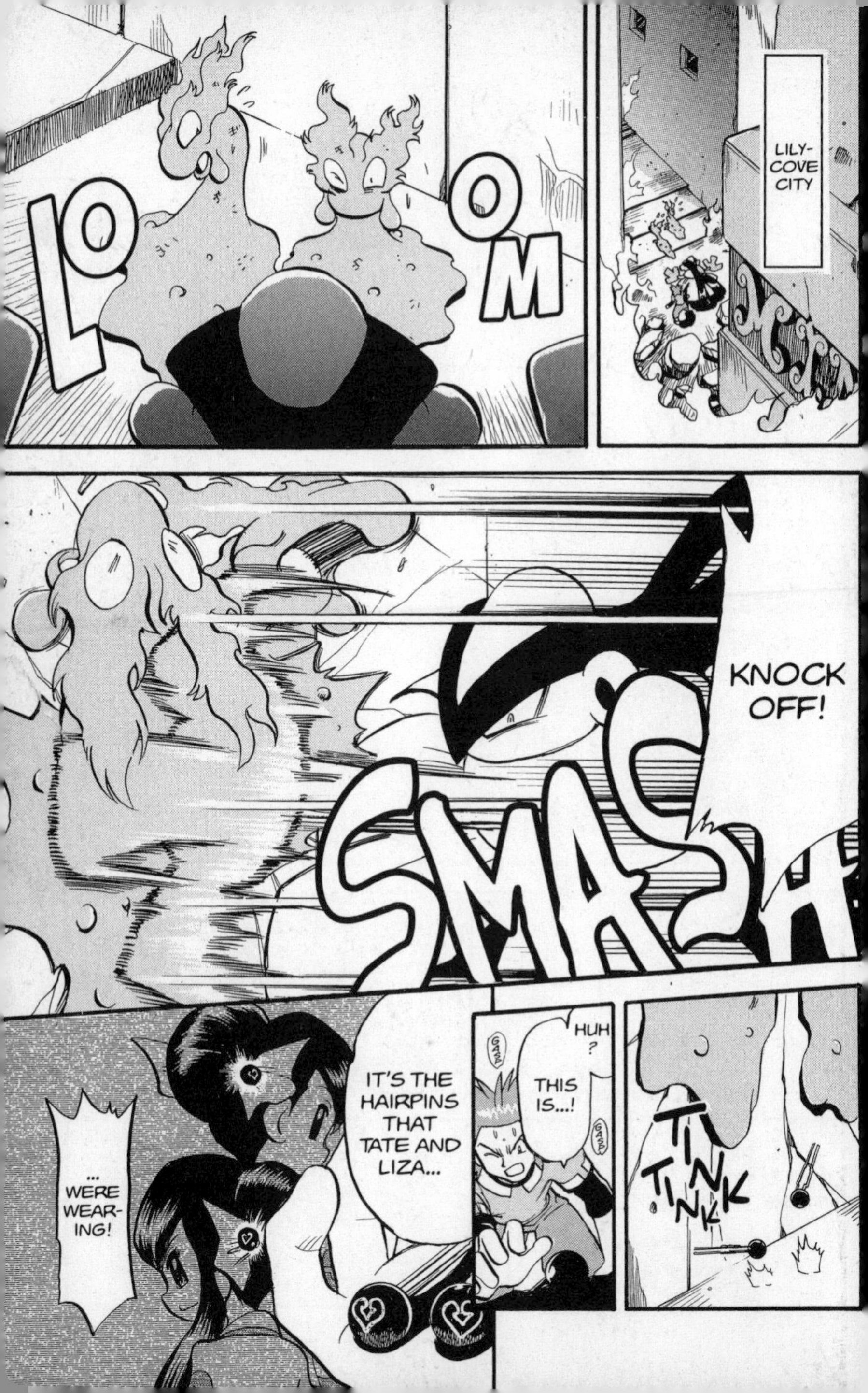
LILY-COVE CITY
LOOM
KNOCK OFF!
SMASH
TINK TINK
HUH? THIS IS...!
IT'S THE HAIRPINS THAT TATE AND LIZA...
...WERE WEARING!

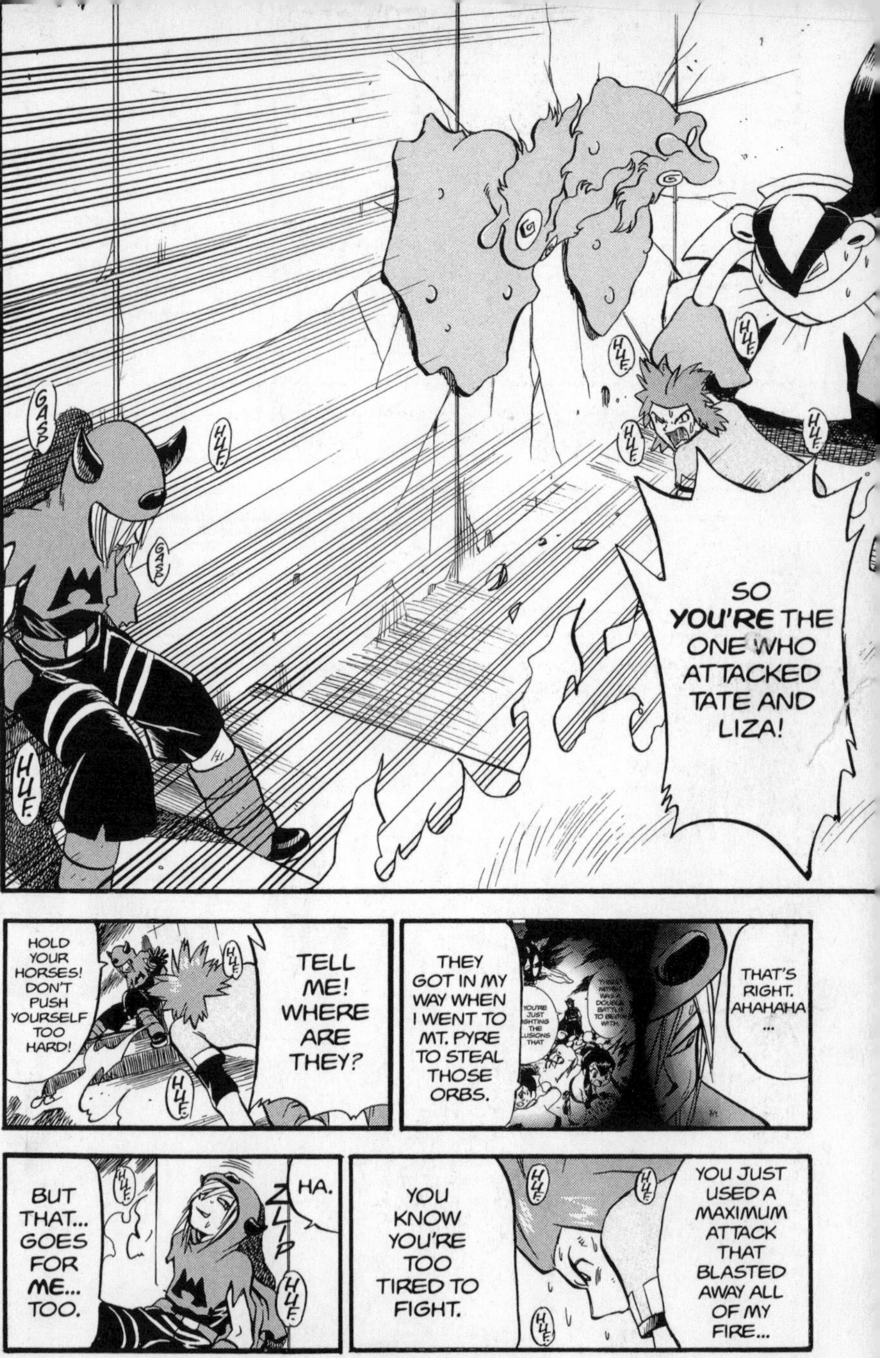
HUF
HUF
HUF
SO YOU'RE THE ONE WHO ATTACKED TATE AND LIZA!
HUF
GASP
GASP
HUF
THAT'S RIGHT. AHAHAHA ...
THEY GOT IN MY WAY WHEN I WENT TO MT. PYRE TO STEAL THOSE ORBS.
HUF
TELL ME! WHERE ARE THEY?
HOLD YOUR HORSES! DON'T PUSH YOURSELF TOO HARD!
HUF
HUF
YOU JUST USED A MAXIMUM ATTACK THAT BLASTED AWAY ALL OF MY FIRE...
YOU KNOW YOU'RE TOO TIRED TO FIGHT.
HUF
HA.
ZLIP
HUF
BUT THAT... GOES FOR ME... TOO.
HUF

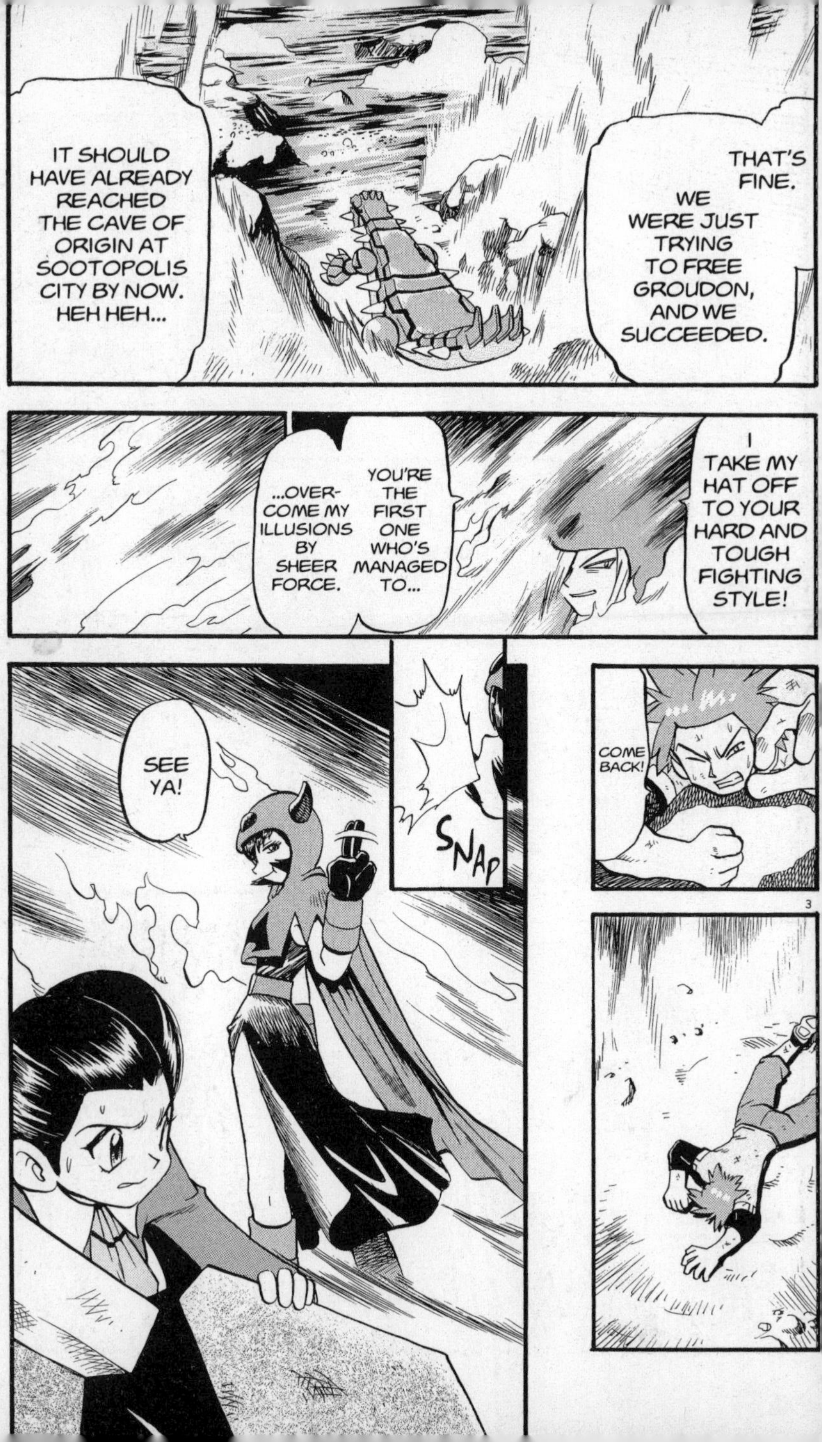
THAT'S FINE. WE WERE JUST TRYING TO FREE GROUDON, AND WE SUCCEEDED.
IT SHOULD HAVE ALREADY REACHED THE CAVE OF ORIGIN AT SOOTOPOLIS CITY BY NOW. HEH HEH...
I TAKE MY HAT OFF TO YOUR HARD AND TOUGH FIGHTING STYLE!
YOU'RE THE FIRST ONE WHO'S MANAGED TO...
...OVER-COME MY ILLUSIONS BY SHEER FORCE.
COME BACK!
SNAP
SEE YA!

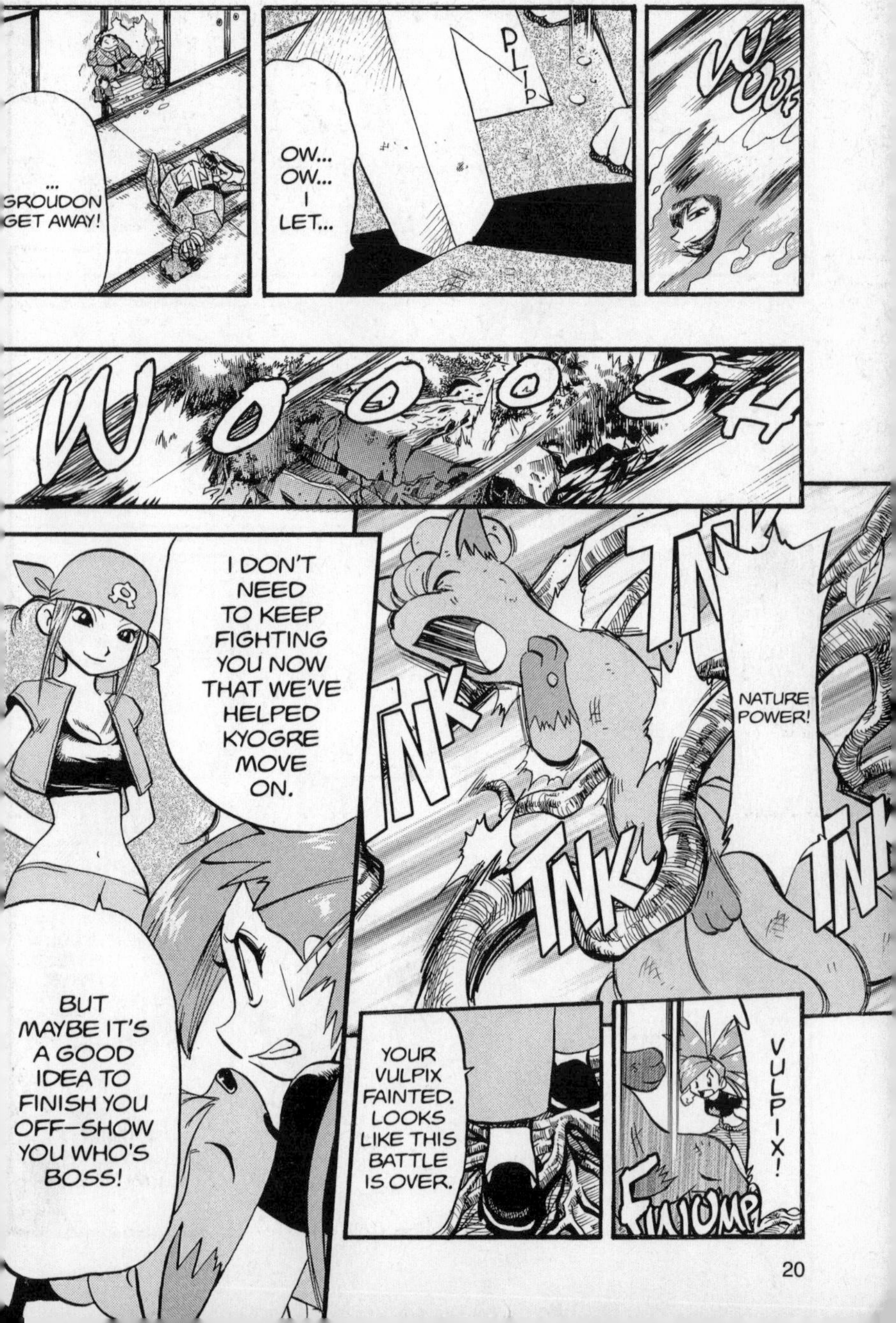
PLIP
OW... OW... I LET...
... GROUDON GET AWAY!
WOOOSH
TNK
NATURE POWER!
TNK
TNK
TNK
I DON'T NEED TO KEEP FIGHTING YOU NOW THAT WE'VE HELPED KYOGRE MOVE ON.
VULPIX!
YOUR VULPIX FAINTED. LOOKS LIKE THIS BATTLE IS OVER.
BUT MAYBE IT'S A GOOD IDEA TO FINISH YOU OFF—SHOW YOU WHO'S BOSS!

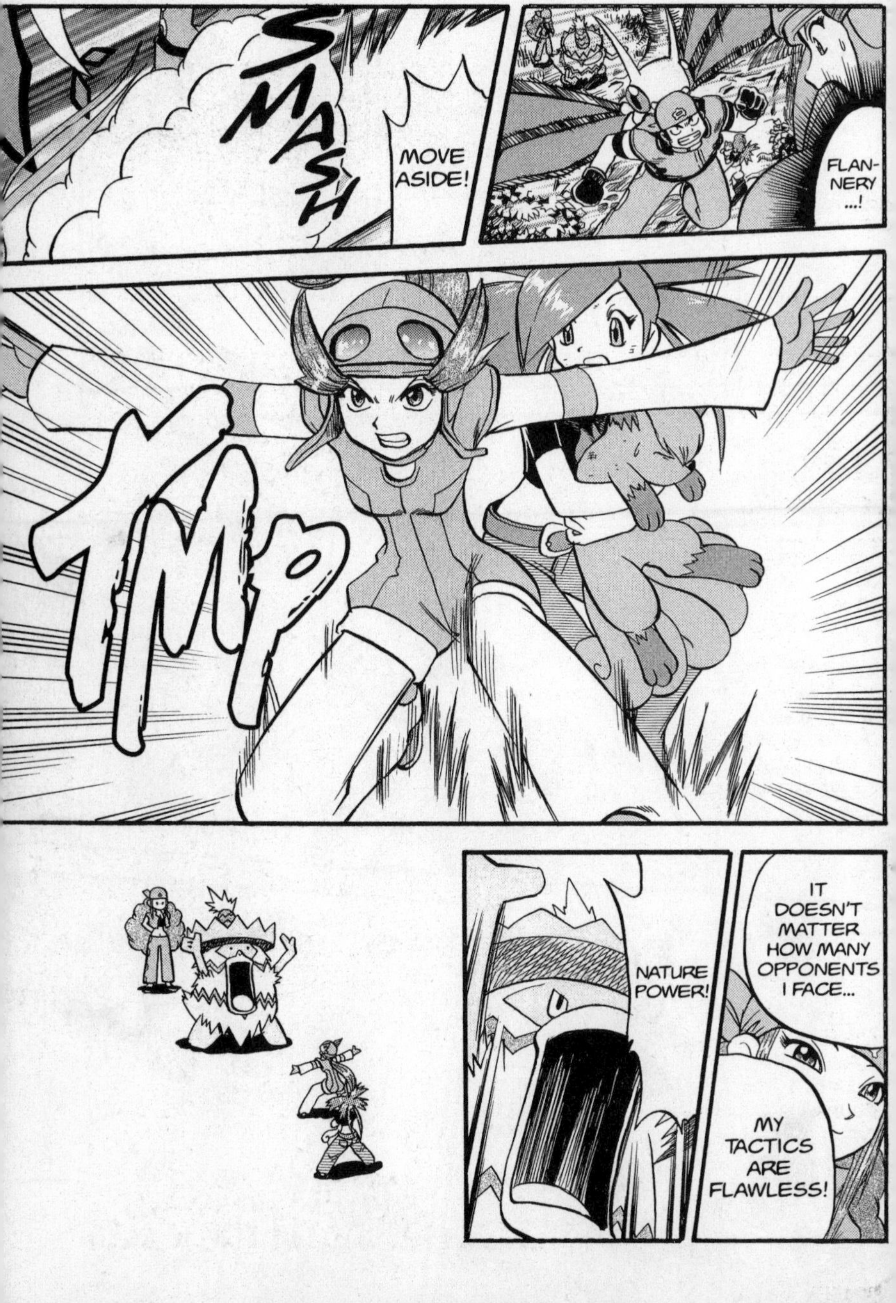
FLAN-NERY ...!
MOVE ASIDE!
SMASH
TMP
IT DOESN'T MATTER HOW MANY OPPONENTS I FACE...
MY TACTICS ARE FLAWLESS!
NATURE POWER!

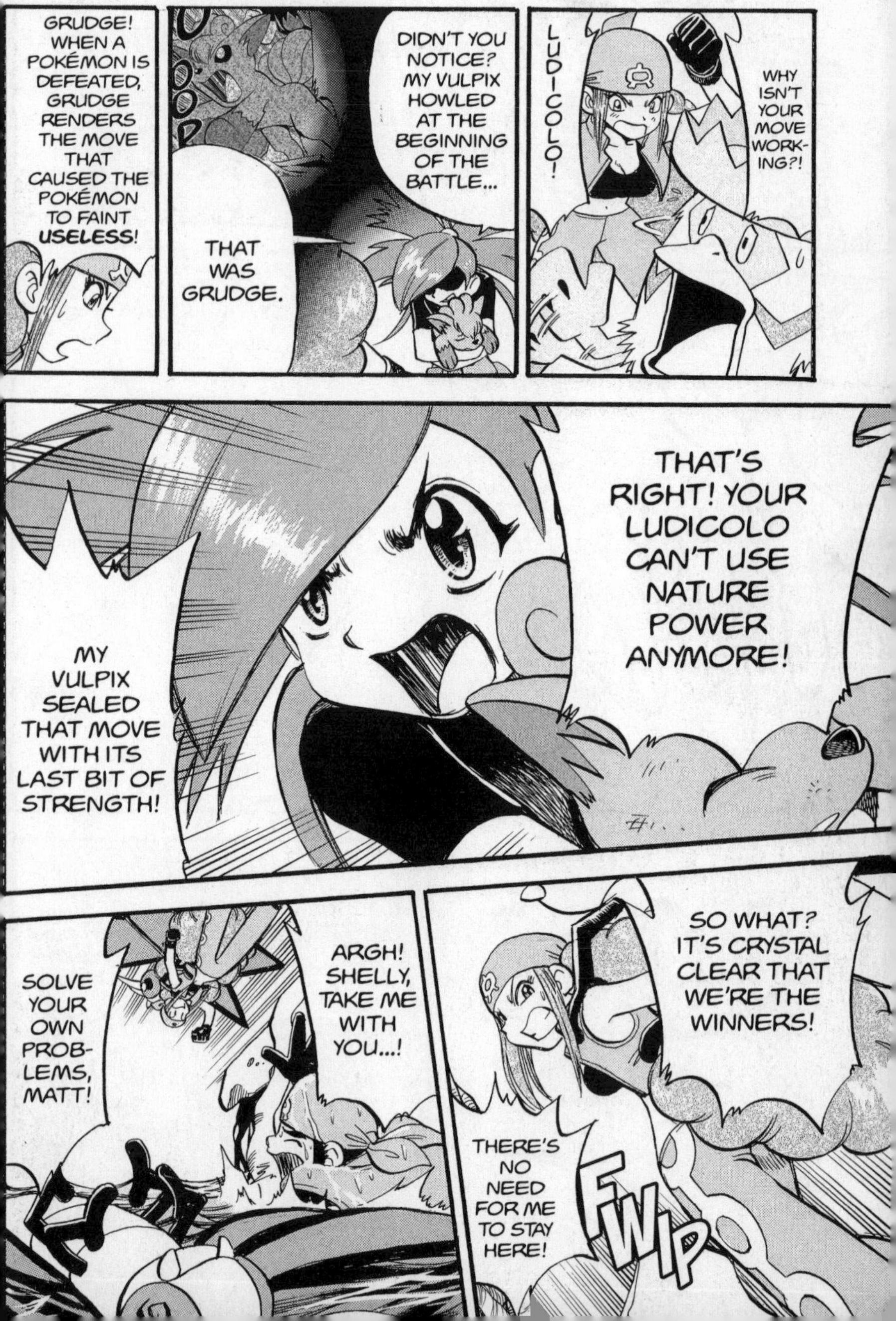
LUDICOLO!
WHY ISN'T YOUR MOVE WORKING?!
DIDN'T YOU NOTICE? MY VULPIX HOWLED AT THE BEGINNING OF THE BATTLE...
THAT WAS GRUDGE.
GRUDGE! WHEN A POKÉMON IS DEFEATED, GRUDGE RENDERS THE MOVE THAT CAUSED THE POKÉMON TO FAINT **USELESS**!
THAT'S RIGHT! YOUR LUDICOLO CAN'T USE NATURE POWER ANYMORE!
MY VULPIX SEALED THAT MOVE WITH ITS LAST BIT OF STRENGTH!
SO WHAT? IT'S CRYSTAL CLEAR THAT WE'RE THE WINNERS!
THERE'S NO NEED FOR ME TO STAY HERE!
FWIP
ARGH! SHELLY, TAKE ME WITH YOU...!
SOLVE YOUR OWN PROBLEMS, MATT!

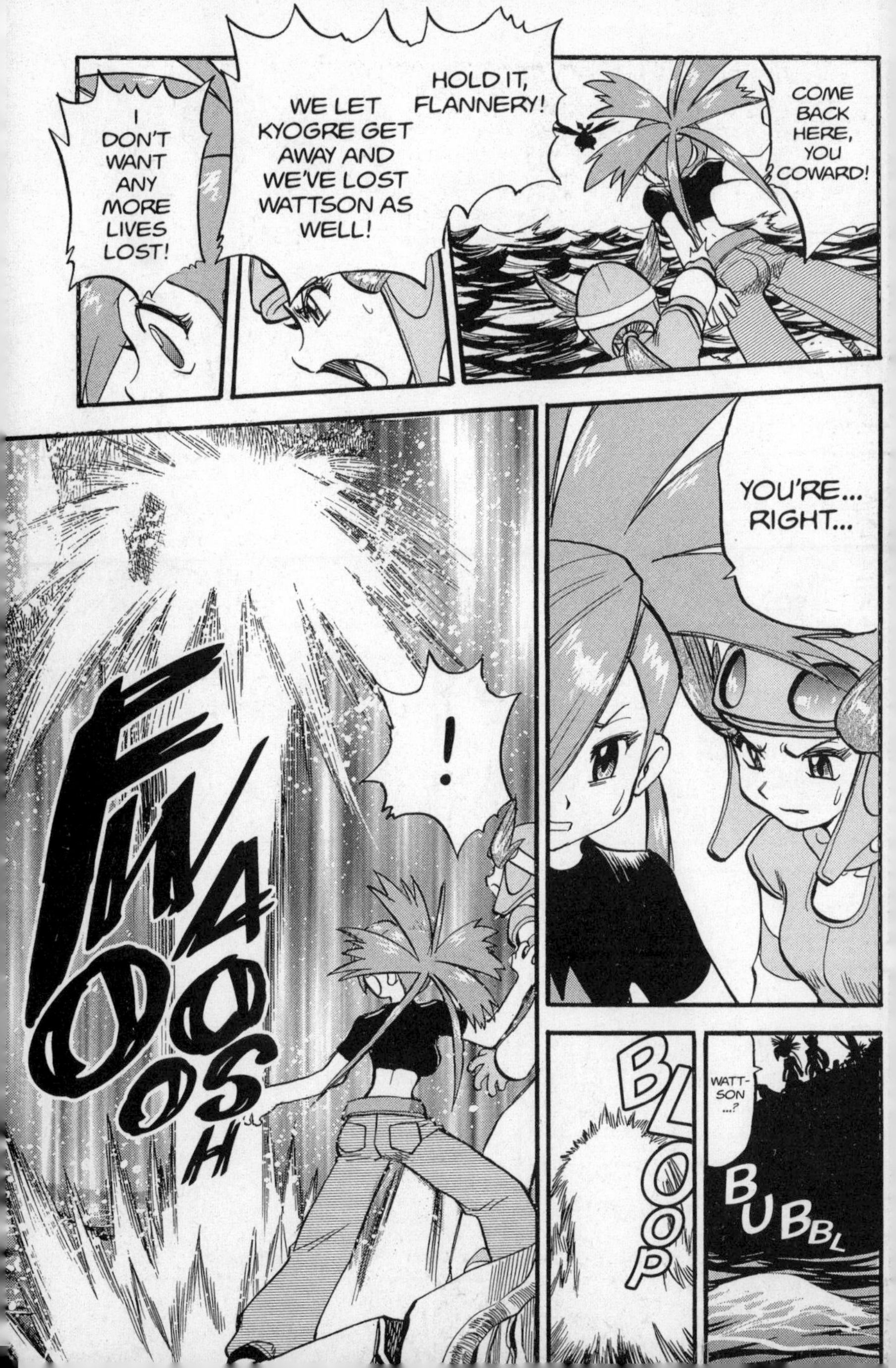
COME BACK HERE, YOU COWARD!
HOLD IT, FLANNERY!
WE LET KYOGRE GET AWAY AND WE'VE LOST WATTSON AS WELL!
I DON'T WANT ANY MORE LIVES LOST!
YOU'RE... RIGHT...
WATT-SON ...?
BUBBL
BLOOP
!
FWOOOOSH

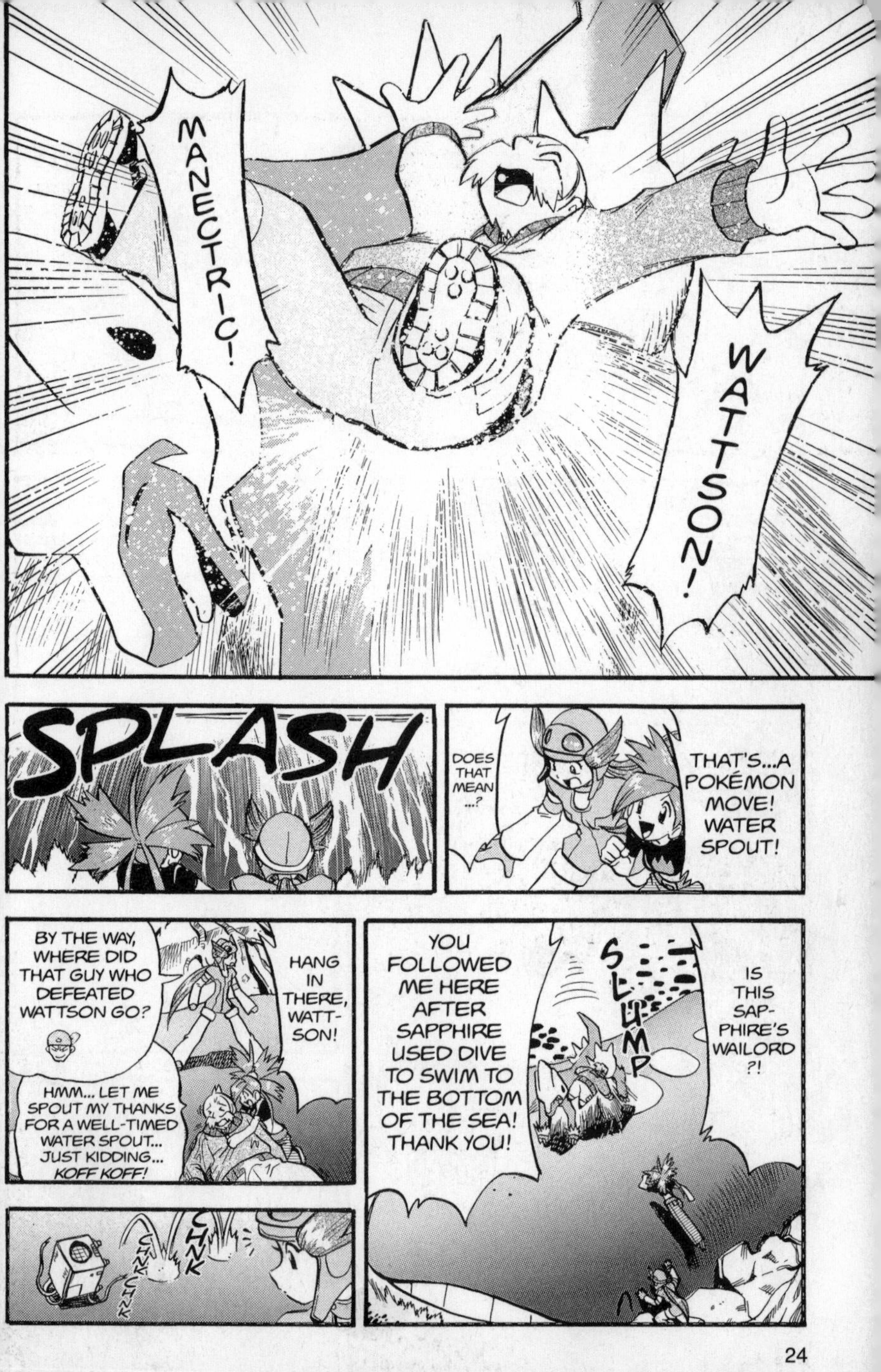
WATTSON!
MANECTRIC!
THAT'S...A POKÉMON MOVE! WATER SPOUT!
DOES THAT MEAN ...?
SPLASH
IS THIS SAPPHIRE'S WAILORD ?!
SLUMP
YOU FOLLOWED ME HERE AFTER SAPPHIRE USED DIVE TO SWIM TO THE BOTTOM OF THE SEA! THANK YOU!
HANG IN THERE, WATTSON!
BY THE WAY, WHERE DID THAT GUY WHO DEFEATED WATTSON GO?
HMM... LET ME SPOUT MY THANKS FOR A WELL-TIMED WATER SPOUT... JUST KIDDING... *KOFF KOFF!*
CHNK
CHNK CHNK

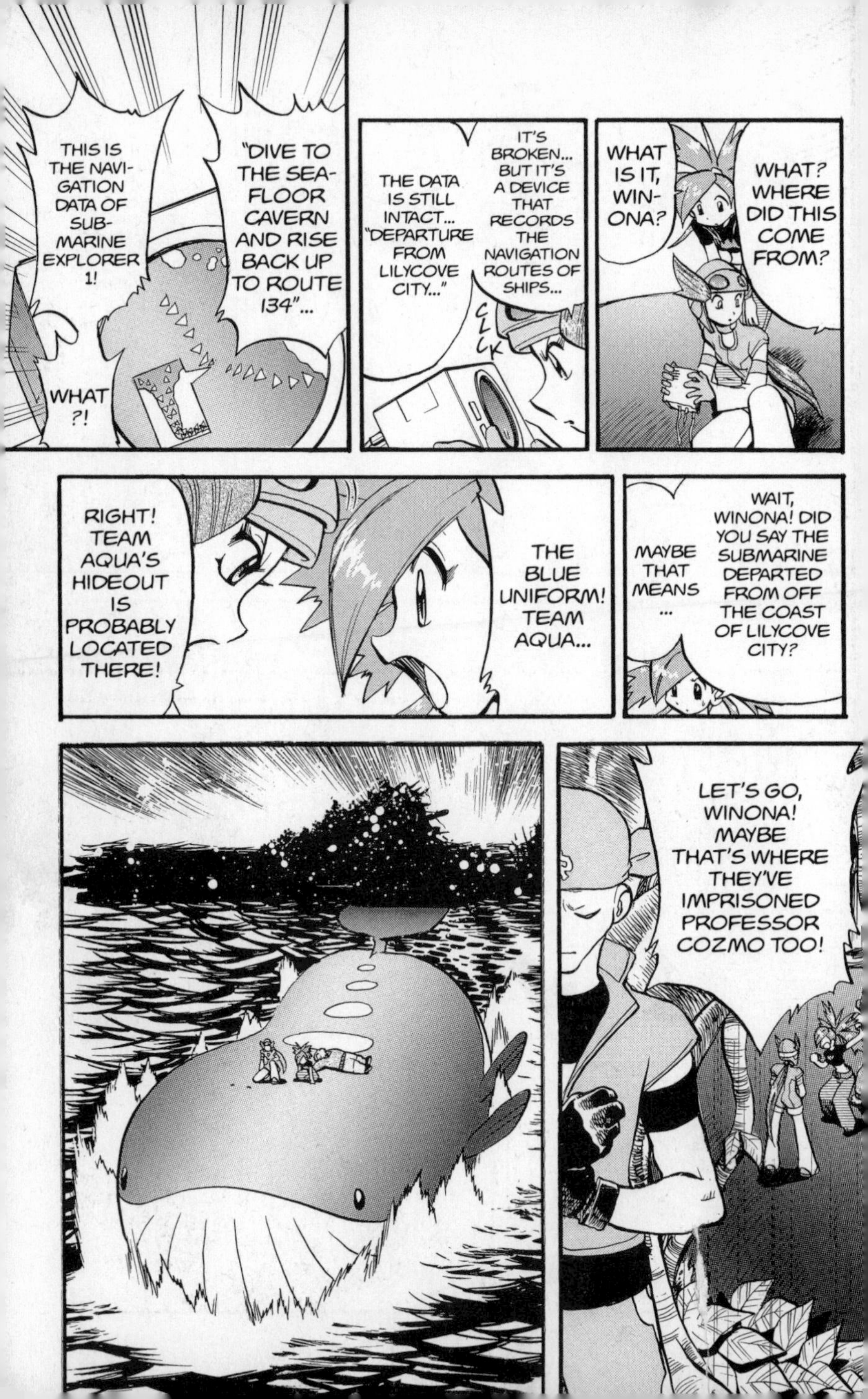
WHAT? WHERE DID THIS COME FROM?
WHAT IS IT, WINONA?
IT'S BROKEN... BUT IT'S A DEVICE THAT RECORDS THE NAVIGATION ROUTES OF SHIPS...
THE DATA IS STILL INTACT... "DEPARTURE FROM LILYCOVE CITY..."
CLICK
"DIVE TO THE SEAFLOOR CAVERN AND RISE BACK UP TO ROUTE 134"...
THIS IS THE NAVIGATION DATA OF SUBMARINE EXPLORER 1!
WHAT?!
WAIT, WINONA! DID YOU SAY THE SUBMARINE DEPARTED FROM OFF THE COAST OF LILYCOVE CITY?
MAYBE THAT MEANS...
THE BLUE UNIFORM! TEAM AQUA...
RIGHT! TEAM AQUA'S HIDEOUT IS PROBABLY LOCATED THERE!
LET'S GO, WINONA! MAYBE THAT'S WHERE THEY'VE IMPRISONED PROFESSOR COZMO TOO!

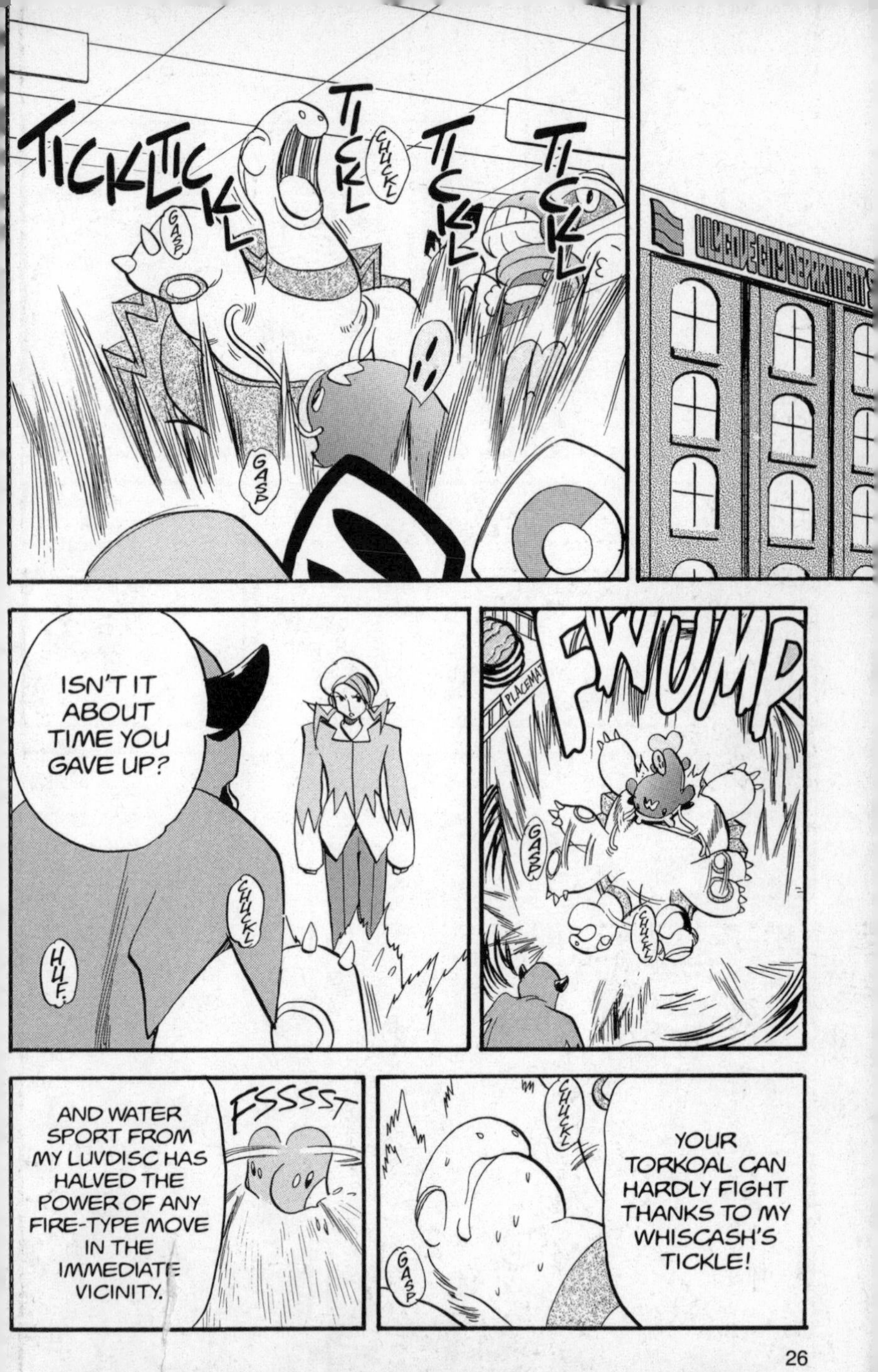

TICKL
TICKL
CHUCKL
TICKL
TICKL
TICKL
GASP
GASP
FWUMP
PLACEMAT
GASP
CHUCKL
ISN'T IT ABOUT TIME YOU GAVE UP?
CHUCKL
HUF.
CHUCKL
YOUR TORKOAL CAN HARDLY FIGHT THANKS TO MY WHISCASH'S TICKLE!
GASP
FSSSST
AND WATER SPORT FROM MY LUVDISC HAS HALVED THE POWER OF ANY FIRE-TYPE MOVE IN THE IMMEDIATE VICINITY.

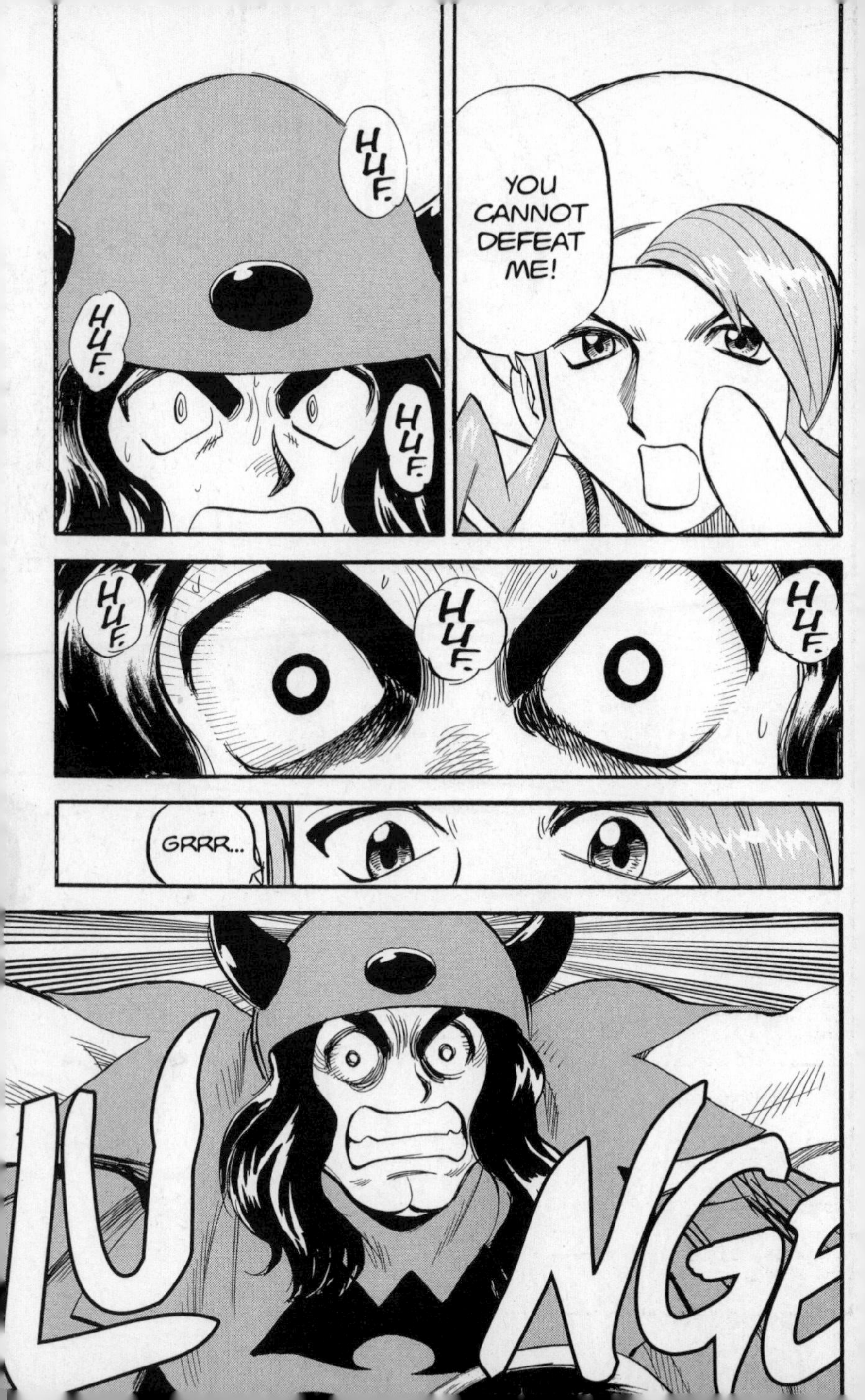
YOU CANNOT DEFEAT ME!
HUF.
HUF.
HUF.
HUF.
HUF.
HUF.
GRRR...
LU NG

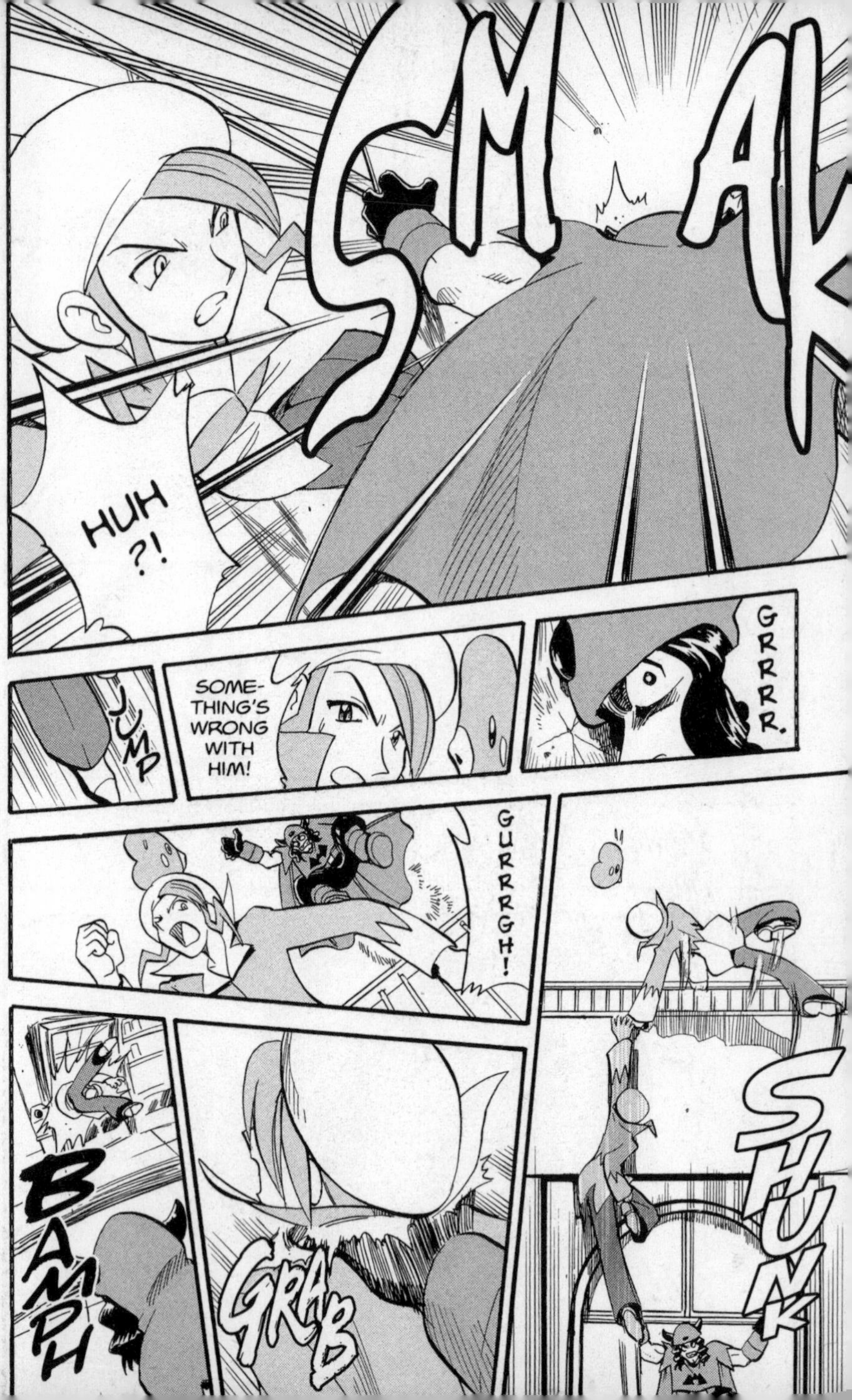
SMAK
HUH ?!
GRRRR.
SOME-THING'S WRONG WITH HIM!
JUMP
SHUNK
GURRRGH!
GRAB
BAMPH

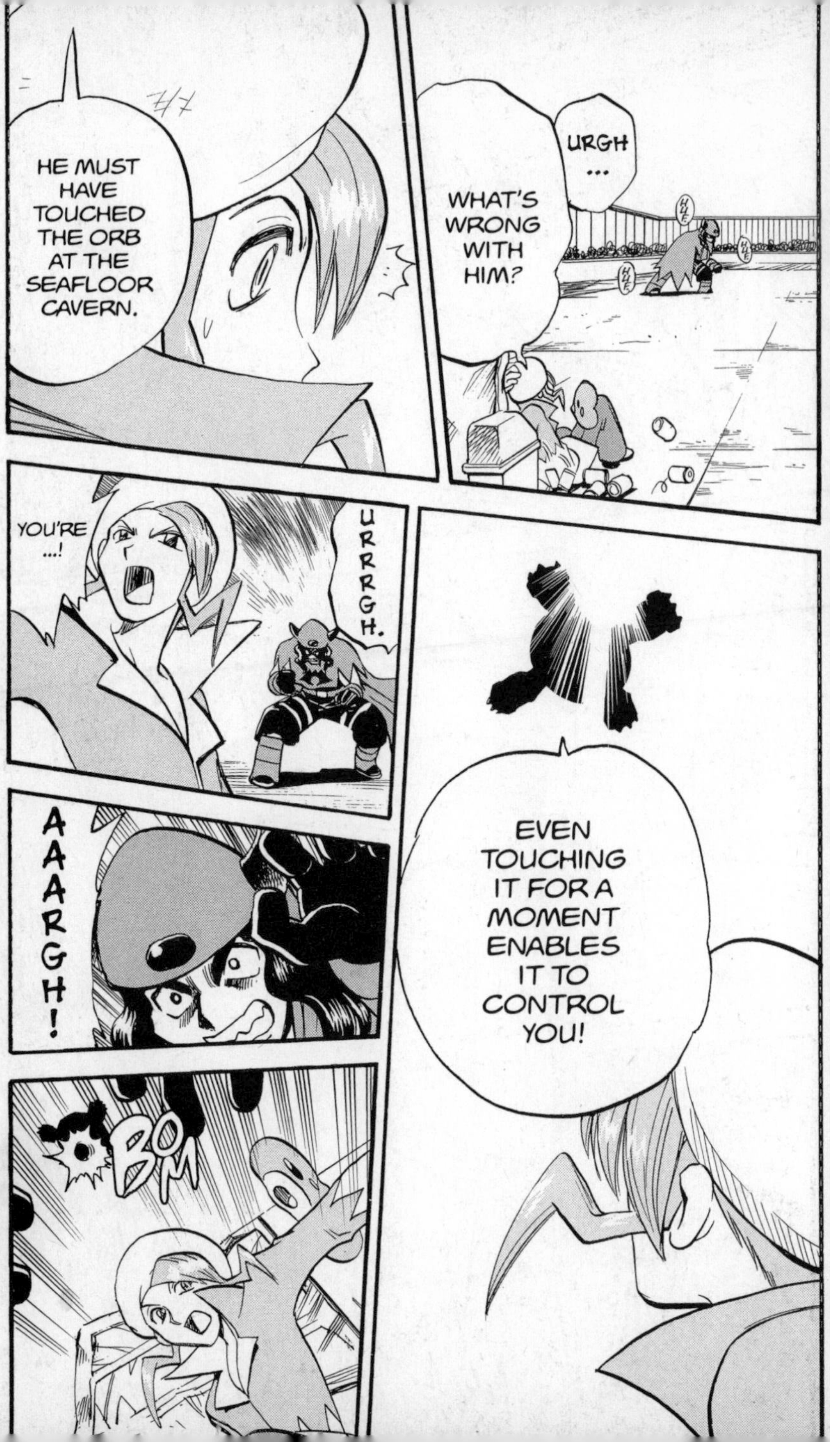
URGH ...
WHAT'S WRONG WITH HIM?
HE MUST HAVE TOUCHED THE ORB AT THE SEAFLOOR CAVERN.
EVEN TOUCHING IT FOR A MOMENT ENABLES IT TO CONTROL YOU!
URRRGH.
YOU'RE ...!
AAAARGH!
BOOM

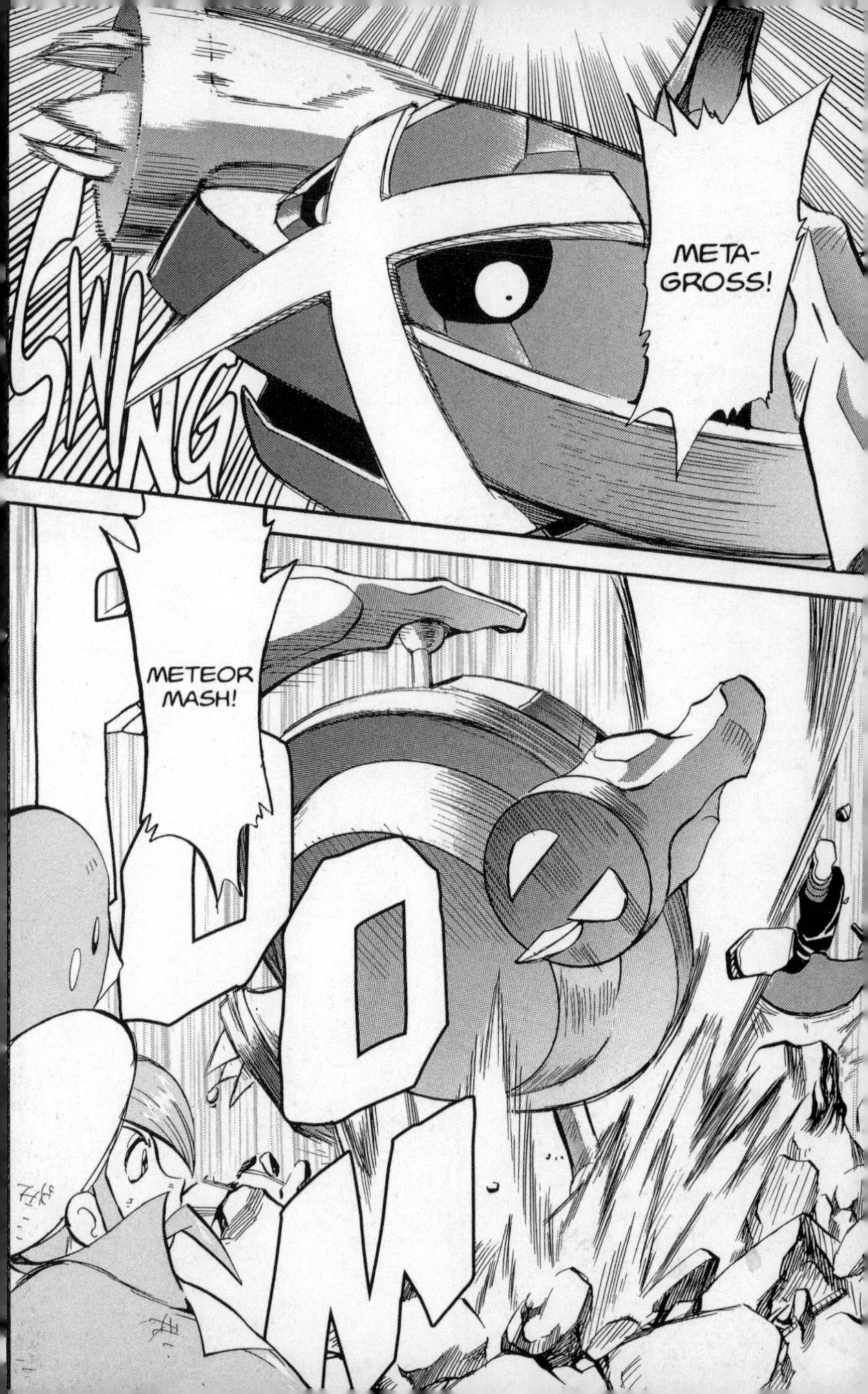
META-GROSS!
SWING
METEOR MASH!

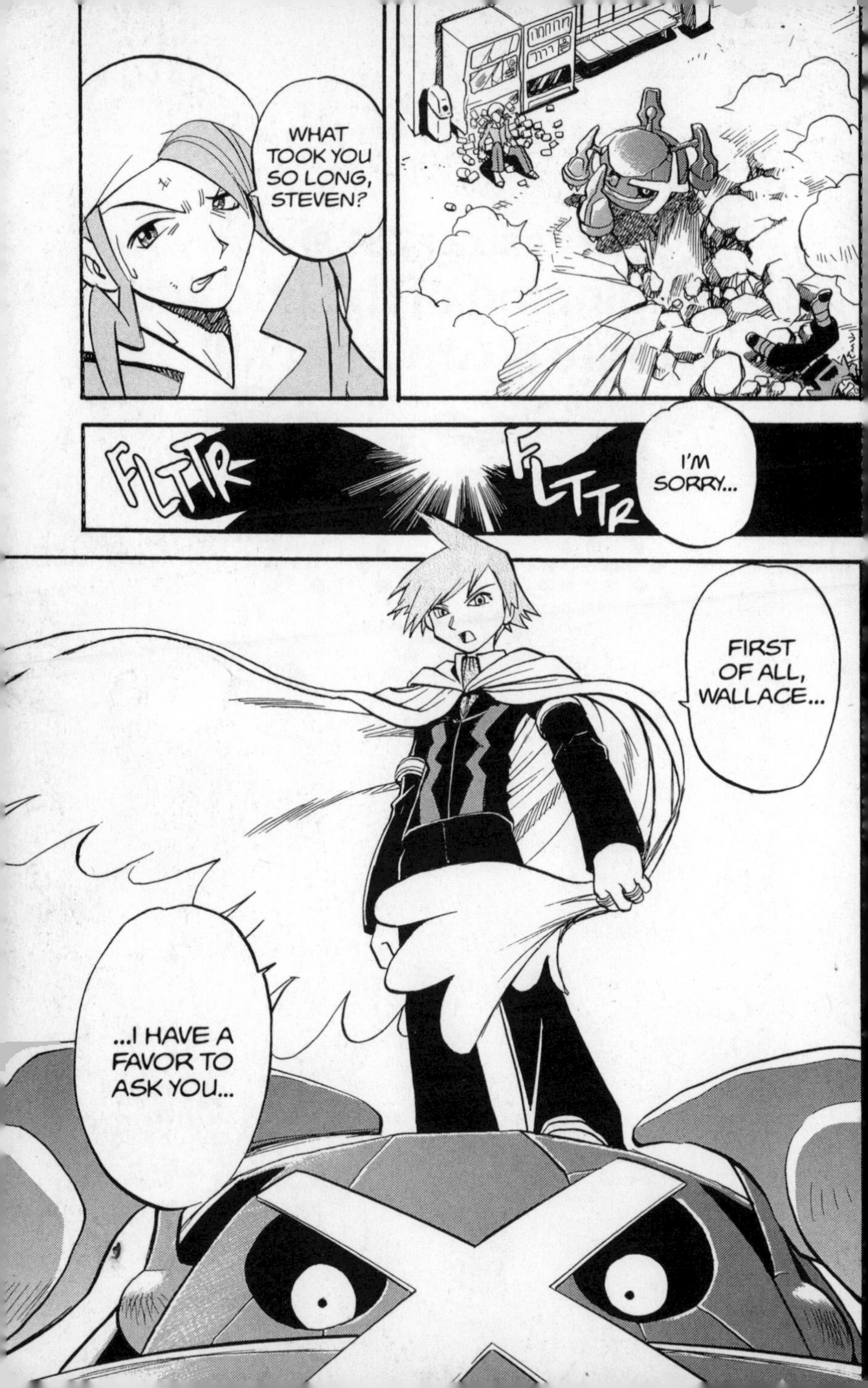
WHAT TOOK YOU SO LONG, STEVEN?
I'M SORRY...
FLTTR
FLTR
FIRST OF ALL, WALLACE...
...I HAVE A FAVOR TO ASK YOU...

# ● Chapter 251 ●
# The Beginning of the End with Kyogre & Groudon XIII

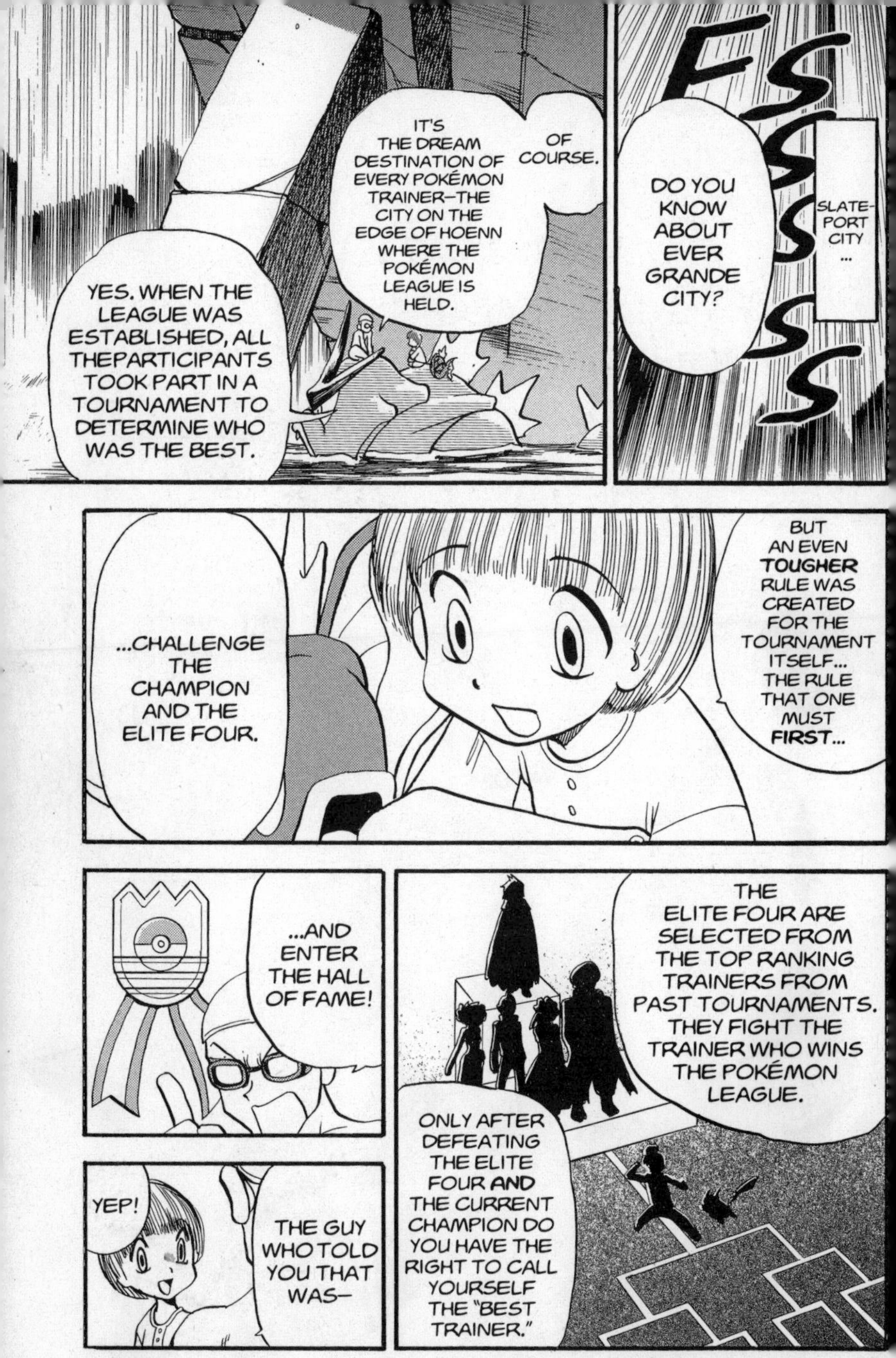
FSSSSS
SLATEPORT CITY...
DO YOU KNOW ABOUT EVER GRANDE CITY?
OF COURSE.
IT'S THE DREAM DESTINATION OF EVERY POKÉMON TRAINER—THE CITY ON THE EDGE OF HOENN WHERE THE POKÉMON LEAGUE IS HELD.
YES. WHEN THE LEAGUE WAS ESTABLISHED, ALL THEPARTICIPANTS TOOK PART IN A TOURNAMENT TO DETERMINE WHO WAS THE BEST.
BUT AN EVEN **TOUGHER** RULE WAS CREATED FOR THE TOURNAMENT ITSELF... THE RULE THAT ONE MUST **FIRST**...
...CHALLENGE THE CHAMPION AND THE ELITE FOUR.
THE ELITE FOUR ARE SELECTED FROM THE TOP RANKING TRAINERS FROM PAST TOURNAMENTS. THEY FIGHT THE TRAINER WHO WINS THE POKÉMON LEAGUE.
ONLY AFTER DEFEATING THE ELITE FOUR **AND** THE CURRENT CHAMPION DO YOU HAVE THE RIGHT TO CALL YOURSELF THE "BEST TRAINER."
...AND ENTER THE HALL OF FAME!
THE GUY WHO TOLD YOU THAT WAS—
YEP!

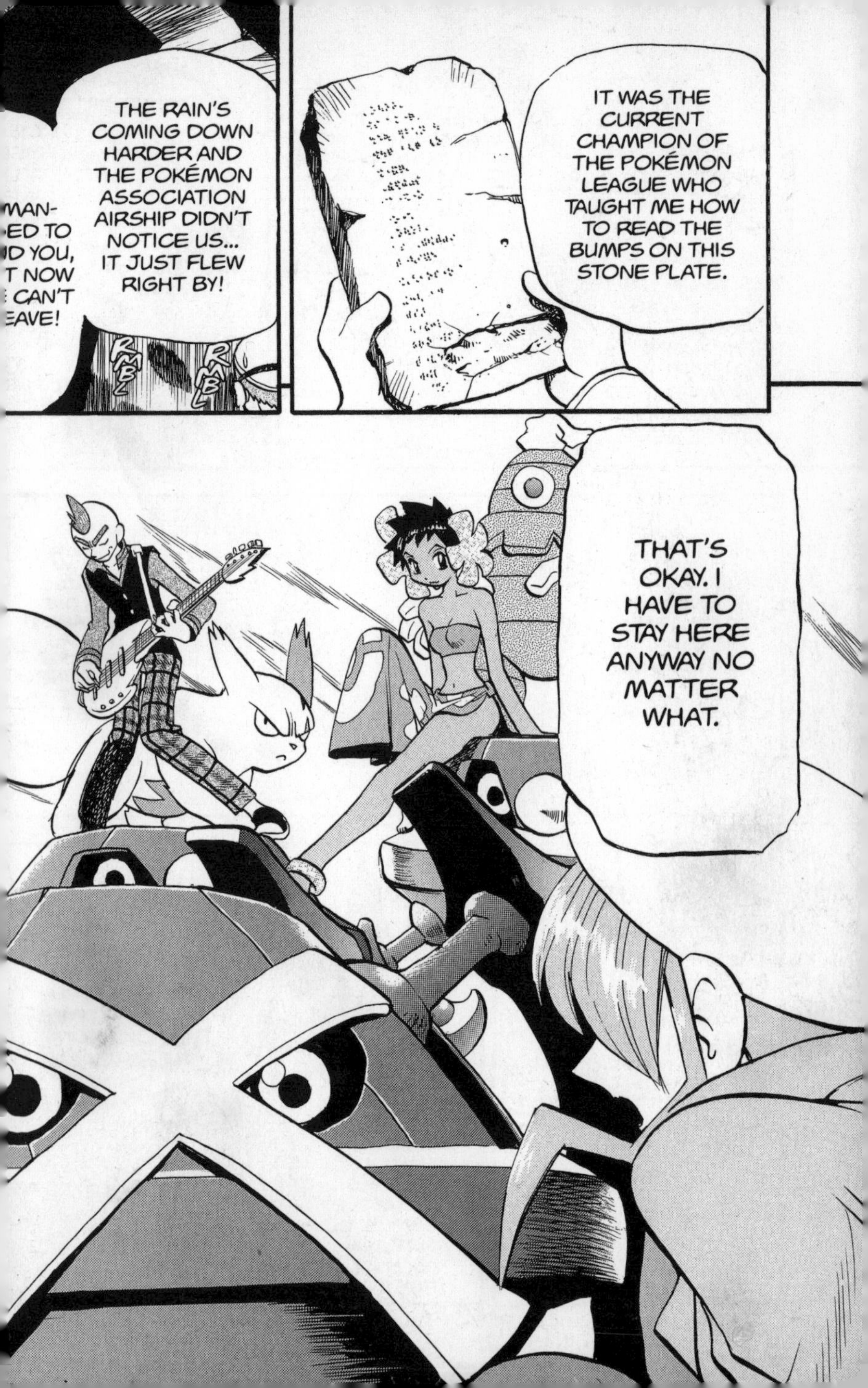
IT WAS THE CURRENT CHAMPION OF THE POKÉMON LEAGUE WHO TAUGHT ME HOW TO READ THE BUMPS ON THIS STONE PLATE.
THE RAIN'S COMING DOWN HARDER AND THE POKÉMON ASSOCIATION AIRSHIP DIDN'T NOTICE US... IT JUST FLEW RIGHT BY!
MAN- ED TO ND YOU, T NOW CAN'T EAVE!
RMBL RMBL
THAT'S OKAY. I HAVE TO STAY HERE ANYWAY NO MATTER WHAT.

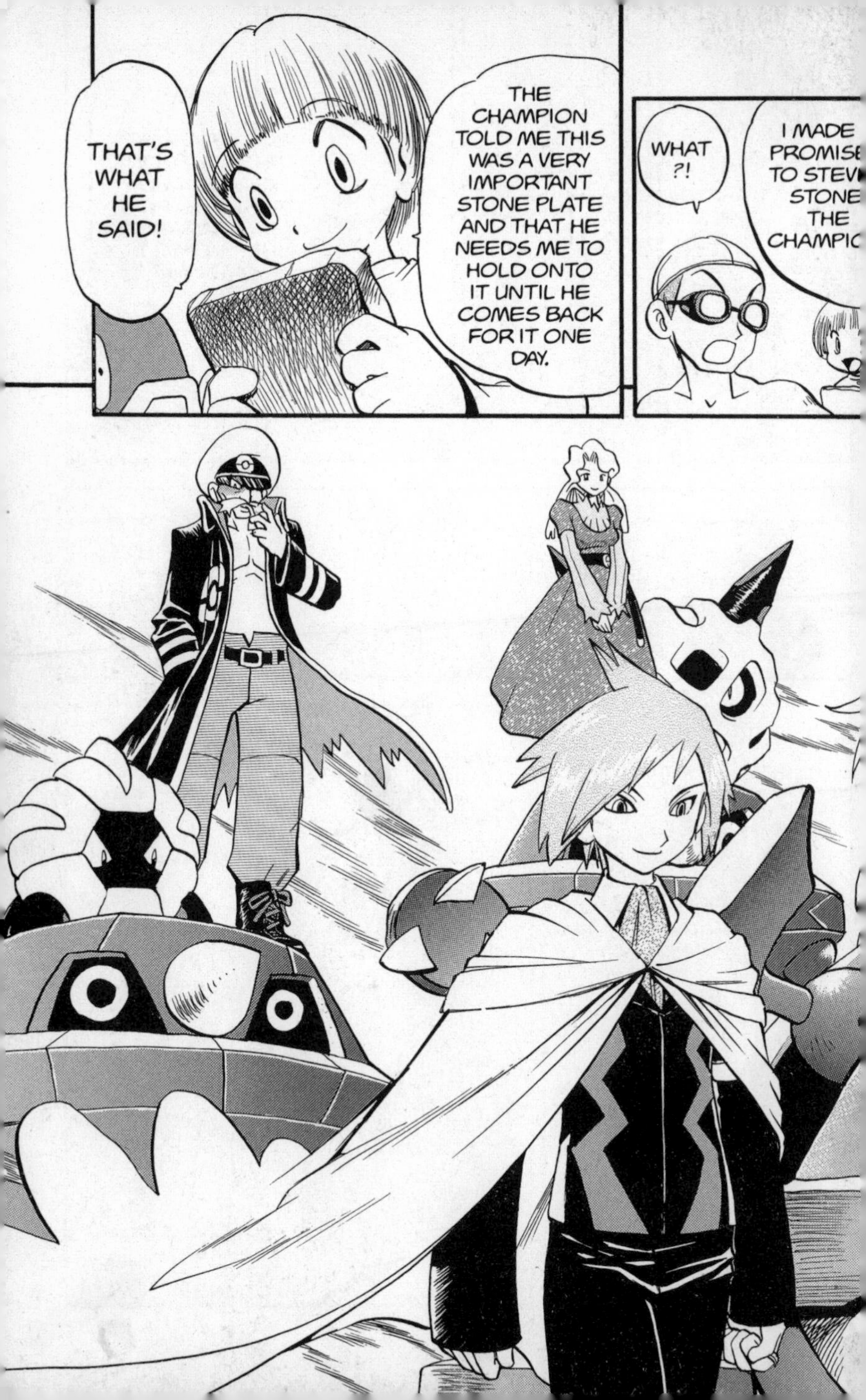
I MADE PROMISE TO STEV STONE THE CHAMPIO
WHAT ?!
THE CHAMPION TOLD ME THIS WAS A VERY IMPORTANT STONE PLATE AND THAT HE NEEDS ME TO HOLD ONTO IT UNTIL HE COMES BACK FOR IT ONE DAY.
THAT'S WHAT HE SAID!

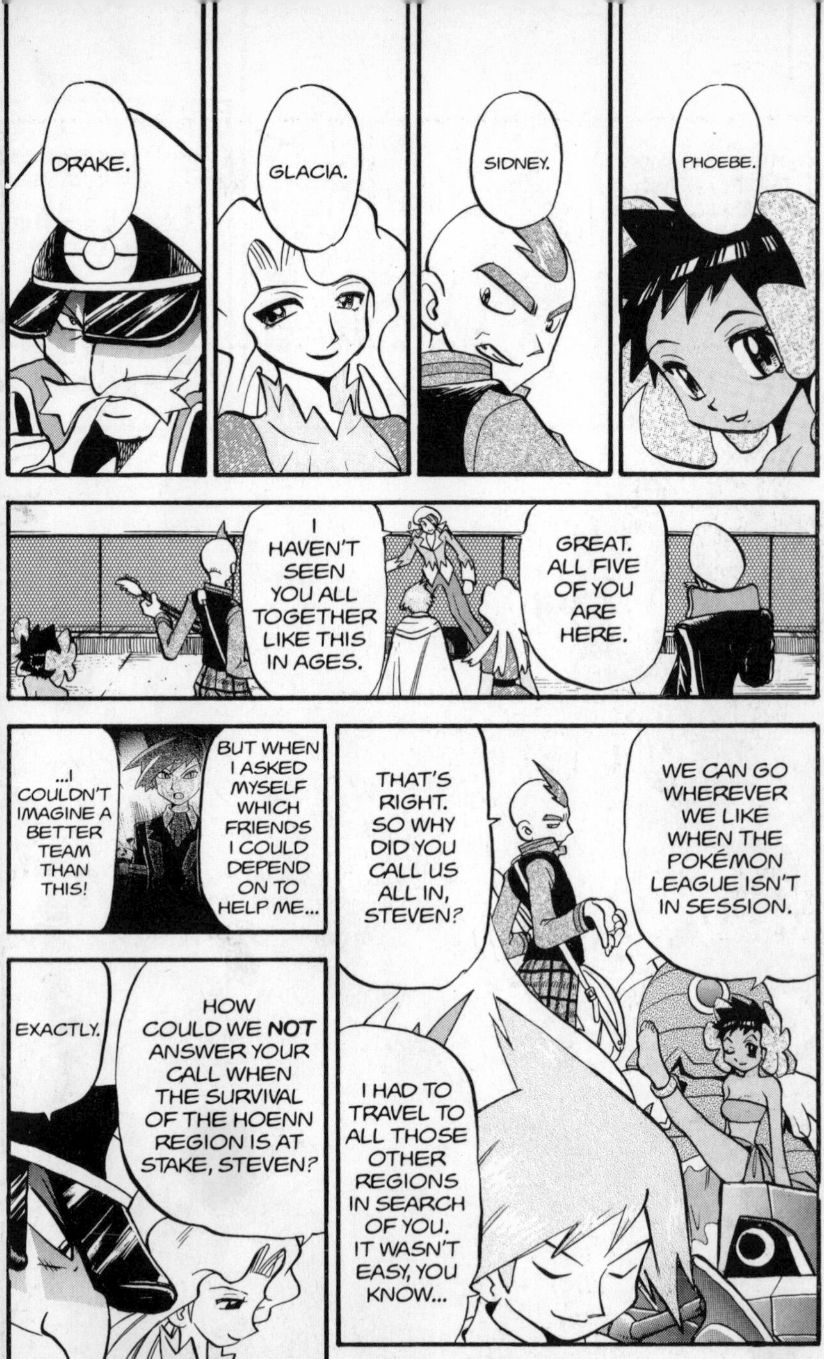
PHOEBE.
SIDNEY.
GLACIA.
DRAKE.
GREAT. ALL FIVE OF YOU ARE HERE.
I HAVEN'T SEEN YOU ALL TOGETHER LIKE THIS IN AGES.
WE CAN GO WHEREVER WE LIKE WHEN THE POKÉMON LEAGUE ISN'T IN SESSION.
THAT'S RIGHT. SO WHY DID YOU CALL US ALL IN, STEVEN?
I HAD TO TRAVEL TO ALL THOSE OTHER REGIONS IN SEARCH OF YOU. IT WASN'T EASY, YOU KNOW...
BUT WHEN I ASKED MYSELF WHICH FRIENDS I COULD DEPEND ON TO HELP ME...
...I COULDN'T IMAGINE A BETTER TEAM THAN THIS!
HOW COULD WE **NOT** ANSWER YOUR CALL WHEN THE SURVIVAL OF THE HOENN REGION IS AT STAKE, STEVEN?
EXACTLY.

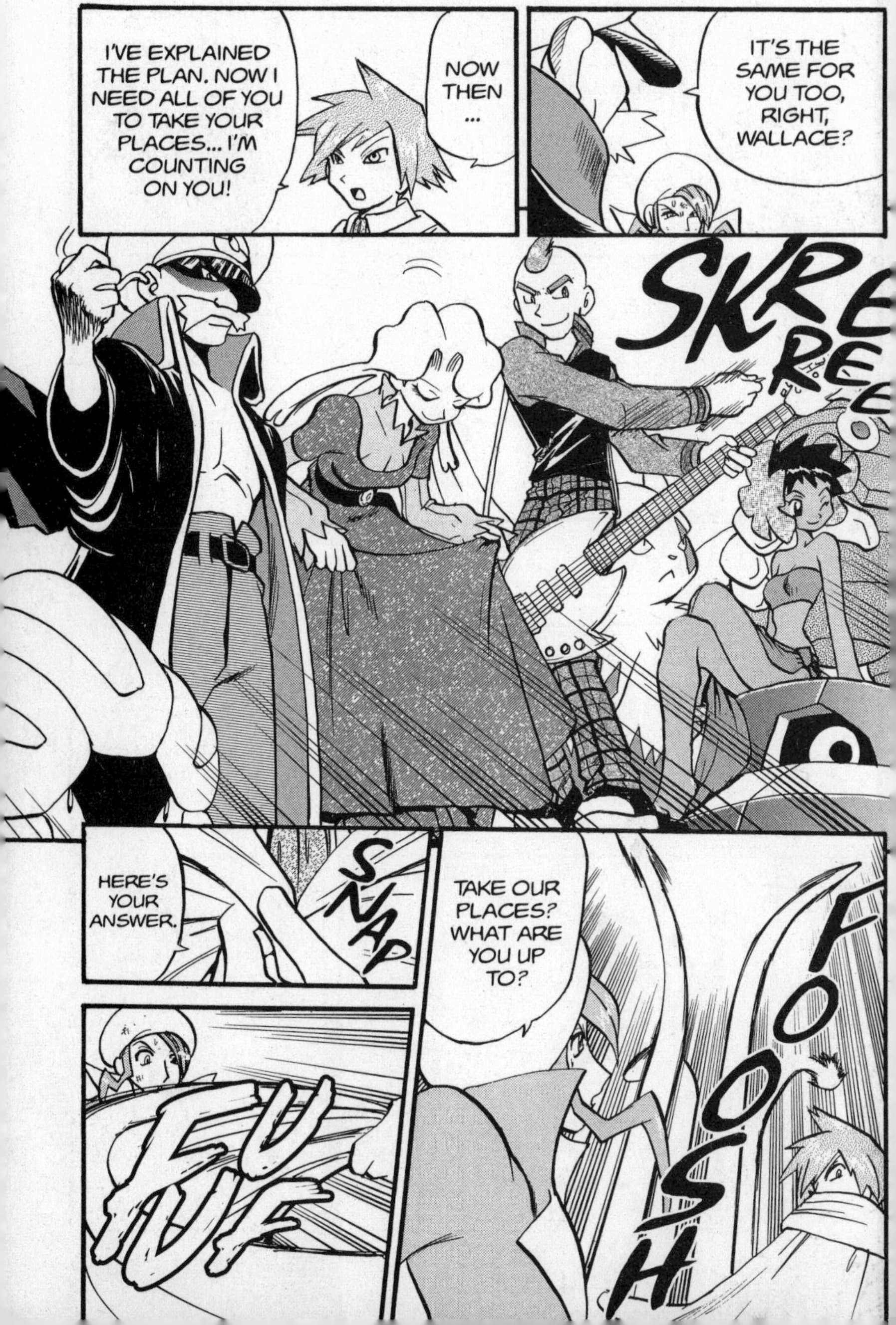
IT'S THE SAME FOR YOU TOO, RIGHT, WALLACE?
NOW THEN ...
I'VE EXPLAINED THE PLAN. NOW I NEED ALL OF YOU TO TAKE YOUR PLACES... I'M COUNTING ON YOU!
SKREEEE
FOOOSH
TAKE OUR PLACES? WHAT ARE YOU UP TO?
SNAP
HERE'S YOUR ANSWER.

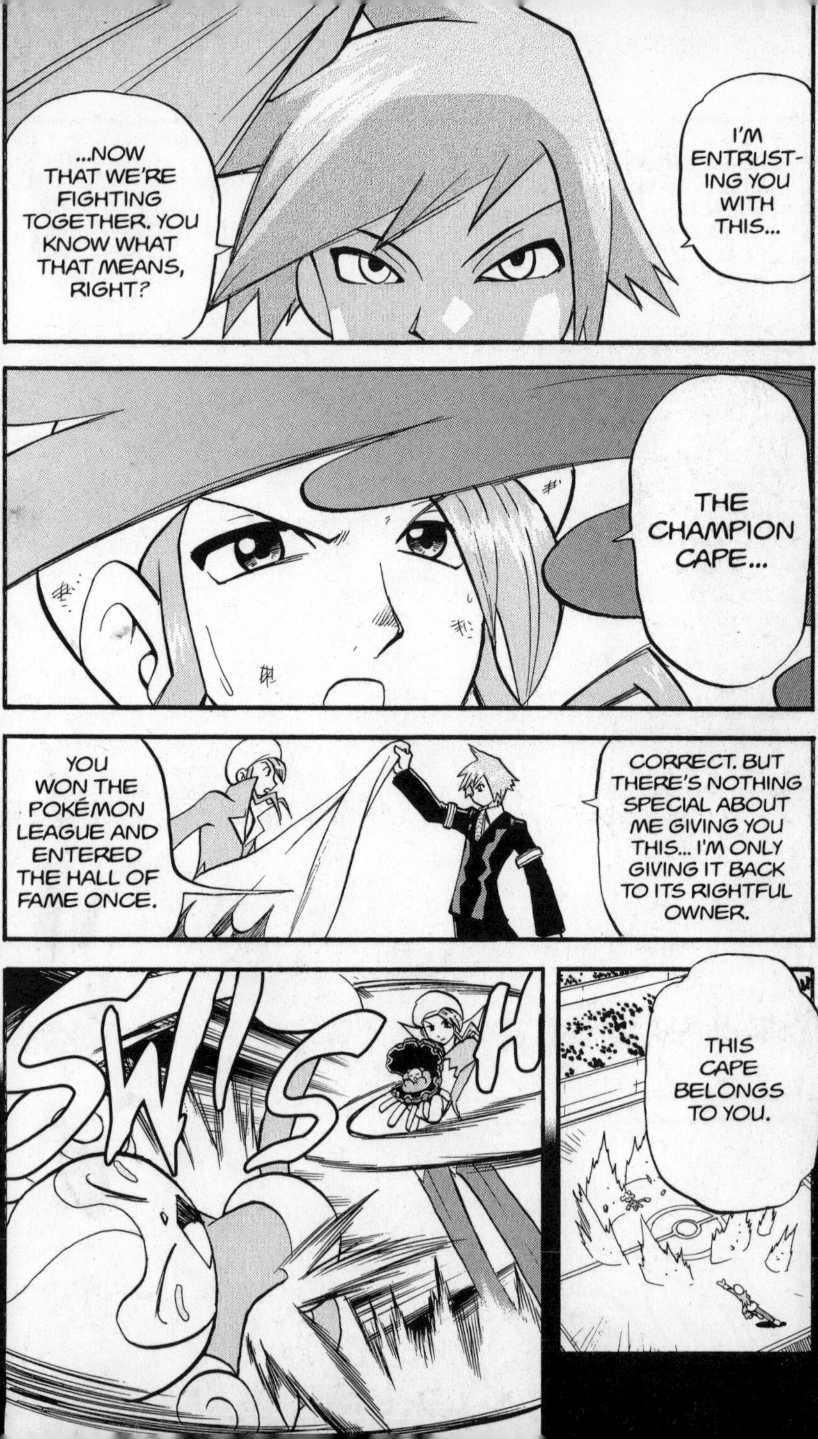
I'M ENTRUST-ING YOU WITH THIS...
...NOW THAT WE'RE FIGHTING TOGETHER. YOU KNOW WHAT THAT MEANS, RIGHT?
THE CHAMPION CAPE...
YOU WON THE POKÉMON LEAGUE AND ENTERED THE HALL OF FAME ONCE.
CORRECT. BUT THERE'S NOTHING SPECIAL ABOUT ME GIVING YOU THIS... I'M ONLY GIVING IT BACK TO ITS RIGHTFUL OWNER.
THIS CAPE BELONGS TO YOU.
SWISH

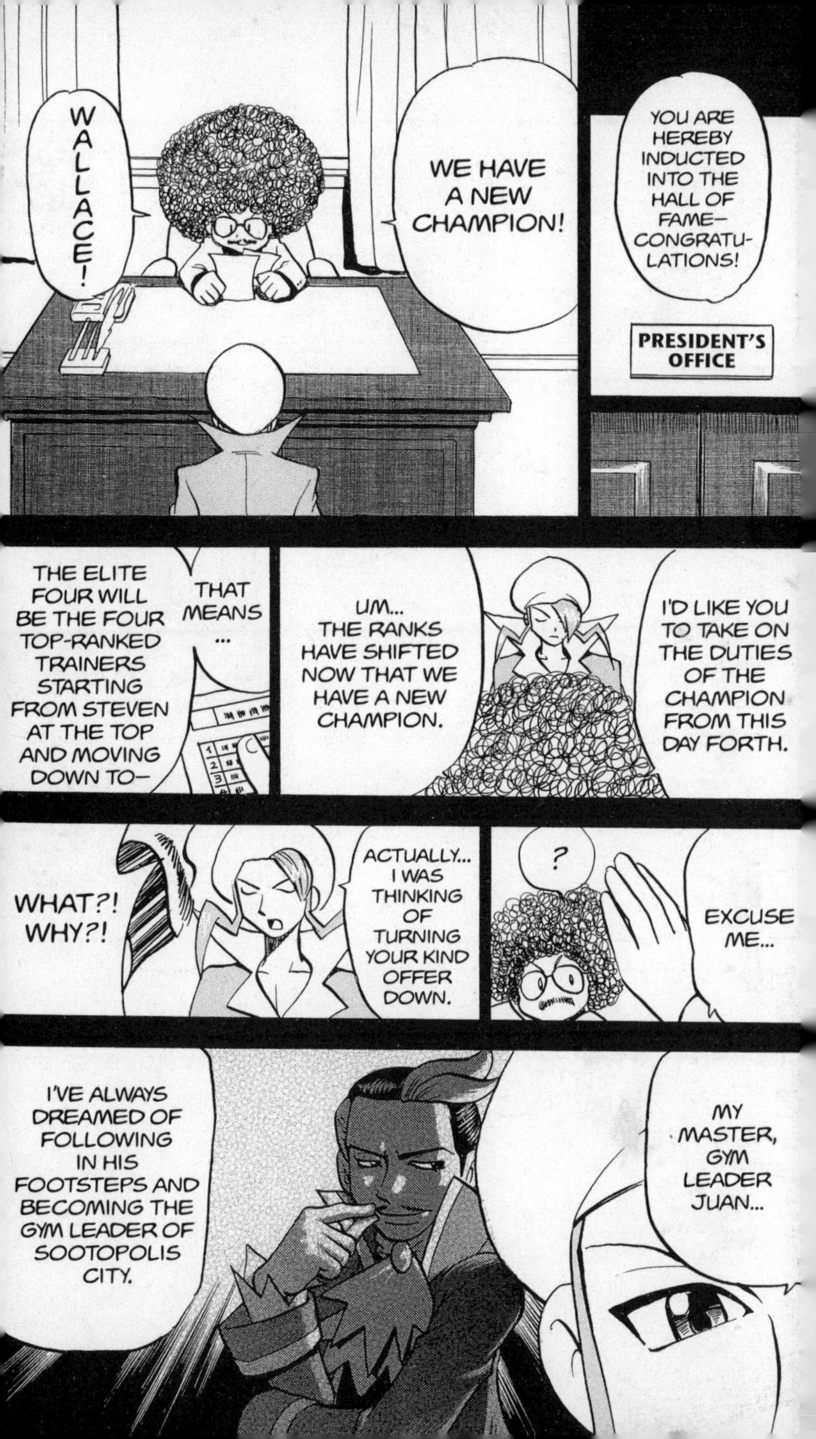
YOU ARE HEREBY INDUCTED INTO THE HALL OF FAME— CONGRATULATIONS!
PRESIDENT'S OFFICE
WE HAVE A NEW CHAMPION!
WALLACE!
I'D LIKE YOU TO TAKE ON THE DUTIES OF THE CHAMPION FROM THIS DAY FORTH.
UM... THE RANKS HAVE SHIFTED NOW THAT WE HAVE A NEW CHAMPION.
THAT MEANS...
THE ELITE FOUR WILL BE THE FOUR TOP-RANKED TRAINERS STARTING FROM STEVEN AT THE TOP AND MOVING DOWN TO—
EXCUSE ME...
?
ACTUALLY... I WAS THINKING OF TURNING YOUR KIND OFFER DOWN.
WHAT?! WHY?!
MY MASTER, GYM LEADER JUAN...
I'VE ALWAYS DREAMED OF FOLLOWING IN HIS FOOTSTEPS AND BECOMING THE GYM LEADER OF SOOTOPOLIS CITY.

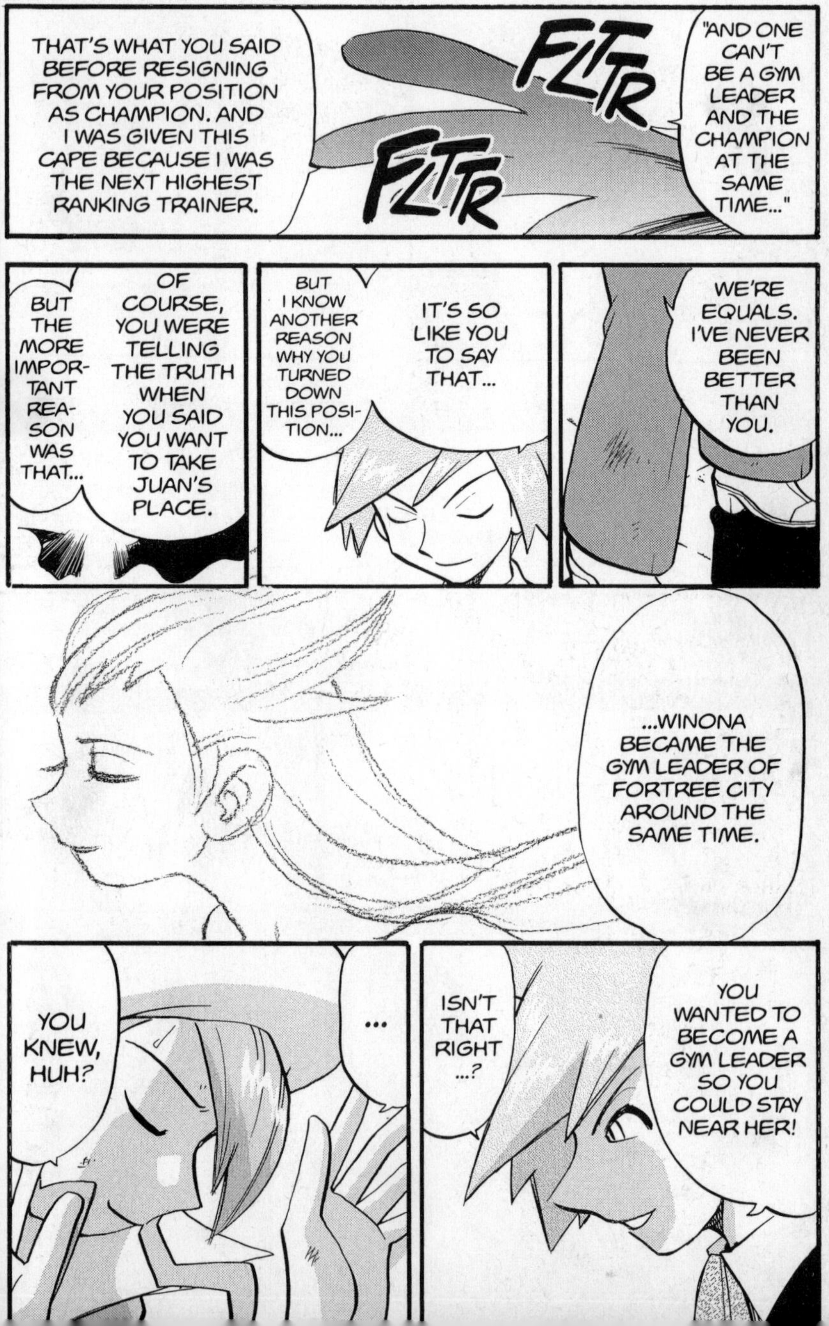
"AND ONE CAN'T BE A GYM LEADER AND THE CHAMPION AT THE SAME TIME..."
FLTTR
FLTTR
THAT'S WHAT YOU SAID BEFORE RESIGNING FROM YOUR POSITION AS CHAMPION. AND I WAS GIVEN THIS CAPE BECAUSE I WAS THE NEXT HIGHEST RANKING TRAINER.
WE'RE EQUALS. I'VE NEVER BEEN BETTER THAN YOU.
IT'S SO LIKE YOU TO SAY THAT...
BUT I KNOW ANOTHER REASON WHY YOU TURNED DOWN THIS POSI-TION...
OF COURSE, YOU WERE TELLING THE TRUTH WHEN YOU SAID YOU WANT TO TAKE JUAN'S PLACE.
BUT THE MORE IMPOR-TANT REA-SON WAS THAT...
...WINONA BECAME THE GYM LEADER OF FORTREE CITY AROUND THE SAME TIME.
YOU WANTED TO BECOME A GYM LEADER SO YOU COULD STAY NEAR HER!
ISN'T THAT RIGHT ...?
...
YOU KNEW, HUH?

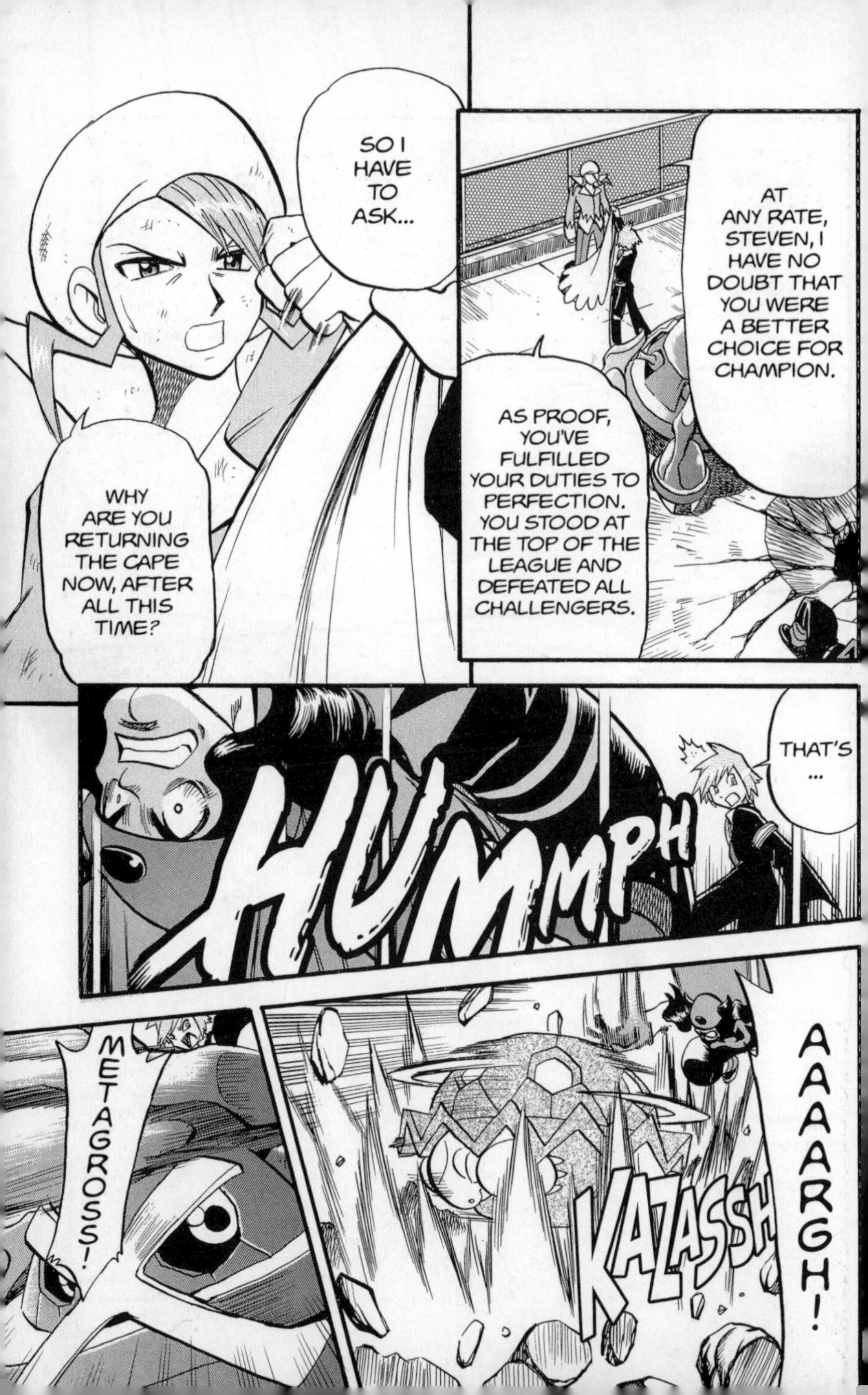
AT ANY RATE, STEVEN, I HAVE NO DOUBT THAT YOU WERE A BETTER CHOICE FOR CHAMPION.
AS PROOF, YOU'VE FULFILLED YOUR DUTIES TO PERFECTION. YOU STOOD AT THE TOP OF THE LEAGUE AND DEFEATED ALL CHALLENGERS.
SO I HAVE TO ASK...
WHY ARE YOU RETURNING THE CAPE NOW, AFTER ALL THIS TIME?
THAT'S ...
HUMMPH
AAAARGH!
KAZASSH
METAGROSS!

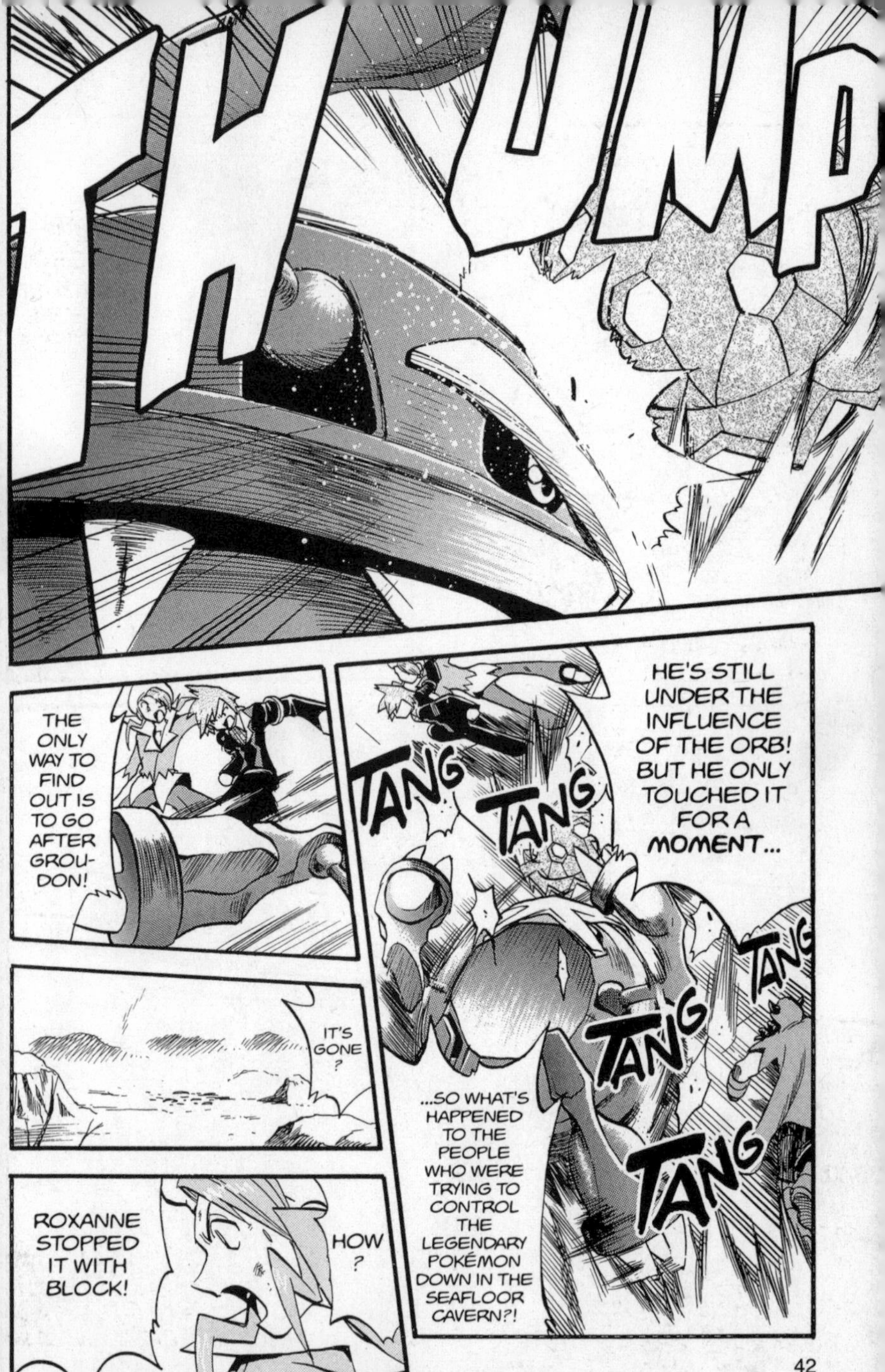
THUMP
HE'S STILL UNDER THE INFLUENCE OF THE ORB! BUT HE ONLY TOUCHED IT FOR A MOMENT...
TANG TANG
TANG TANG
TANG TANG
...SO WHAT'S HAPPENED TO THE PEOPLE WHO WERE TRYING TO CONTROL THE LEGENDARY POKÉMON DOWN IN THE SEAFLOOR CAVERN?!
THE ONLY WAY TO FIND OUT IS TO GO AFTER GROU- DON!
IT'S GONE ?
HOW ?
ROXANNE STOPPED IT WITH BLOCK!

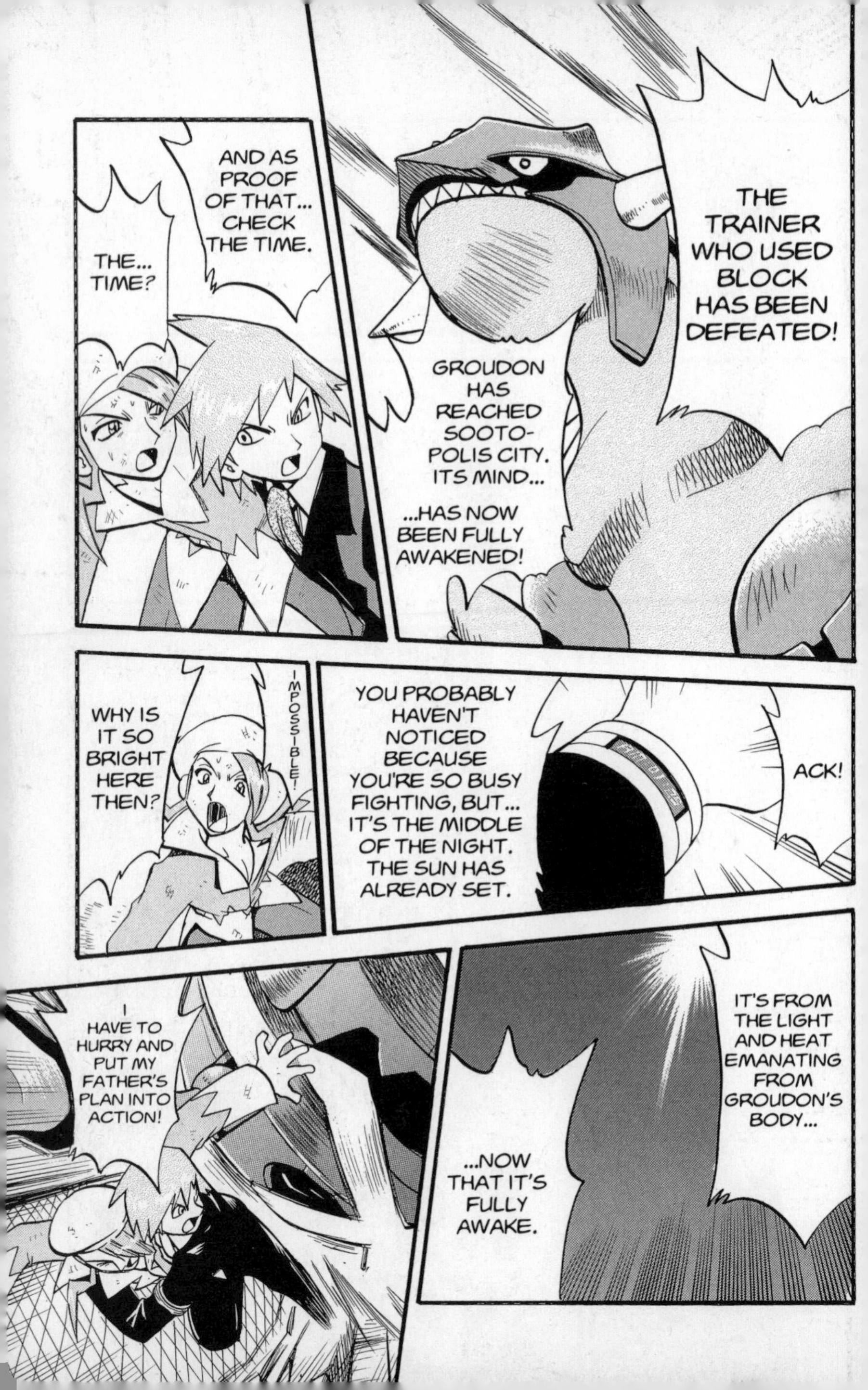
THE TRAINER WHO USED BLOCK HAS BEEN DEFEATED!
GROUDON HAS REACHED SOOTO-POLIS CITY. ITS MIND...
...HAS NOW BEEN FULLY AWAKENED!
AND AS PROOF OF THAT... CHECK THE TIME.
THE... TIME?
ACK!
YOU PROBABLY HAVEN'T NOTICED BECAUSE YOU'RE SO BUSY FIGHTING, BUT... IT'S THE MIDDLE OF THE NIGHT. THE SUN HAS ALREADY SET.
IMPOSSIBLE!
WHY IS IT SO BRIGHT HERE THEN?
IT'S FROM THE LIGHT AND HEAT EMANATING FROM GROUDON'S BODY...
...NOW THAT IT'S FULLY AWAKE.
I HAVE TO HURRY AND PUT MY FATHER'S PLAN INTO ACTION!

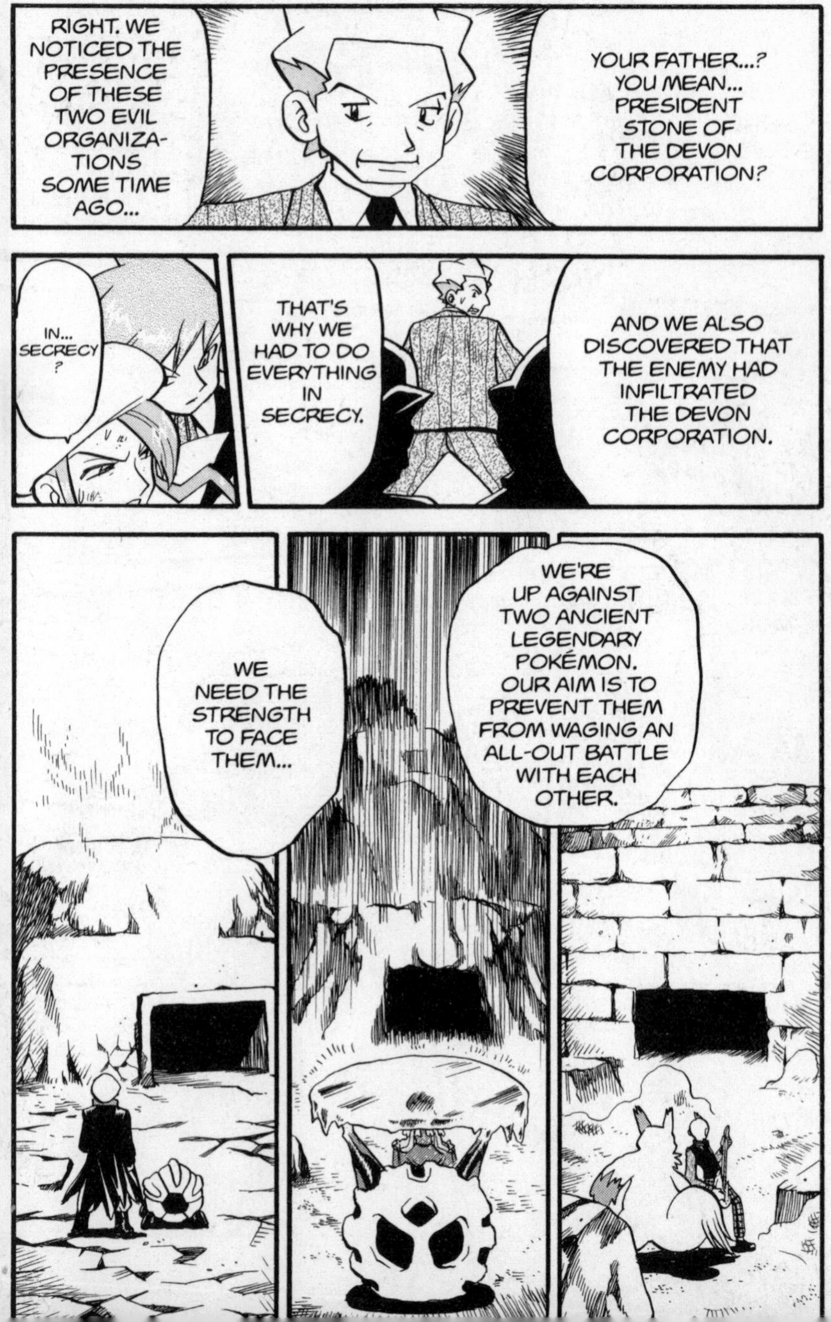
YOUR FATHER...? YOU MEAN... PRESIDENT STONE OF THE DEVON CORPORATION?
RIGHT. WE NOTICED THE PRESENCE OF THESE TWO EVIL ORGANIZA-TIONS SOME TIME AGO...
AND WE ALSO DISCOVERED THAT THE ENEMY HAD INFILTRATED THE DEVON CORPORATION.
THAT'S WHY WE HAD TO DO EVERYTHING IN SECRECY.
IN... SECRECY?
WE'RE UP AGAINST TWO ANCIENT LEGENDARY POKÉMON. OUR AIM IS TO PREVENT THEM FROM WAGING AN ALL-OUT BATTLE WITH EACH OTHER.
WE NEED THE STRENGTH TO FACE THEM...

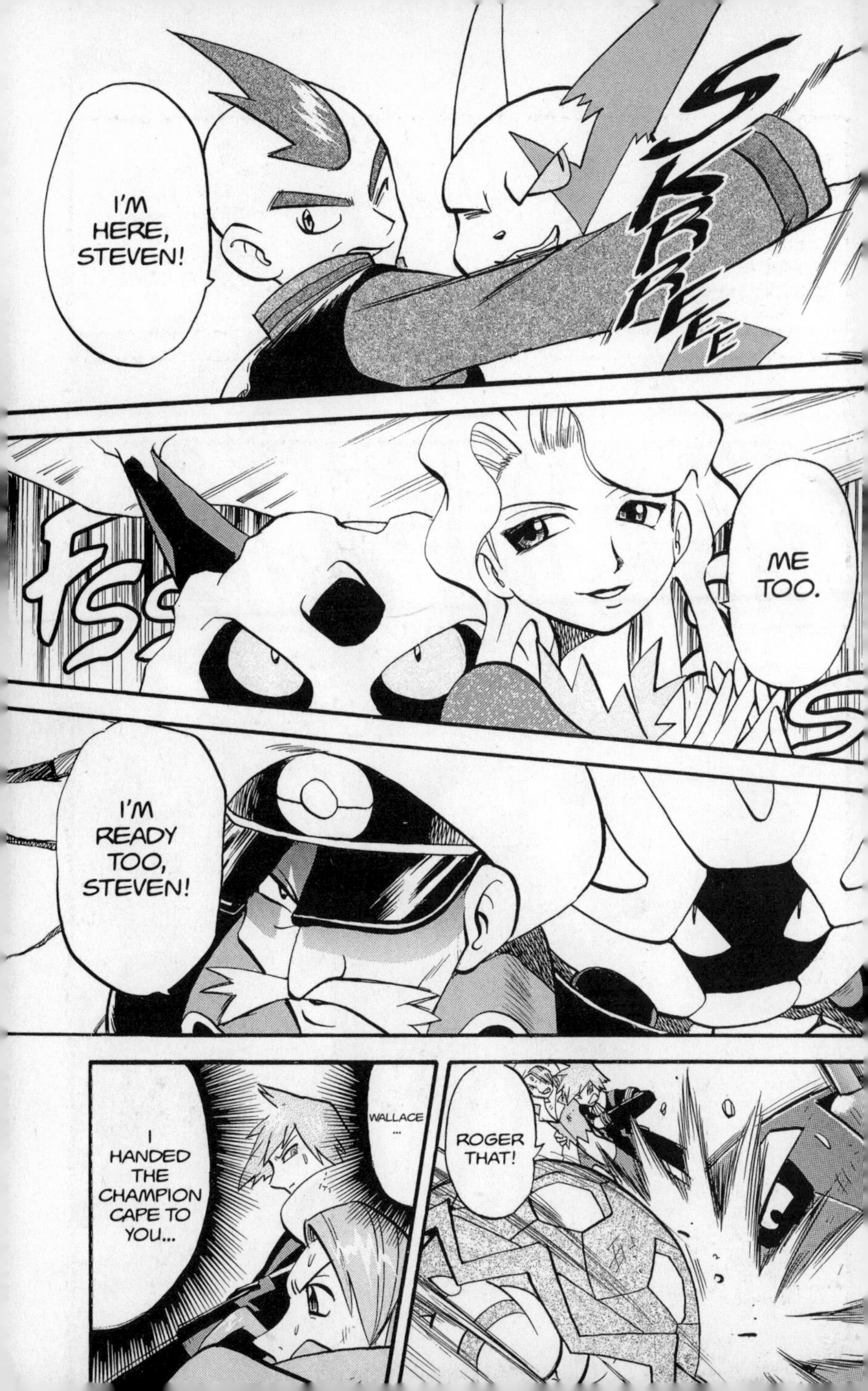
I'M HERE, STEVEN!
SKREEE
ME TOO.
FSS
I'M READY TOO, STEVEN!
ROGER THAT!
WALLACE...
I HANDED THE CHAMPION CAPE TO YOU...

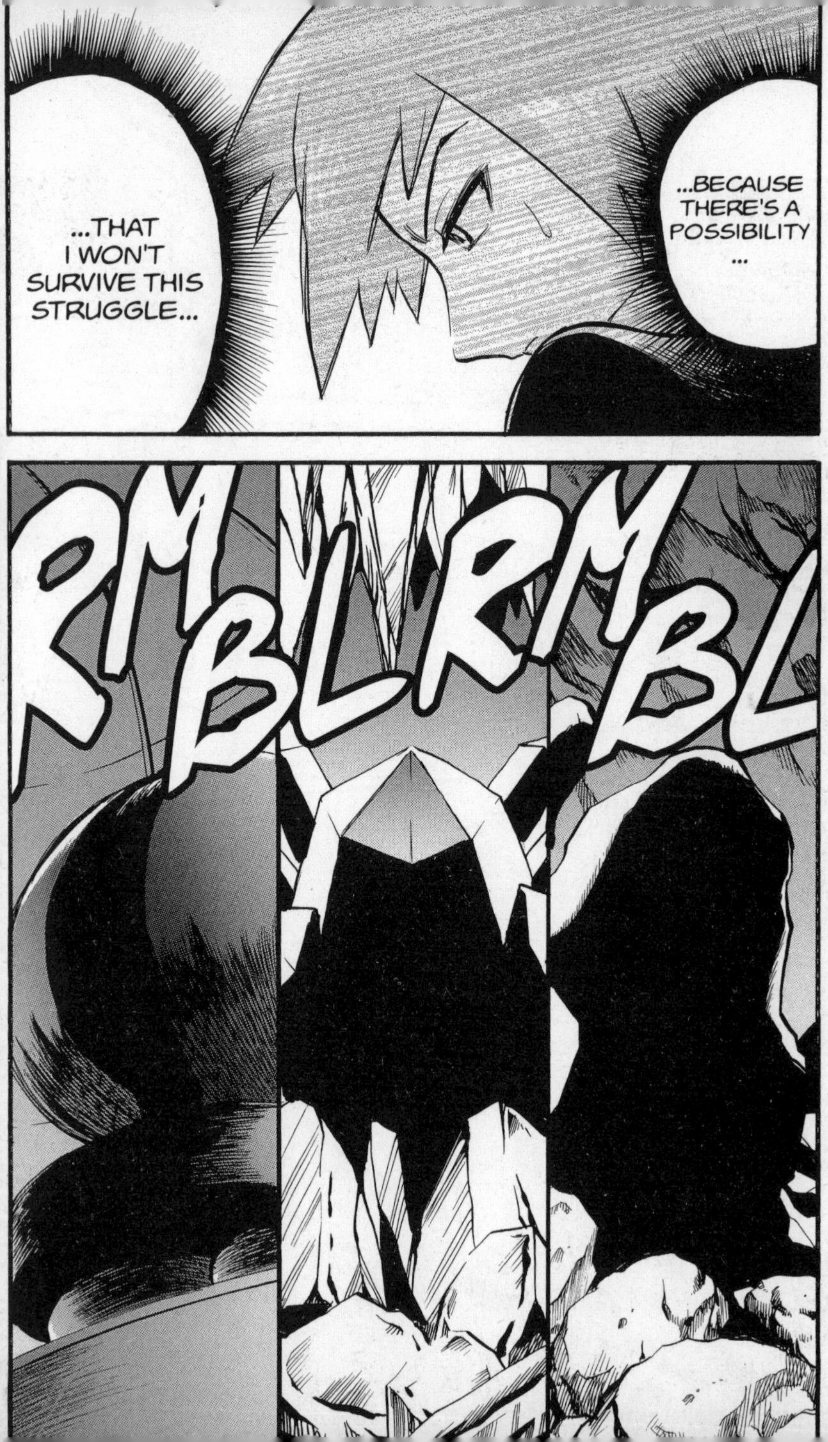
...BECAUSE THERE'S A POSSIBILITY...
...THAT I WON'T SURVIVE THIS STRUGGLE...
RM BLRM BL

# ADVENTURE MAP

# SAPPHIRE

CHIC
Blaziken ♀
**Lv40**

RONO
Lairon ♂
**Lv41**

RELLY
Relicanth ♂
**Lv47**

PHADO
Donphan ♂
**Lv48**

TROPPY
Tropius ♂
**Lv46**

LORRY
Wailord ♂
**Lv48**

| Route 126 |
| --- |

↓

| Seafloor Cavern |
| --- |

| Sootopolis City |
| --- |

# RUBY

MUMU
Swampert ♂

NANA
Mightyena ♀

KIKI
Delcatty ♀

FOFO
Castform ♀

| | | | | |
| --- | --- | --- | --- | --- |
| Stone Badge | Knuckle Badge | Dynamo Badge | Heat Badge |
|  | | |  |
| Balance Badge | Feather Badge | Mind Badge | Rain Badge |
|  | | |  |

| | | Cool | Beauty | Cute | Smart | Tou |
| --- | --- | --- | --- | --- | --- | --- |
| Normal | | ⊕ | ⊕ | ⊕ | ⊕ | ⊕ |
| Super | | ⊕ | ⊕ | ⊕ | ⊕ | ⊕ |
| Hyper | | ⊕ | ★ | ⊕ | ⊕ | ⊕ |
| Master | | ★ | ★ | ★ | ★ | ★ |

# ● Chapter 252 ●
# The Beginning of the End with Kyogre & Groudon XIV

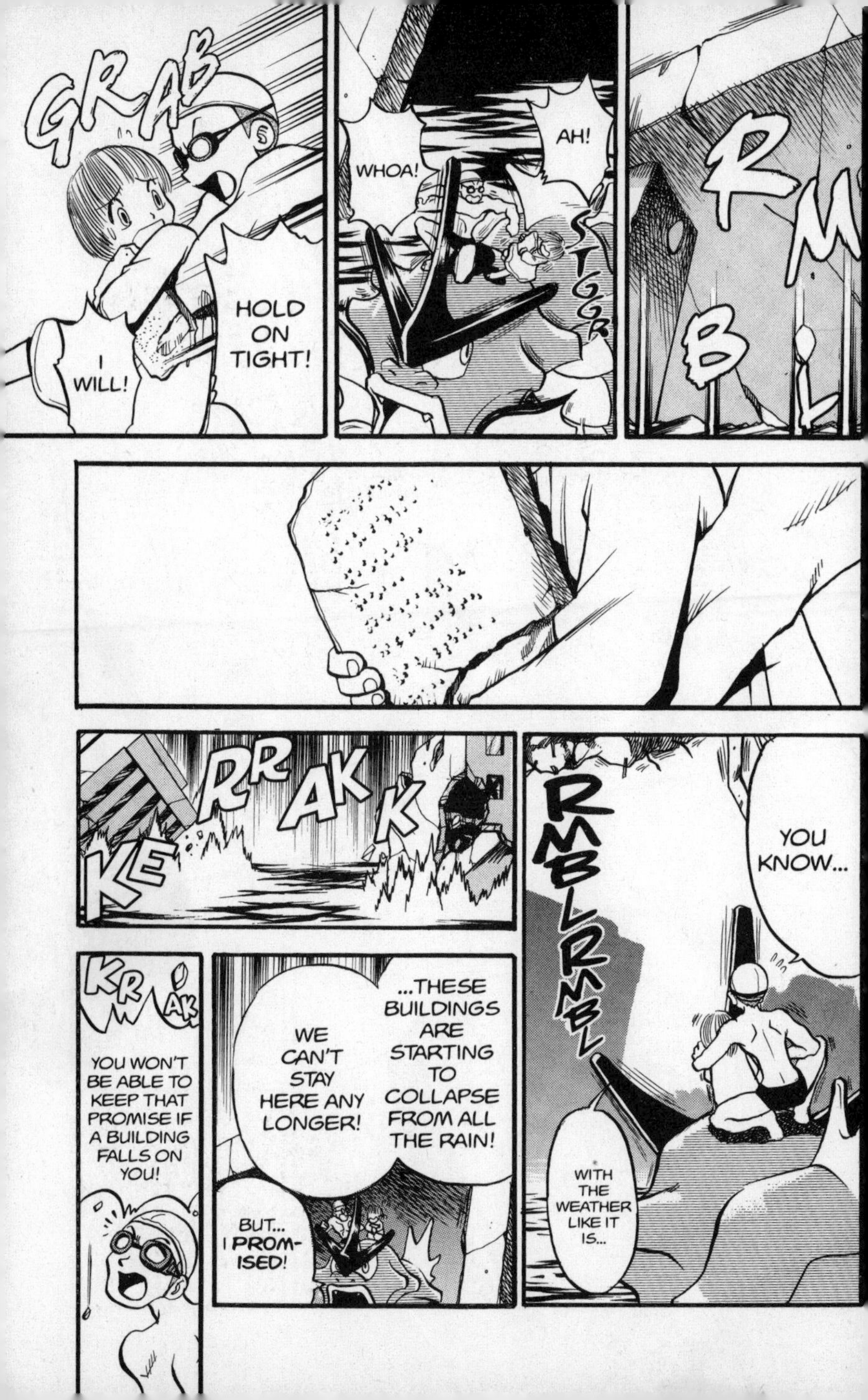
RMBL
AH!
WHOA!
STGGR
GRAB
HOLD ON TIGHT!
I WILL!
YOU KNOW...
RMBLRMBL
WITH THE WEATHER LIKE IT IS...
KERRAKK
...THESE BUILDINGS ARE STARTING TO COLLAPSE FROM ALL THE RAIN!
WE CAN'T STAY HERE ANY LONGER!
BUT... I **PROM-ISED**!
KRAK
YOU WON'T BE ABLE TO KEEP THAT PROMISE IF A BUILDING FALLS ON YOU!

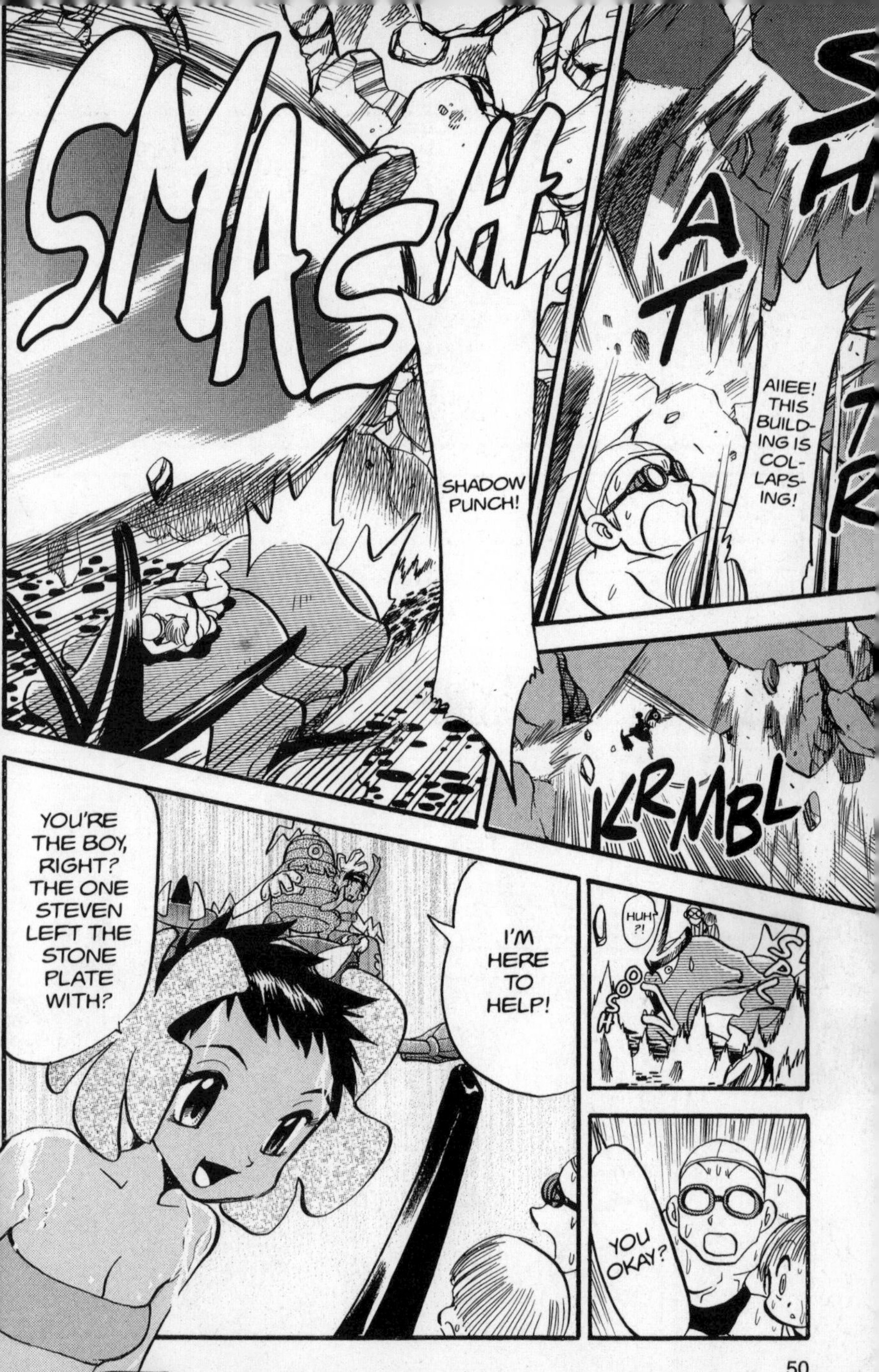
AIIEE! THIS BUILDING IS COLLAPSING!
KRMBL
SMASH
SHADOW PUNCH!
HUH?!
SPL
SHOOSH
YOU OKAY?
I'M HERE TO HELP!
YOU'RE THE BOY, RIGHT? THE ONE STEVEN LEFT THE STONE PLATE WITH?

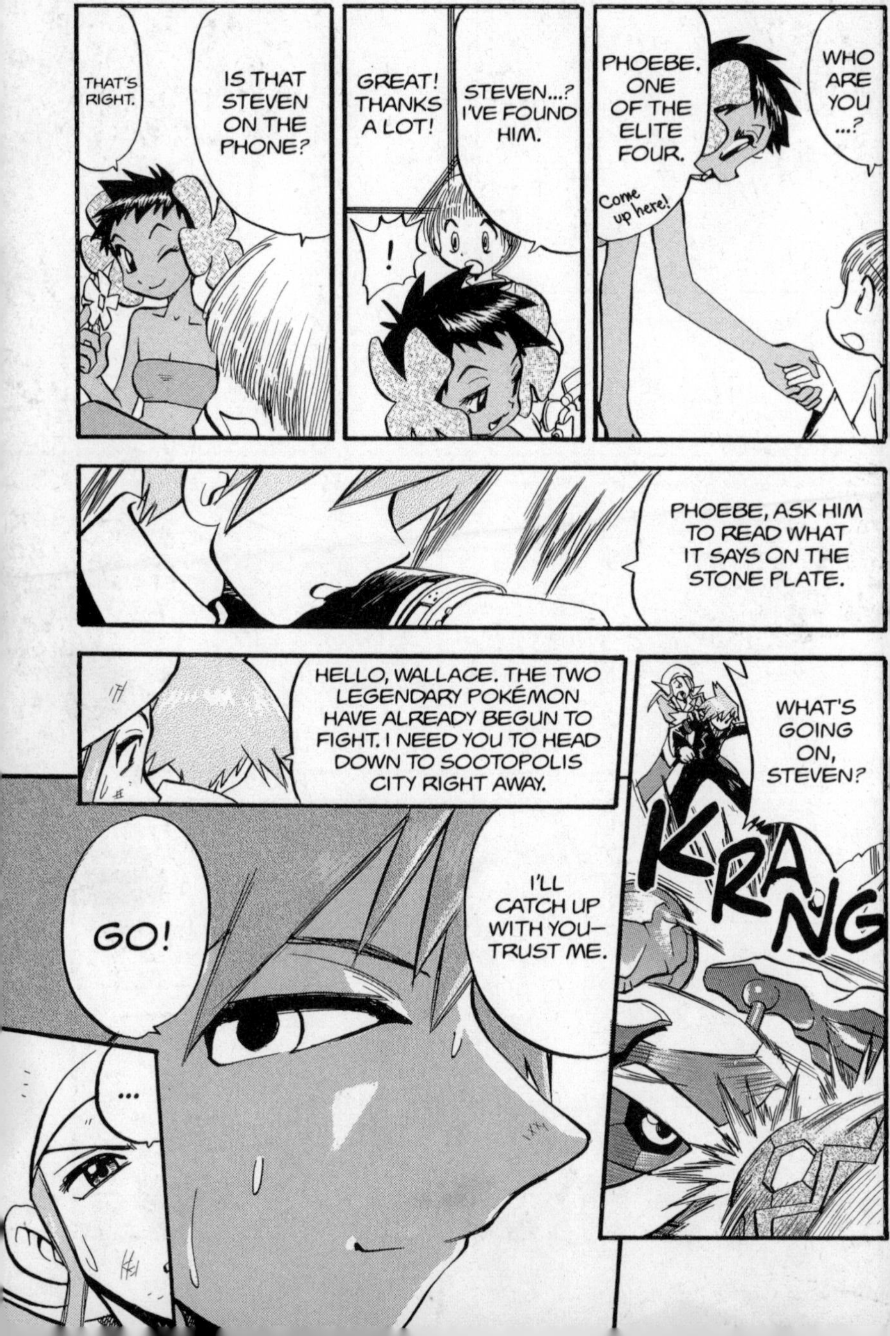
WHO ARE YOU ...?
PHOEBE. ONE OF THE ELITE FOUR.
Come up here!
STEVEN...? I'VE FOUND HIM.
GREAT! THANKS A LOT!
!
IS THAT STEVEN ON THE PHONE?
THAT'S RIGHT.
PHOEBE, ASK HIM TO READ WHAT IT SAYS ON THE STONE PLATE.
WHAT'S GOING ON, STEVEN?
KRANG
HELLO, WALLACE. THE TWO LEGENDARY POKÉMON HAVE ALREADY BEGUN TO FIGHT. I NEED YOU TO HEAD DOWN TO SOOTOPOLIS CITY RIGHT AWAY.
I'LL CATCH UP WITH YOU— TRUST ME.
GO!
...

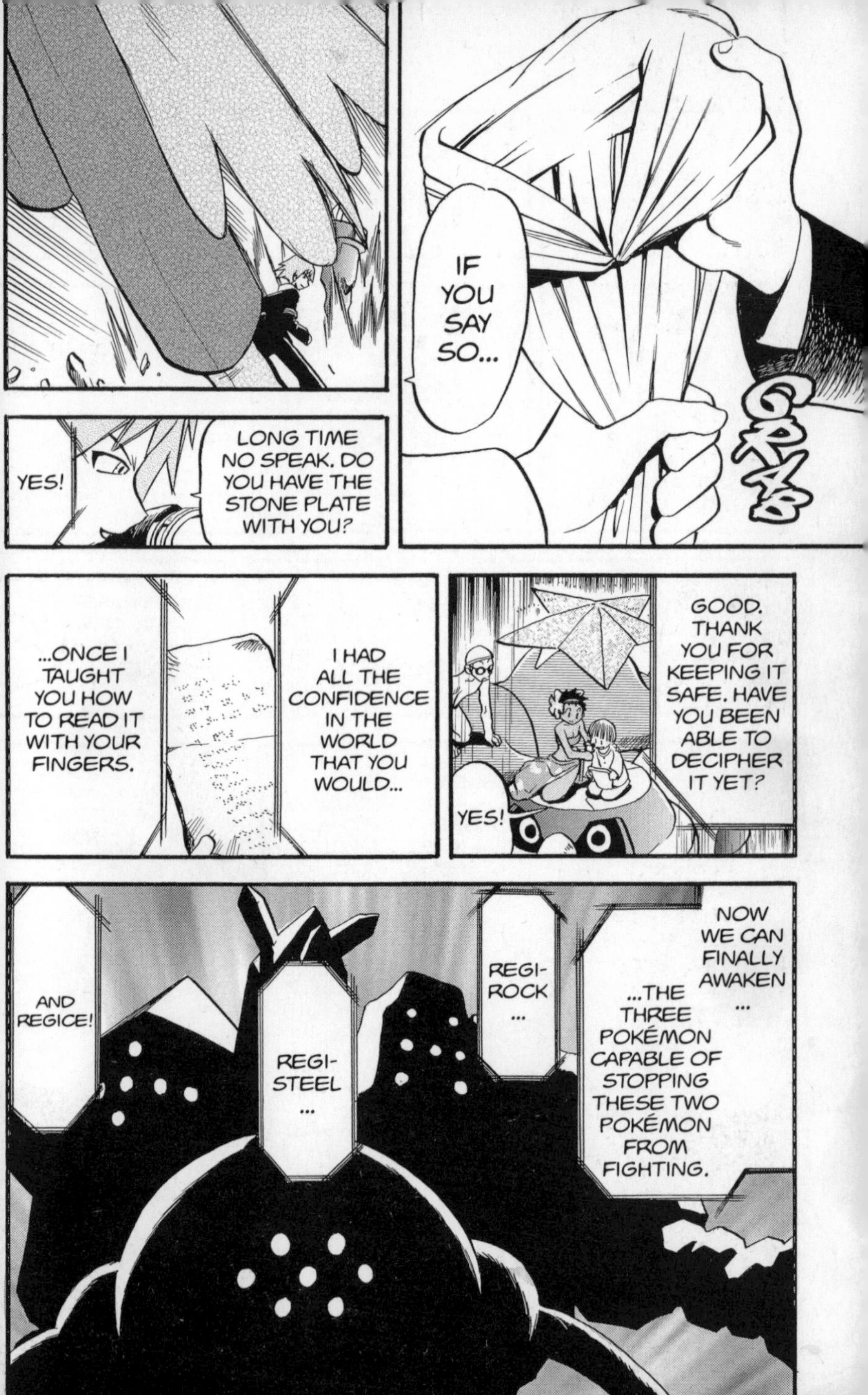
IF YOU SAY SO...
GRAB
LONG TIME NO SPEAK. DO YOU HAVE THE STONE PLATE WITH YOU?
YES!
GOOD. THANK YOU FOR KEEPING IT SAFE. HAVE YOU BEEN ABLE TO DECIPHER IT YET?
YES!
I HAD ALL THE CONFIDENCE IN THE WORLD THAT YOU WOULD...
...ONCE I TAUGHT YOU HOW TO READ IT WITH YOUR FINGERS.
NOW WE CAN FINALLY AWAKEN ...
...THE THREE POKÉMON CAPABLE OF STOPPING THESE TWO POKÉMON FROM FIGHTING.
REGI-ROCK ...
REGI-STEEL ...
AND REGICE!

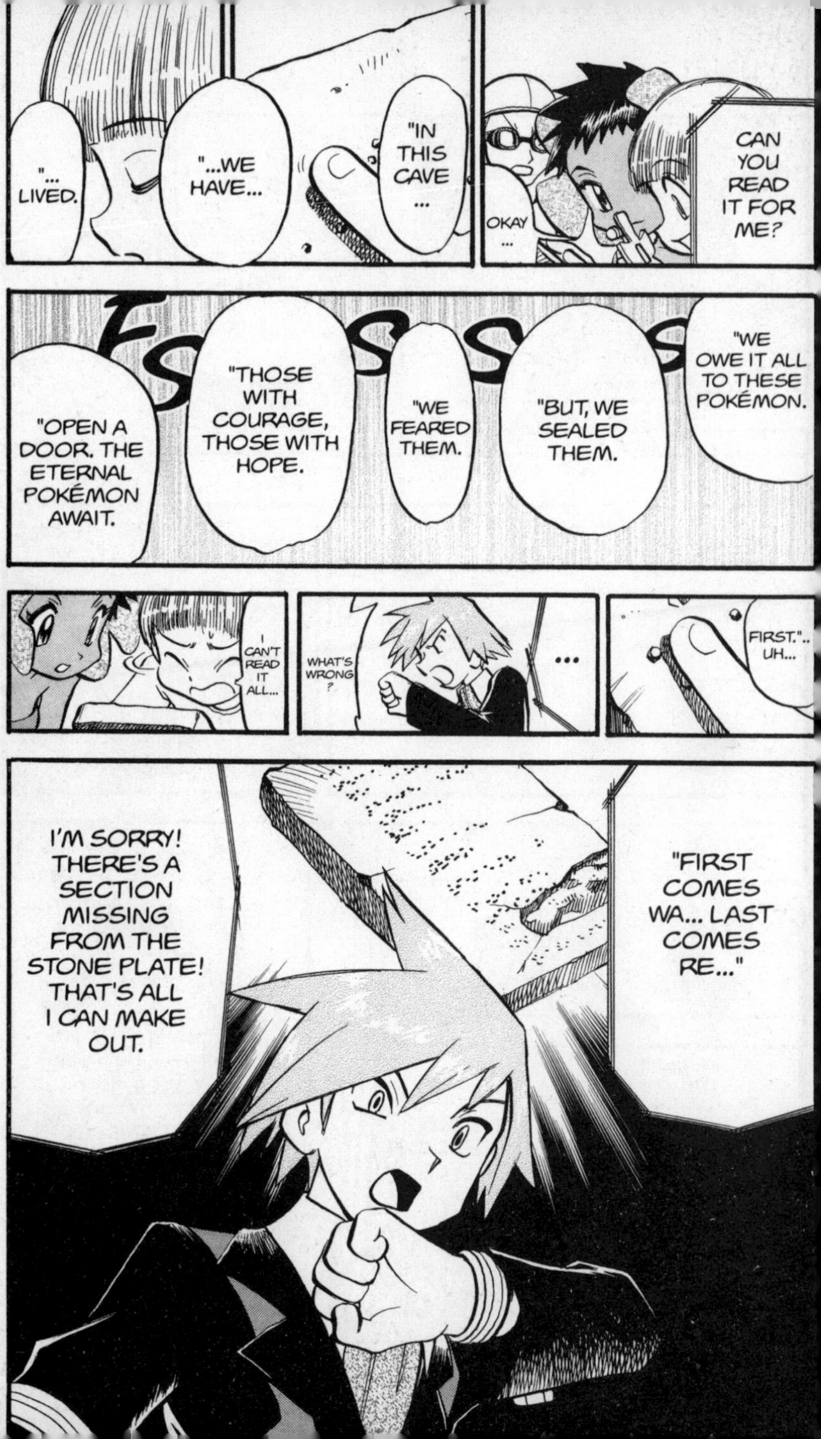
CAN YOU READ IT FOR ME?
OKAY ...
"IN THIS CAVE ...
"...WE HAVE...
"... LIVED.
"WE OWE IT ALL TO THESE POKÉMON.
"BUT, WE SEALED THEM.
"WE FEARED THEM.
"THOSE WITH COURAGE, THOSE WITH HOPE.
"OPEN A DOOR. THE ETERNAL POKÉMON AWAIT.
FSSSS
FIRST." .. UH...
...
WHAT'S WRONG?
I CAN'T READ IT ALL...
"FIRST COMES WA... LAST COMES RE..."
I'M SORRY! THERE'S A SECTION MISSING FROM THE STONE PLATE! THAT'S ALL I CAN MAKE OUT.

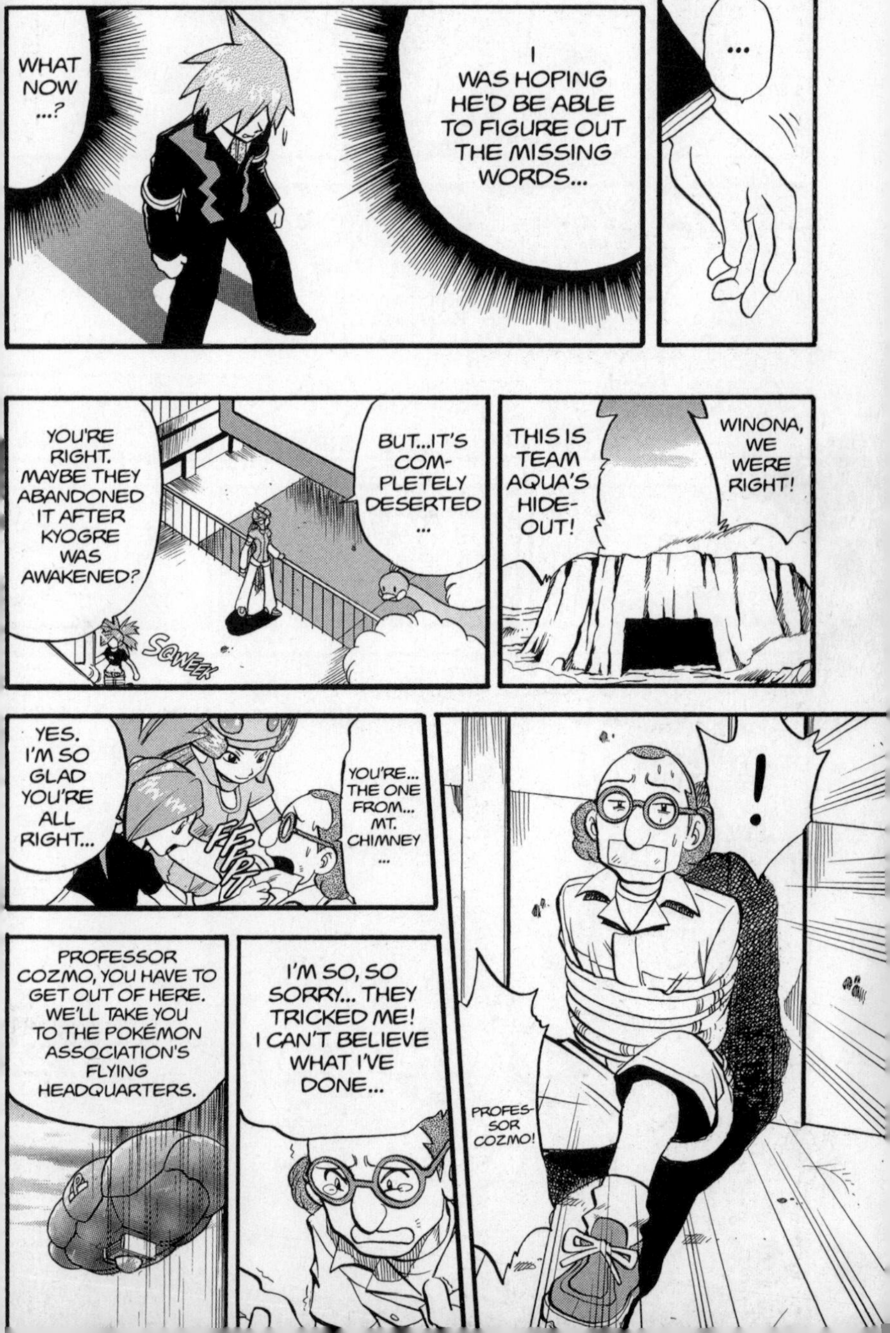
...
I WAS HOPING HE'D BE ABLE TO FIGURE OUT THE MISSING WORDS...
WHAT NOW ...?
WINONA, WE WERE RIGHT!
THIS IS TEAM AQUA'S HIDE-OUT!
BUT...IT'S COM-PLETELY DESERTED ...
YOU'RE RIGHT. MAYBE THEY ABANDONED IT AFTER KYOGRE WAS AWAKENED?
SQWEEK
!
PROFES-SOR COZMO!
YOU'RE... THE ONE FROM... MT. CHIMNEY ...
YES. I'M SO GLAD YOU'RE ALL RIGHT...
I'M SO, SO SORRY... THEY TRICKED ME! I CAN'T BELIEVE WHAT I'VE DONE...
PROFESSOR COZMO, YOU HAVE TO GET OUT OF HERE. WE'LL TAKE YOU TO THE POKÉMON ASSOCIATION'S FLYING HEADQUARTERS.

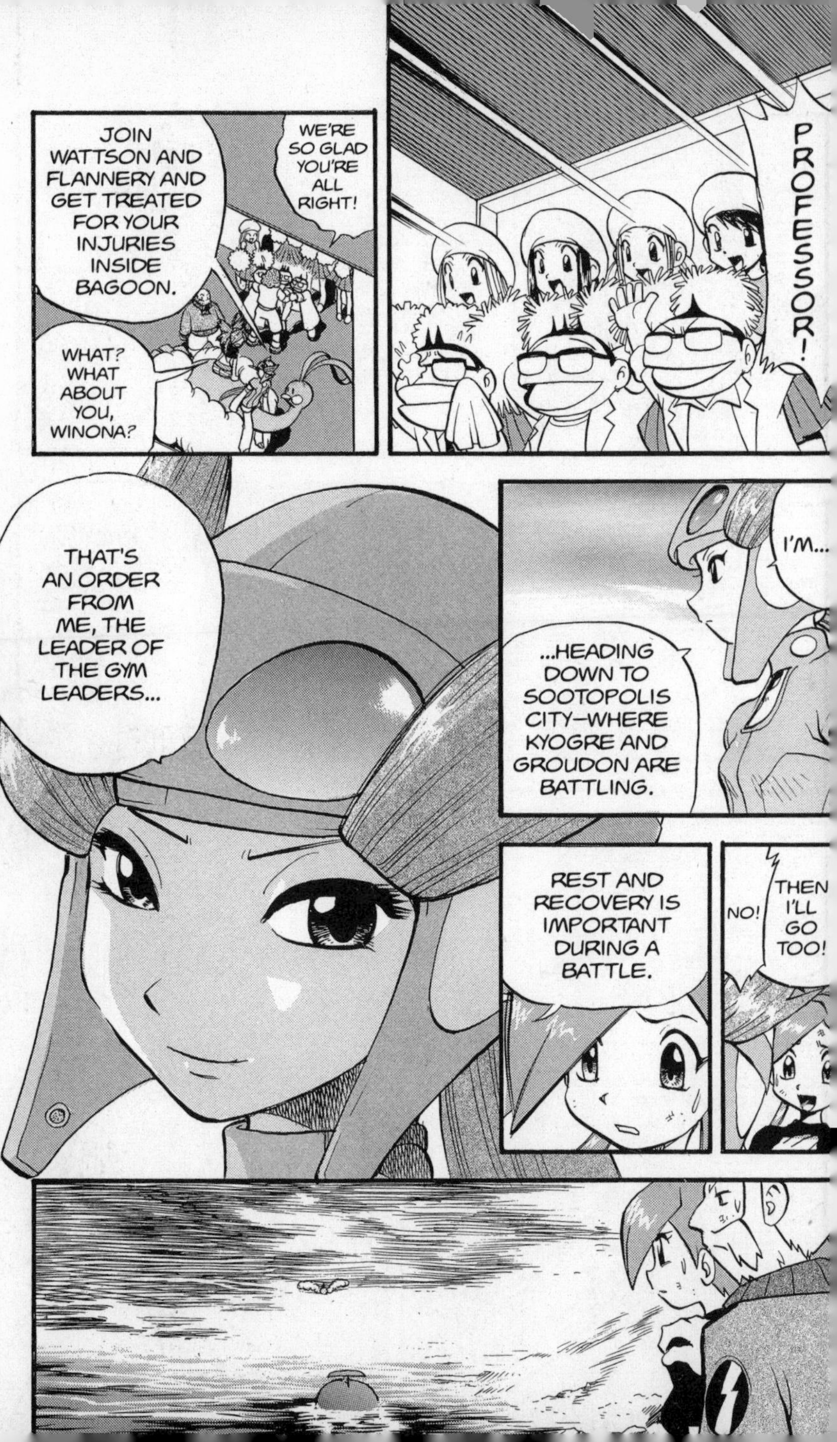
PROFESSOR!
WE'RE SO GLAD YOU'RE ALL RIGHT!
JOIN WATTSON AND FLANNERY AND GET TREATED FOR YOUR INJURIES INSIDE BAGOON.
WHAT? WHAT ABOUT YOU, WINONA?
I'M...
...HEADING DOWN TO SOOTOPOLIS CITY—WHERE KYOGRE AND GROUDON ARE BATTLING.
THEN I'LL GO TOO!
NO!
REST AND RECOVERY IS IMPORTANT DURING A BATTLE.
THAT'S AN ORDER FROM ME, THE LEADER OF THE GYM LEADERS...

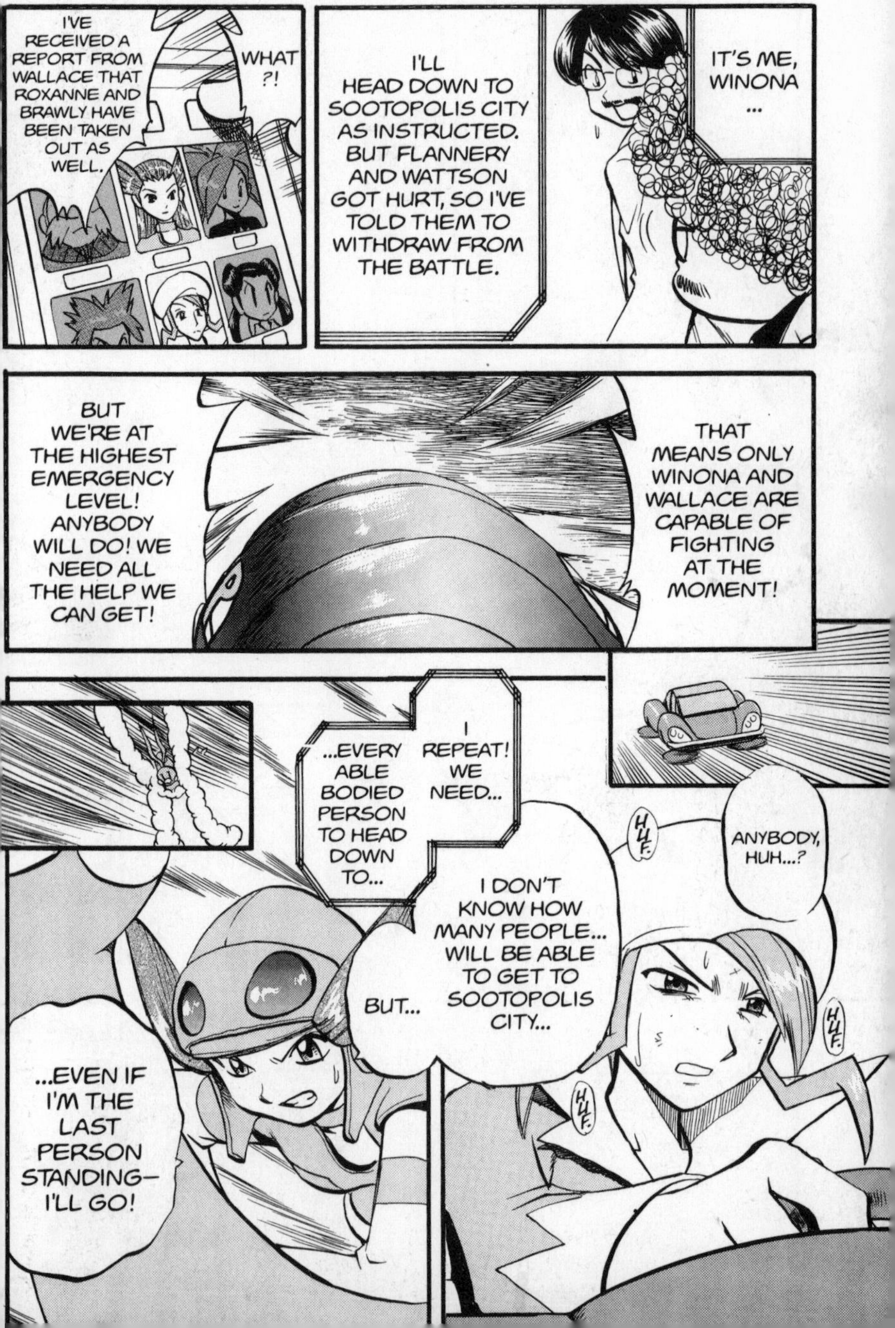
IT'S ME, WINONA ...
I'LL HEAD DOWN TO SOOTOPOLIS CITY AS INSTRUCTED. BUT FLANNERY AND WATTSON GOT HURT, SO I'VE TOLD THEM TO WITHDRAW FROM THE BATTLE.
WHAT ?!
I'VE RECEIVED A REPORT FROM WALLACE THAT ROXANNE AND BRAWLY HAVE BEEN TAKEN OUT AS WELL.
THAT MEANS ONLY WINONA AND WALLACE ARE CAPABLE OF FIGHTING AT THE MOMENT!
BUT WE'RE AT THE HIGHEST EMERGENCY LEVEL! ANYBODY WILL DO! WE NEED ALL THE HELP WE CAN GET!
I REPEAT! WE NEED...
...EVERY ABLE BODIED PERSON TO HEAD DOWN TO...
ANYBODY, HUH...?
HUF
I DON'T KNOW HOW MANY PEOPLE... WILL BE ABLE TO GET TO SOOTOPOLIS CITY...
HUF
HUF
BUT...
...EVEN IF I'M THE LAST PERSON STANDING— I'LL GO!

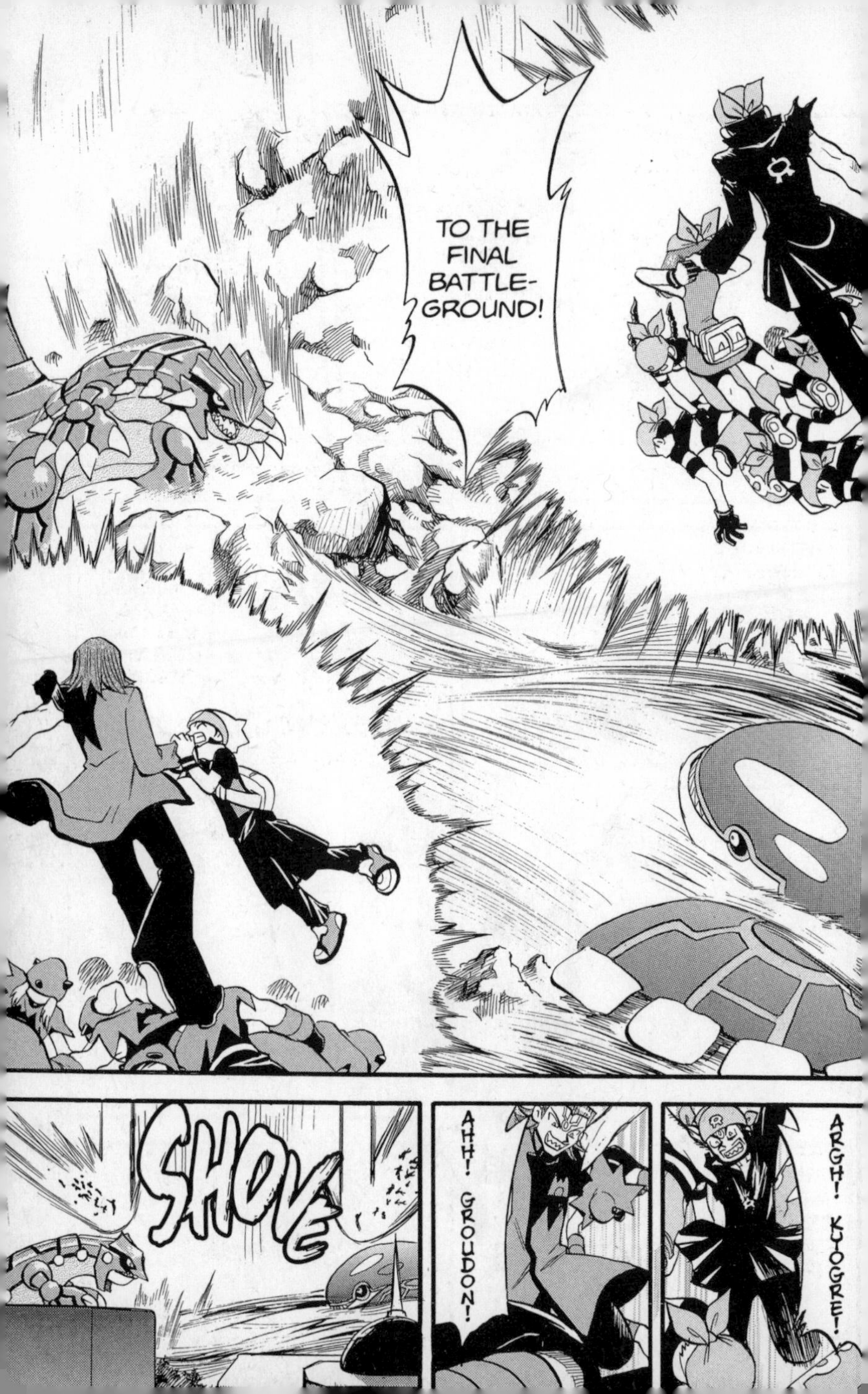
TO THE FINAL BATTLE-GROUND!
ARGH! KYOGRE!
AHH! GROUDON!
SHOVE

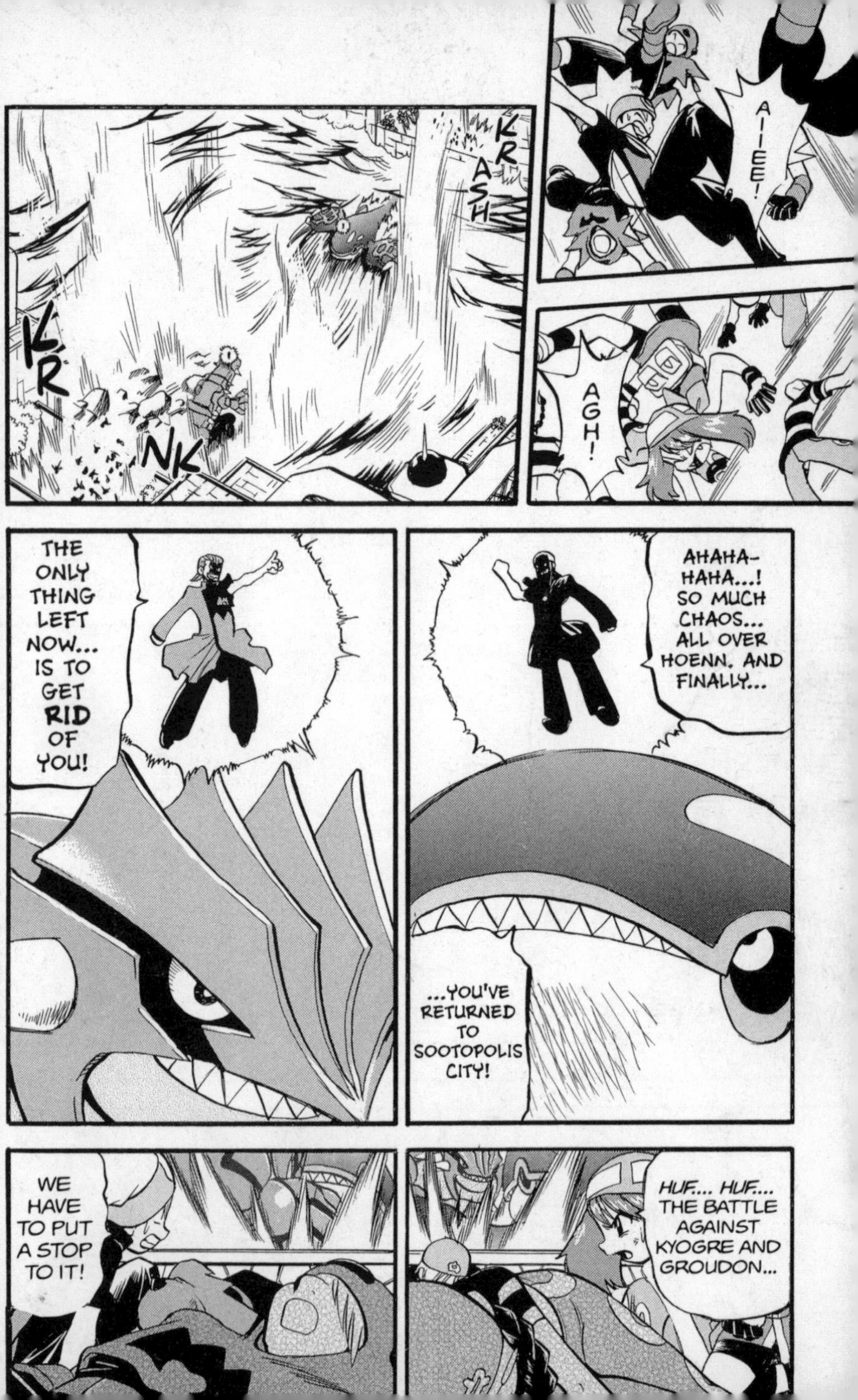
AIIEE!
AGH!
KRASH
KRNK
AHAHA-HAHA...! SO MUCH CHAOS... ALL OVER HOENN. AND FINALLY...
...YOU'VE RETURNED TO SOOTOPOLIS CITY!
THE ONLY THING LEFT NOW... IS TO GET RID OF YOU!
HUF... HUF... THE BATTLE AGAINST KYOGRE AND GROUDON...
WE HAVE TO PUT A STOP TO IT!

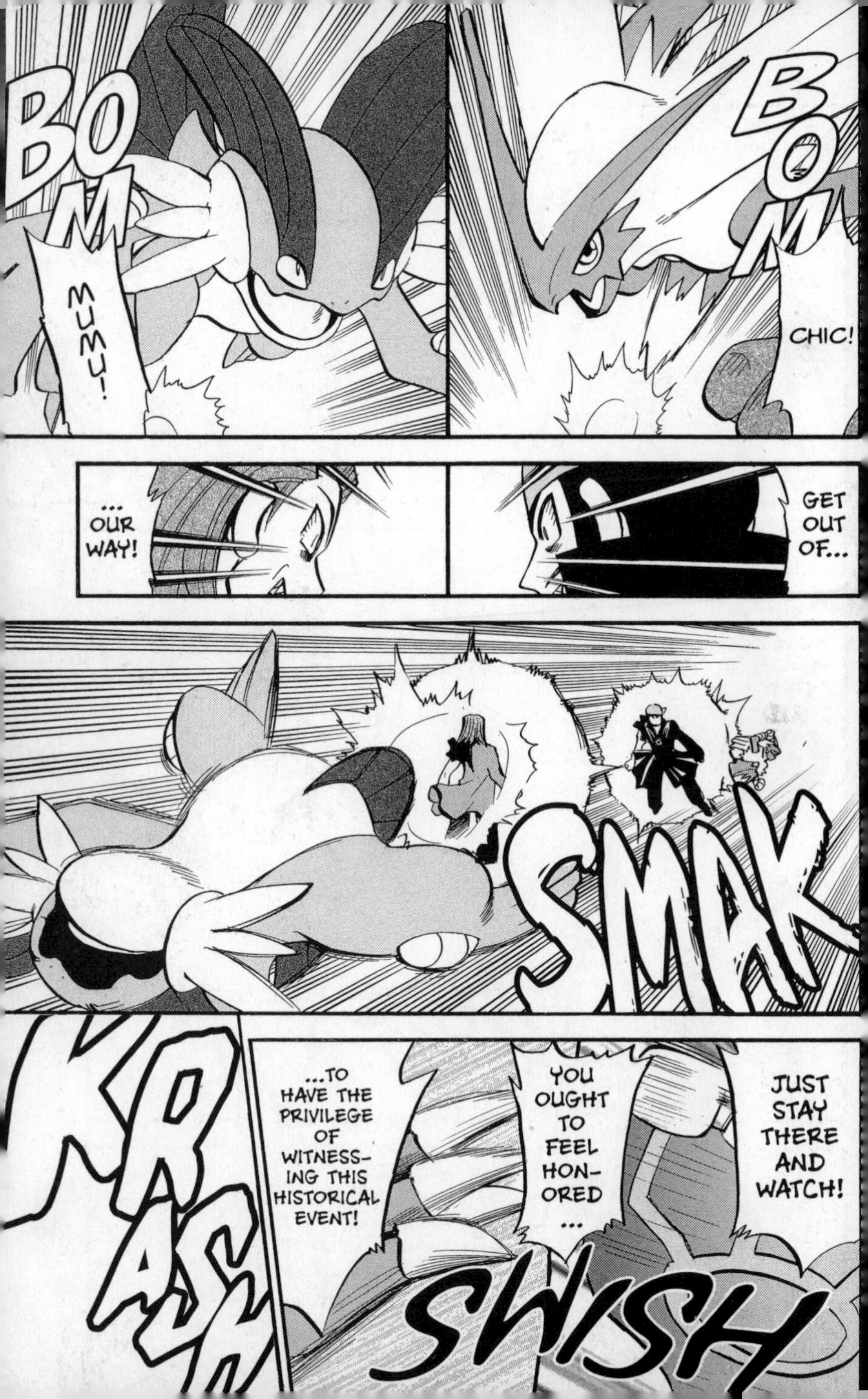
BOOM
CHIC!
BOOM
MUMU!
GET OUT OF...
...OUR WAY!
SMAK
JUST STAY THERE AND WATCH!
YOU OUGHT TO FEEL HON-ORED...
...TO HAVE THE PRIVILEGE OF WITNESS-ING THIS HISTORICAL EVENT!
SWISH
KRASH

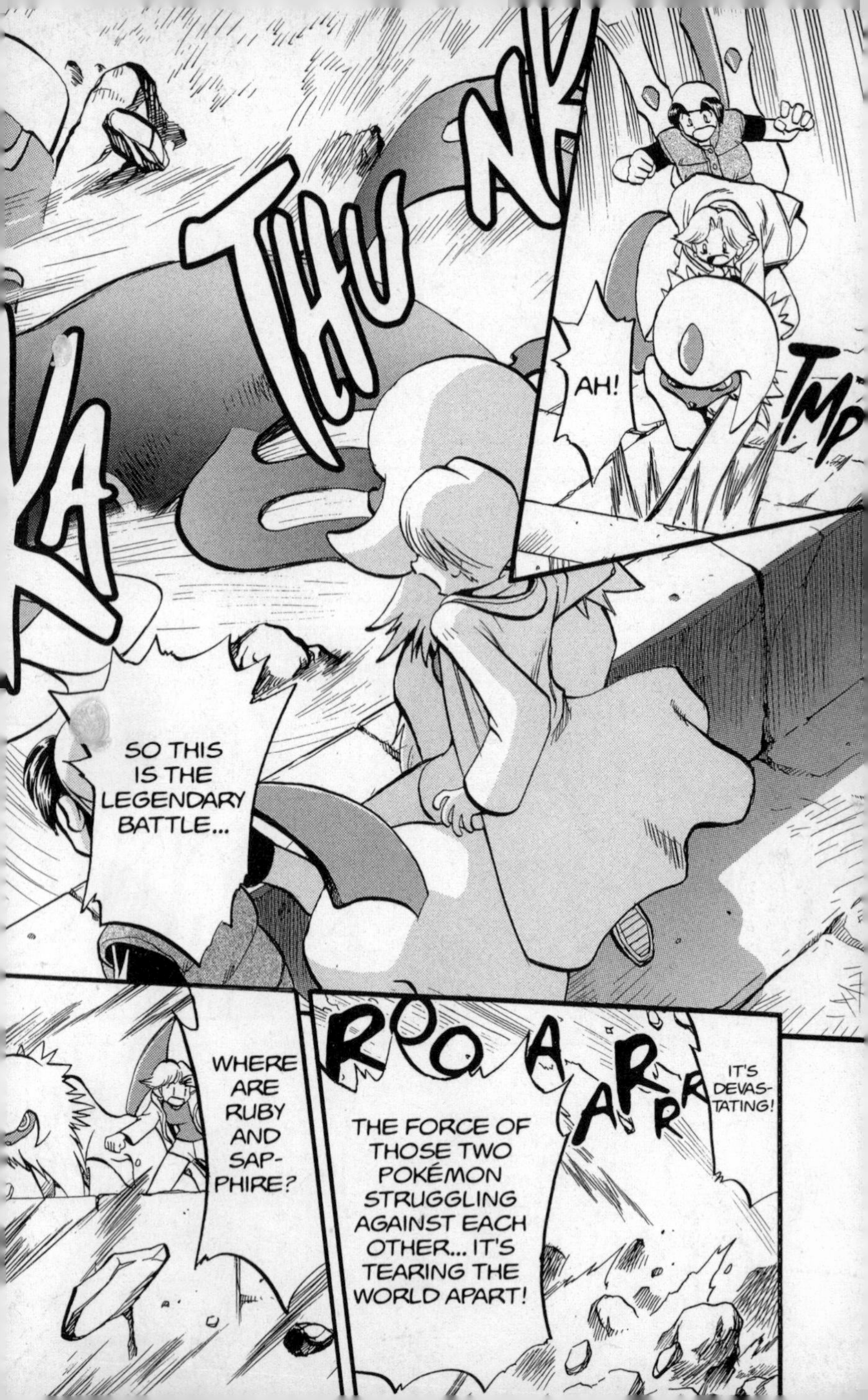
AH!
TMP
KA THUNK
SO THIS IS THE LEGENDARY BATTLE...
ROOAARRR
IT'S DEVAS-TATING!
THE FORCE OF THOSE TWO POKÉMON STRUGGLING AGAINST EACH OTHER... IT'S TEARING THE WORLD APART!
WHERE ARE RUBY AND SAP-PHIRE?

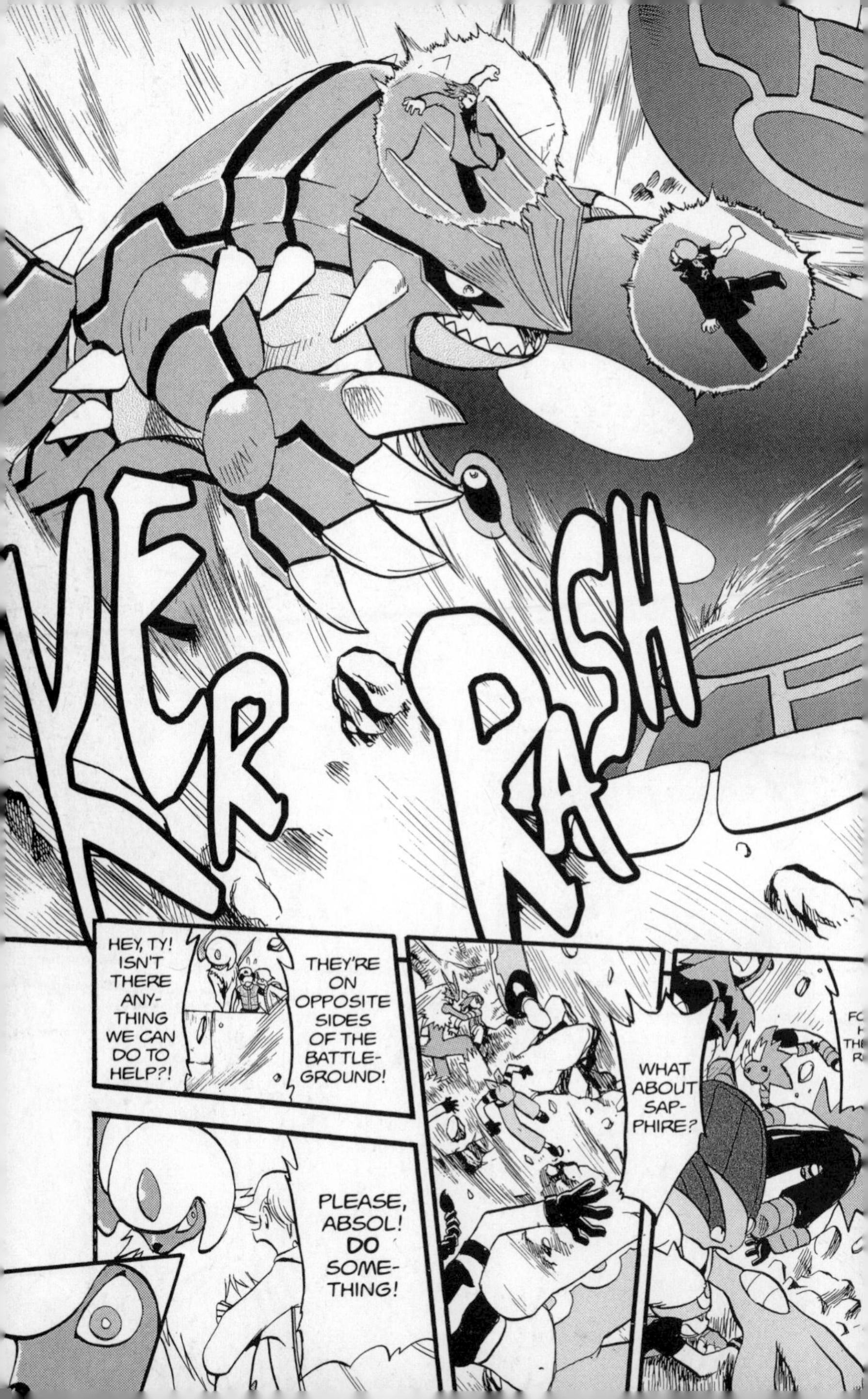
KRRASH
WHAT ABOUT SAP-PHIRE?
HEY, TY! ISN'T THERE ANY-THING WE CAN DO TO HELP?!
THEY'RE ON OPPOSITE SIDES OF THE BATTLE-GROUND!
PLEASE, ABSOL! DO SOME-THING!

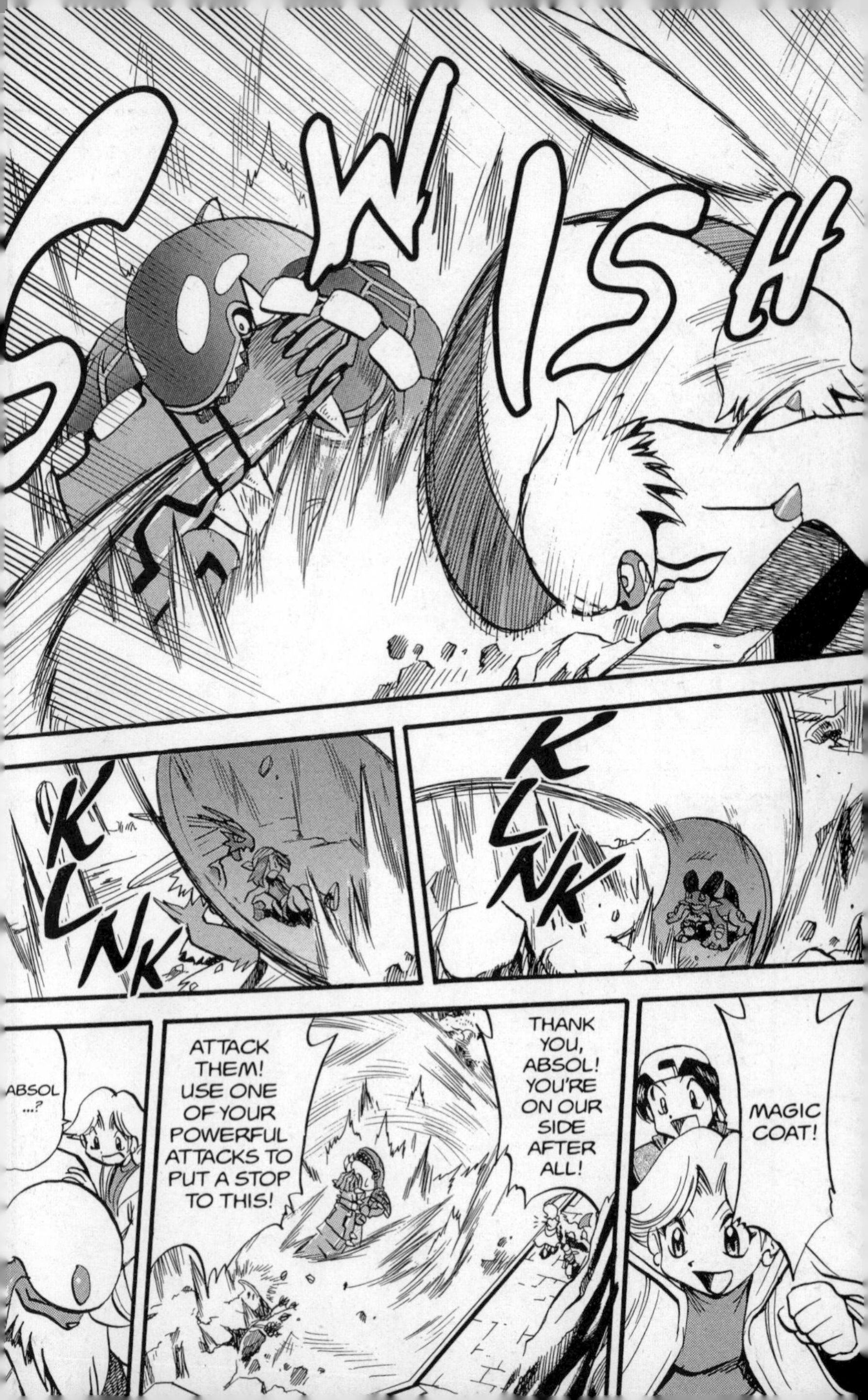
SWISH
KLINK
KLINK
MAGIC COAT!
THANK YOU, ABSOL! YOU'RE ON OUR SIDE AFTER ALL!
ATTACK THEM! USE ONE OF YOUR POWERFUL ATTACKS TO PUT A STOP TO THIS!
ABSOL ...?

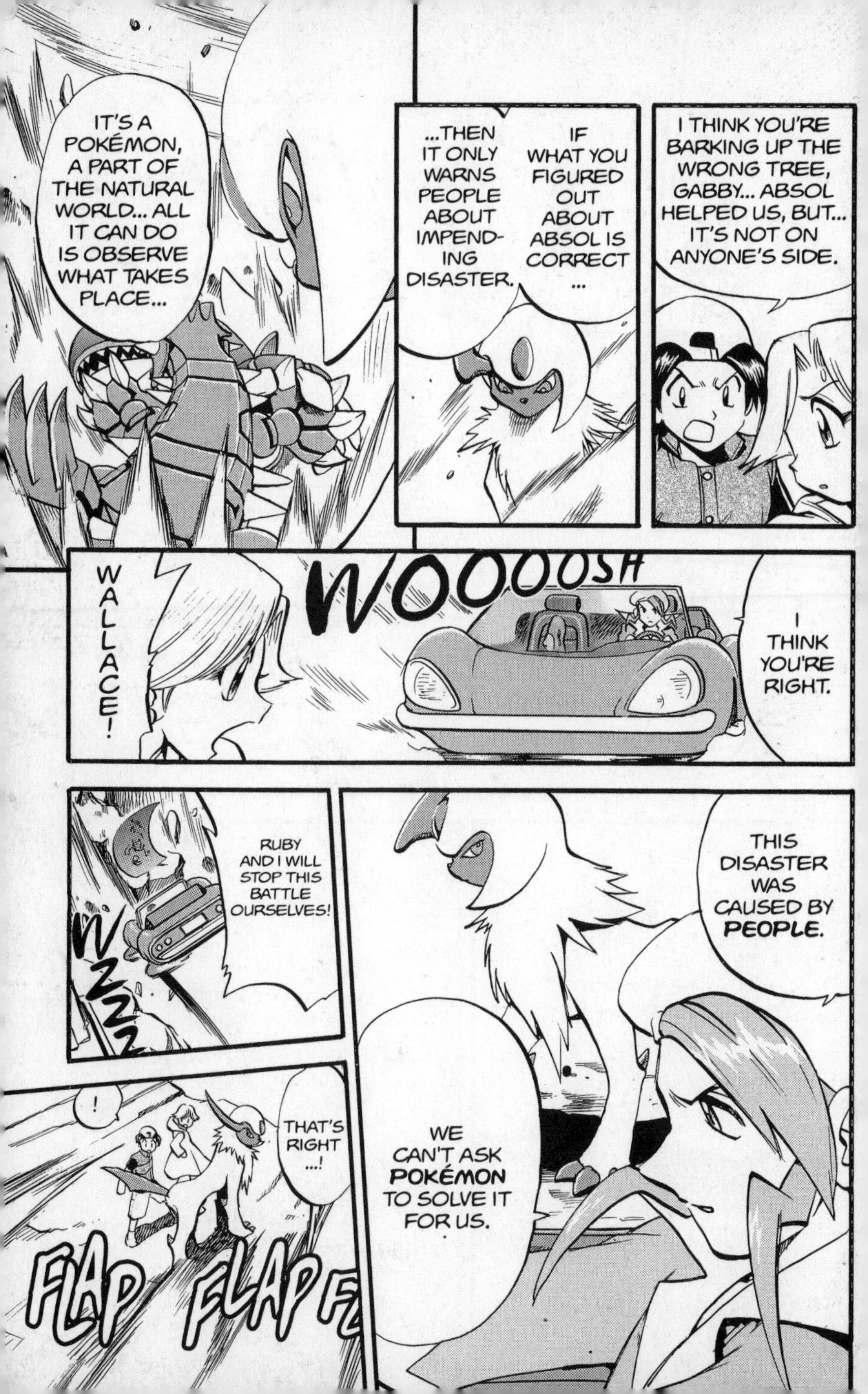
I THINK YOU'RE BARKING UP THE WRONG TREE, GABBY... ABSOL HELPED US, BUT... IT'S NOT ON ANYONE'S SIDE.
IF WHAT YOU FIGURED OUT ABOUT ABSOL IS CORRECT...
...THEN IT ONLY WARNS PEOPLE ABOUT IMPENDING DISASTER.
IT'S A POKÉMON, A PART OF THE NATURAL WORLD... ALL IT CAN DO IS OBSERVE WHAT TAKES PLACE...
I THINK YOU'RE RIGHT.
WOOOOSH
WALLACE!
THIS DISASTER WAS CAUSED BY **PEOPLE**.
WE CAN'T ASK **POKÉMON** TO SOLVE IT FOR US.
RUBY AND I WILL STOP THIS BATTLE OURSELVES!
WZZZ
THAT'S RIGHT...!
!
FLAP FLAP FL

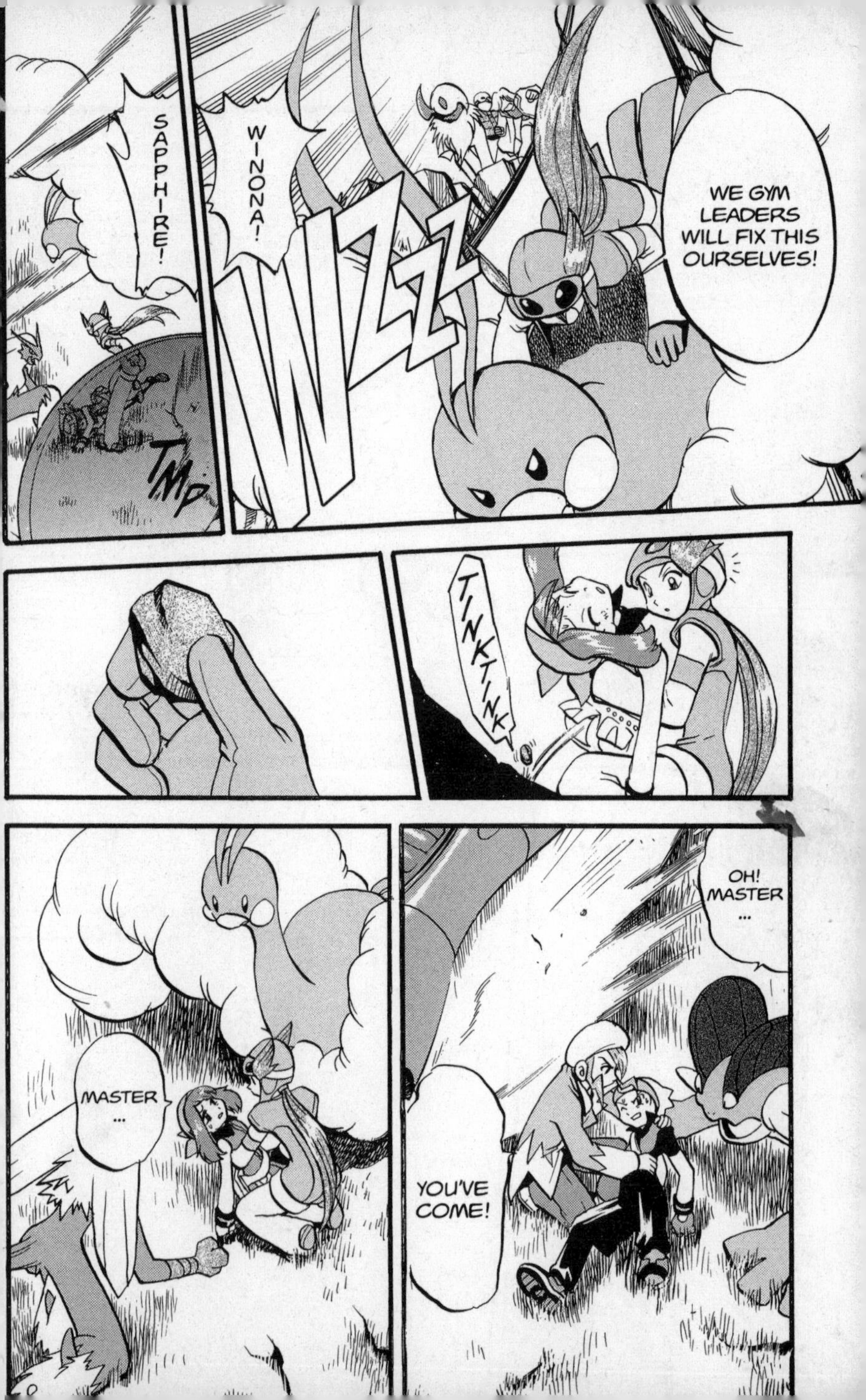
WE GYM LEADERS WILL FIX THIS OURSELVES!
WINONA!
WZZZ
SAPPHIRE!
TMP
TINK TINK
OH! MASTER ...
YOU'VE COME!
MASTER ...

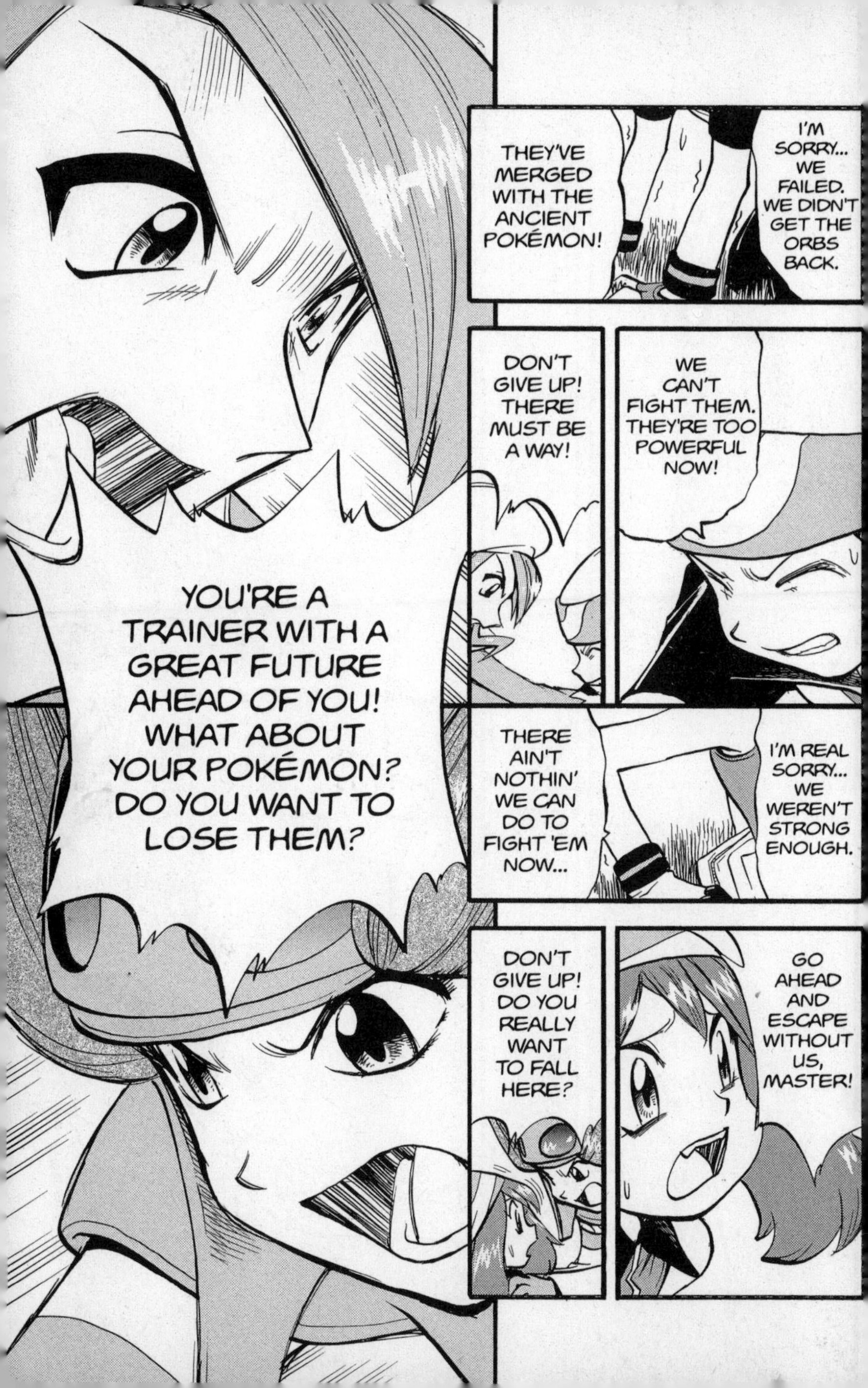
I'M SORRY... WE FAILED. WE DIDN'T GET THE ORBS BACK.
THEY'VE MERGED WITH THE ANCIENT POKÉMON!
WE CAN'T FIGHT THEM. THEY'RE TOO POWERFUL NOW!
DON'T GIVE UP! THERE MUST BE A WAY!
I'M REAL SORRY... WE WEREN'T STRONG ENOUGH.
THERE AIN'T NOTHIN' WE CAN DO TO FIGHT 'EM NOW...
GO AHEAD AND ESCAPE WITHOUT US, MASTER!
DON'T GIVE UP! DO YOU REALLY WANT TO FALL HERE?
YOU'RE A TRAINER WITH A GREAT FUTURE AHEAD OF YOU! WHAT ABOUT YOUR POKÉMON? DO YOU WANT TO LOSE THEM?

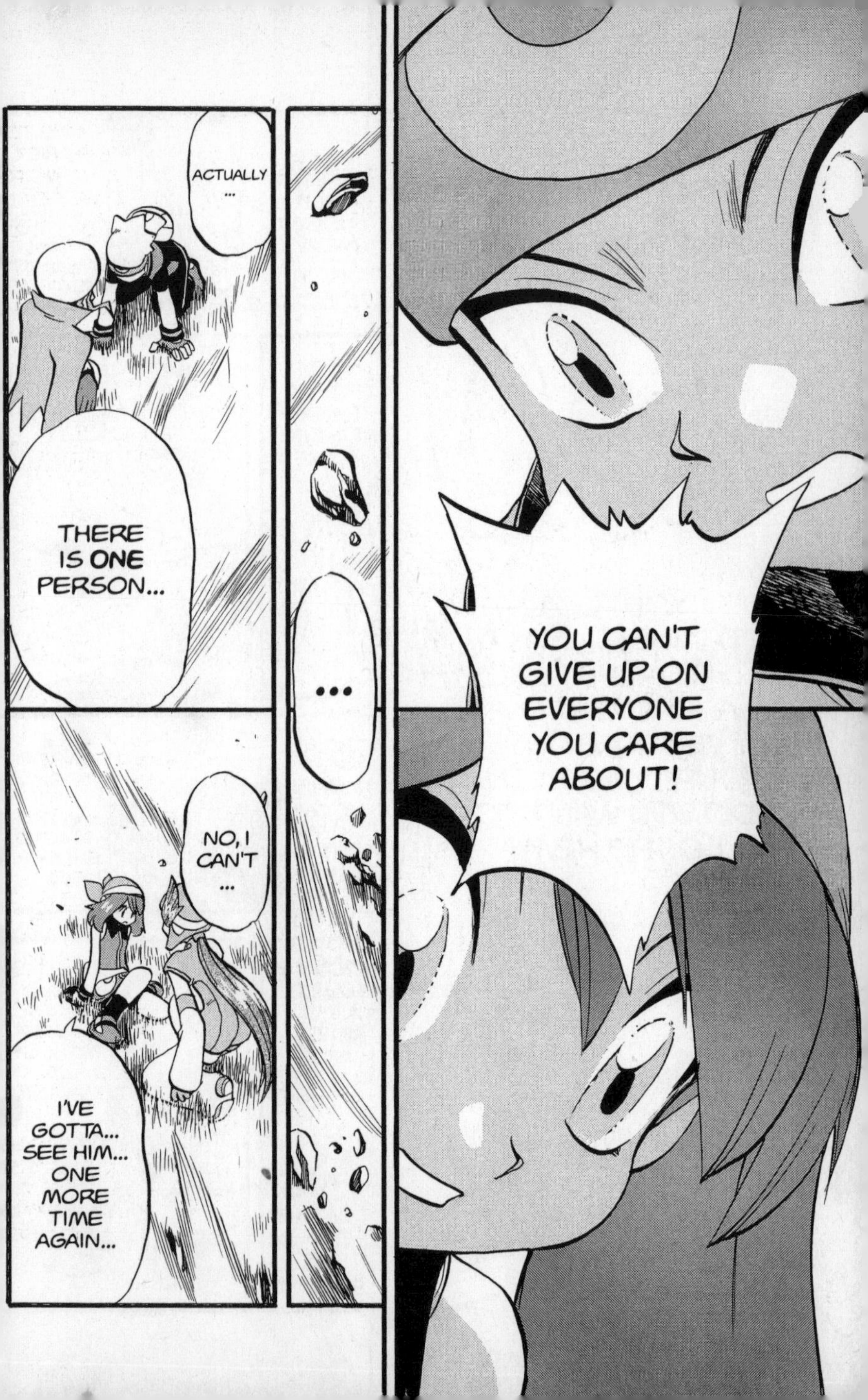
YOU CAN'T GIVE UP ON EVERYONE YOU CARE ABOUT!
...
ACTUALLY ...
THERE IS ONE PERSON...
NO, I CAN'T ...
I'VE GOTTA... SEE HIM... ONE MORE TIME AGAIN...

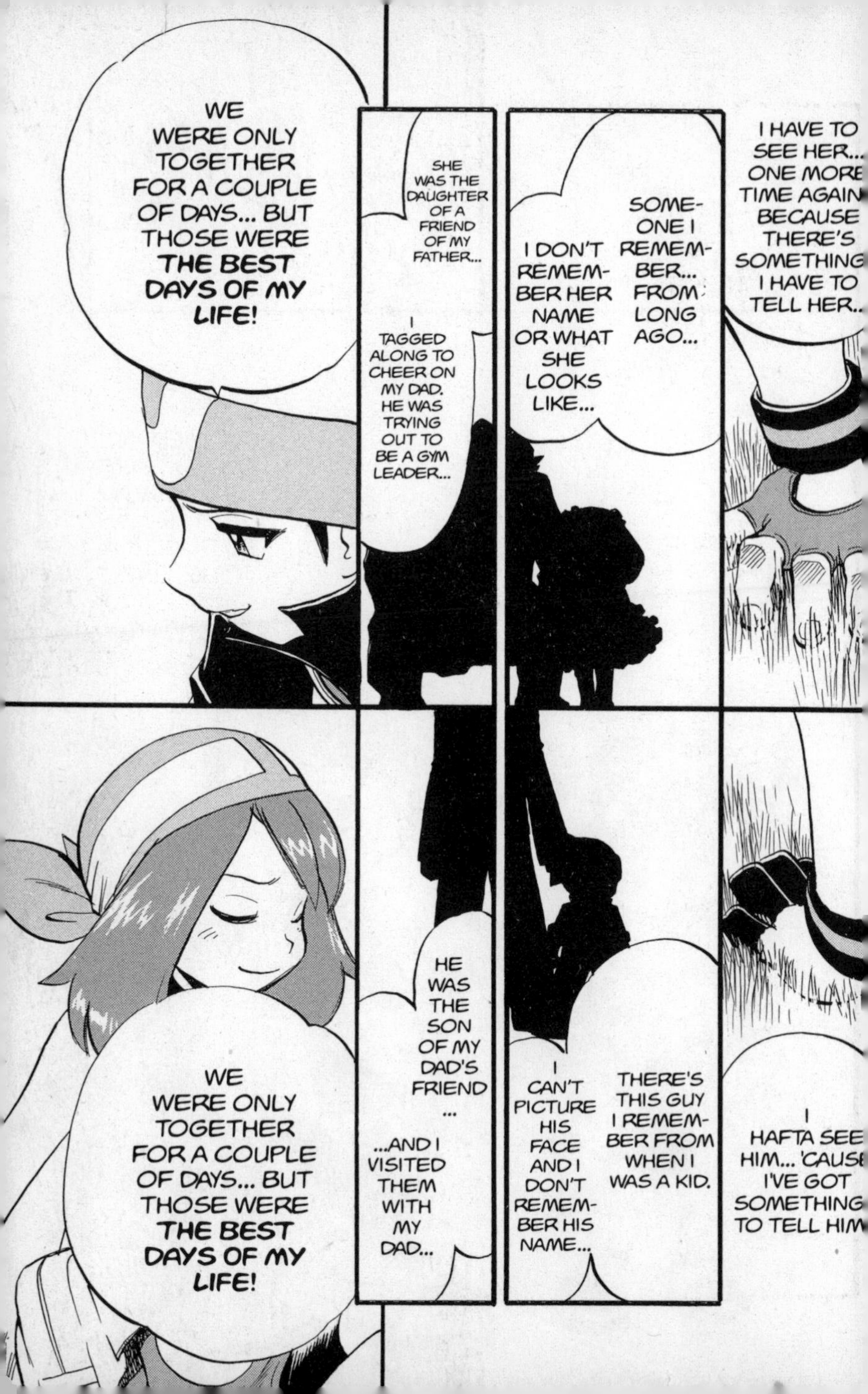
I HAVE TO SEE HER... ONE MORE TIME AGAIN BECAUSE THERE'S SOMETHING I HAVE TO TELL HER...
SOME-ONE I REMEM-BER... FROM LONG AGO...
I DON'T REMEM-BER HER NAME OR WHAT SHE LOOKS LIKE...
SHE WAS THE DAUGHTER OF A FRIEND OF MY FATHER...
I TAGGED ALONG TO CHEER ON MY DAD. HE WAS TRYING OUT TO BE A GYM LEADER...
WE WERE ONLY TOGETHER FOR A COUPLE OF DAYS... BUT THOSE WERE **THE BEST DAYS OF MY LIFE!**
I HAFTA SEE HIM... 'CAUSE I'VE GOT SOMETHING TO TELL HIM
THERE'S THIS GUY I REMEM-BER FROM WHEN I WAS A KID.
I CAN'T PICTURE HIS FACE AND I DON'T REMEM-BER HIS NAME...
HE WAS THE SON OF MY DAD'S FRIEND...
...AND I VISITED THEM WITH MY DAD...
WE WERE ONLY TOGETHER FOR A COUPLE OF DAYS... BUT THOSE WERE **THE BEST DAYS OF MY LIFE!**

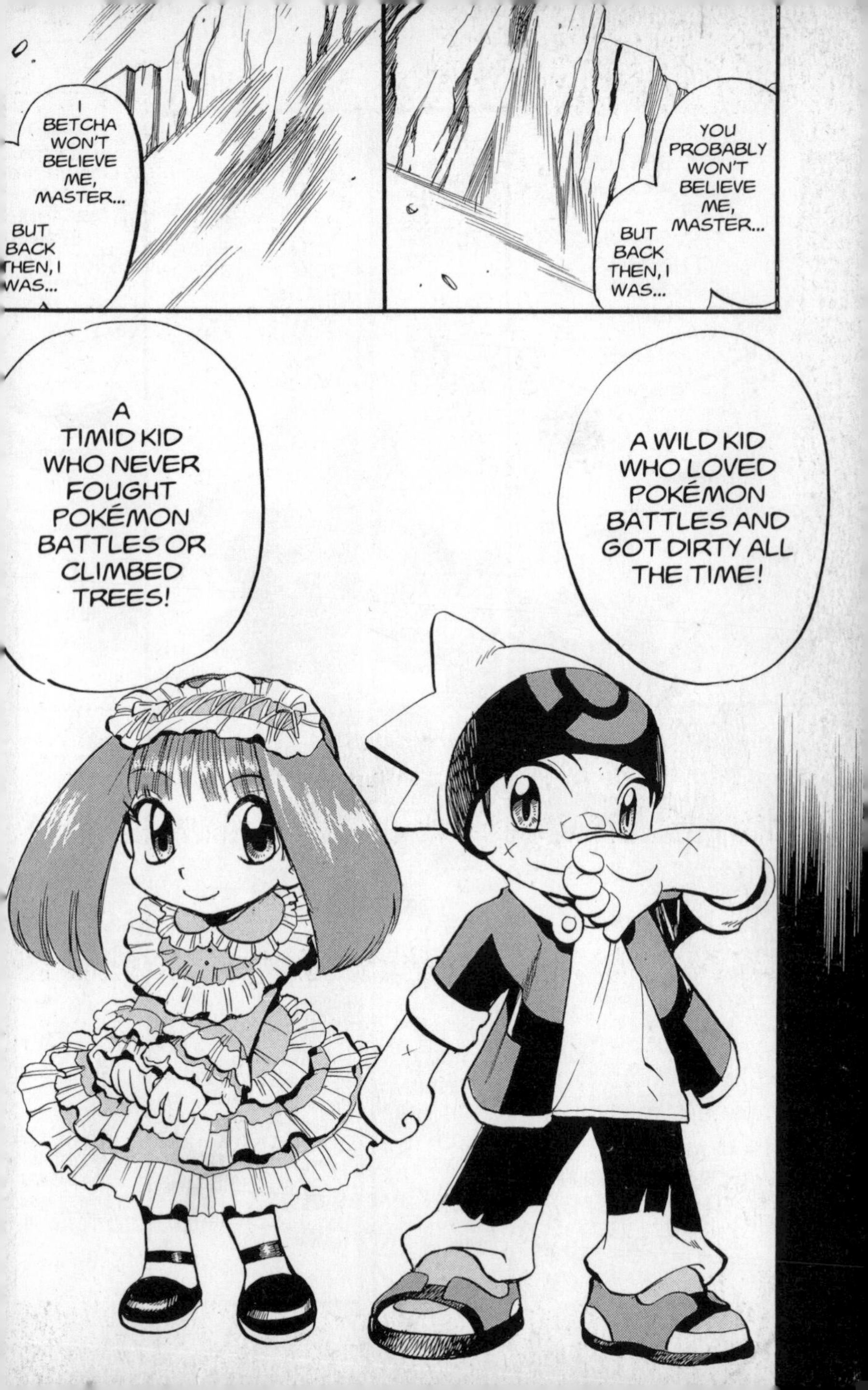
YOU PROBABLY WON'T BELIEVE ME, MASTER...
BUT BACK THEN, I WAS...
I BETCHA WON'T BELIEVE ME, MASTER...
BUT BACK THEN, I WAS...
A WILD KID WHO LOVED POKÉMON BATTLES AND GOT DIRTY ALL THE TIME!
A TIMID KID WHO NEVER FOUGHT POKÉMON BATTLES OR CLIMBED TREES!

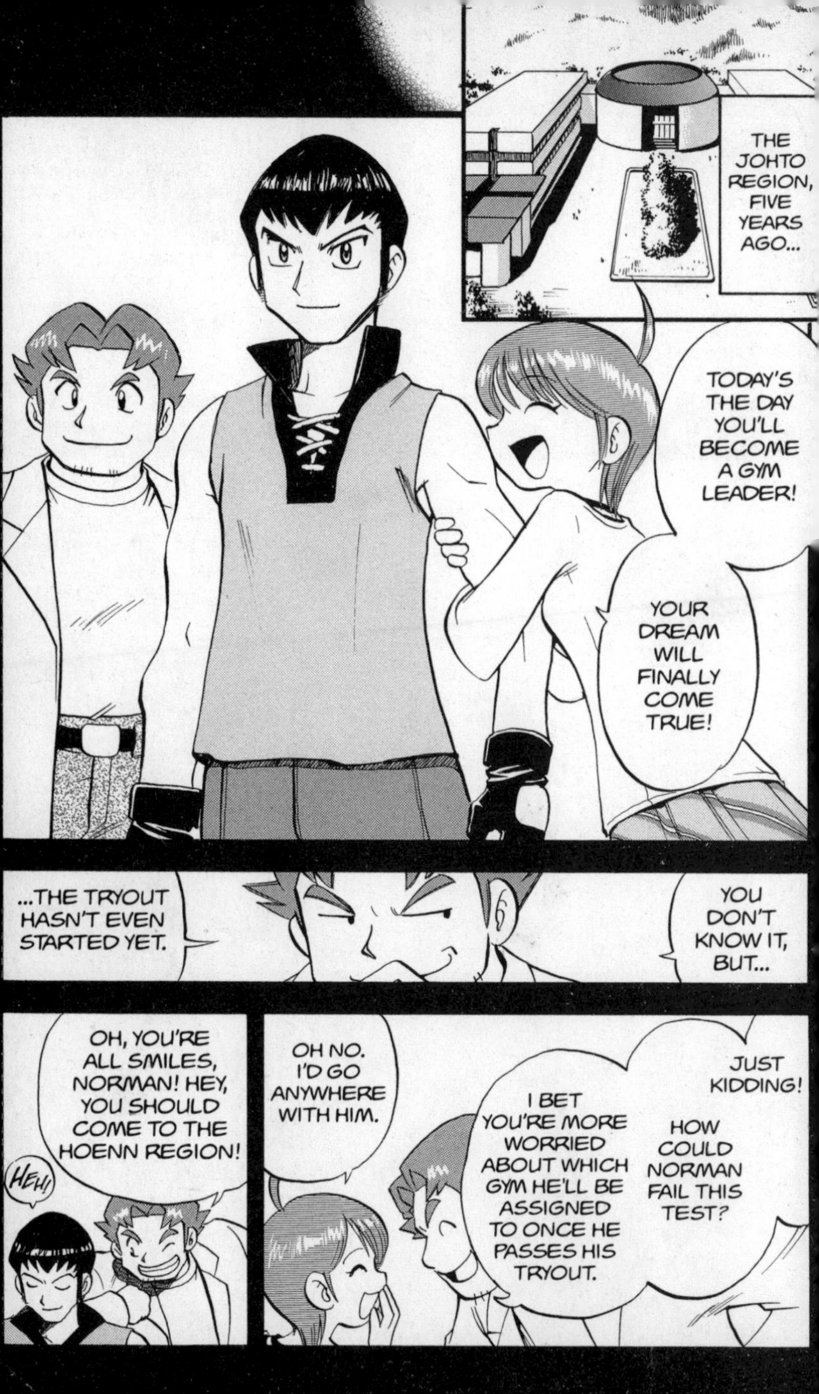
THE JOHTO REGION, FIVE YEARS AGO...
TODAY'S THE DAY YOU'LL BECOME A GYM LEADER!
YOUR DREAM WILL FINALLY COME TRUE!
YOU DON'T KNOW IT, BUT...
...THE TRYOUT HASN'T EVEN STARTED YET.
JUST KIDDING!
HOW COULD NORMAN FAIL THIS TEST?
I BET YOU'RE MORE WORRIED ABOUT WHICH GYM HE'LL BE ASSIGNED TO ONCE HE PASSES HIS TRYOUT.
OH NO. I'D GO ANYWHERE WITH HIM.
OH, YOU'RE ALL SMILES, NORMAN! HEY, YOU SHOULD COME TO THE HOENN REGION!
HEH!

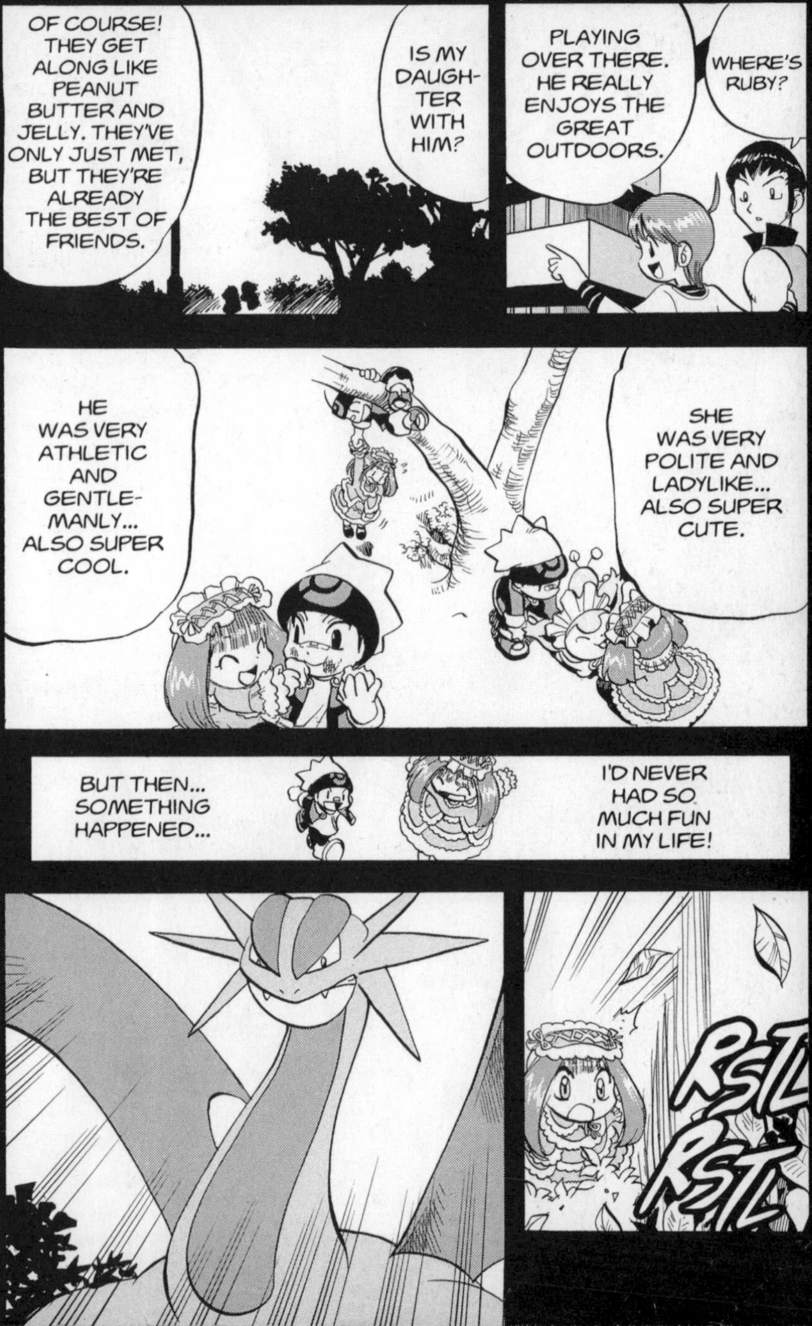
WHERE'S RUBY?
PLAYING OVER THERE. HE REALLY ENJOYS THE GREAT OUTDOORS.
IS MY DAUGHTER WITH HIM?
OF COURSE! THEY GET ALONG LIKE PEANUT BUTTER AND JELLY. THEY'VE ONLY JUST MET, BUT THEY'RE ALREADY THE BEST OF FRIENDS.
SHE WAS VERY POLITE AND LADYLIKE... ALSO SUPER CUTE.
HE WAS VERY ATHLETIC AND GENTLEMANLY... ALSO SUPER COOL.
I'D NEVER HAD SO MUCH FUN IN MY LIFE!
BUT THEN... SOMETHING HAPPENED...
RSTL
RSTL

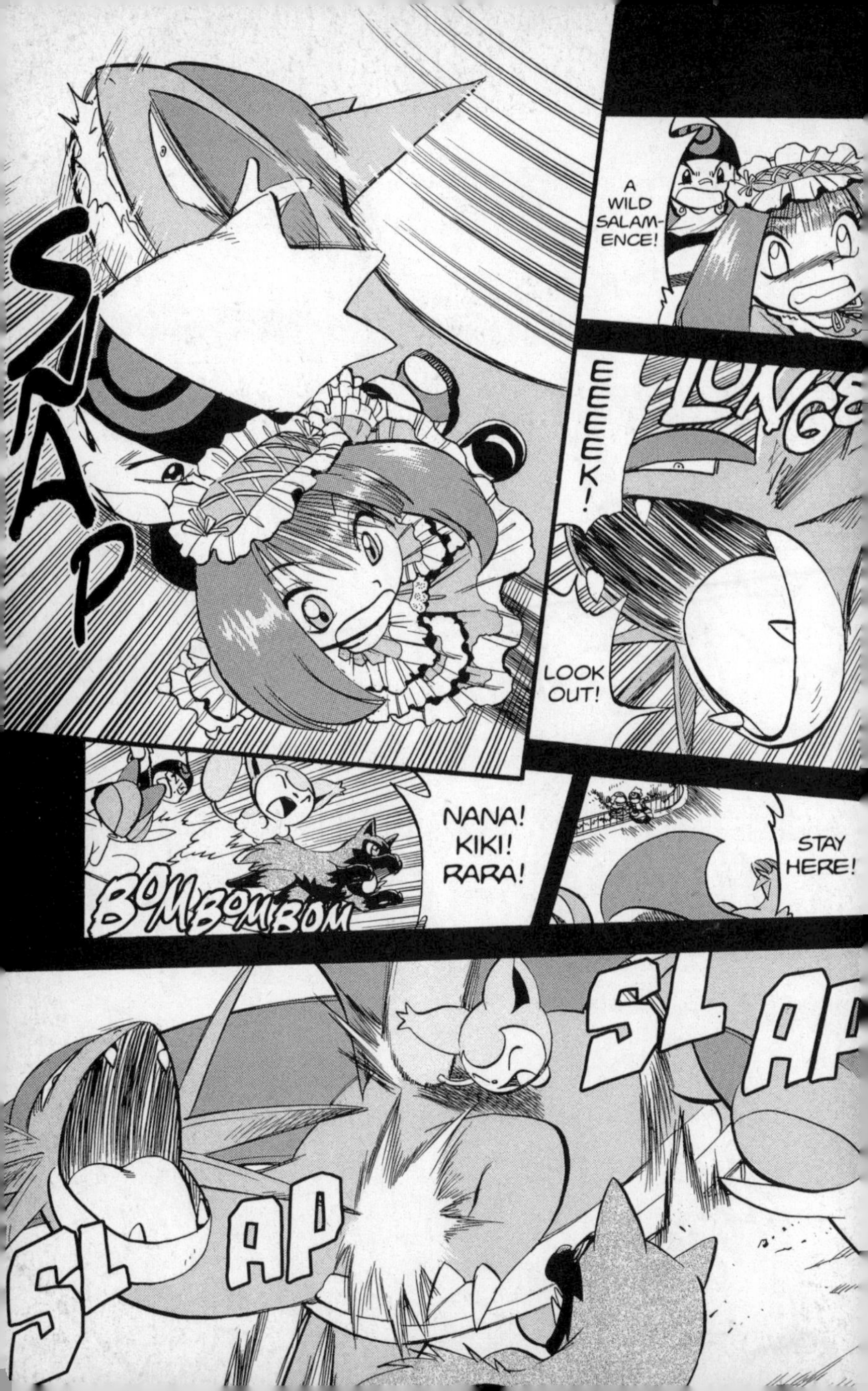
A WILD SALAMENCE!
LUNGE
EEEEEK!
LOOK OUT!
SLAP
STAY HERE!
NANA! KIKI! RARA!
BOMBOMBOM
SLAP
SLAP

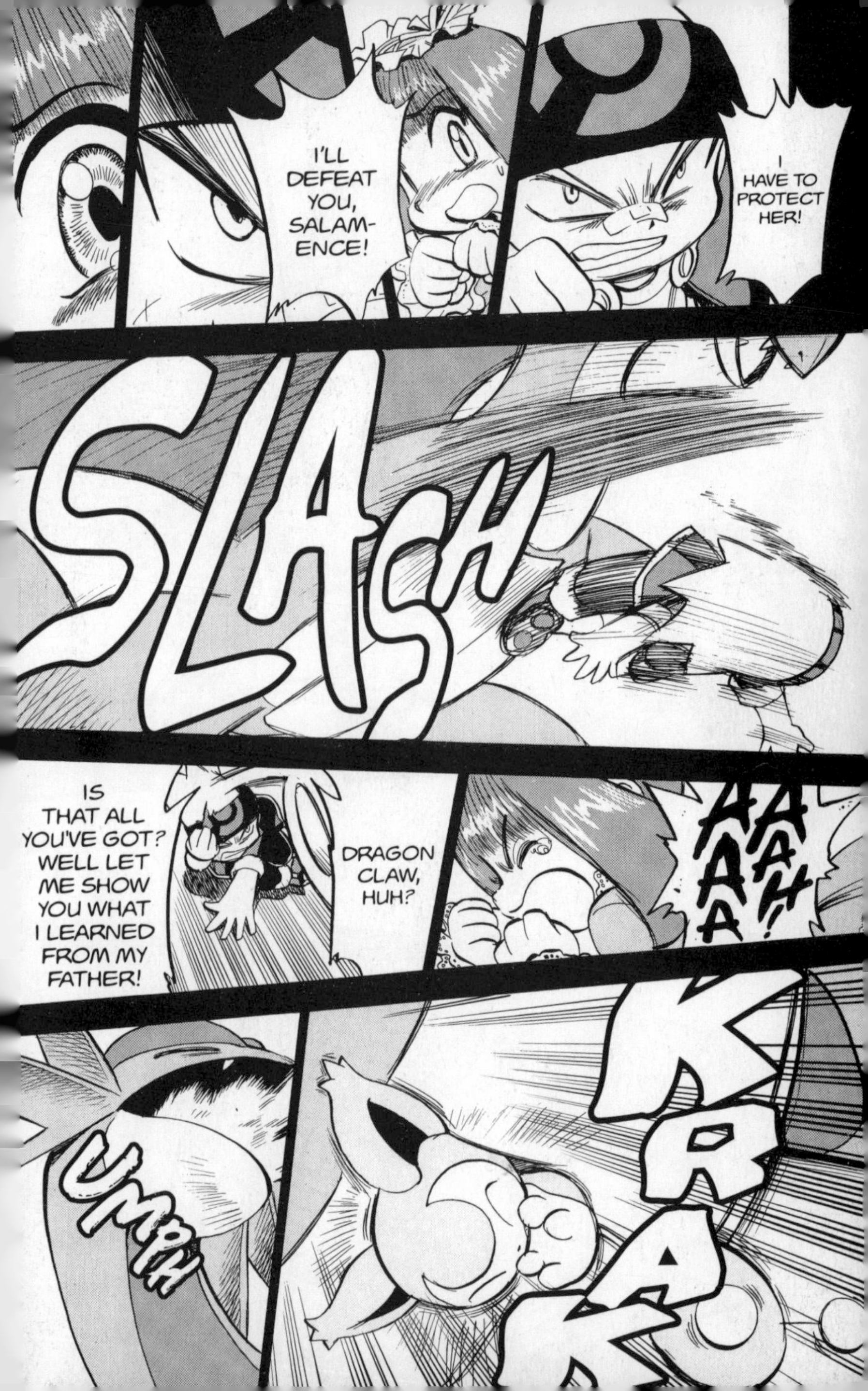
I HAVE TO PROTECT HER!
I'LL DEFEAT YOU, SALAM-ENCE!
SLASH
AAAAAAH!
DRAGON CLAW, HUH?
IS THAT ALL YOU'VE GOT? WELL LET ME SHOW YOU WHAT I LEARNED FROM MY FATHER!
KRAK
UMPH

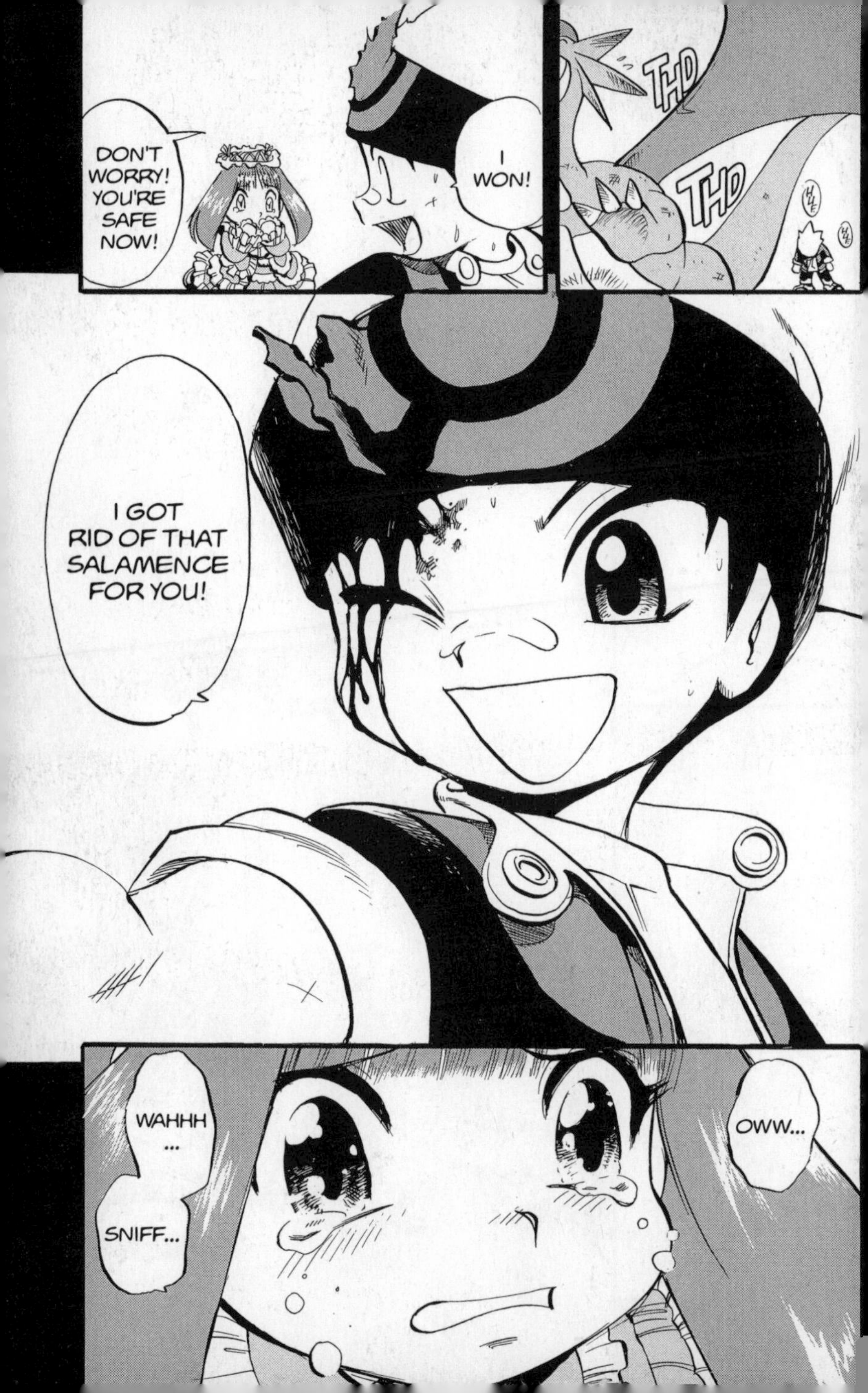
THD
THD
I WON!
DON'T WORRY! YOU'RE SAFE NOW!
I GOT RID OF THAT SALAMENCE FOR YOU!
OWW...
WAHHH ...
SNIFF...

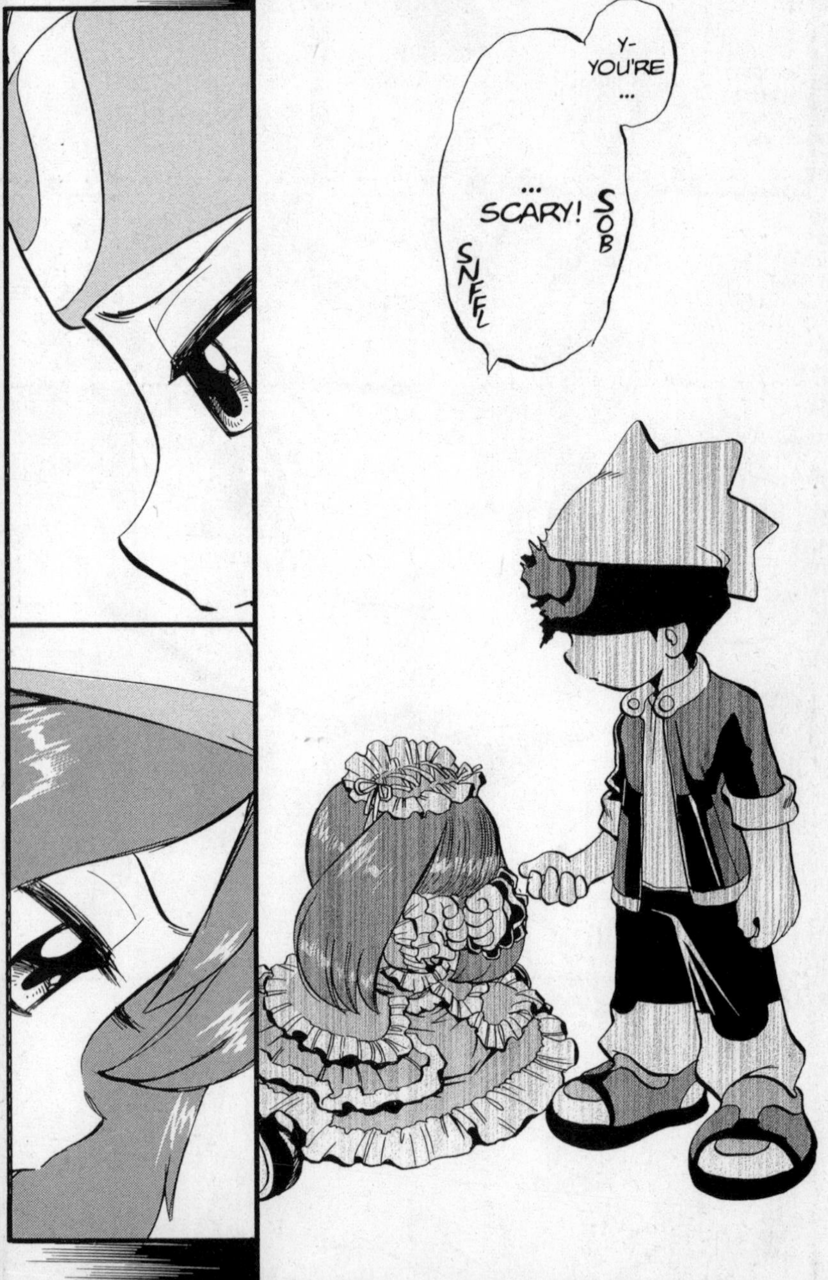
Y-YOU'RE ...
... SCARY!
SOB
SNFFL

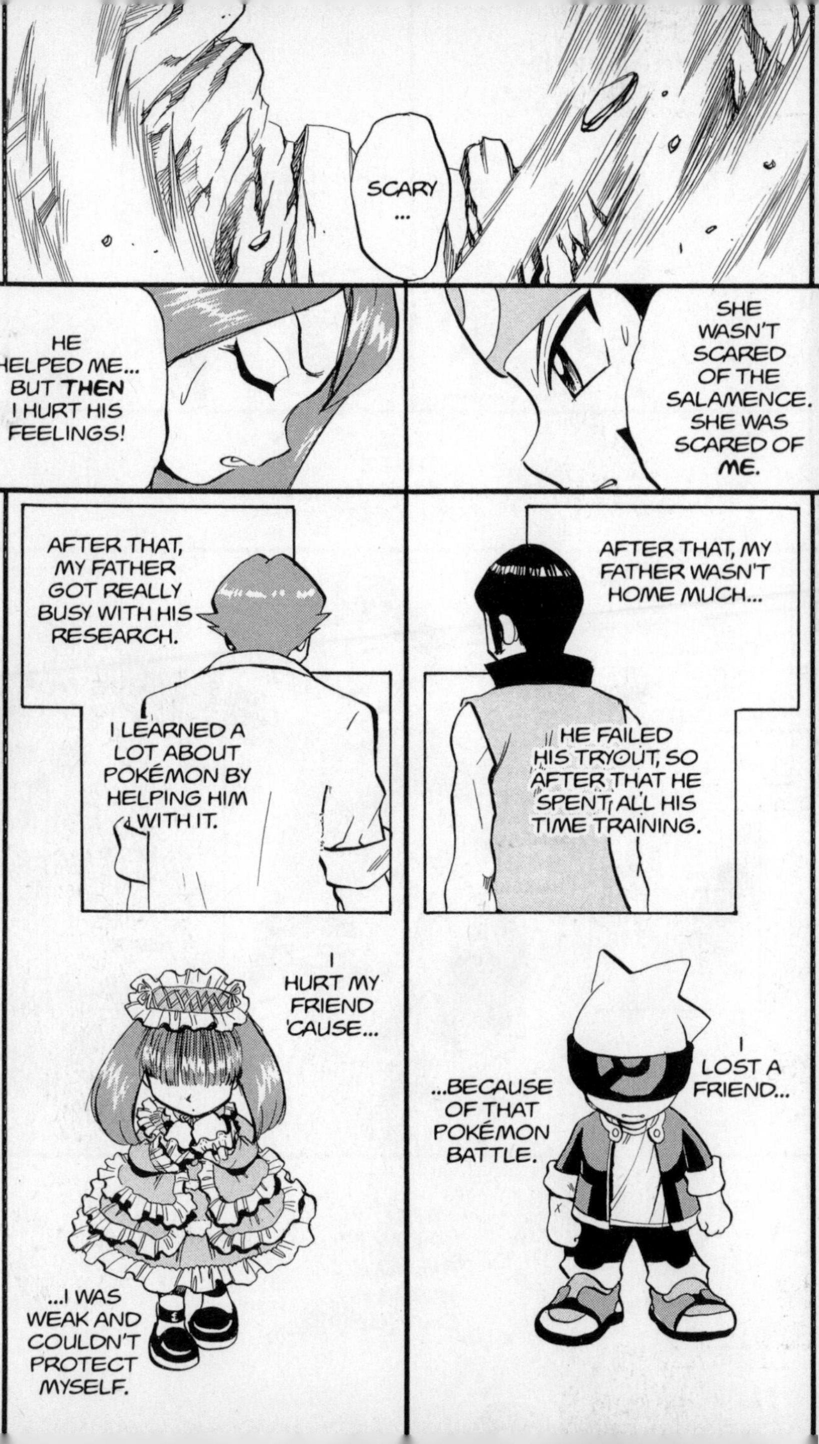
SCARY...
SHE WASN'T SCARED OF THE SALAMENCE. SHE WAS SCARED OF **ME**.
HE HELPED ME... BUT **THEN** I HURT HIS FEELINGS!
AFTER THAT, MY FATHER WASN'T HOME MUCH...
HE FAILED HIS TRYOUT, SO AFTER THAT HE SPENT ALL HIS TIME TRAINING.
AFTER THAT, MY FATHER GOT REALLY BUSY WITH HIS RESEARCH.
I LEARNED A LOT ABOUT POKÉMON BY HELPING HIM WITH IT.
I LOST A FRIEND...
...BECAUSE OF THAT POKÉMON BATTLE.
I HURT MY FRIEND 'CAUSE...
...I WAS WEAK AND COULDN'T PROTECT MYSELF.

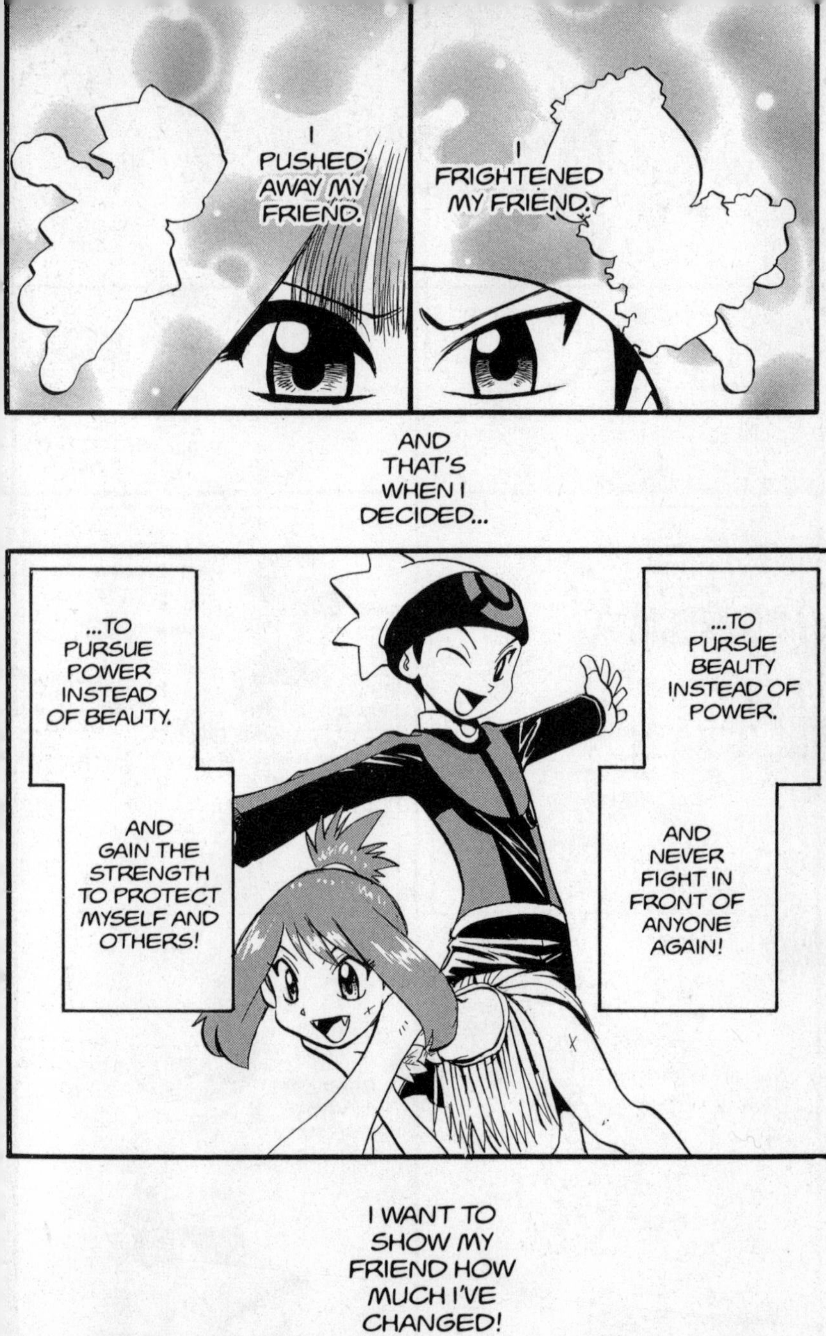
I FRIGHTENED MY FRIEND.
I PUSHED AWAY MY FRIEND.
AND THAT'S WHEN I DECIDED...
...TO PURSUE BEAUTY INSTEAD OF POWER.
AND NEVER FIGHT IN FRONT OF ANYONE AGAIN!
...TO PURSUE POWER INSTEAD OF BEAUTY.
AND GAIN THE STRENGTH TO PROTECT MYSELF AND OTHERS!
I WANT TO SHOW MY FRIEND HOW MUCH I'VE CHANGED!

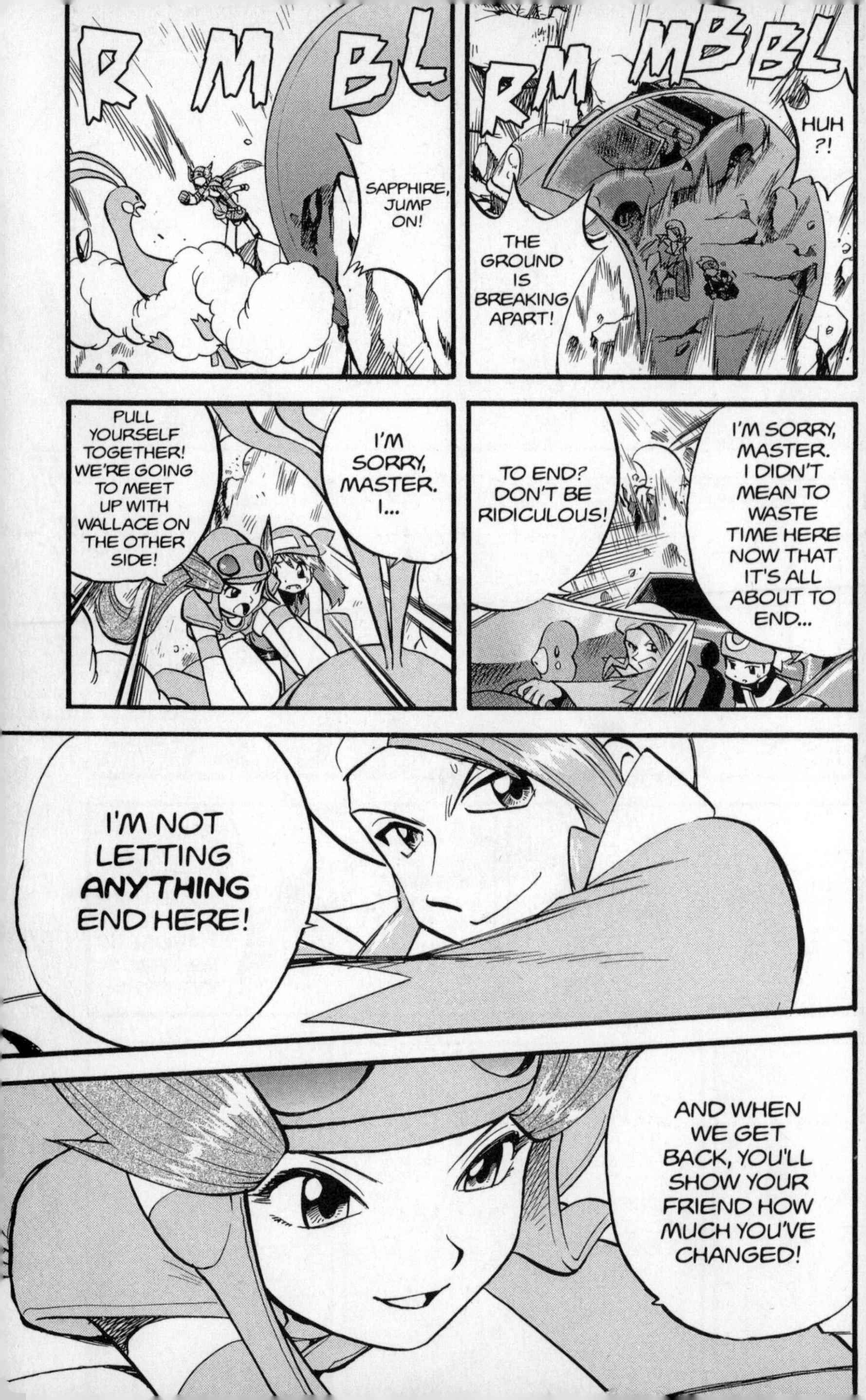
RM MBBL
HUH ?!
THE GROUND IS BREAKING APART!
R M BL
SAPPHIRE, JUMP ON!
I'M SORRY, MASTER. I DIDN'T MEAN TO WASTE TIME HERE NOW THAT IT'S ALL ABOUT TO END...
TO END? DON'T BE RIDICULOUS!
I'M SORRY, MASTER. I...
PULL YOURSELF TOGETHER! WE'RE GOING TO MEET UP WITH WALLACE ON THE OTHER SIDE!
I'M NOT LETTING **ANYTHING** END HERE!
AND WHEN WE GET BACK, YOU'LL SHOW YOUR FRIEND HOW MUCH YOU'VE CHANGED!

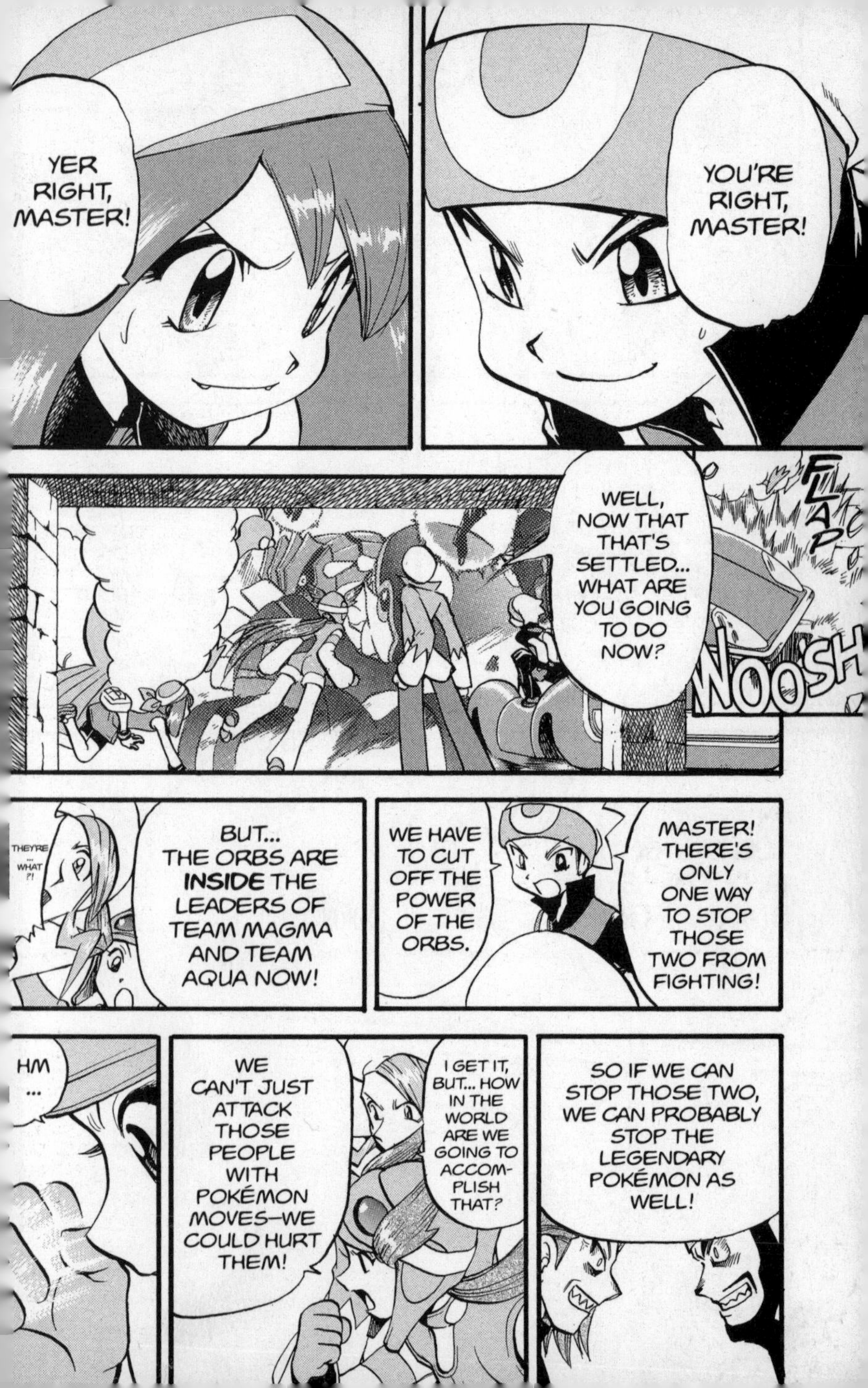
YOU'RE RIGHT, MASTER!
YER RIGHT, MASTER!
FLAP
WELL, NOW THAT THAT'S SETTLED... WHAT ARE YOU GOING TO DO NOW?
WOOSH
MASTER! THERE'S ONLY ONE WAY TO STOP THOSE TWO FROM FIGHTING!
WE HAVE TO CUT OFF THE POWER OF THE ORBS.
BUT... THE ORBS ARE **INSIDE** THE LEADERS OF TEAM MAGMA AND TEAM AQUA NOW!
THEY'RE ... WHAT ?!
SO IF WE CAN STOP THOSE TWO, WE CAN PROBABLY STOP THE LEGENDARY POKÉMON AS WELL!
I GET IT, BUT... HOW IN THE WORLD ARE WE GOING TO ACCOMPLISH THAT?
WE CAN'T JUST ATTACK THOSE PEOPLE WITH POKÉMON MOVES—WE COULD HURT THEM!
HM ...

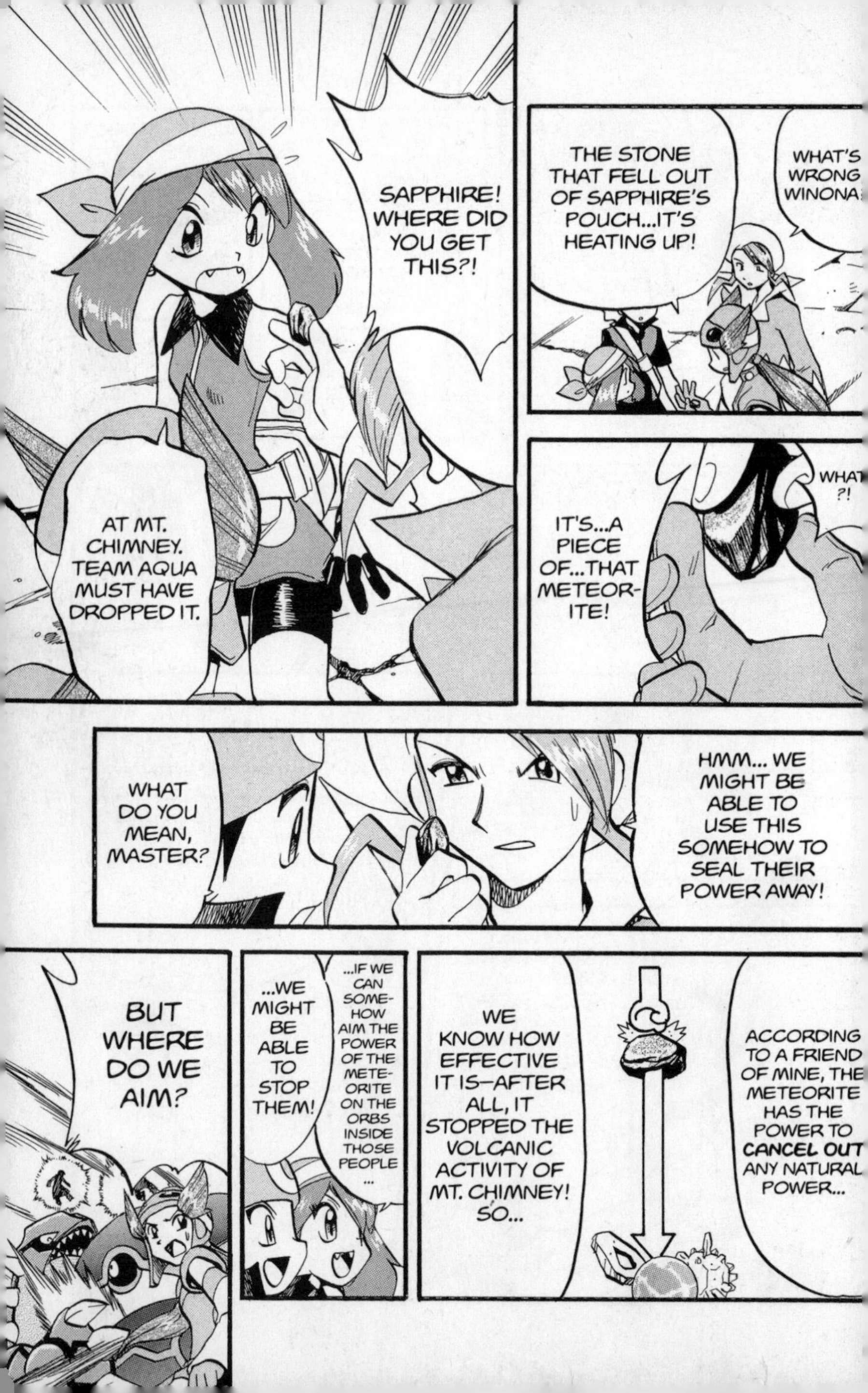
WHAT'S WRONG WINONA
THE STONE THAT FELL OUT OF SAPPHIRE'S POUCH...IT'S HEATING UP!
WHAT?!
IT'S...A PIECE OF...THAT METEOR-ITE!
SAPPHIRE! WHERE DID YOU GET THIS?!
AT MT. CHIMNEY. TEAM AQUA MUST HAVE DROPPED IT.
HMM... WE MIGHT BE ABLE TO USE THIS SOMEHOW TO SEAL THEIR POWER AWAY!
WHAT DO YOU MEAN, MASTER?
ACCORDING TO A FRIEND OF MINE, THE METEORITE HAS THE POWER TO **CANCEL OUT** ANY NATURAL POWER...
WE KNOW HOW EFFECTIVE IT IS—AFTER ALL, IT STOPPED THE VOLCANIC ACTIVITY OF MT. CHIMNEY! SO...
...IF WE CAN SOME-HOW AIM THE POWER OF THE METE-ORITE ON THE ORBS INSIDE THOSE PEOPLE...
...WE MIGHT BE ABLE TO STOP THEM!
BUT WHERE DO WE AIM?

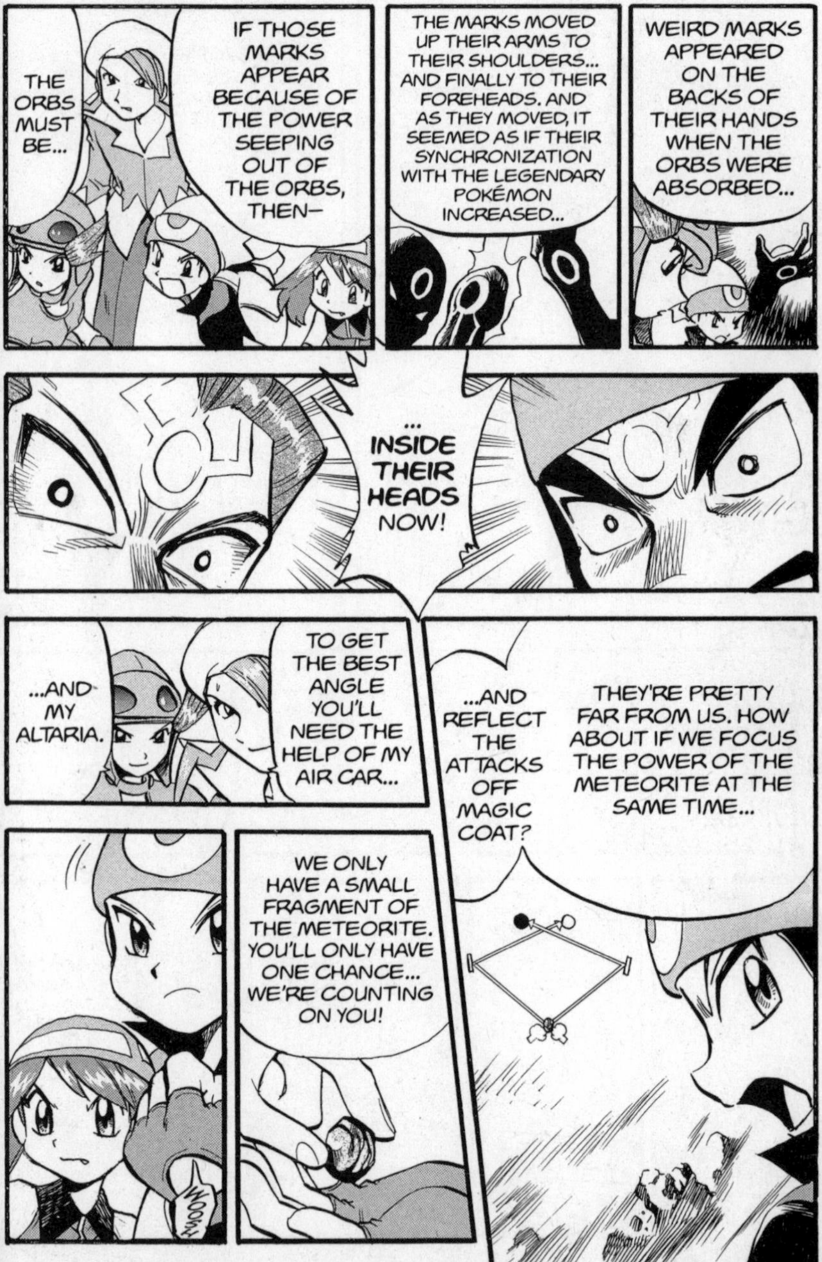
WEIRD MARKS APPEARED ON THE BACKS OF THEIR HANDS WHEN THE ORBS WERE ABSORBED...
THE MARKS MOVED UP THEIR ARMS TO THEIR SHOULDERS... AND FINALLY TO THEIR FOREHEADS. AND AS THEY MOVED, IT SEEMED AS IF THEIR SYNCHRONIZATION WITH THE LEGENDARY POKÉMON INCREASED...
IF THOSE MARKS APPEAR BECAUSE OF THE POWER SEEPING OUT OF THE ORBS, THEN—
THE ORBS MUST BE...
... INSIDE THEIR HEADS NOW!
THEY'RE PRETTY FAR FROM US. HOW ABOUT IF WE FOCUS THE POWER OF THE METEORITE AT THE SAME TIME...
...AND REFLECT THE ATTACKS OFF MAGIC COAT?
TO GET THE BEST ANGLE YOU'LL NEED THE HELP OF MY AIR CAR...
...AND MY ALTARIA.
WE ONLY HAVE A SMALL FRAGMENT OF THE METEORITE. YOU'LL ONLY HAVE ONE CHANCE... WE'RE COUNTING ON YOU!
WOOSH

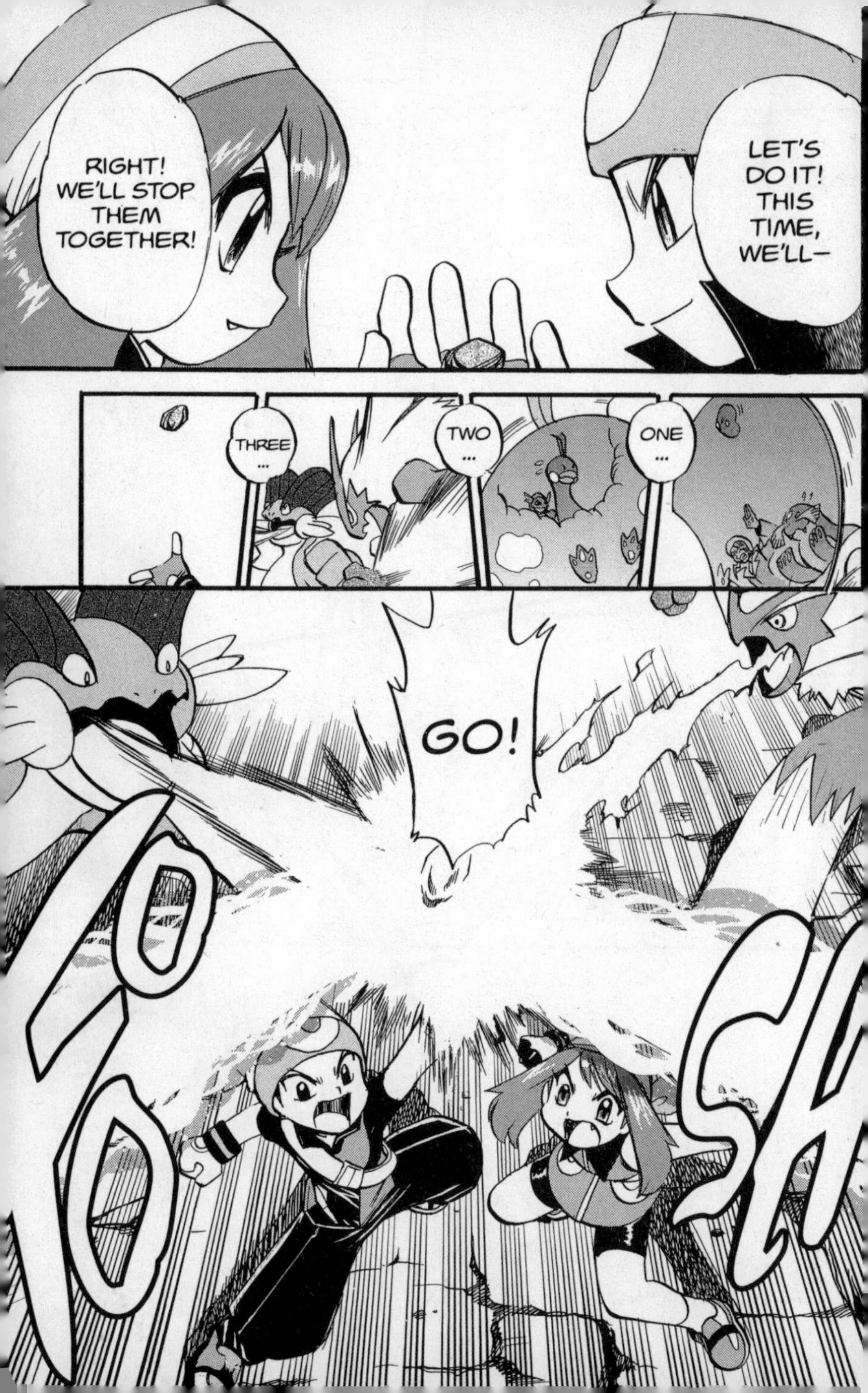
RIGHT! WE'LL STOP THEM TOGETHER!
LET'S DO IT! THIS TIME, WE'LL—
THREE ...
TWO ...
ONE ...
GO!

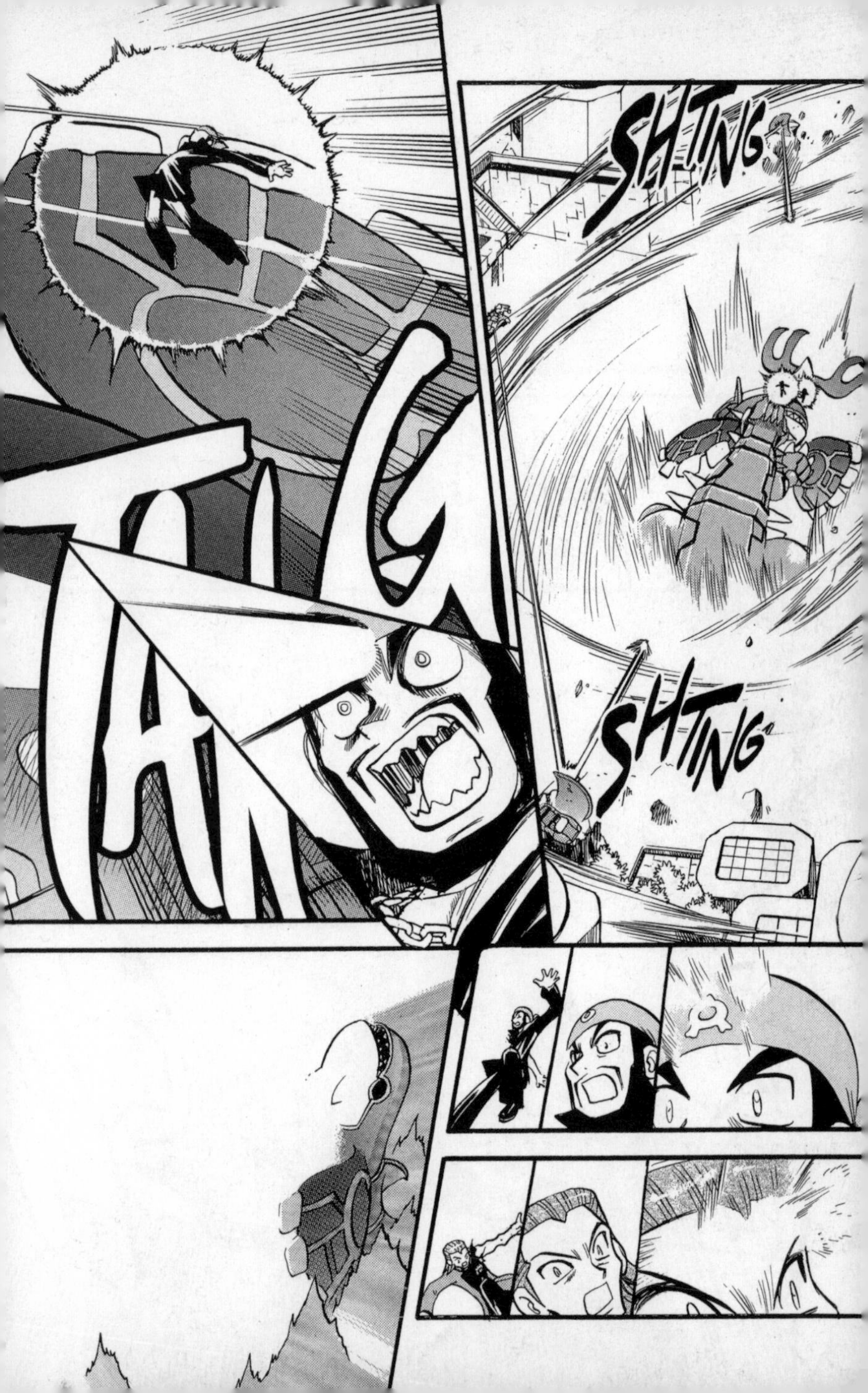
SHING
SHING

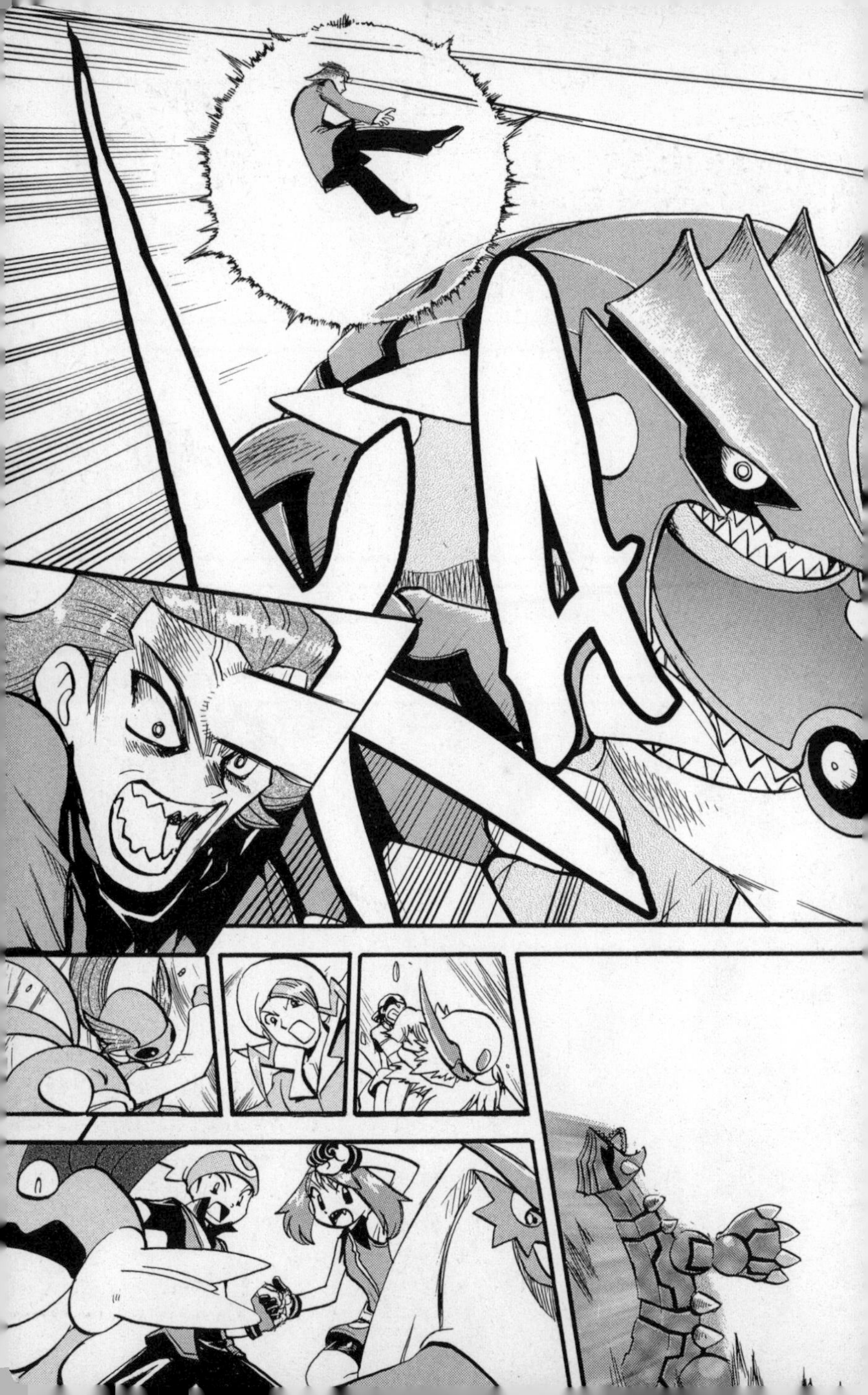

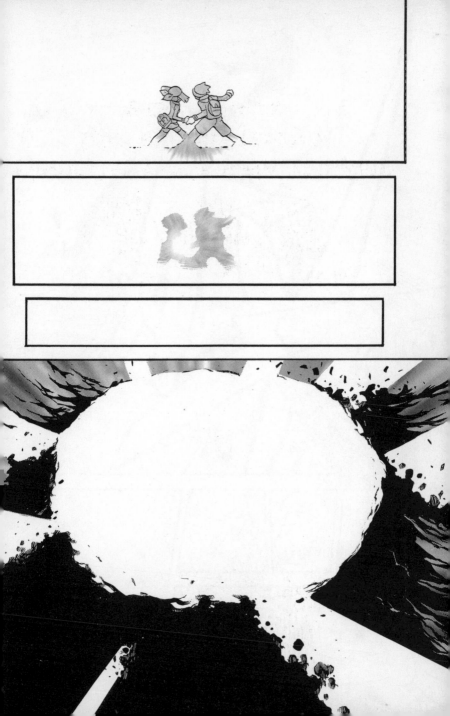

● Chapter 253 ●

# A Royal Rumble with Regirock, Regice and Registeel I

Pokémon™ Adventures
Ruby & Sapphire
The Fourth Chapter

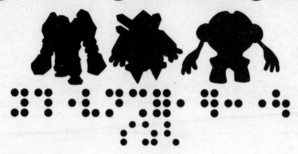

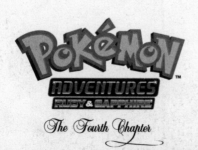

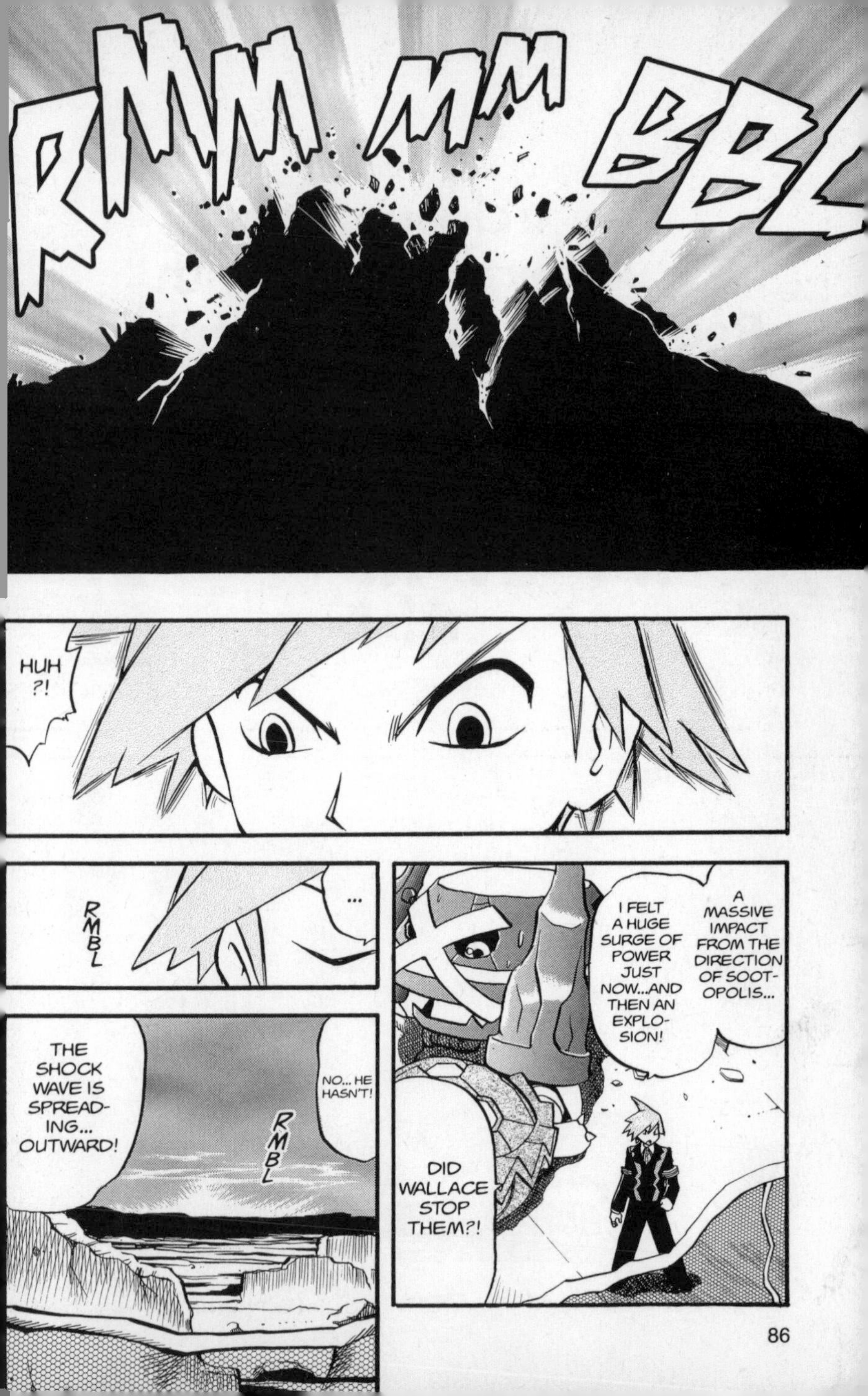

RMMMMBBL
HUH ?!
A MASSIVE IMPACT FROM THE DIRECTION OF SOOT-OPOLIS...
I FELT A HUGE SURGE OF POWER JUST NOW...AND THEN AN EXPLO-SION!
DID WALLACE STOP THEM?!
...
RMBL
NO... HE HASN'T!
RMBL
THE SHOCK WAVE IS SPREAD-ING... OUTWARD!

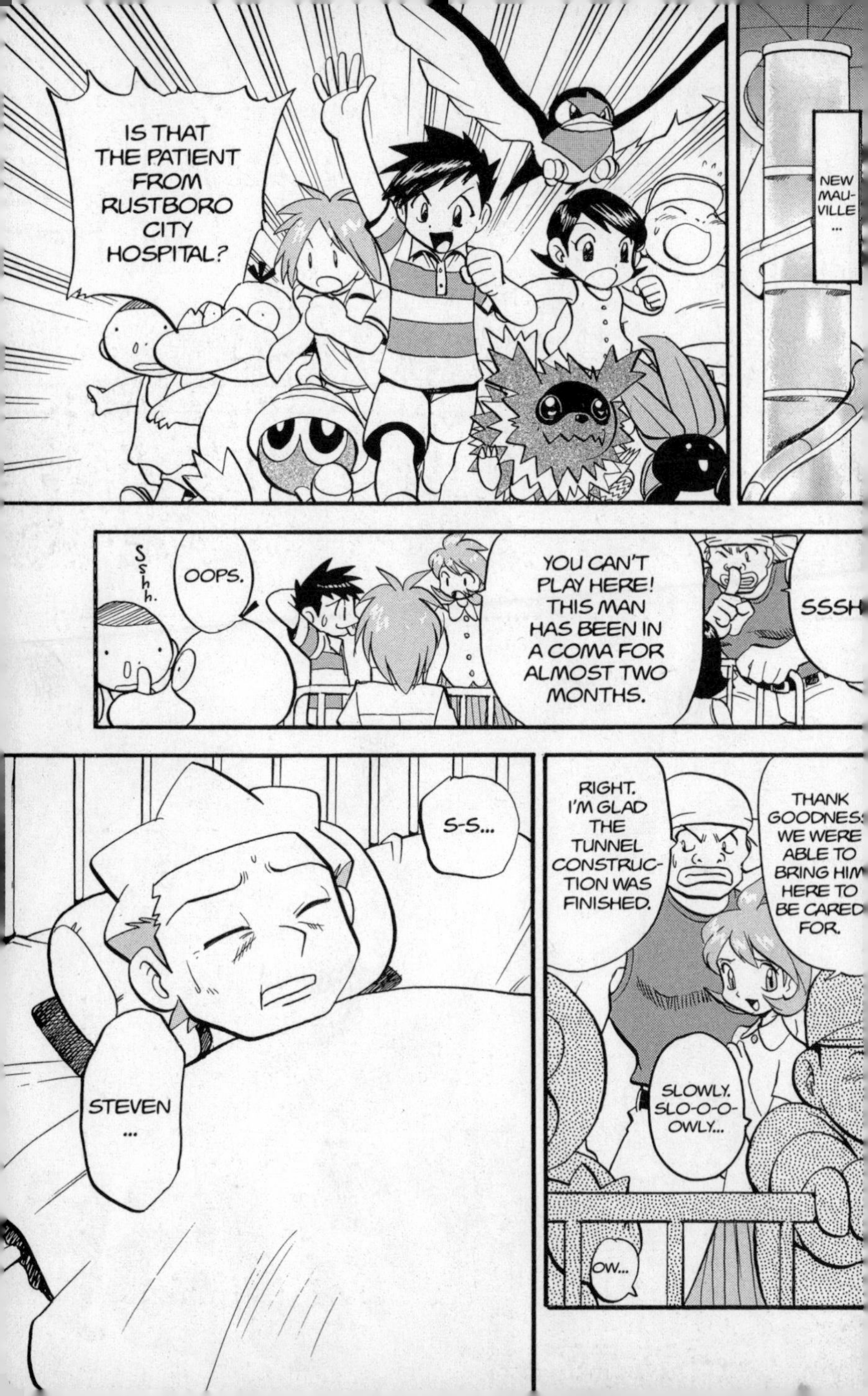
NEW MAUVILLE...
IS THAT THE PATIENT FROM RUSTBORO CITY HOSPITAL?
SSSH
YOU CAN'T PLAY HERE! THIS MAN HAS BEEN IN A COMA FOR ALMOST TWO MONTHS.
OOPS.
Sshh.
THANK GOODNES WE WERE ABLE TO BRING HIM HERE TO BE CARED FOR.
RIGHT. I'M GLAD THE TUNNEL CONSTRUCTION WAS FINISHED.
SLOWLY. SLO-O-O-OWLY...
OW...
S-S...
STEVEN...

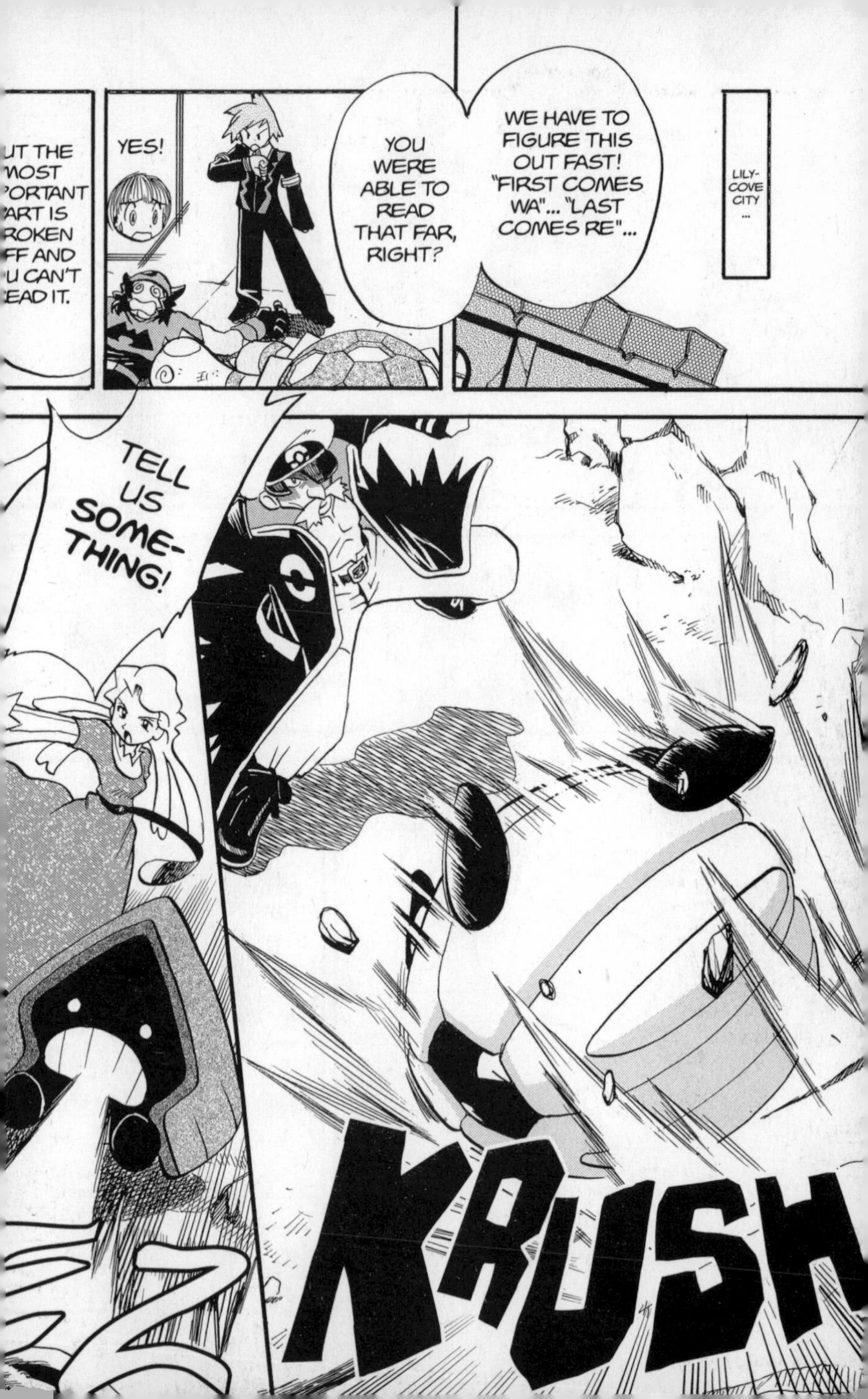
LILY-COVE CITY ...
WE HAVE TO FIGURE THIS OUT FAST! "FIRST COMES WA"... "LAST COMES RE"...
YOU WERE ABLE TO READ THAT FAR, RIGHT?
YES!
UT THE MOST PORTANT ART IS ROKEN FF AND U CAN'T EAD IT.
TELL US SOME-THING!
KRUSH

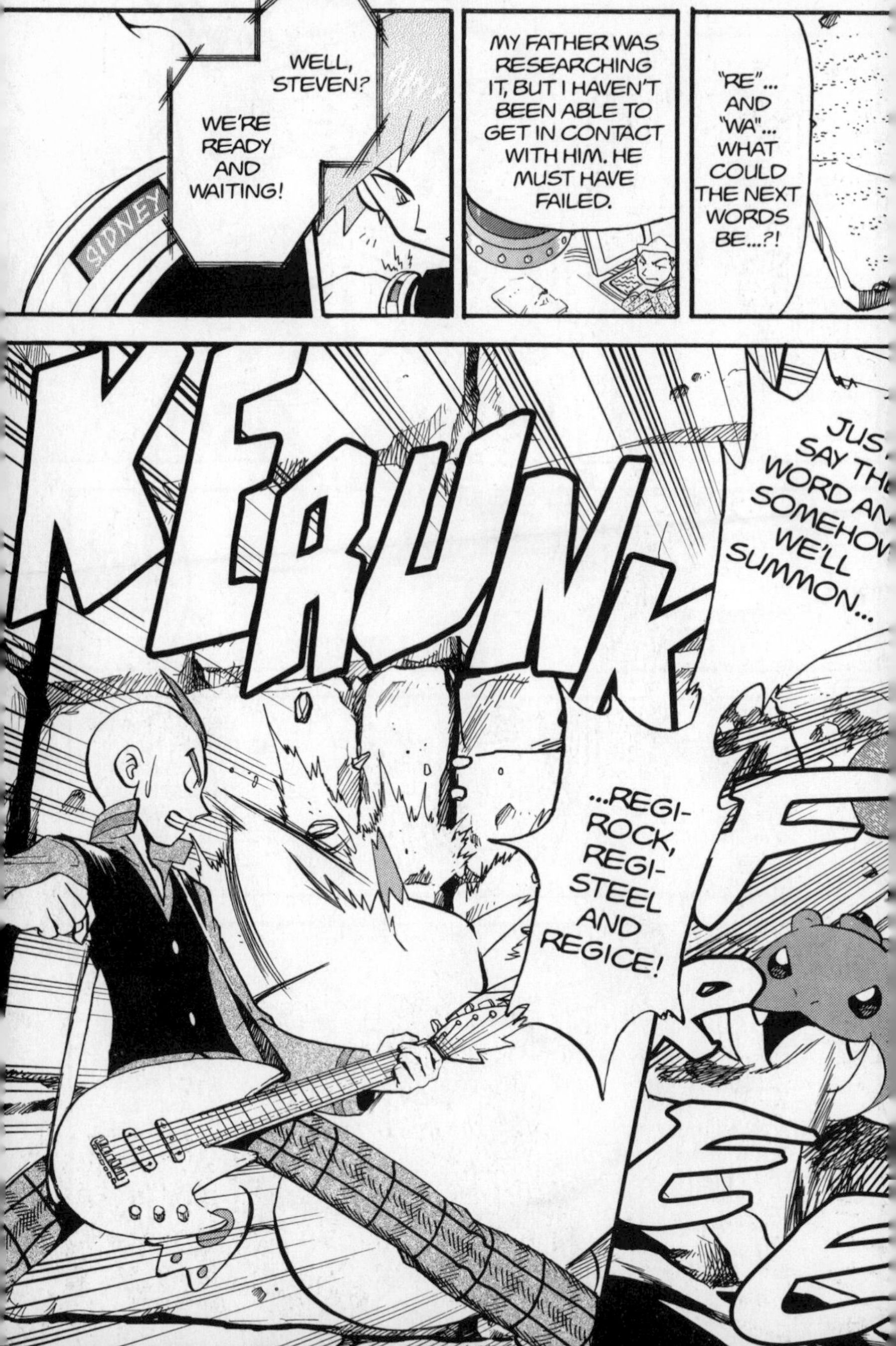
"RE"... AND "WA"... WHAT COULD THE NEXT WORDS BE...?!
MY FATHER WAS RESEARCHING IT, BUT I HAVEN'T BEEN ABLE TO GET IN CONTACT WITH HIM. HE MUST HAVE FAILED.
WELL, STEVEN?
WE'RE READY AND WAITING!
SIDNEY
JUS SAY TH WORD AN SOMEHOW WE'LL SUMMON...
KLRUNK
...REGI-ROCK, REGI-STEEL AND REGICE!

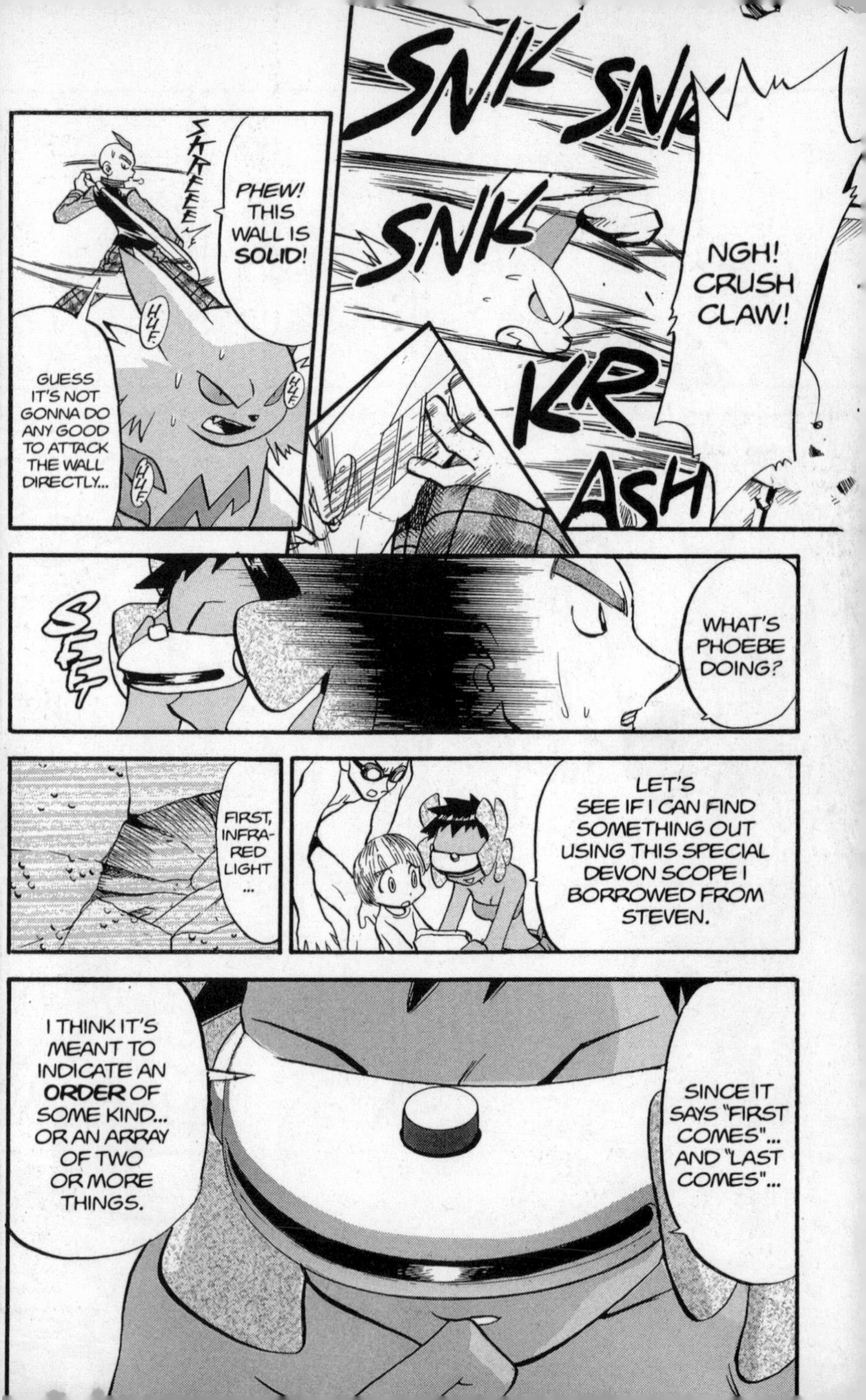
SNK
SNK
NGH! CRUSH CLAW!
KRASH
SKREEEE
PHEW! THIS WALL IS **SOLID**!
HUF
HUF
HUF
HUF
GUESS IT'S NOT GONNA DO ANY GOOD TO ATTACK THE WALL DIRECTLY...
WHAT'S PHOEBE DOING?
LET'S SEE IF I CAN FIND SOMETHING OUT USING THIS SPECIAL DEVON SCOPE I BORROWED FROM STEVEN.
FIRST, INFRA-RED LIGHT...
SINCE IT SAYS "FIRST COMES"... AND "LAST COMES"...
I THINK IT'S MEANT TO INDICATE AN **ORDER** OF SOME KIND... OR AN ARRAY OF TWO OR MORE THINGS.

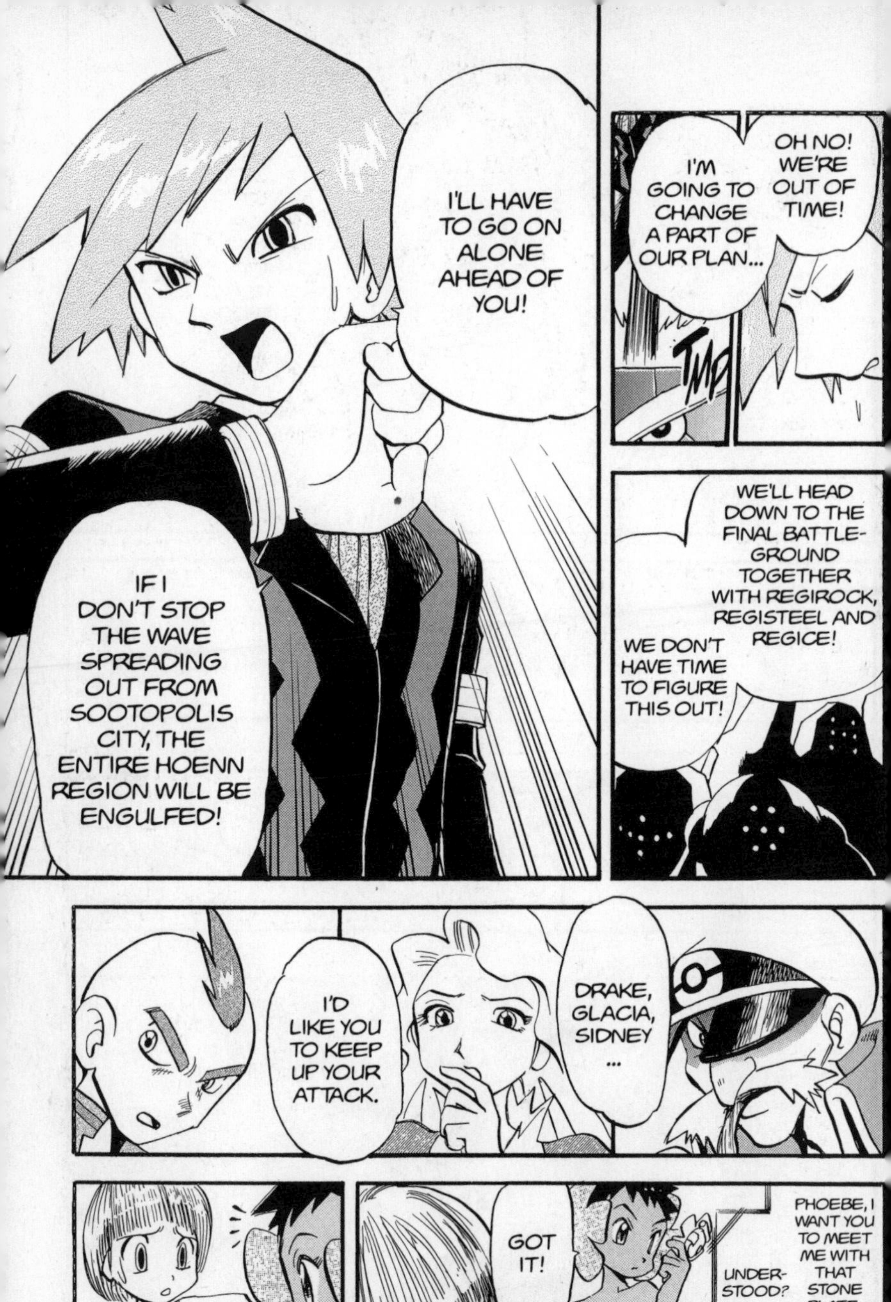
OH NO! WE'RE OUT OF TIME!
I'M GOING TO CHANGE A PART OF OUR PLAN...
TMP
WE'LL HEAD DOWN TO THE FINAL BATTLE-GROUND TOGETHER WITH REGIROCK, REGISTEEL AND REGICE!
WE DON'T HAVE TIME TO FIGURE THIS OUT!
I'LL HAVE TO GO ON ALONE AHEAD OF YOU!
IF I DON'T STOP THE WAVE SPREADING OUT FROM SOOTOPOLIS CITY, THE ENTIRE HOENN REGION WILL BE ENGULFED!
DRAKE, GLACIA, SIDNEY ...
I'D LIKE YOU TO KEEP UP YOUR ATTACK.
PHOEBE, I WANT YOU TO MEET ME WITH THAT STONE PLATE.
UNDER-STOOD?
GOT IT!

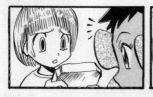

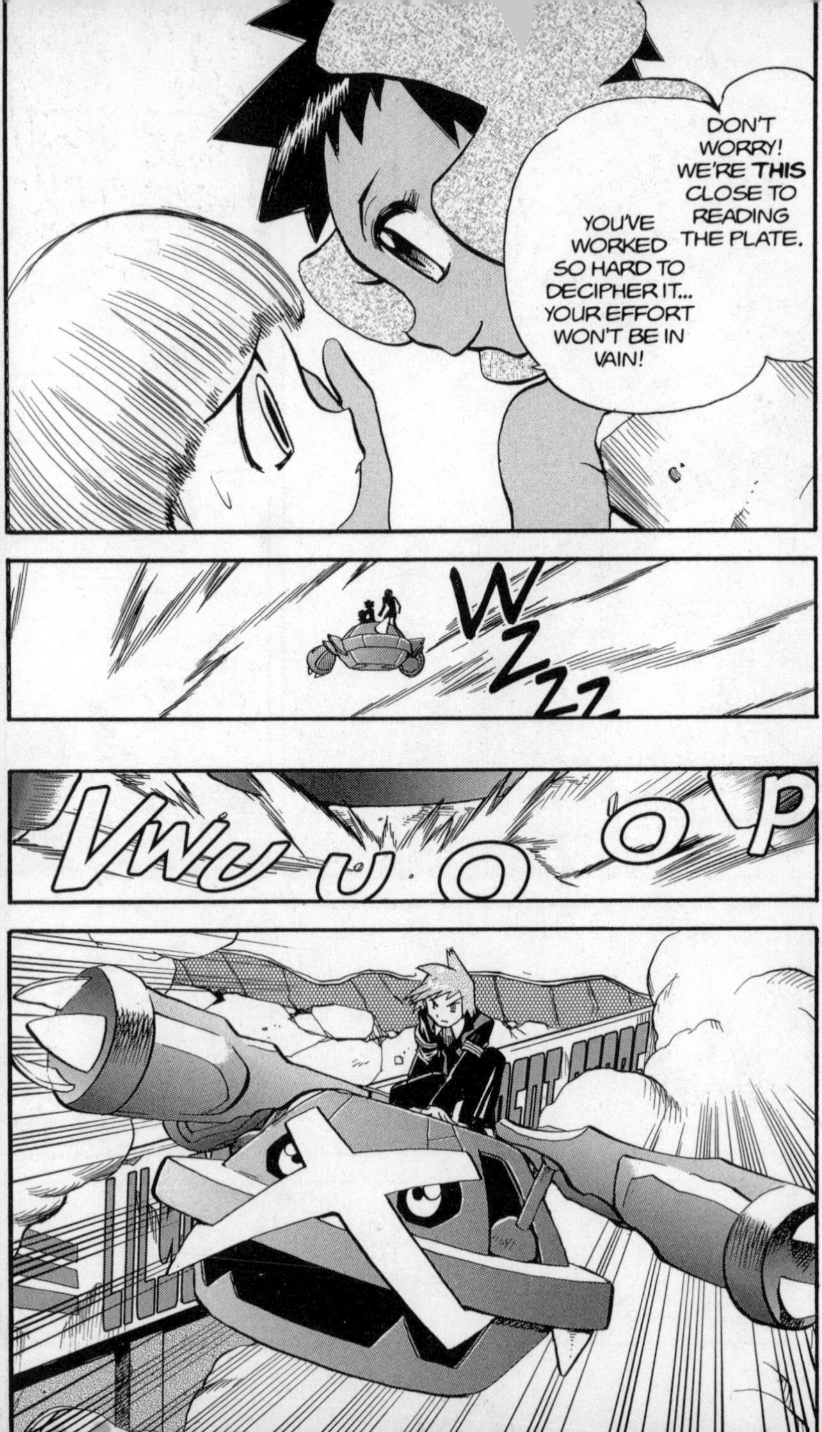
DON'T WORRY! WE'RE THIS CLOSE TO READING THE PLATE.
YOU'VE WORKED SO HARD TO DECIPHER IT... YOUR EFFORT WON'T BE IN VAIN!
WZZZ
VWUUOOOP

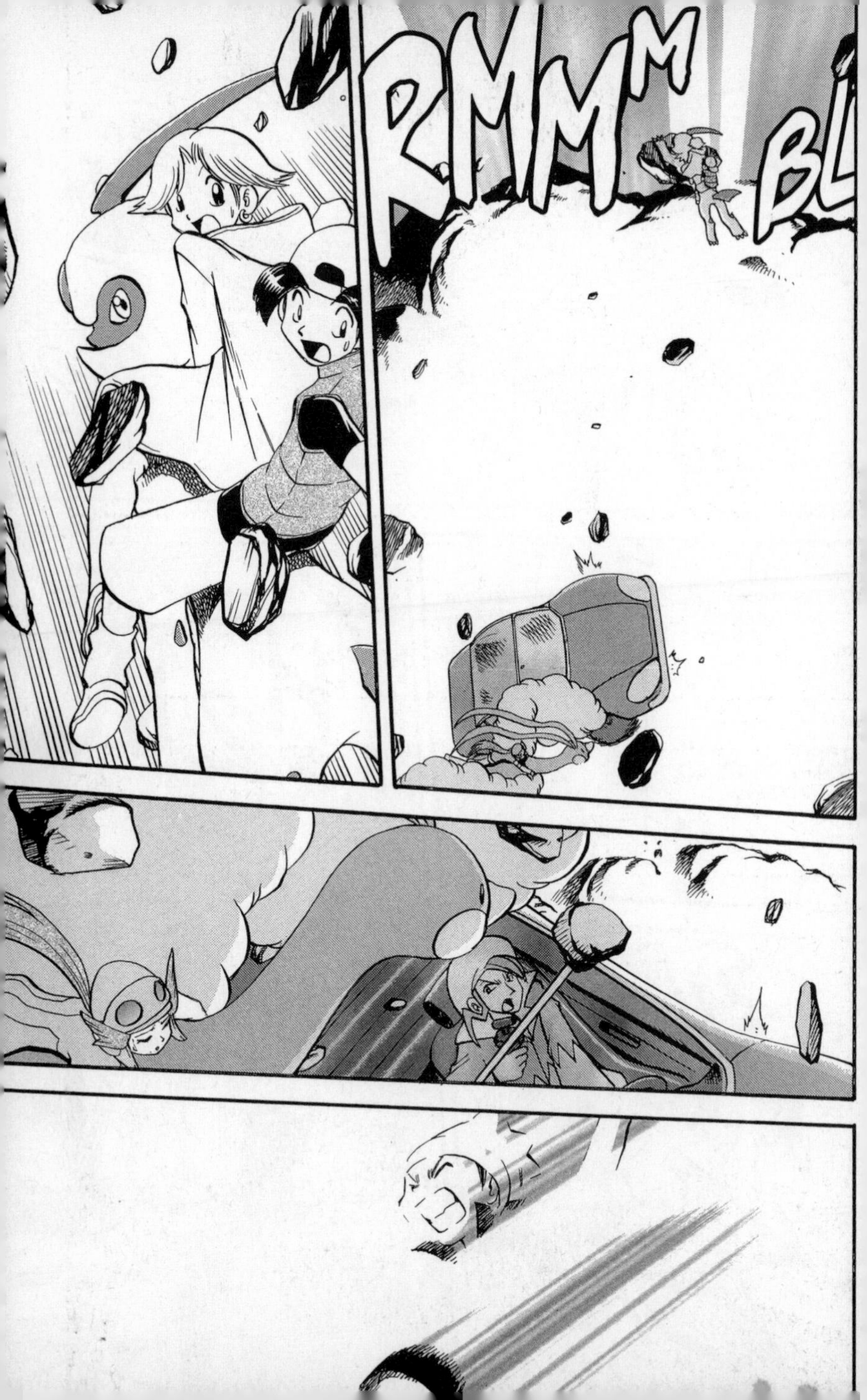
RMMM
BL

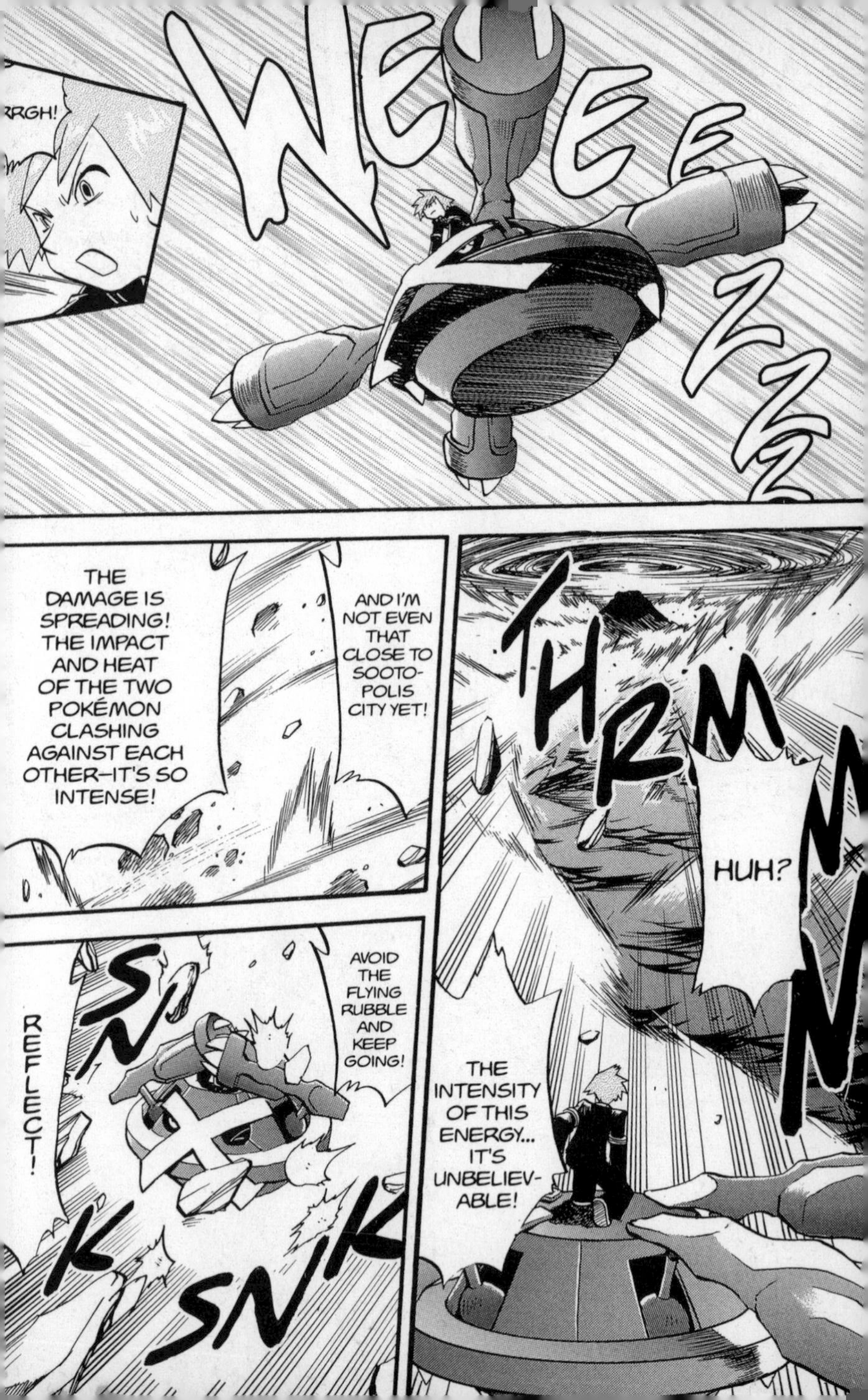
WEEEZZZZ
RRGH!
THRMMMM
HUH?
THE INTENSITY OF THIS ENERGY... IT'S UNBELIEVABLE!
AND I'M NOT EVEN THAT CLOSE TO SOOTOPOLIS CITY YET!
THE DAMAGE IS SPREADING! THE IMPACT AND HEAT OF THE TWO POKÉMON CLASHING AGAINST EACH OTHER—IT'S SO INTENSE!
AVOID THE FLYING RUBBLE AND KEEP GOING!
SNK
REFLECT!
SNK

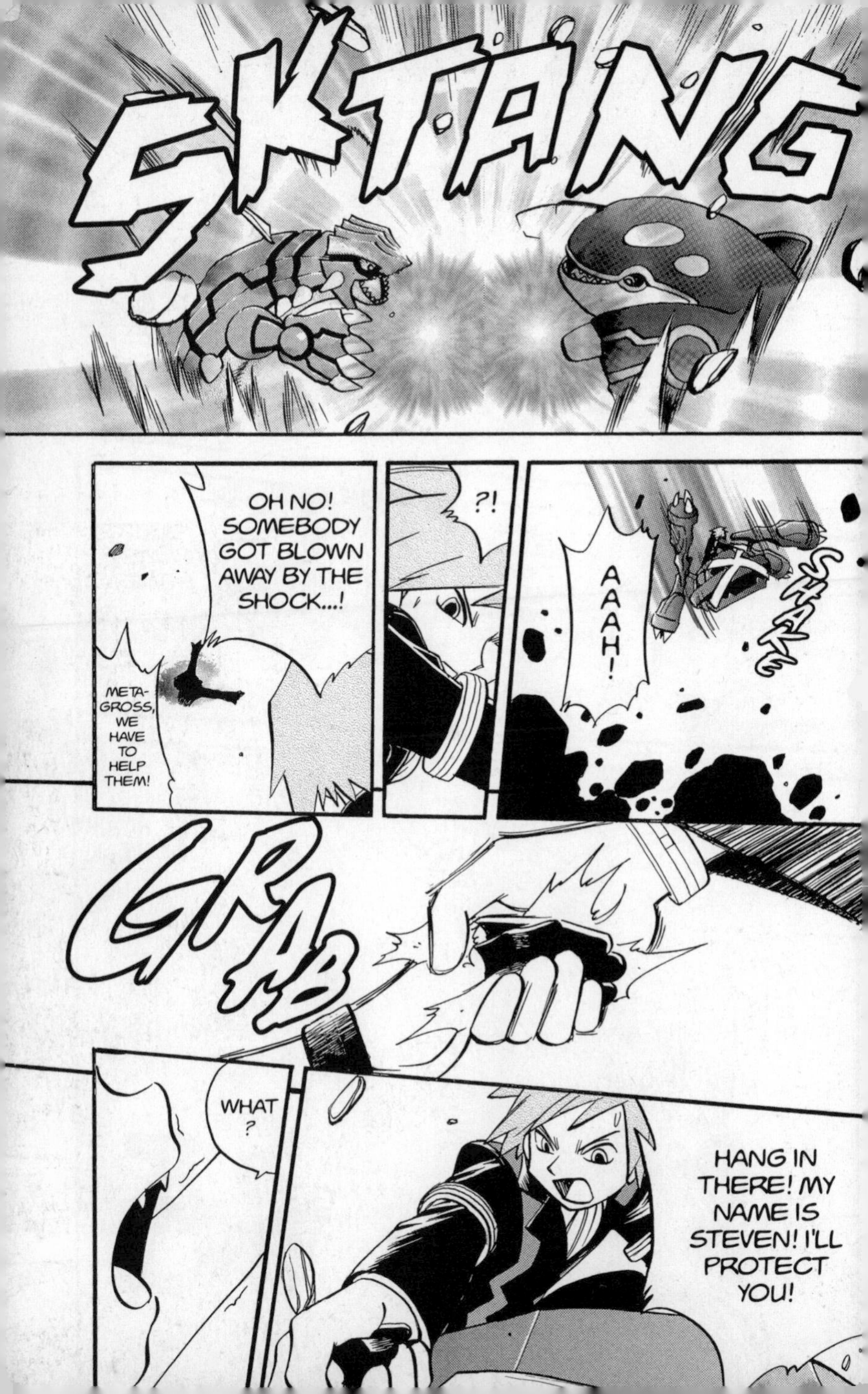
SKTANG
AAAH!
SHAKE
?!
OH NO! SOMEBODY GOT BLOWN AWAY BY THE SHOCK...!
METAGROSS, WE HAVE TO HELP THEM!
GRAB
HANG IN THERE! MY NAME IS STEVEN! I'LL PROTECT YOU!
WHAT?

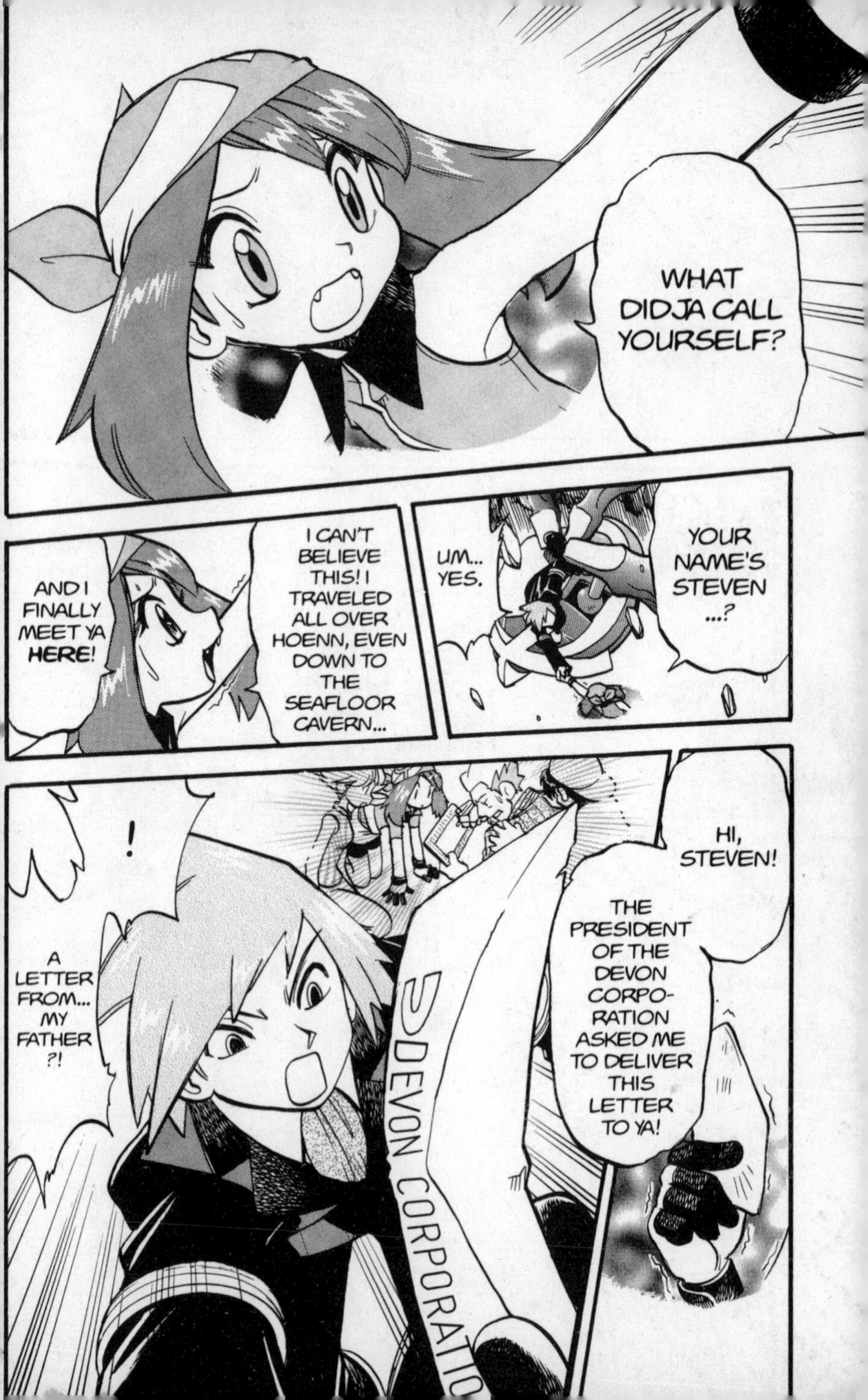
WHAT DIDJA CALL YOURSELF?
YOUR NAME'S STEVEN ...?
UM... YES.
I CAN'T BELIEVE THIS! I TRAVELED ALL OVER HOENN, EVEN DOWN TO THE SEAFLOOR CAVERN...
AND I FINALLY MEET YA HERE!
HI, STEVEN!
THE PRESIDENT OF THE DEVON CORPORATION ASKED ME TO DELIVER THIS LETTER TO YA!
DEVON CORPORATIO
!
A LETTER FROM... MY FATHER ?!

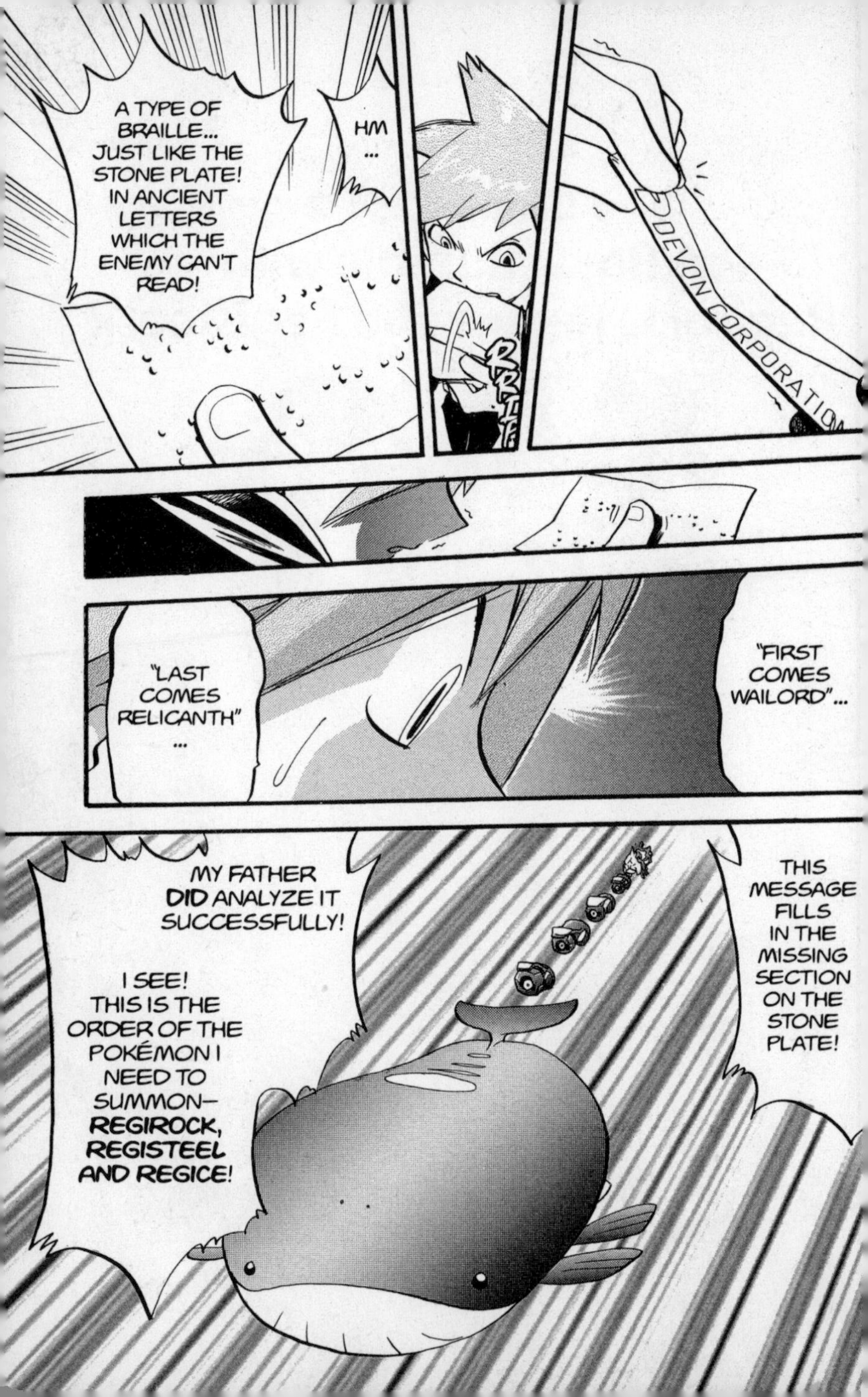
DEVON CORPORATION
HM ...
A TYPE OF BRAILLE... JUST LIKE THE STONE PLATE! IN ANCIENT LETTERS WHICH THE ENEMY CAN'T READ!
"FIRST COMES WAILORD"...
"LAST COMES RELICANTH" ...
THIS MESSAGE FILLS IN THE MISSING SECTION ON THE STONE PLATE!
MY FATHER **DID** ANALYZE IT SUCCESSFULLY!
I SEE! THIS IS THE ORDER OF THE POKÉMON I NEED TO SUMMON– **REGIROCK, REGISTEEL AND REGICE!**

# ● Chapter 254 ●
# A Royal Rumble with
# Regirock, Regice and Registeel II

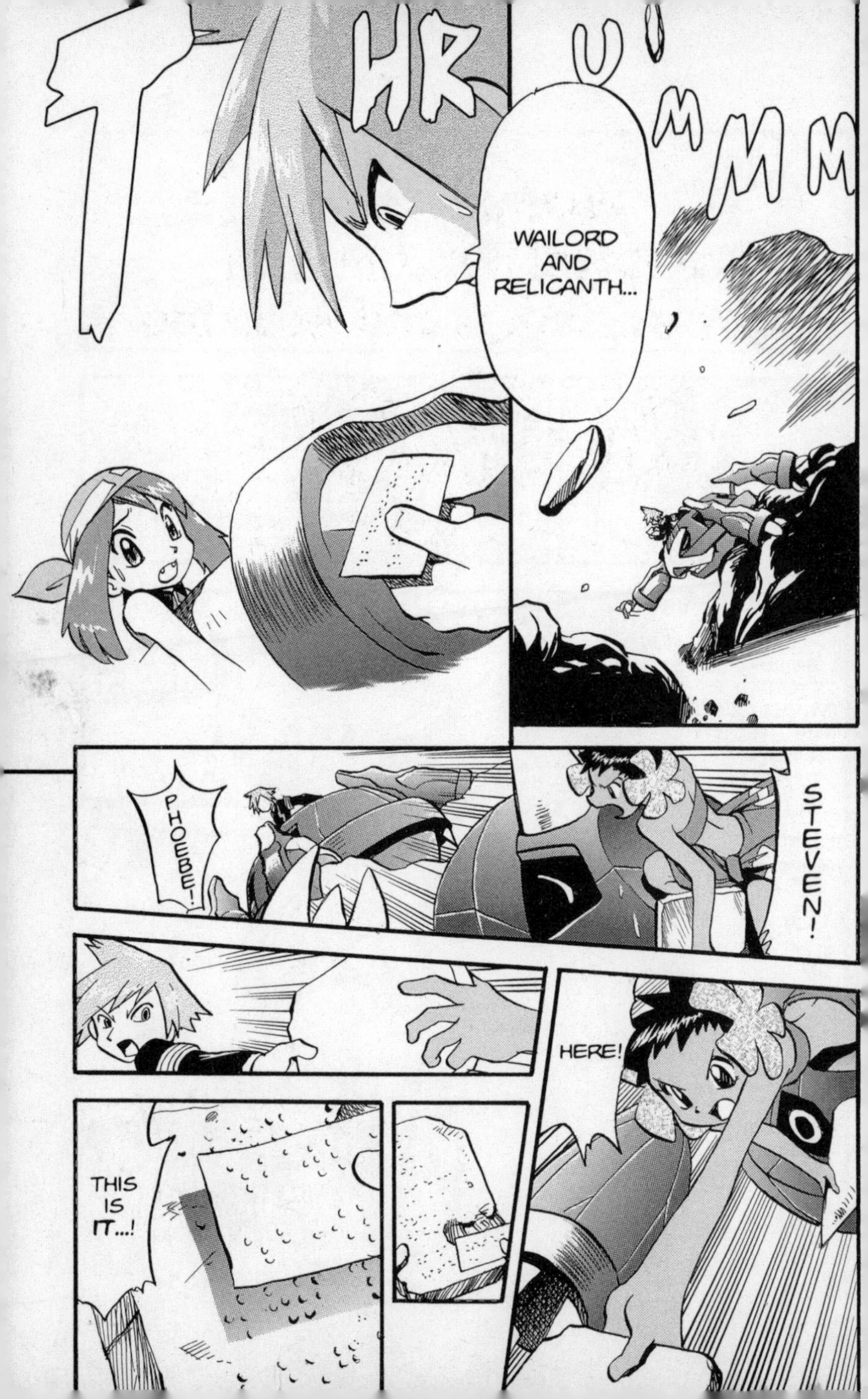

THRUMMMM
WAILORD AND RELICANTH...
STEVEN!
PHOEBE!
HERE!
THIS IS IT...!

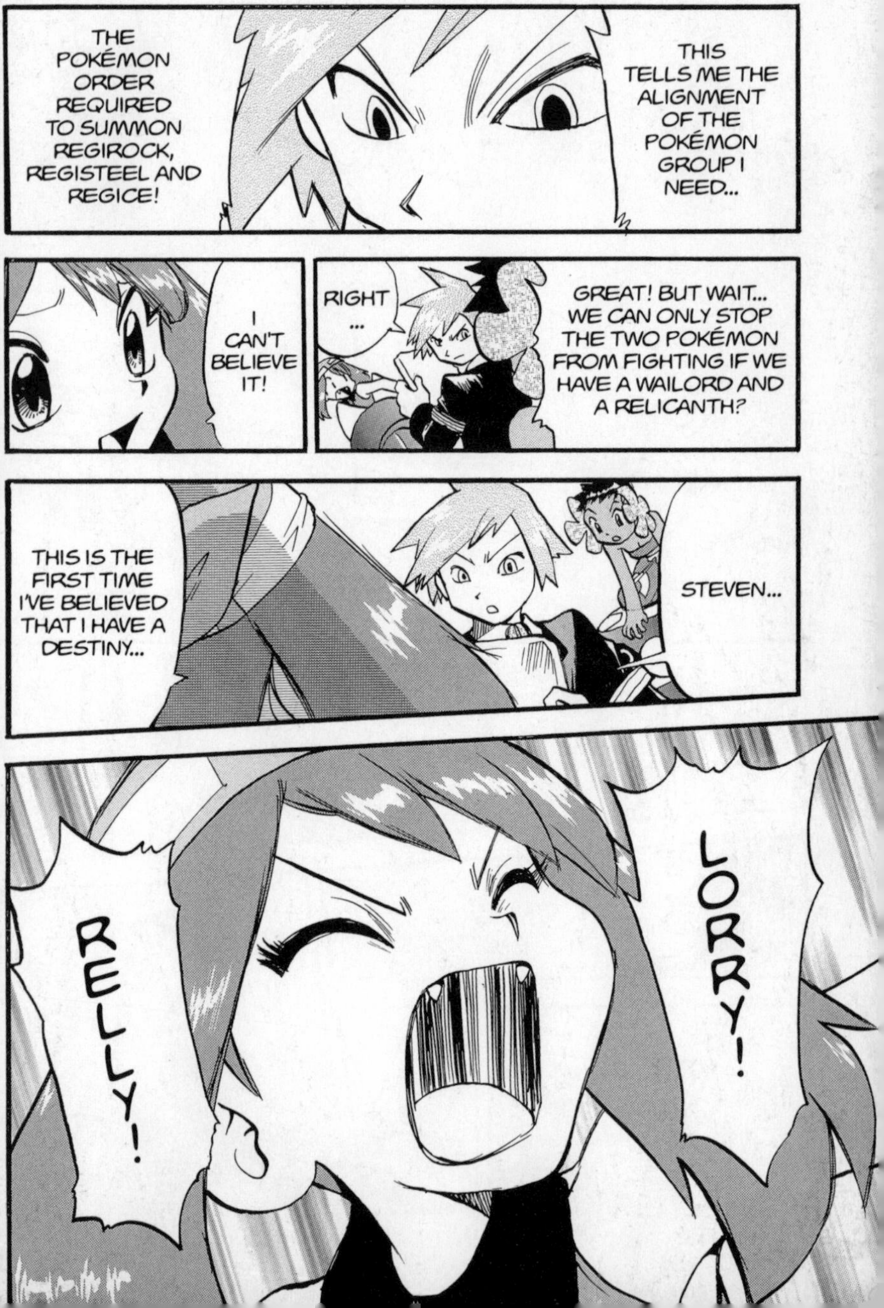
THIS TELLS ME THE ALIGNMENT OF THE POKÉMON GROUP I NEED...
THE POKÉMON ORDER REQUIRED TO SUMMON REGIROCK, REGISTEEL AND REGICE!
GREAT! BUT WAIT... WE CAN ONLY STOP THE TWO POKÉMON FROM FIGHTING IF WE HAVE A WAILORD AND A RELICANTH?
RIGHT ...
I CAN'T BELIEVE IT!
STEVEN...
THIS IS THE FIRST TIME I'VE BELIEVED THAT I HAVE A DESTINY...
LORRY!
RELLY!

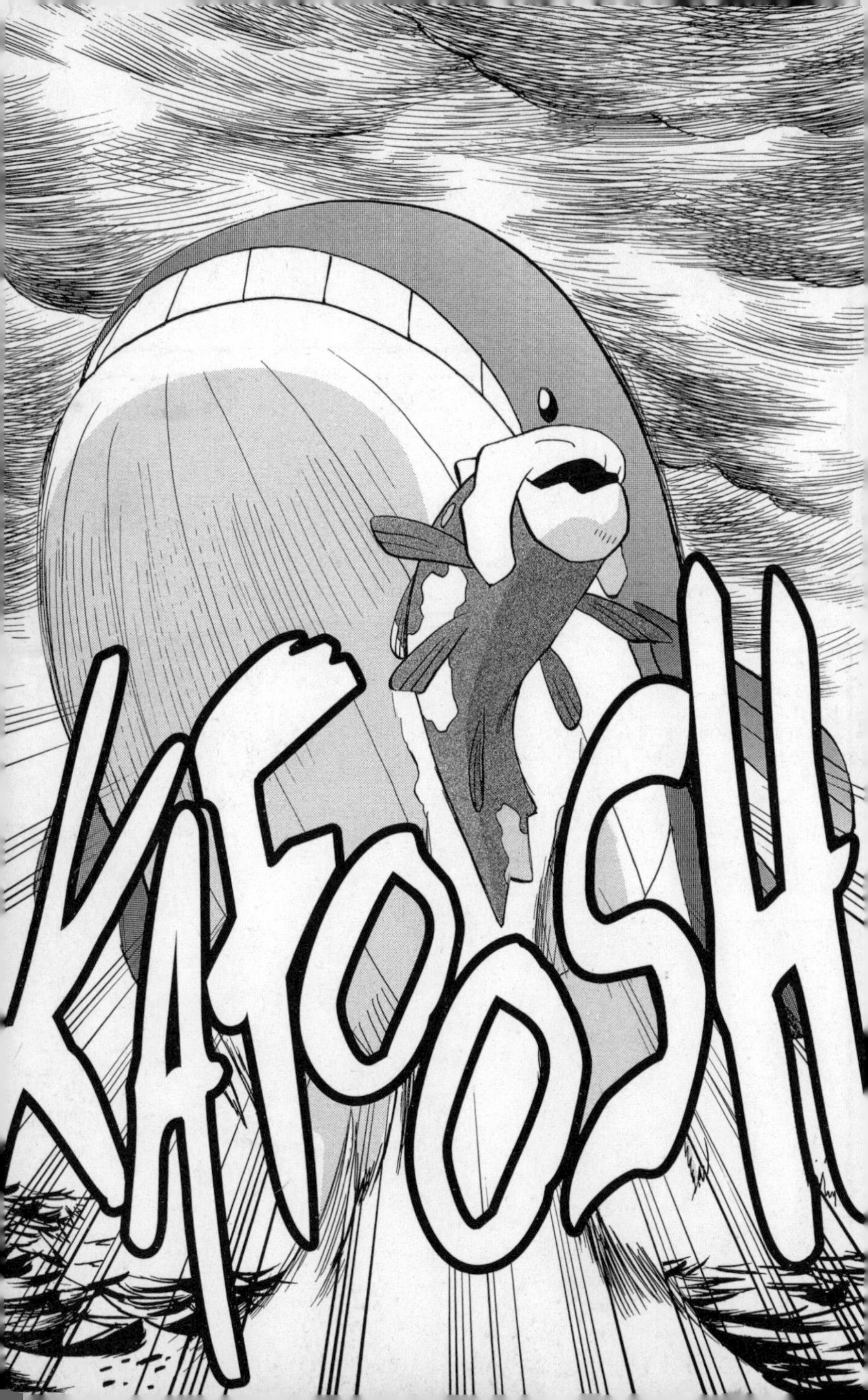
KAFOOSH

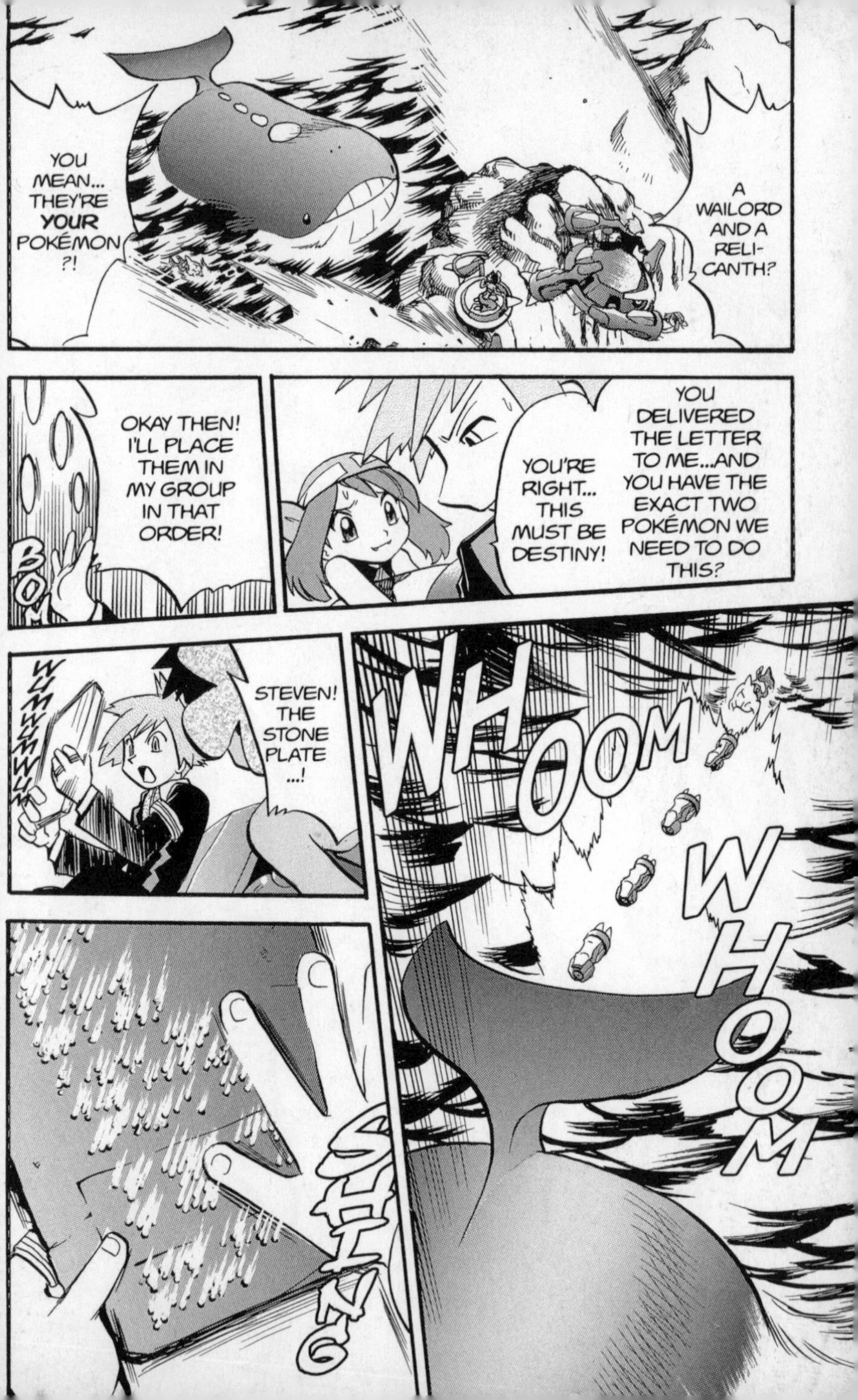
A WAILORD AND A RELI- CANTH?
YOU MEAN... THEY'RE **YOUR** POKÉMON ?!
YOU DELIVERED THE LETTER TO ME...AND YOU HAVE THE EXACT TWO POKÉMON WE NEED TO DO THIS?
YOU'RE RIGHT... THIS MUST BE DESTINY!
OKAY THEN! I'LL PLACE THEM IN MY GROUP IN THAT ORDER!
WHOOM
WHOOOM
STEVEN! THE STONE PLATE ...!
SHING

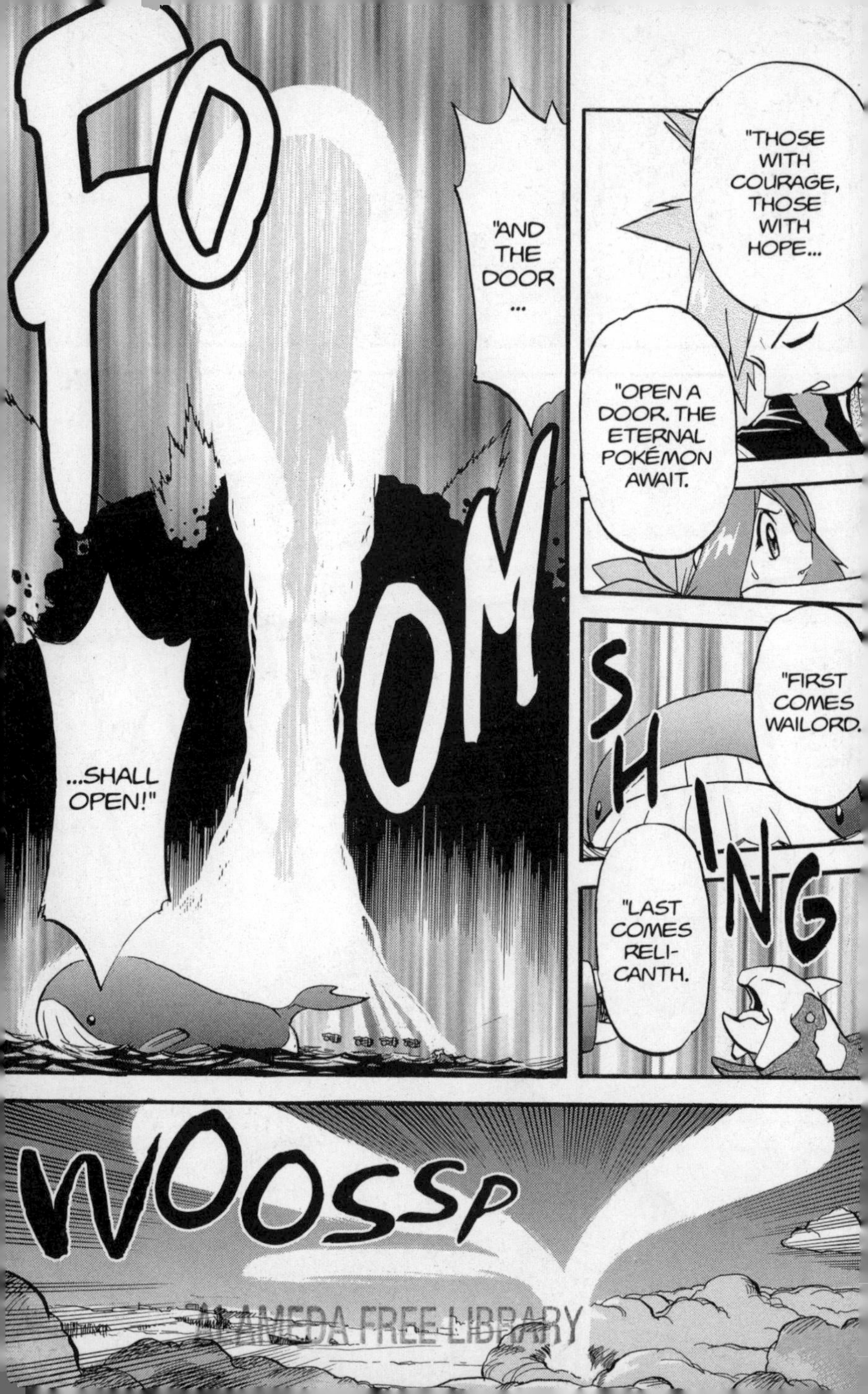
"THOSE WITH COURAGE, THOSE WITH HOPE...
"OPEN A DOOR. THE ETERNAL POKÉMON AWAIT.
"FIRST COMES WAILORD.
SHING
"LAST COMES RELI-CANTH.
"AND THE DOOR ...
FOOM
...SHALL OPEN!"
WOOSSP

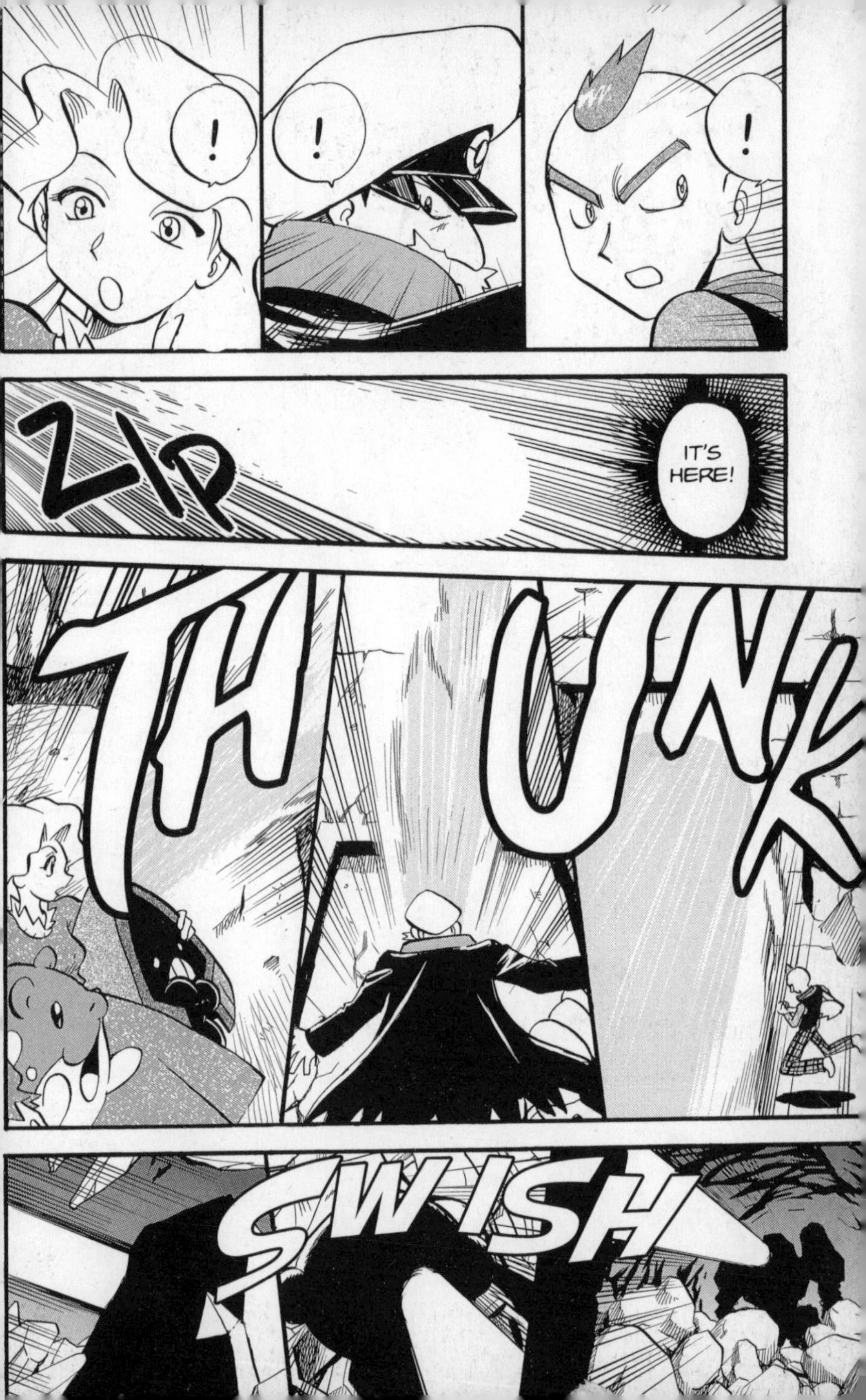
!
!
!
IT'S HERE!
ZIP
THUNK
SWISH

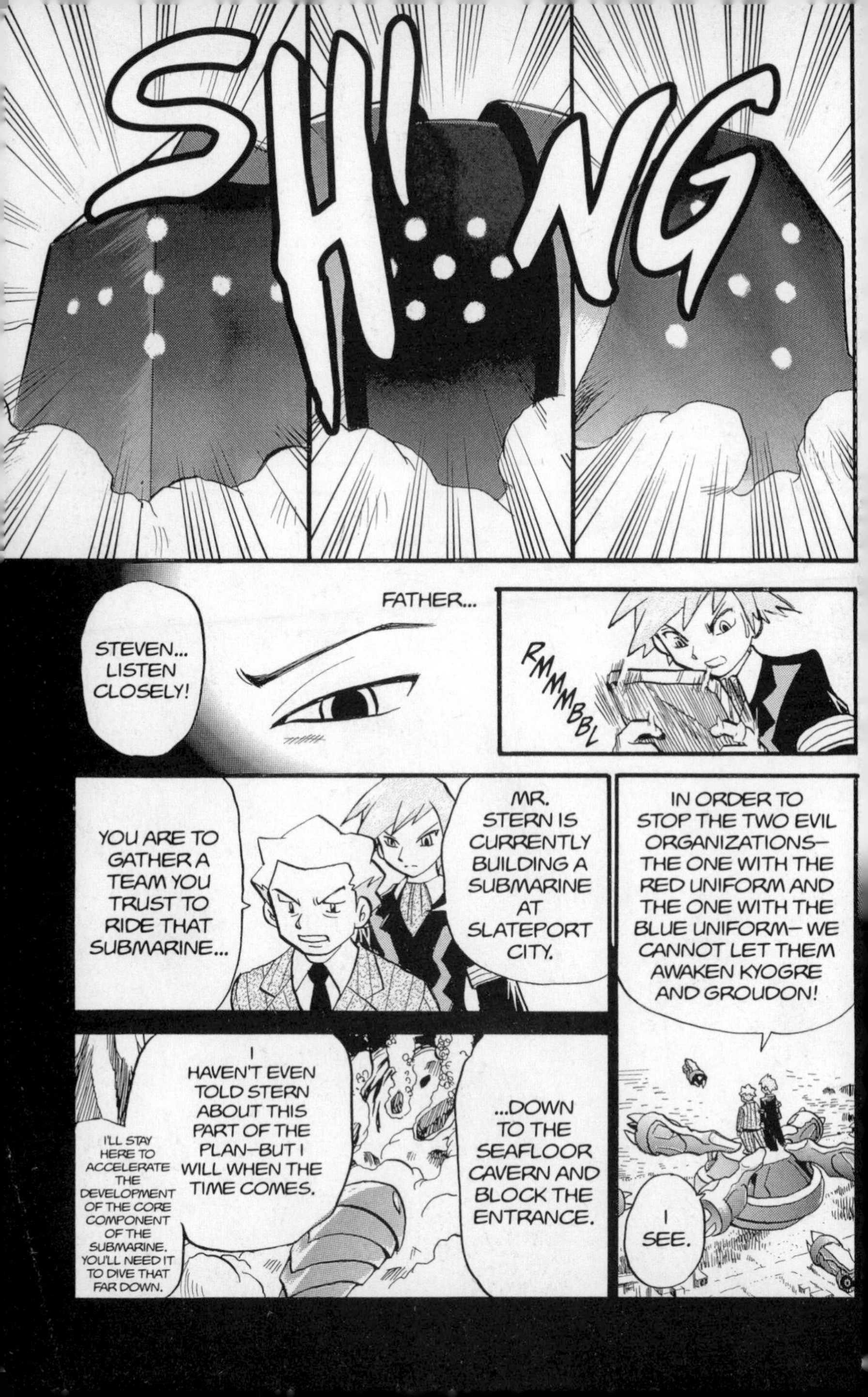
SHING
RMMMBBL
FATHER...
STEVEN... LISTEN CLOSELY!
IN ORDER TO STOP THE TWO EVIL ORGANIZATIONS— THE ONE WITH THE RED UNIFORM AND THE ONE WITH THE BLUE UNIFORM— WE CANNOT LET THEM AWAKEN KYOGRE AND GROUDON!
I SEE.
MR. STERN IS CURRENTLY BUILDING A SUBMARINE AT SLATEPORT CITY.
YOU ARE TO GATHER A TEAM YOU TRUST TO RIDE THAT SUBMARINE...
...DOWN TO THE SEAFLOOR CAVERN AND BLOCK THE ENTRANCE.
I HAVEN'T EVEN TOLD STERN ABOUT THIS PART OF THE PLAN—BUT I WILL WHEN THE TIME COMES.
I'LL STAY HERE TO ACCELERATE THE DEVELOPMENT OF THE CORE COMPONENT OF THE SUBMARINE. YOU'LL NEED IT TO DIVE THAT FAR DOWN.

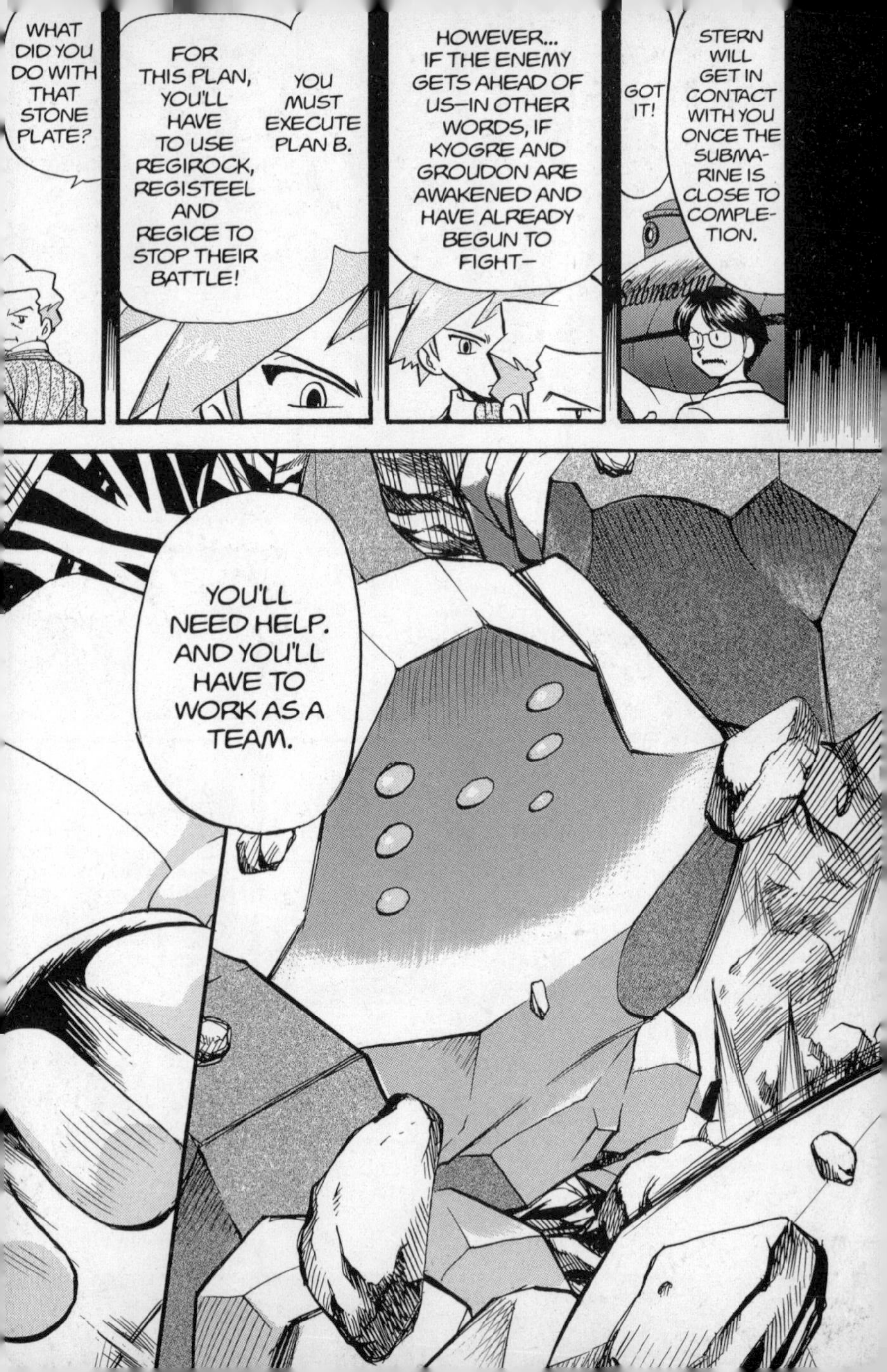
STERN WILL GET IN CONTACT WITH YOU ONCE THE SUBMARINE IS CLOSE TO COMPLETION.
GOT IT!
HOWEVER... IF THE ENEMY GETS AHEAD OF US—IN OTHER WORDS, IF KYOGRE AND GROUDON ARE AWAKENED AND HAVE ALREADY BEGUN TO FIGHT—
YOU MUST EXECUTE PLAN B.
FOR THIS PLAN, YOU'LL HAVE TO USE REGIROCK, REGISTEEL AND REGICE TO STOP THEIR BATTLE!
WHAT DID YOU DO WITH THAT STONE PLATE?
YOU'LL NEED HELP. AND YOU'LL HAVE TO WORK AS A TEAM.

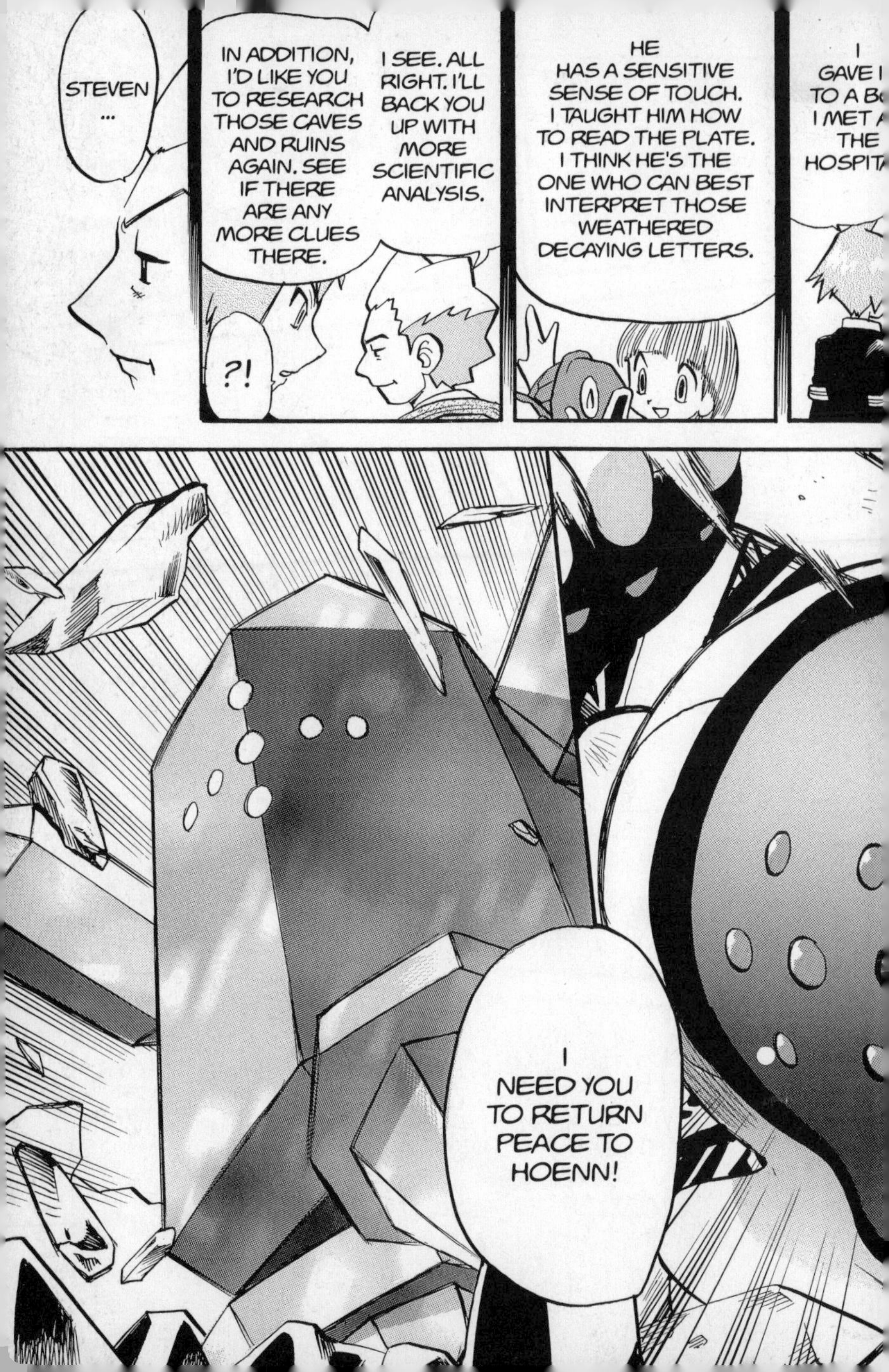
I GAVE I TO A B I MET A THE HOSPITA
HE HAS A SENSITIVE SENSE OF TOUCH. I TAUGHT HIM HOW TO READ THE PLATE. I THINK HE'S THE ONE WHO CAN BEST INTERPRET THOSE WEATHERED DECAYING LETTERS.
IN ADDITION, I'D LIKE YOU TO RESEARCH THOSE CAVES AND RUINS AGAIN. SEE IF THERE ARE ANY MORE CLUES THERE.
I SEE. ALL RIGHT. I'LL BACK YOU UP WITH MORE SCIENTIFIC ANALYSIS.
?!
STEVEN ...
I NEED YOU TO RETURN PEACE TO HOENN!

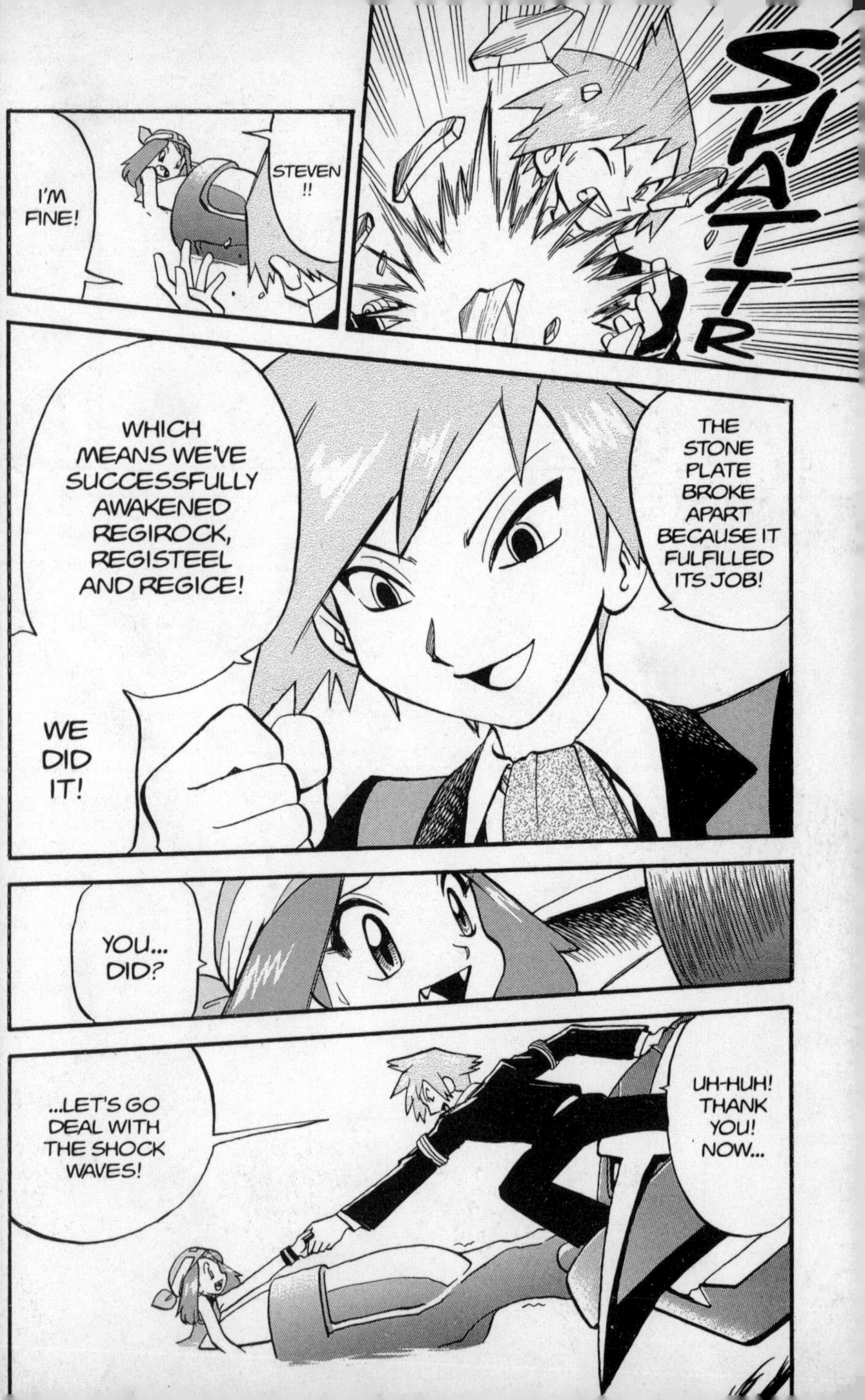
SHATTR
STEVEN!!
I'M FINE!
THE STONE PLATE BROKE APART BECAUSE IT FULFILLED ITS JOB!
WHICH MEANS WE'VE SUCCESSFULLY AWAKENED REGIROCK, REGISTEEL AND REGICE!
WE DID IT!
YOU... DID?
UH-HUH! THANK YOU! NOW...
...LET'S GO DEAL WITH THE SHOCK WAVES!

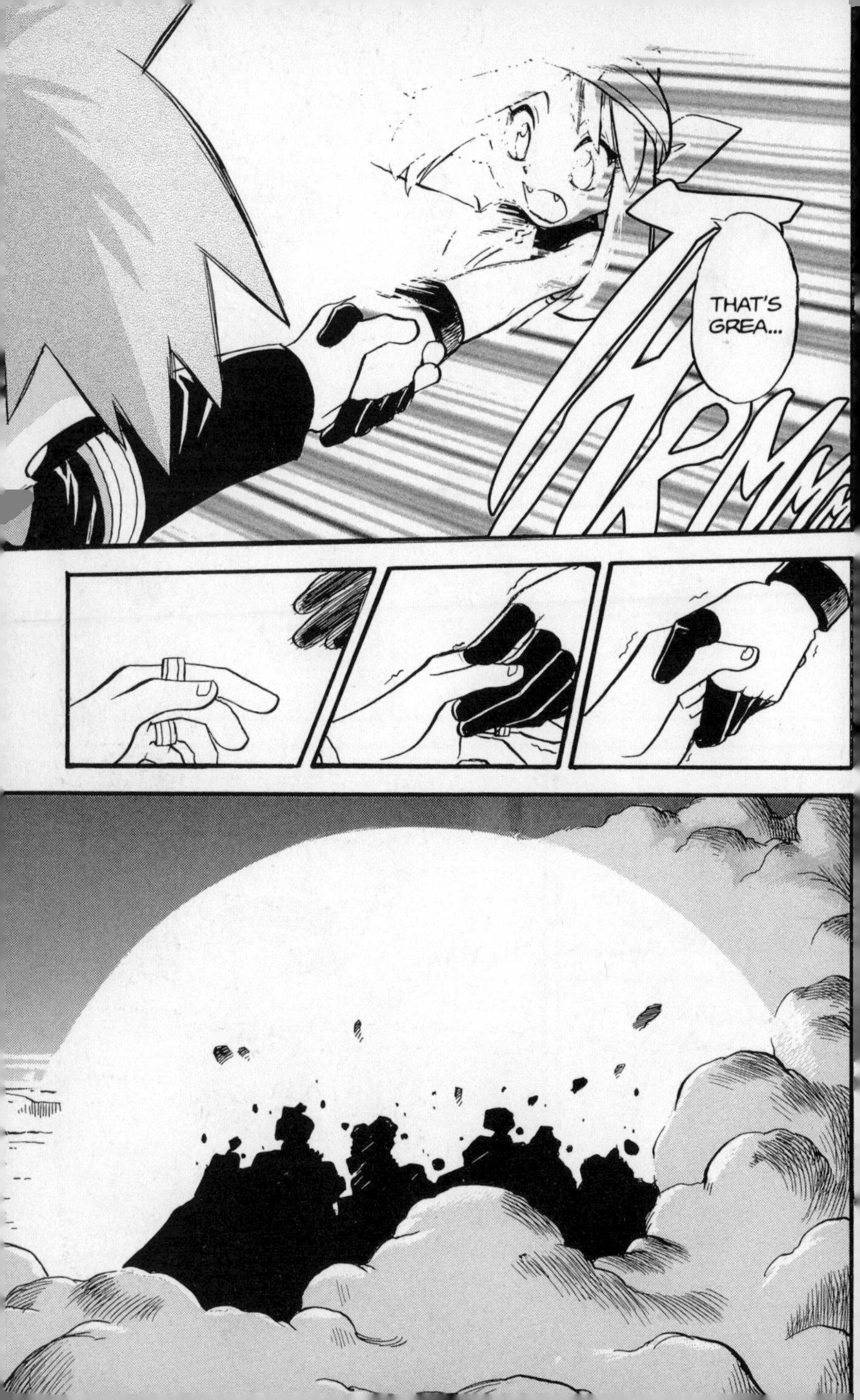
THAT'S GREA...

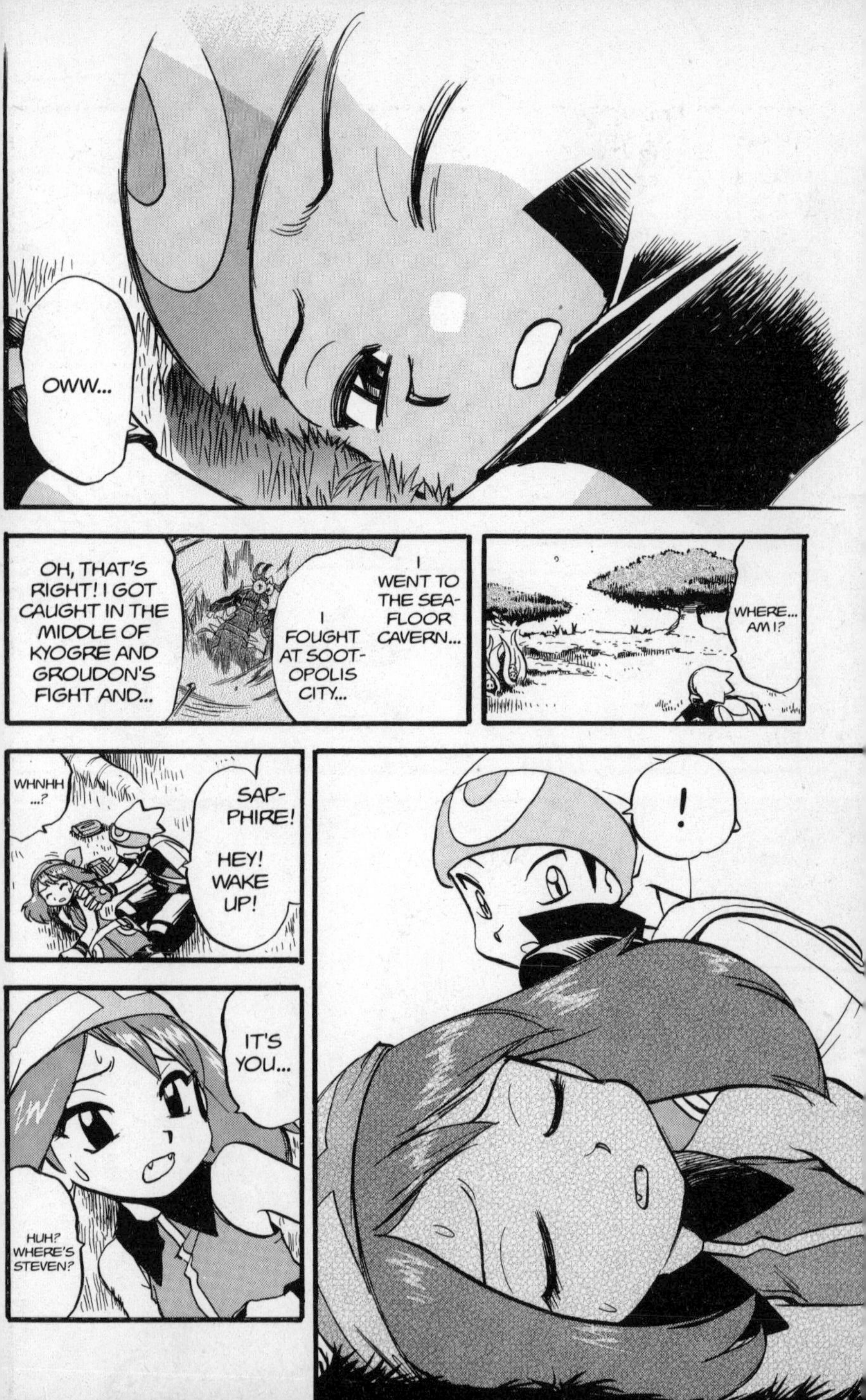
OWW...
WHERE... AM I?
I WENT TO THE SEA-FLOOR CAVERN...
I FOUGHT AT SOOT-OPOLIS CITY...
OH, THAT'S RIGHT! I GOT CAUGHT IN THE MIDDLE OF KYOGRE AND GROUDON'S FIGHT AND...
!
SAP-PHIRE!
HEY! WAKE UP!
WHNHH ...?
IT'S YOU...
HUH? WHERE'S STEVEN?

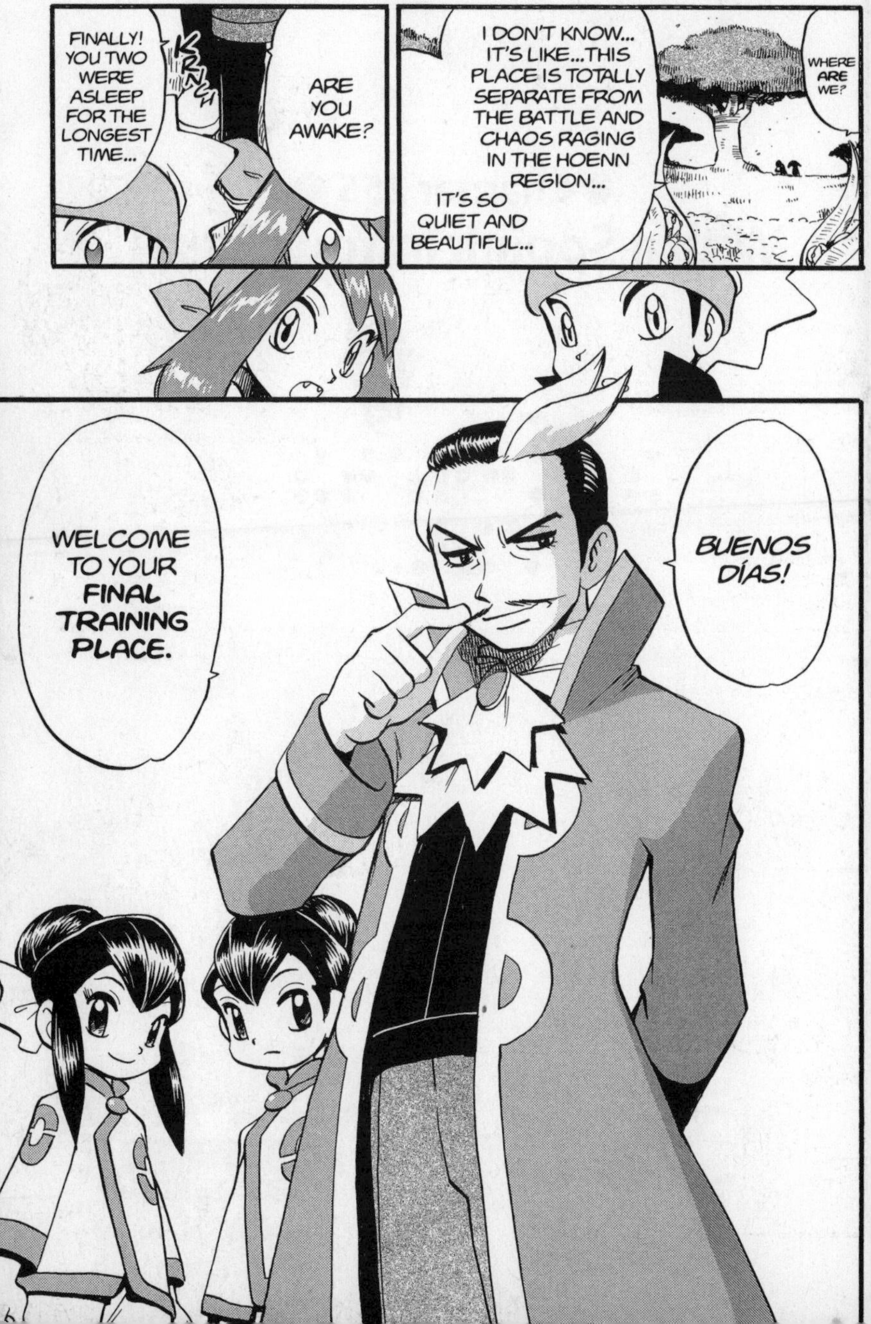
WHERE ARE WE?
I DON'T KNOW... IT'S LIKE...THIS PLACE IS TOTALLY SEPARATE FROM THE BATTLE AND CHAOS RAGING IN THE HOENN REGION...
IT'S SO QUIET AND BEAUTIFUL...
ARE YOU AWAKE?
KRNCH
FINALLY! YOU TWO WERE ASLEEP FOR THE LONGEST TIME...
BUENOS DÍAS!
WELCOME TO YOUR FINAL TRAINING PLACE.

# ● Chapter 255 ●
# With a Spoink in Your Step I

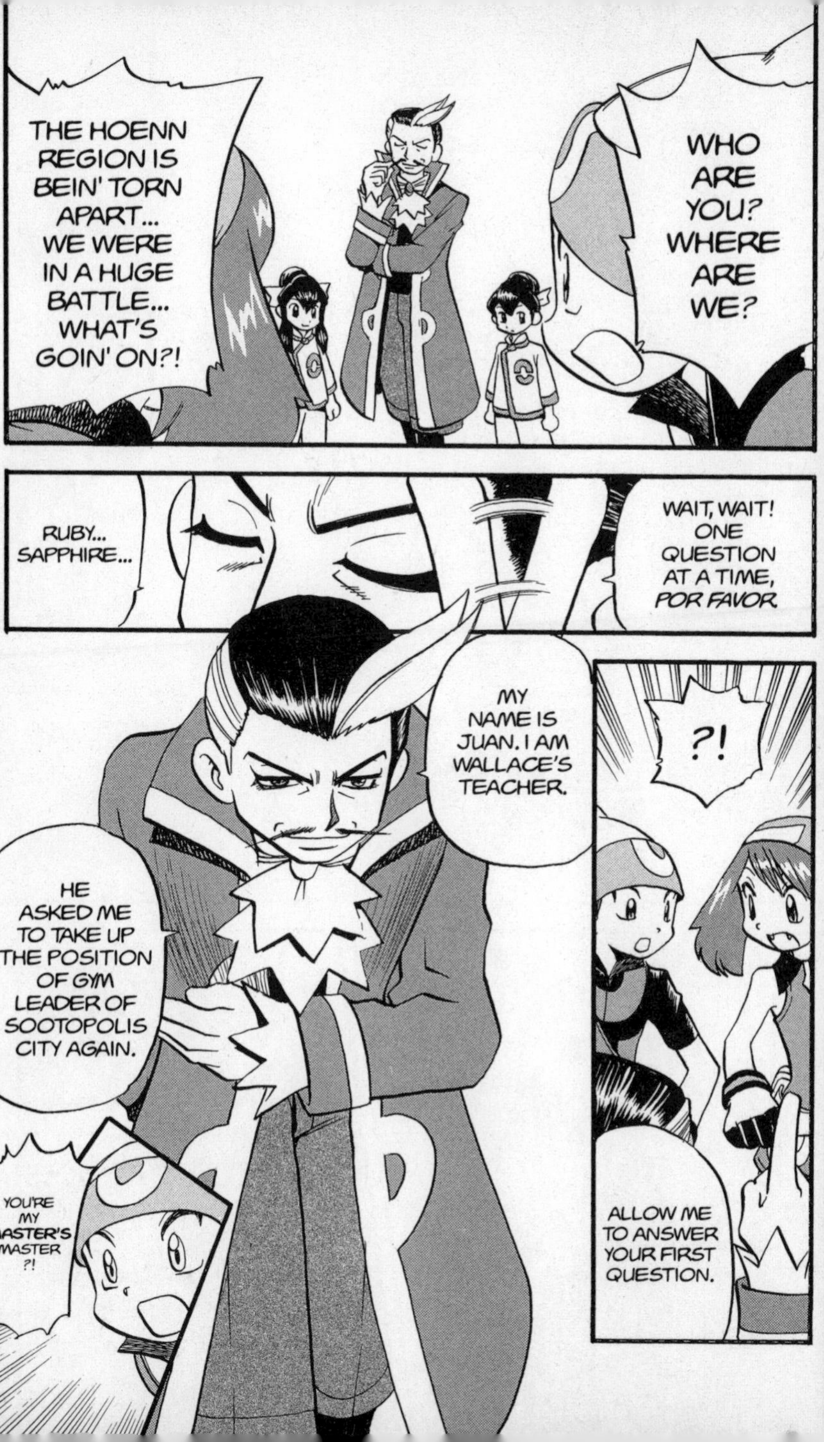
WHO ARE YOU? WHERE ARE WE?
THE HOENN REGION IS BEIN' TORN APART... WE WERE IN A HUGE BATTLE... WHAT'S GOIN' ON?!
WAIT, WAIT! ONE QUESTION AT A TIME, *POR FAVOR.*
RUBY... SAPPHIRE...
?!
ALLOW ME TO ANSWER YOUR FIRST QUESTION.
MY NAME IS JUAN. I AM WALLACE'S TEACHER.
HE ASKED ME TO TAKE UP THE POSITION OF GYM LEADER OF SOOTOPOLIS CITY AGAIN.
YOU'RE MY **MASTER'S** MASTER?!

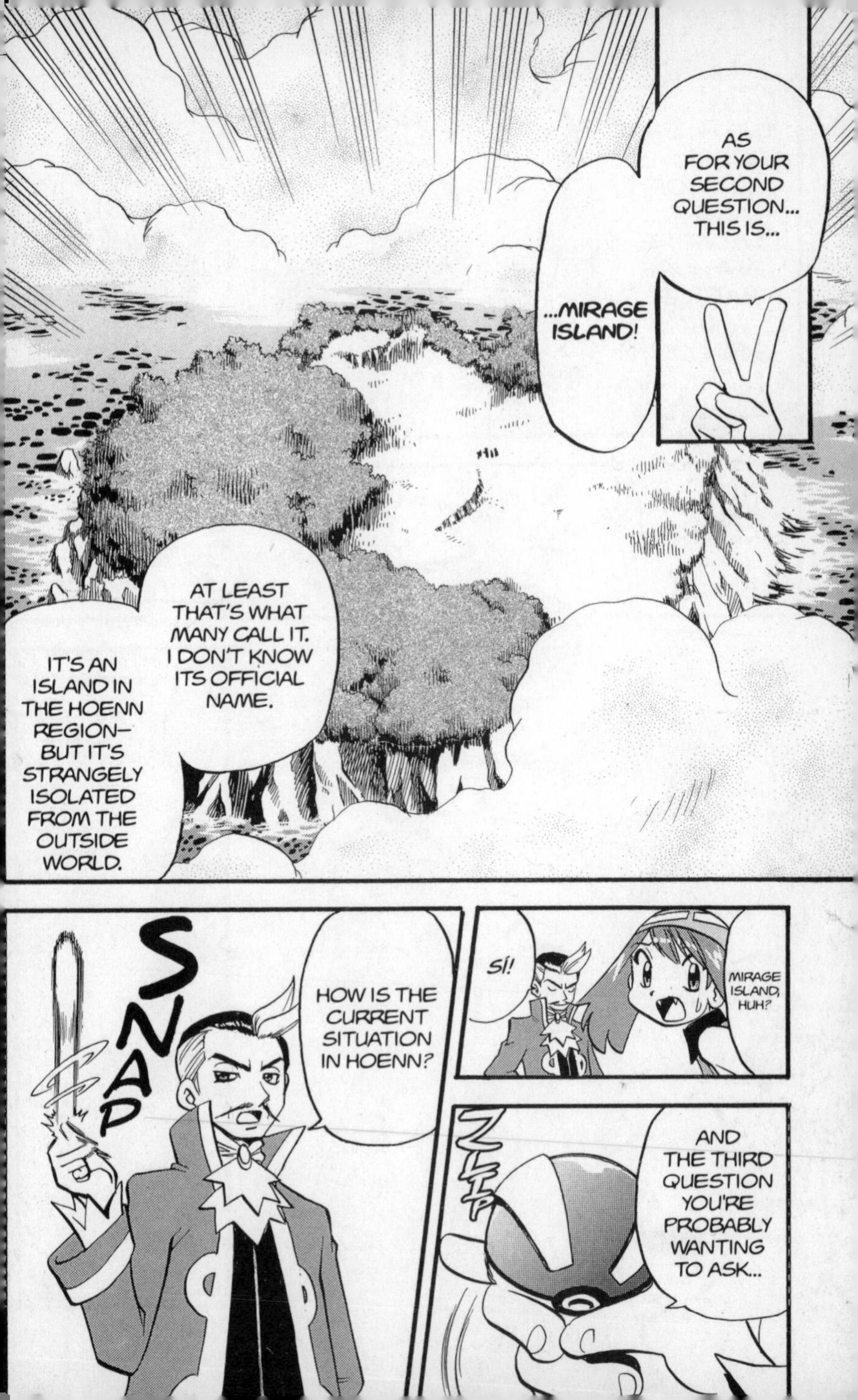
AS FOR YOUR SECOND QUESTION... THIS IS...
...MIRAGE ISLAND!
AT LEAST THAT'S WHAT MANY CALL IT. I DON'T KNOW ITS OFFICIAL NAME.
IT'S AN ISLAND IN THE HOENN REGION—BUT IT'S STRANGELY ISOLATED FROM THE OUTSIDE WORLD.
MIRAGE ISLAND, HUH?
SÍ!
AND THE THIRD QUESTION YOU'RE PROBABLY WANTING TO ASK...
HOW IS THE CURRENT SITUATION IN HOENN?
SNAP

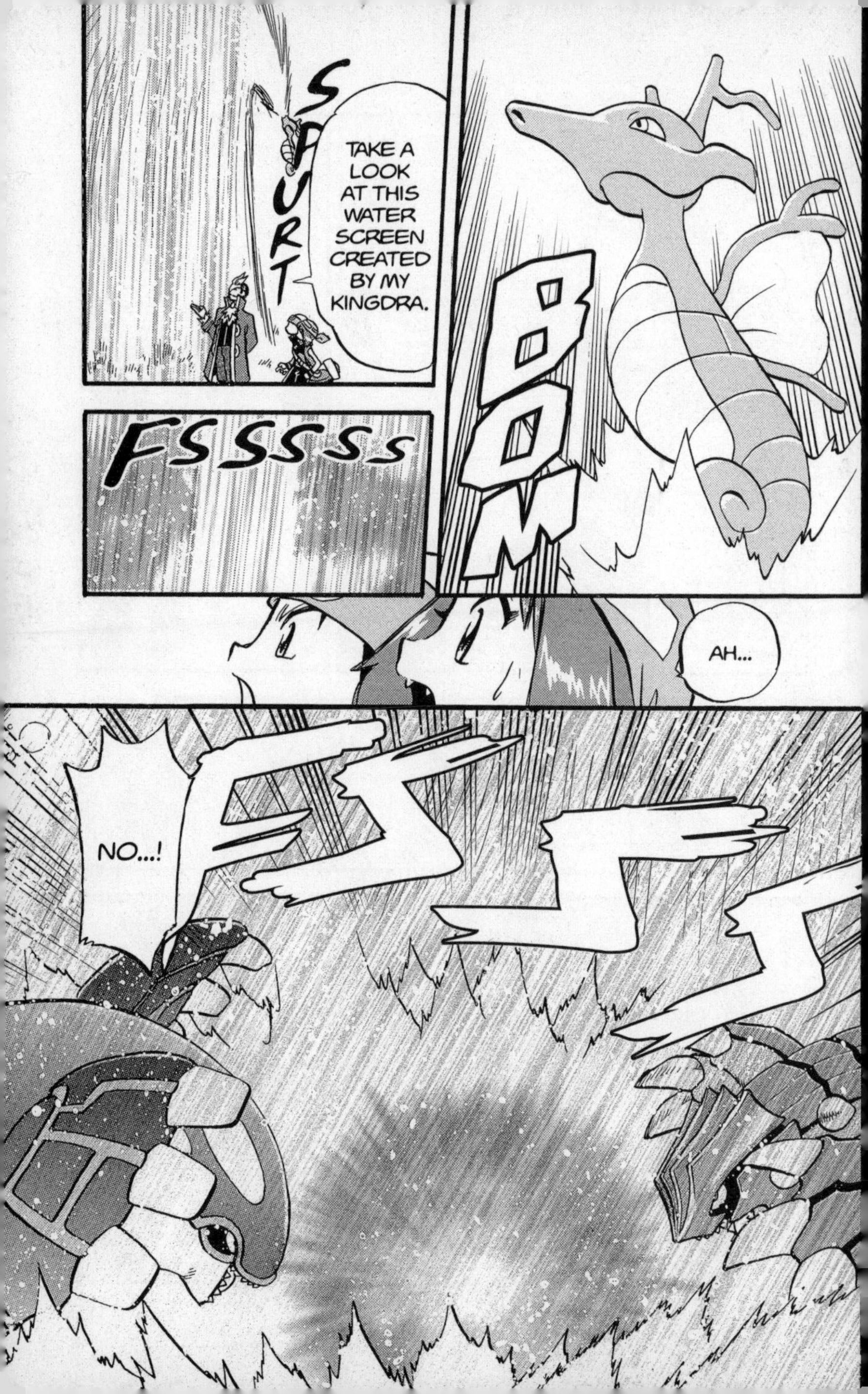
BOOM
TAKE A LOOK AT THIS WATER SCREEN CREATED BY MY KINGDRA.
SPURT
FSSSSS
AH...
NO...!
FSSS

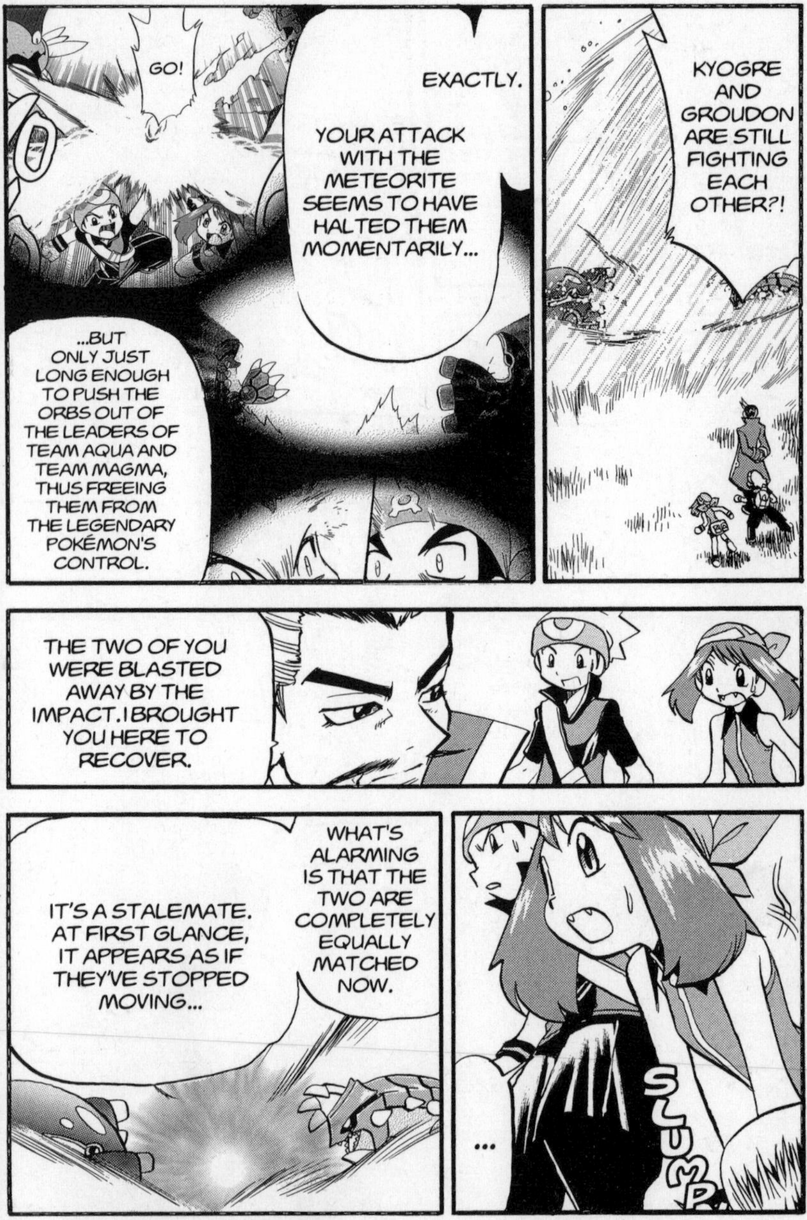
KYOGRE AND GROUDON ARE STILL FIGHTING EACH OTHER?!
EXACTLY.
YOUR ATTACK WITH THE METEORITE SEEMS TO HAVE HALTED THEM MOMENTARILY...
GO!
...BUT ONLY JUST LONG ENOUGH TO PUSH THE ORBS OUT OF THE LEADERS OF TEAM AQUA AND TEAM MAGMA, THUS FREEING THEM FROM THE LEGENDARY POKÉMON'S CONTROL.
THE TWO OF YOU WERE BLASTED AWAY BY THE IMPACT. I BROUGHT YOU HERE TO RECOVER.
...
SLUMP
WHAT'S ALARMING IS THAT THE TWO ARE COMPLETELY EQUALLY MATCHED NOW.
IT'S A STALEMATE. AT FIRST GLANCE, IT APPEARS AS IF THEY'VE STOPPED MOVING...

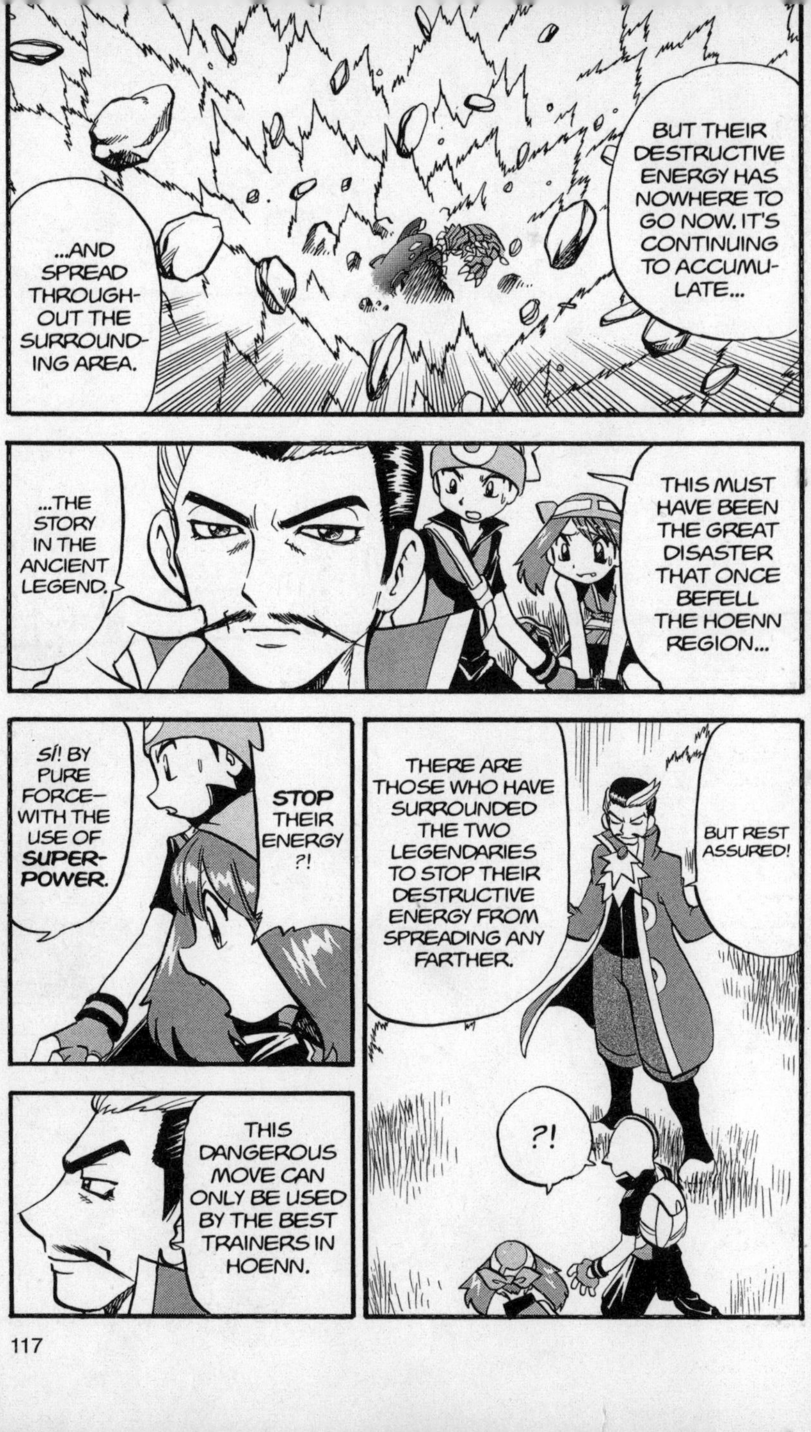
BUT THEIR DESTRUCTIVE ENERGY HAS NOWHERE TO GO NOW. IT'S CONTINUING TO ACCUMULATE...
...AND SPREAD THROUGHOUT THE SURROUNDING AREA.
THIS MUST HAVE BEEN THE GREAT DISASTER THAT ONCE BEFELL THE HOENN REGION...
...THE STORY IN THE ANCIENT LEGEND.
BUT REST ASSURED!
THERE ARE THOSE WHO HAVE SURROUNDED THE TWO LEGENDARIES TO STOP THEIR DESTRUCTIVE ENERGY FROM SPREADING ANY FARTHER.
?!
**STOP** THEIR ENERGY ?!
SÍ! BY PURE FORCE—WITH THE USE OF **SUPERPOWER.**
THIS DANGEROUS MOVE CAN ONLY BE USED BY THE BEST TRAINERS IN HOENN.

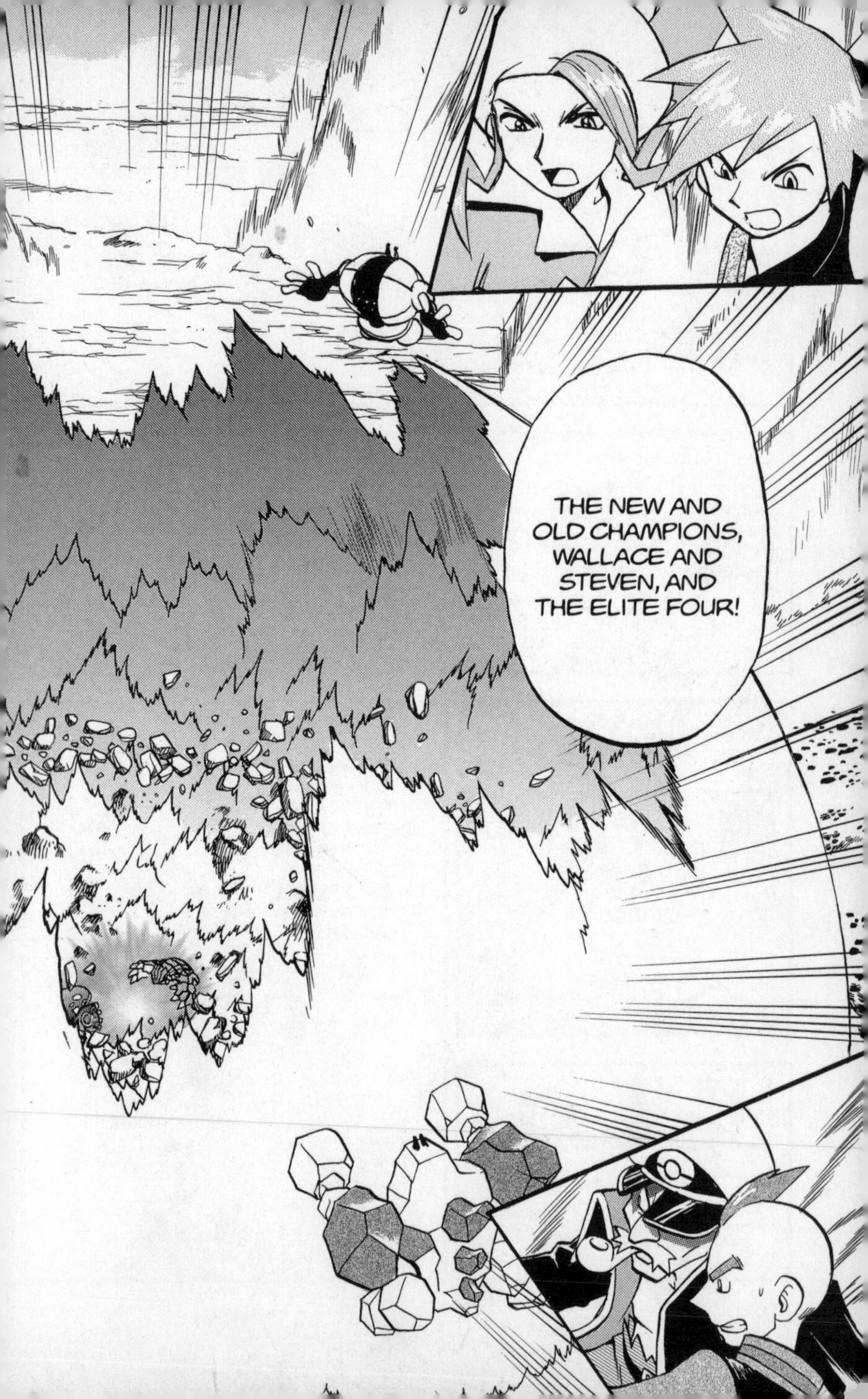
THE NEW AND OLD CHAMPIONS, WALLACE AND STEVEN, AND THE ELITE FOUR!

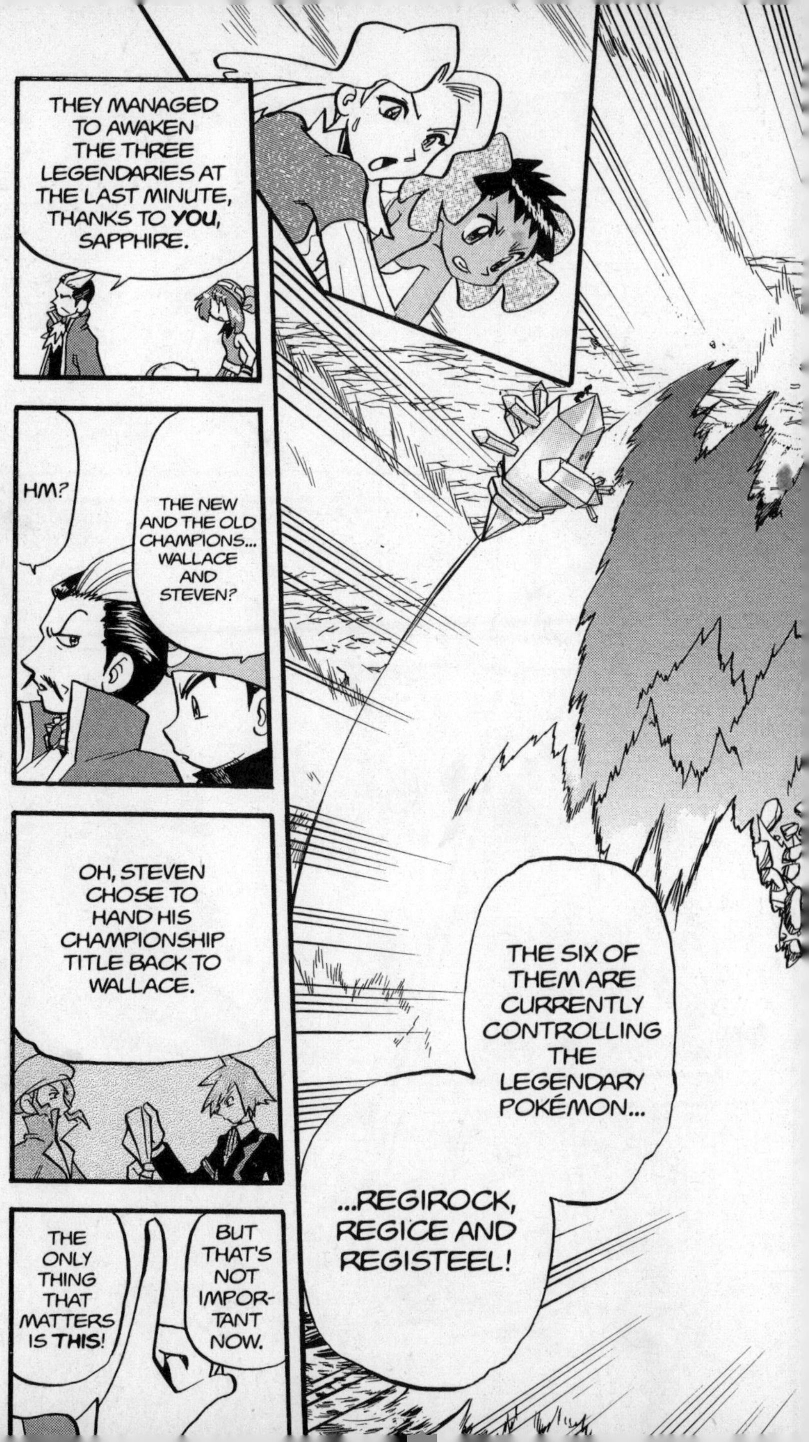
THE SIX OF THEM ARE CURRENTLY CONTROLLING THE LEGENDARY POKÉMON...
...REGIROCK, REGICE AND REGISTEEL!
THEY MANAGED TO AWAKEN THE THREE LEGENDARIES AT THE LAST MINUTE, THANKS TO **YOU**, SAPPHIRE.
THE NEW AND THE OLD CHAMPIONS... WALLACE AND STEVEN?
HM?
OH, STEVEN CHOSE TO HAND HIS CHAMPIONSHIP TITLE BACK TO WALLACE.
BUT THAT'S NOT IMPOR-TANT NOW.
THE ONLY THING THAT MATTERS IS **THIS**!

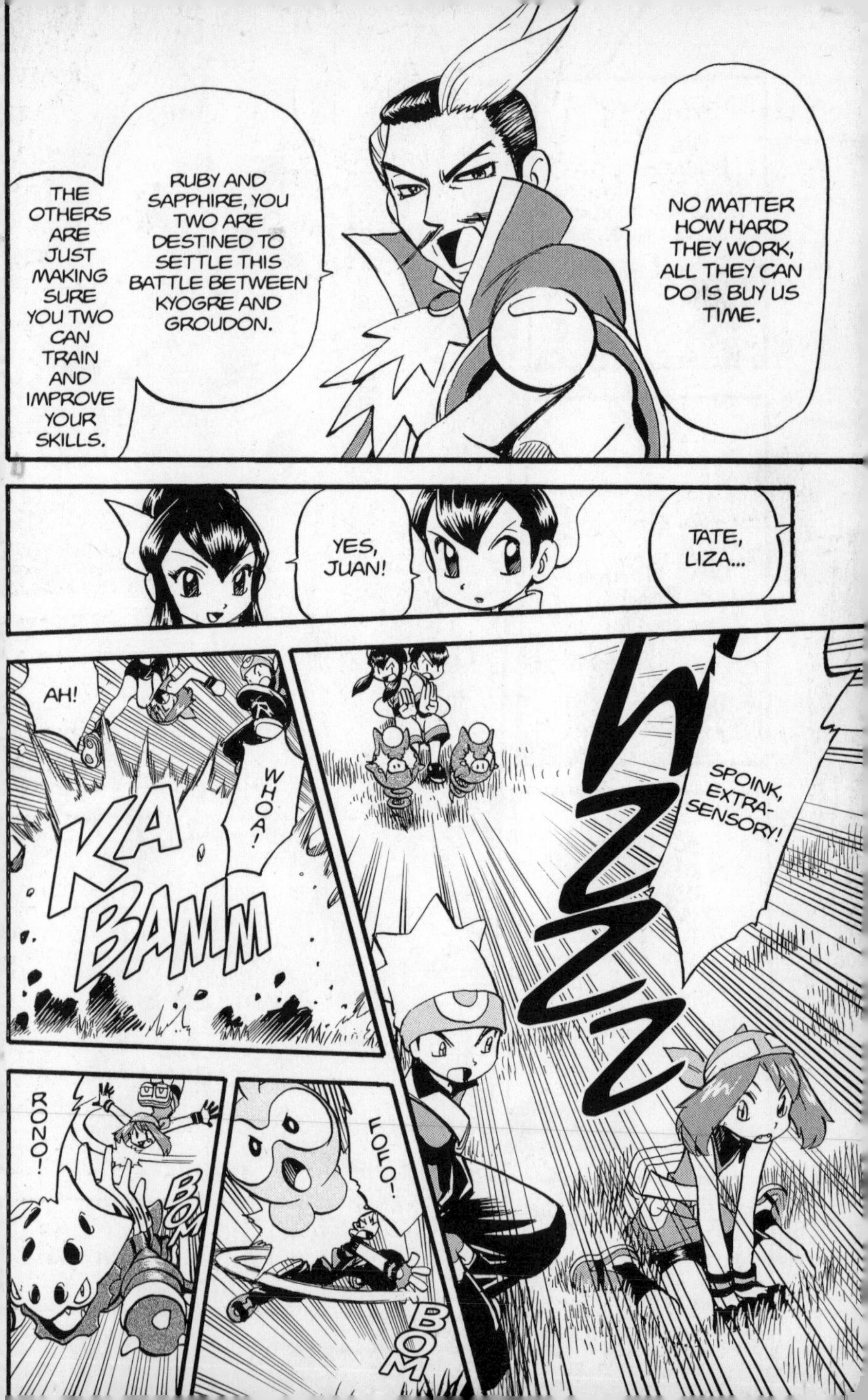
NO MATTER HOW HARD THEY WORK, ALL THEY CAN DO IS BUY US TIME.
RUBY AND SAPPHIRE, YOU TWO ARE DESTINED TO SETTLE THIS BATTLE BETWEEN KYOGRE AND GROUDON.
THE OTHERS ARE JUST MAKING SURE YOU TWO CAN TRAIN AND IMPROVE YOUR SKILLS.
TATE, LIZA...
YES, JUAN!
SPOINK, EXTRA-SENSORY!
AH!
WHOA!
KA BAMM
FOFO!
BOM
RONO!
BOM

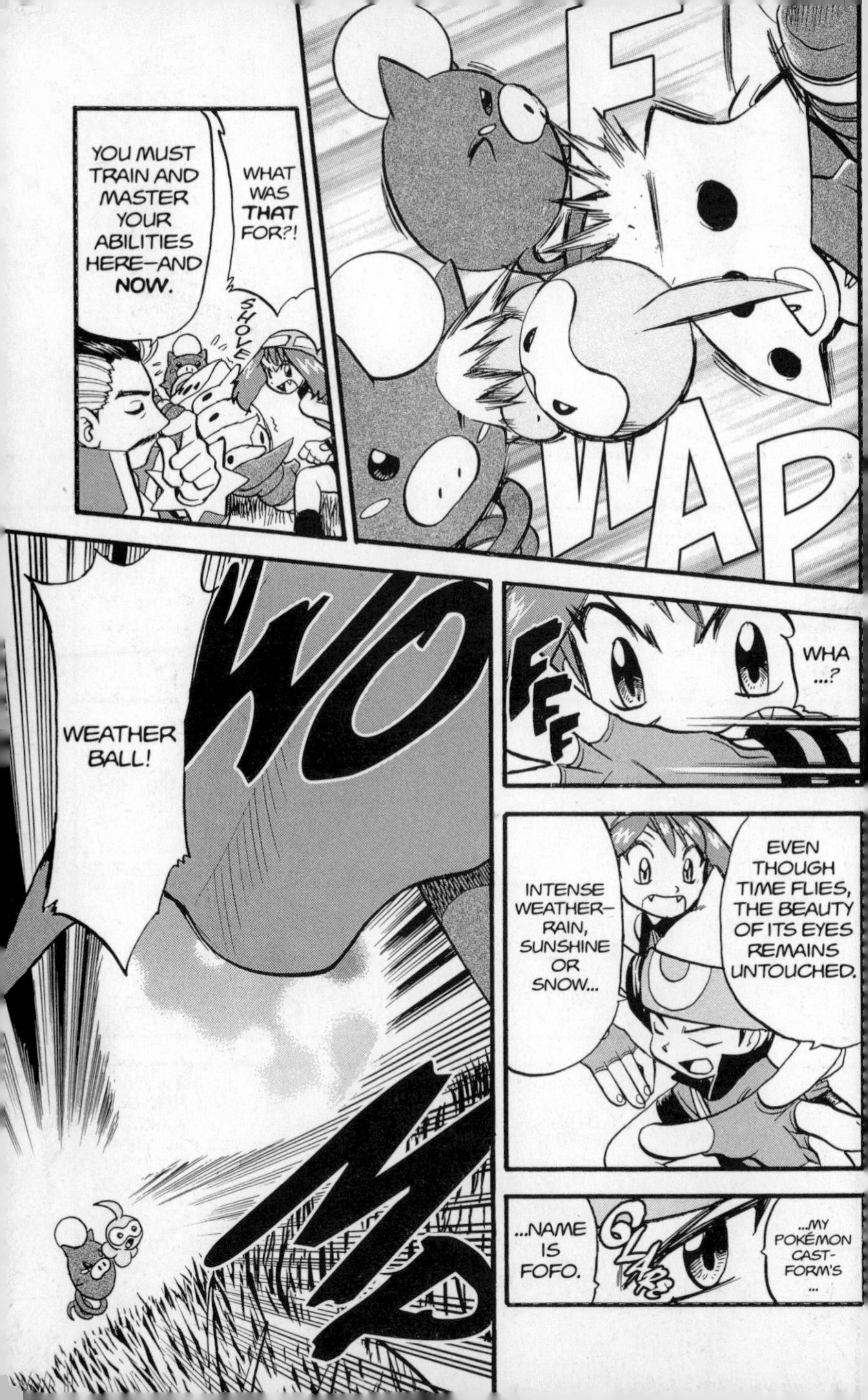
WAP
WHAT WAS THAT FOR?!
SHOVE
YOU MUST TRAIN AND MASTER YOUR ABILITIES HERE—AND NOW.
FFFF
WHA ...?
EVEN THOUGH TIME FLIES, THE BEAUTY OF ITS EYES REMAINS UNTOUCHED.
INTENSE WEATHER—RAIN, SUNSHINE OR SNOW...
...MY POKÉMON CAST-FORM'S ...
...NAME IS FOFO.
WEATHER BALL!
WO
MP

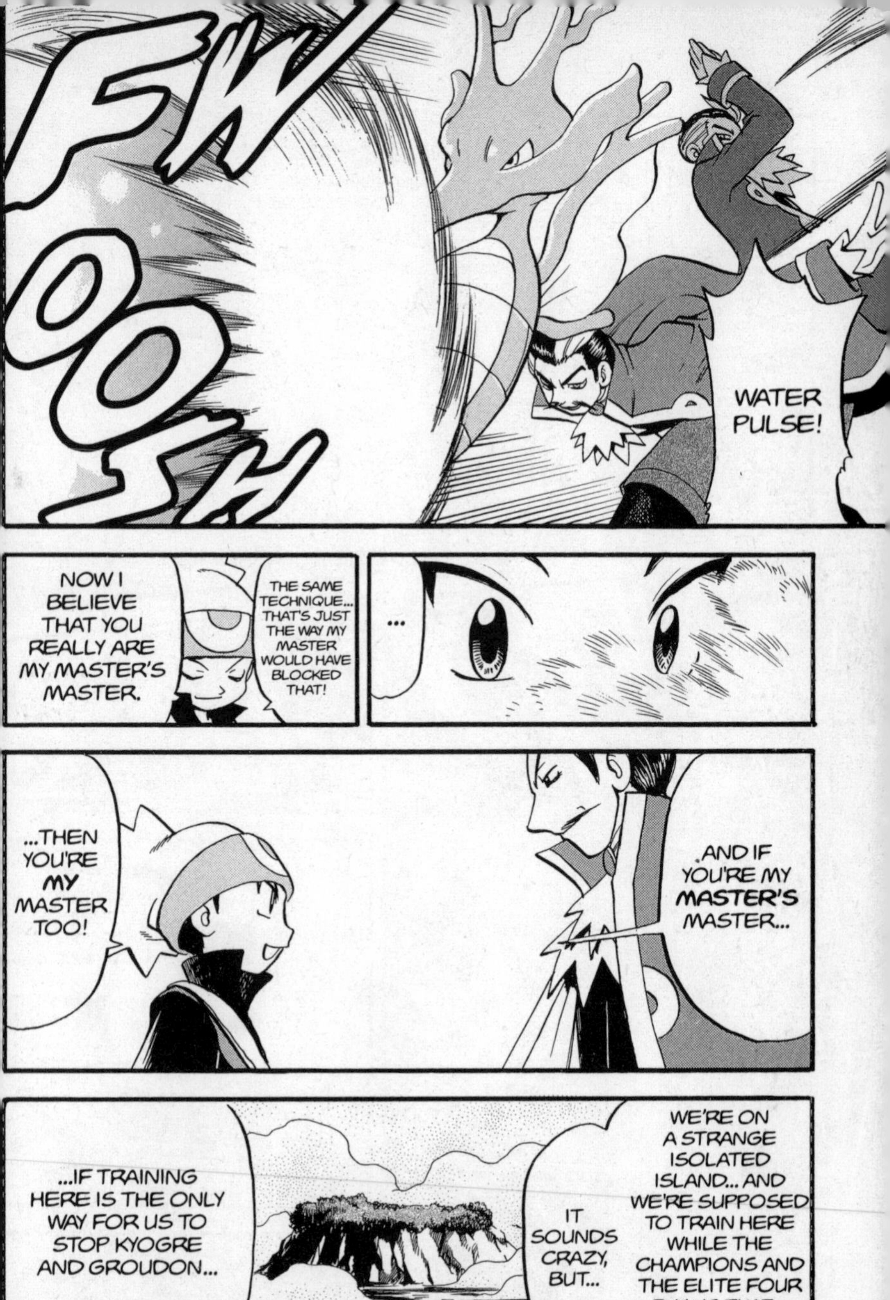
WATER PULSE!
FWOOOSH
...
THE SAME TECHNIQUE... THAT'S JUST THE WAY MY MASTER WOULD HAVE BLOCKED THAT!
NOW I BELIEVE THAT YOU REALLY ARE MY MASTER'S MASTER.
...AND IF YOU'RE MY **MASTER'S** MASTER...
...THEN YOU'RE **MY** MASTER TOO!
WE'RE ON A STRANGE ISOLATED ISLAND... AND WE'RE SUPPOSED TO TRAIN HERE WHILE THE CHAMPIONS AND THE ELITE FOUR BUY US TIME...
IT SOUNDS CRAZY, BUT...
...IF TRAINING HERE IS THE ONLY WAY FOR US TO STOP KYOGRE AND GROUDON...

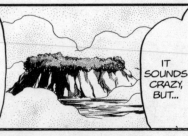

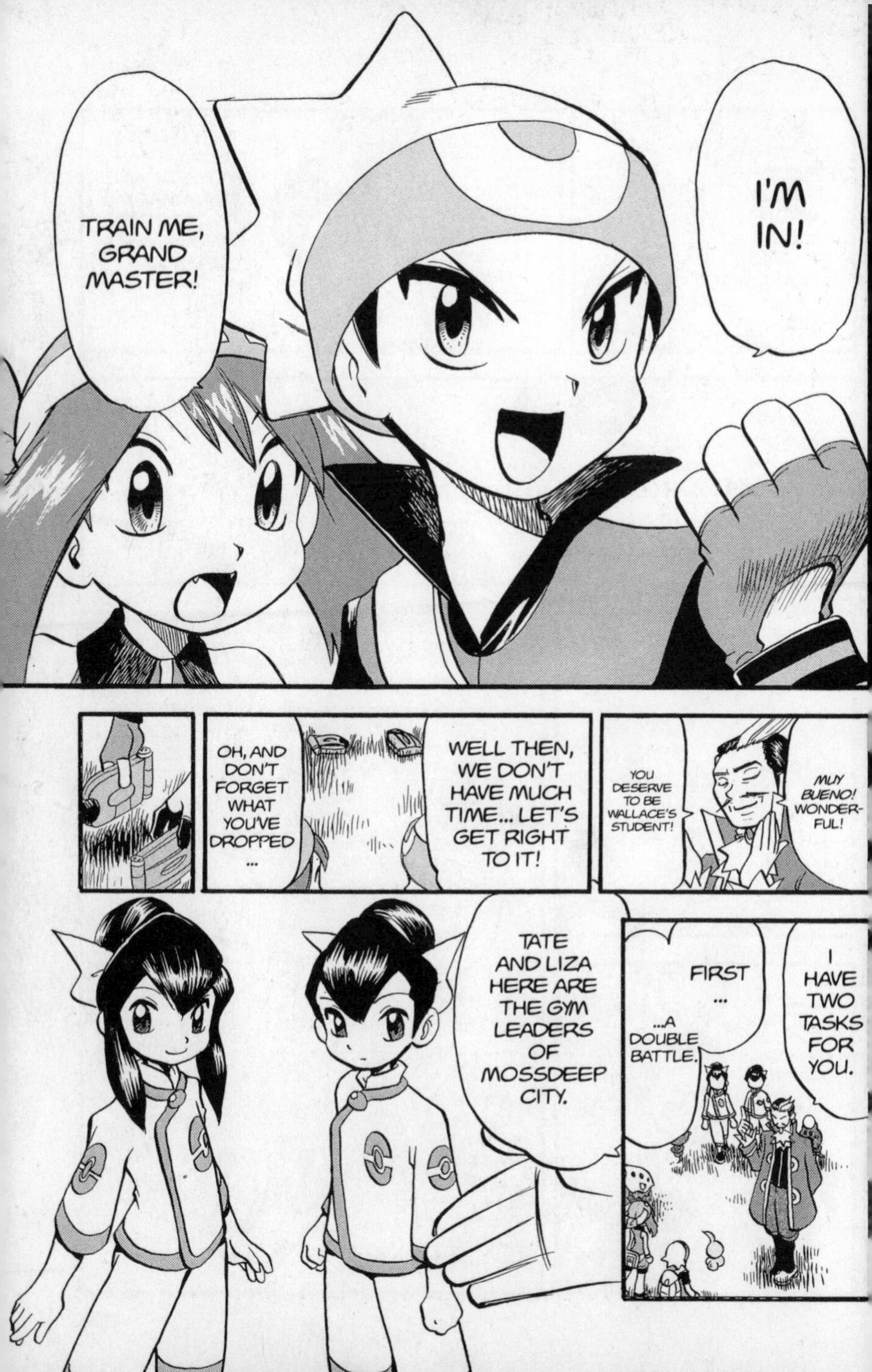
I'M IN!
TRAIN ME, GRAND MASTER!
MUY BUENO! WONDERFUL!
YOU DESERVE TO BE WALLACE'S STUDENT!
WELL THEN, WE DON'T HAVE MUCH TIME... LET'S GET RIGHT TO IT!
OH, AND DON'T FORGET WHAT YOU'VE DROPPED ...
I HAVE TWO TASKS FOR YOU.
FIRST ...
...A DOUBLE BATTLE.
TATE AND LIZA HERE ARE THE GYM LEADERS OF MOSSDEEP CITY.

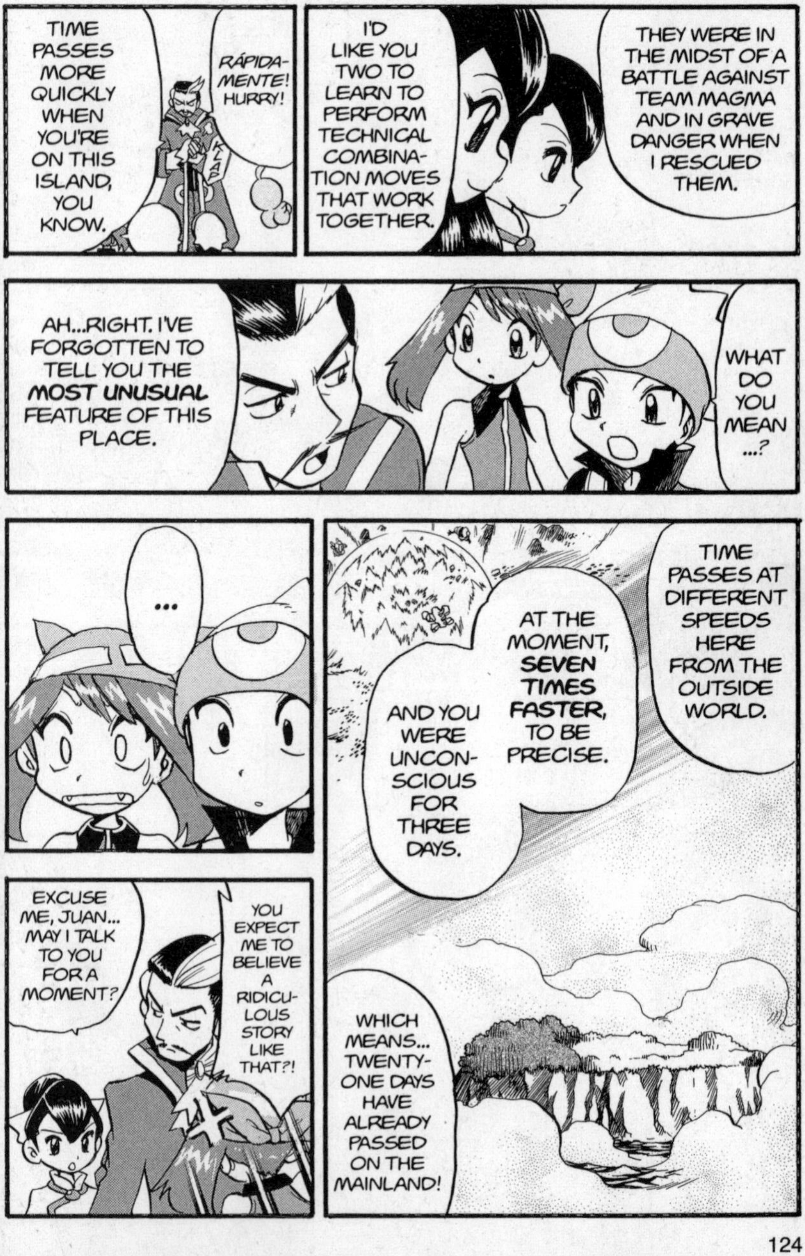
THEY WERE IN THE MIDST OF A BATTLE AGAINST TEAM MAGMA AND IN GRAVE DANGER WHEN I RESCUED THEM.
I'D LIKE YOU TWO TO LEARN TO PERFORM TECHNICAL COMBINATION MOVES THAT WORK TOGETHER.
RÁPIDAMENTE! HURRY!
KLAP
TIME PASSES MORE QUICKLY WHEN YOU'RE ON THIS ISLAND, YOU KNOW.
WHAT DO YOU MEAN ...?
AH...RIGHT. I'VE FORGOTTEN TO TELL YOU THE **MOST UNUSUAL** FEATURE OF THIS PLACE.
TIME PASSES AT DIFFERENT SPEEDS HERE FROM THE OUTSIDE WORLD.
AT THE MOMENT, **SEVEN TIMES FASTER**, TO BE PRECISE.
AND YOU WERE UNCONSCIOUS FOR THREE DAYS.
WHICH MEANS... TWENTY-ONE DAYS HAVE ALREADY PASSED ON THE MAINLAND!
...
YOU EXPECT ME TO BELIEVE A RIDICULOUS STORY LIKE THAT?!
EXCUSE ME, JUAN... MAY I TALK TO YOU FOR A MOMENT?

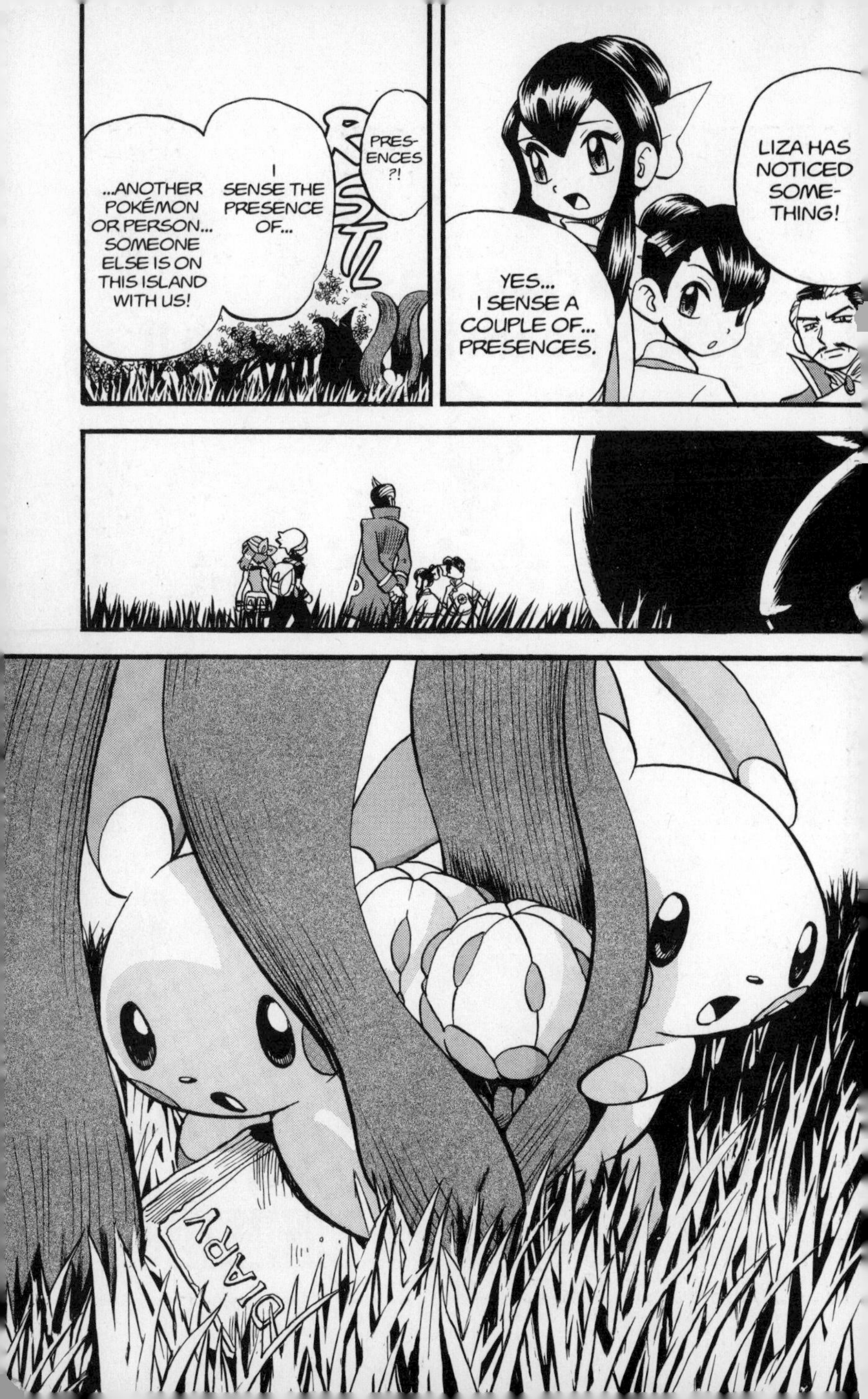
LIZA HAS NOTICED SOME-THING!
YES... I SENSE A COUPLE OF... PRESENCES.
PRES-ENCES ?!
I SENSE THE PRESENCE OF...
...ANOTHER POKÉMON OR PERSON... SOMEONE ELSE IS ON THIS ISLAND WITH US!
DIARY

## ● Chapter 256 ●
# With a Spoink in Your Step II

POKéMON ADVENTURES
RUBY & SAPPHIRE
The Fourth Chapter

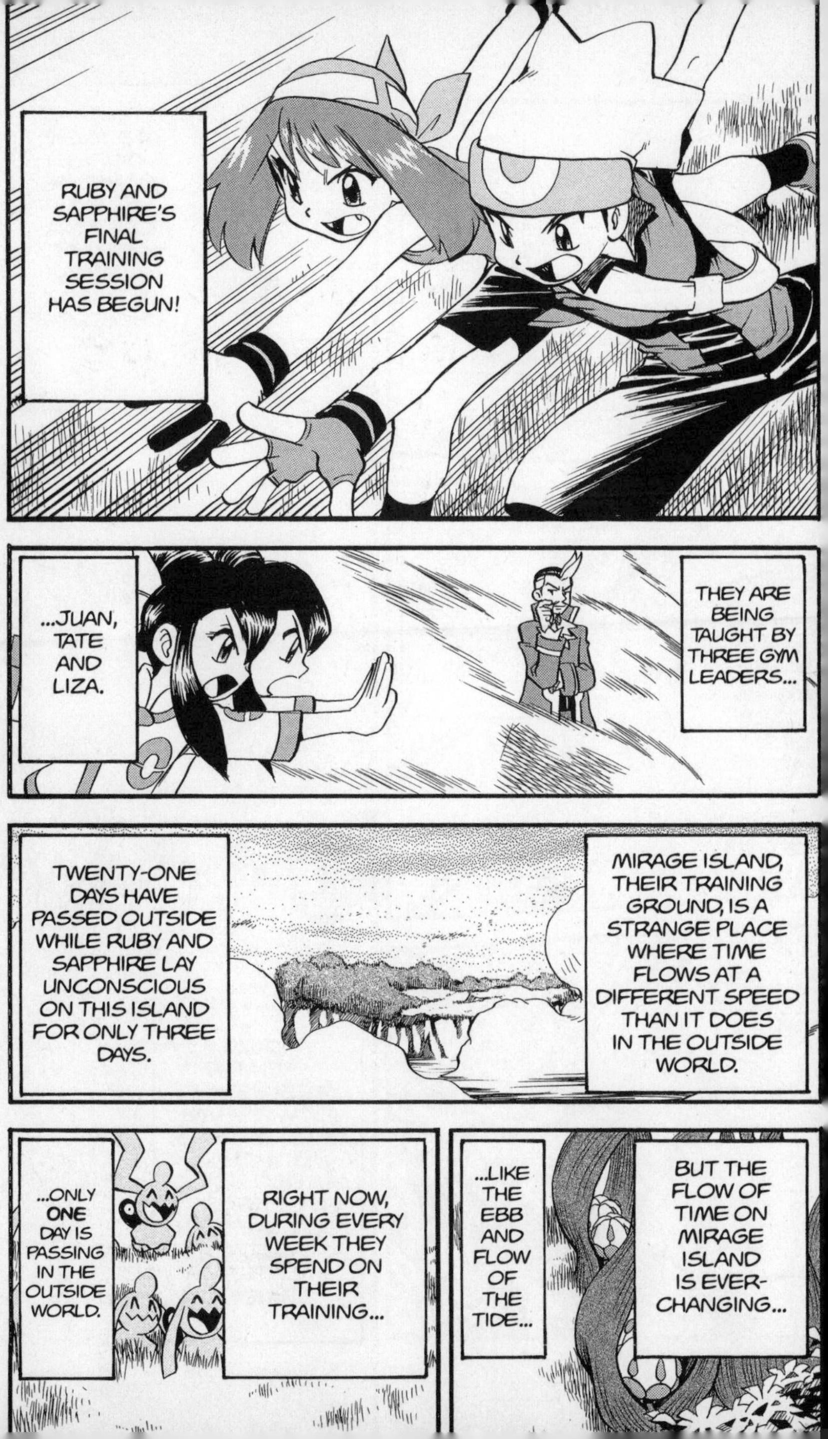
RUBY AND SAPPHIRE'S FINAL TRAINING SESSION HAS BEGUN!
THEY ARE BEING TAUGHT BY THREE GYM LEADERS...
...JUAN, TATE AND LIZA.
MIRAGE ISLAND, THEIR TRAINING GROUND, IS A STRANGE PLACE WHERE TIME FLOWS AT A DIFFERENT SPEED THAN IT DOES IN THE OUTSIDE WORLD.
TWENTY-ONE DAYS HAVE PASSED OUTSIDE WHILE RUBY AND SAPPHIRE LAY UNCONSCIOUS ON THIS ISLAND FOR ONLY THREE DAYS.
BUT THE FLOW OF TIME ON MIRAGE ISLAND IS EVER-CHANGING...
...LIKE THE EBB AND FLOW OF THE TIDE...
RIGHT NOW, DURING EVERY WEEK THEY SPEND ON THEIR TRAINING...
...ONLY **ONE** DAY IS PASSING IN THE OUTSIDE WORLD.

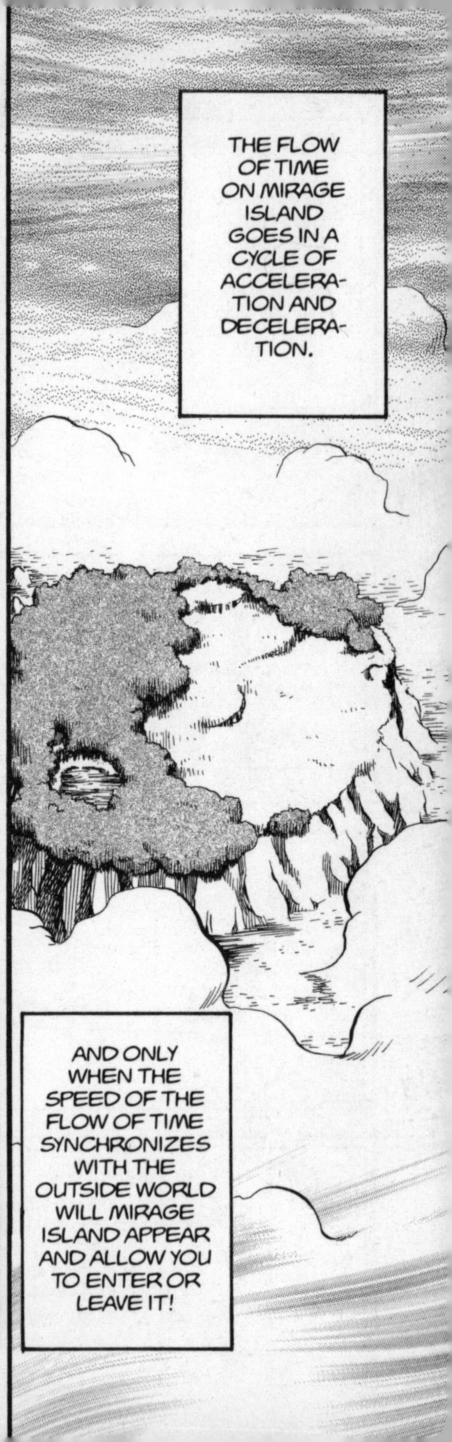
THE FLOW OF TIME ON MIRAGE ISLAND GOES IN A CYCLE OF ACCELERATION AND DECELERATION.
AND ONLY WHEN THE SPEED OF THE FLOW OF TIME SYNCHRONIZES WITH THE OUTSIDE WORLD WILL MIRAGE ISLAND APPEAR AND ALLOW YOU TO ENTER OR LEAVE IT!

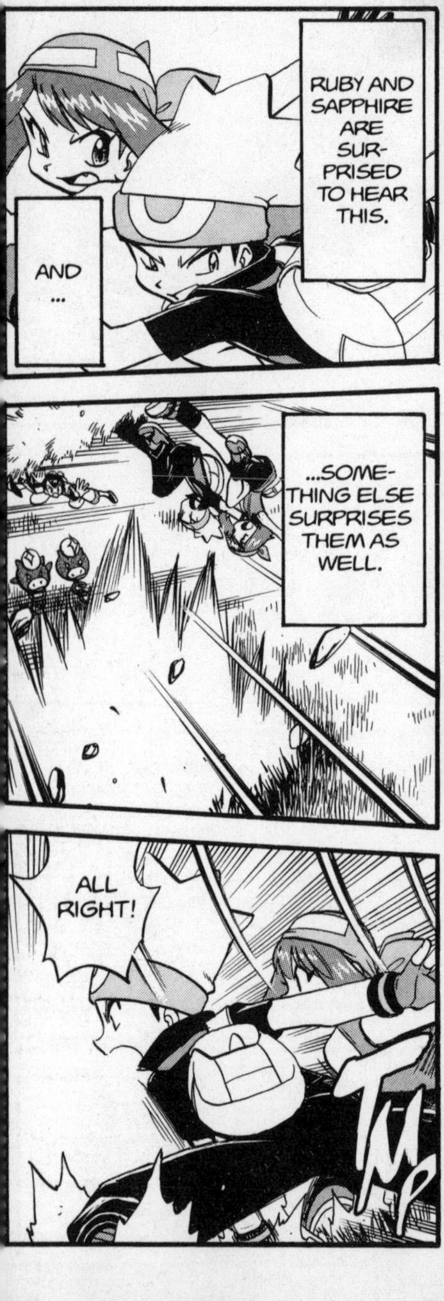
RUBY AND SAPPHIRE ARE SURPRISED TO HEAR THIS.
AND ...
...SOMETHING ELSE SURPRISES THEM AS WELL.
ALL RIGHT!

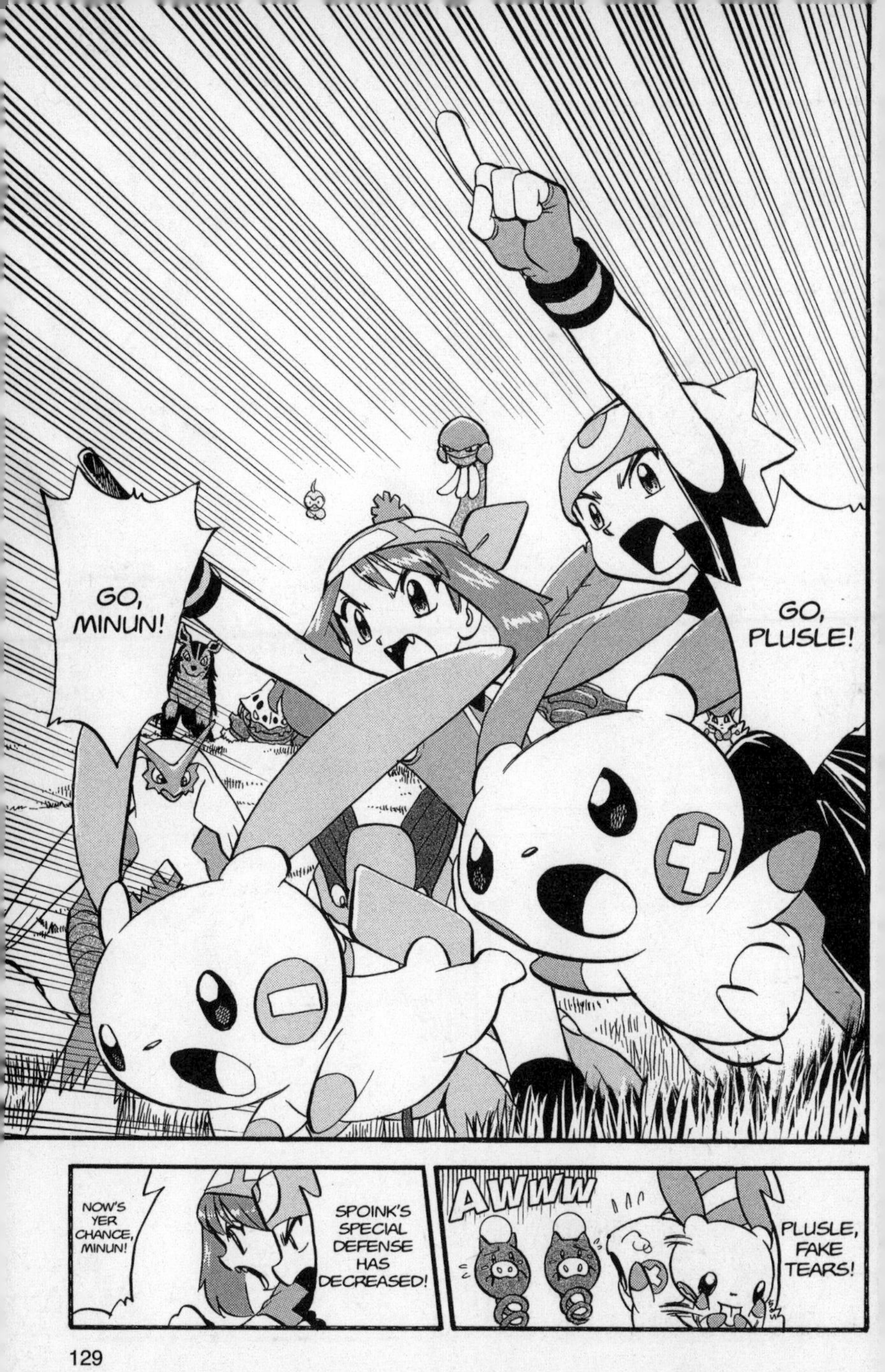
GO, PLUSLE!
GO, MINUN!
PLUSLE, FAKE TEARS!
AWWW
SPOINK'S SPECIAL DEFENSE HAS DECREASED!
NOW'S YER CHANCE, MINUN!

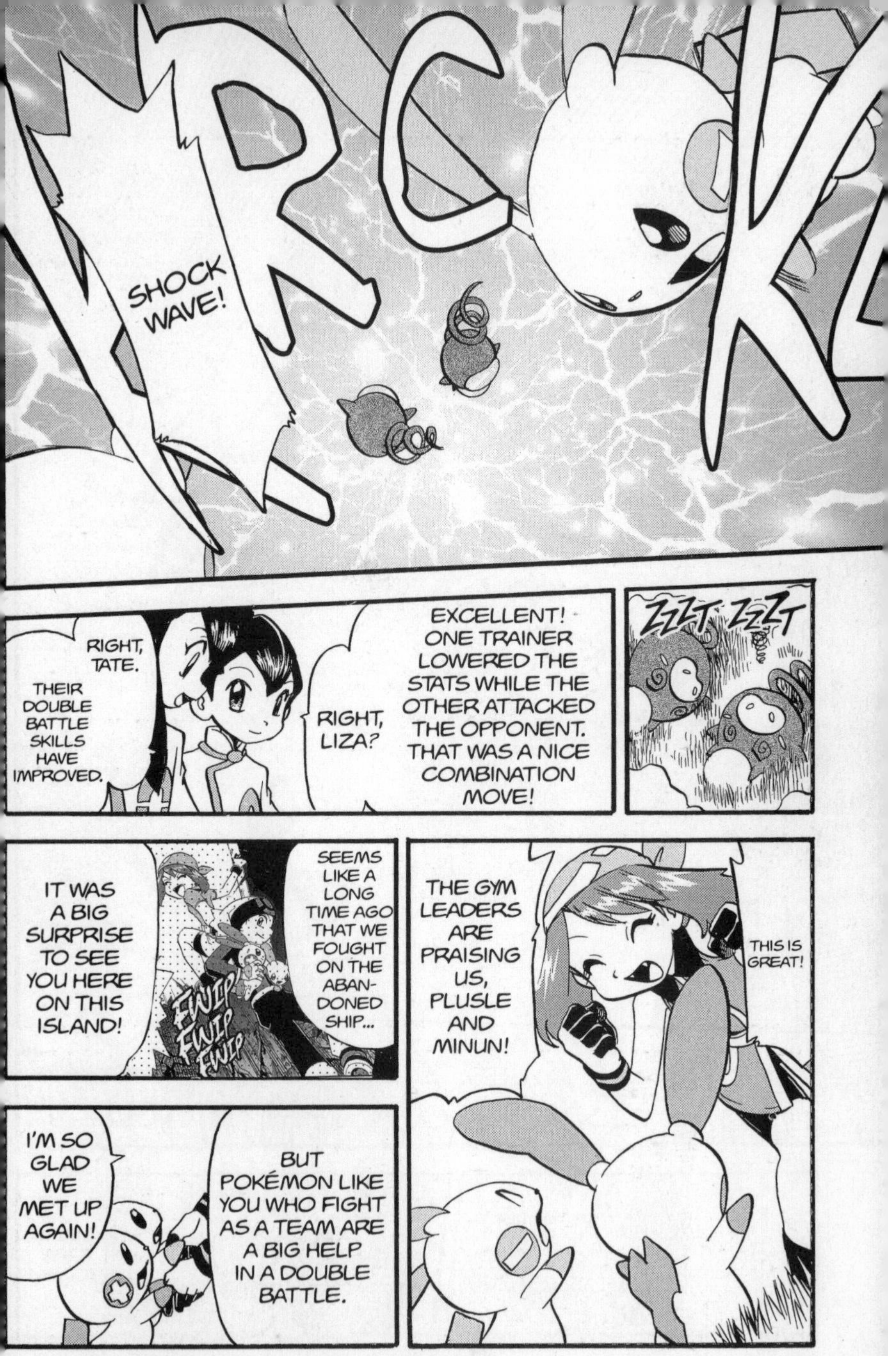
SHOCK WAVE!
ZZZT ZZZT
EXCELLENT! ONE TRAINER LOWERED THE STATS WHILE THE OTHER ATTACKED THE OPPONENT. THAT WAS A NICE COMBINATION MOVE!
RIGHT, LIZA?
RIGHT, TATE.
THEIR DOUBLE BATTLE SKILLS HAVE IMPROVED.
THIS IS GREAT!
THE GYM LEADERS ARE PRAISING US, PLUSLE AND MINUN!
SEEMS LIKE A LONG TIME AGO THAT WE FOUGHT ON THE ABAN-DONED SHIP...
IT WAS A BIG SURPRISE TO SEE YOU HERE ON THIS ISLAND!
FWIP FWIP FWIP
BUT POKÉMON LIKE YOU WHO FIGHT AS A TEAM ARE A BIG HELP IN A DOUBLE BATTLE.
I'M SO GLAD WE MET UP AGAIN!

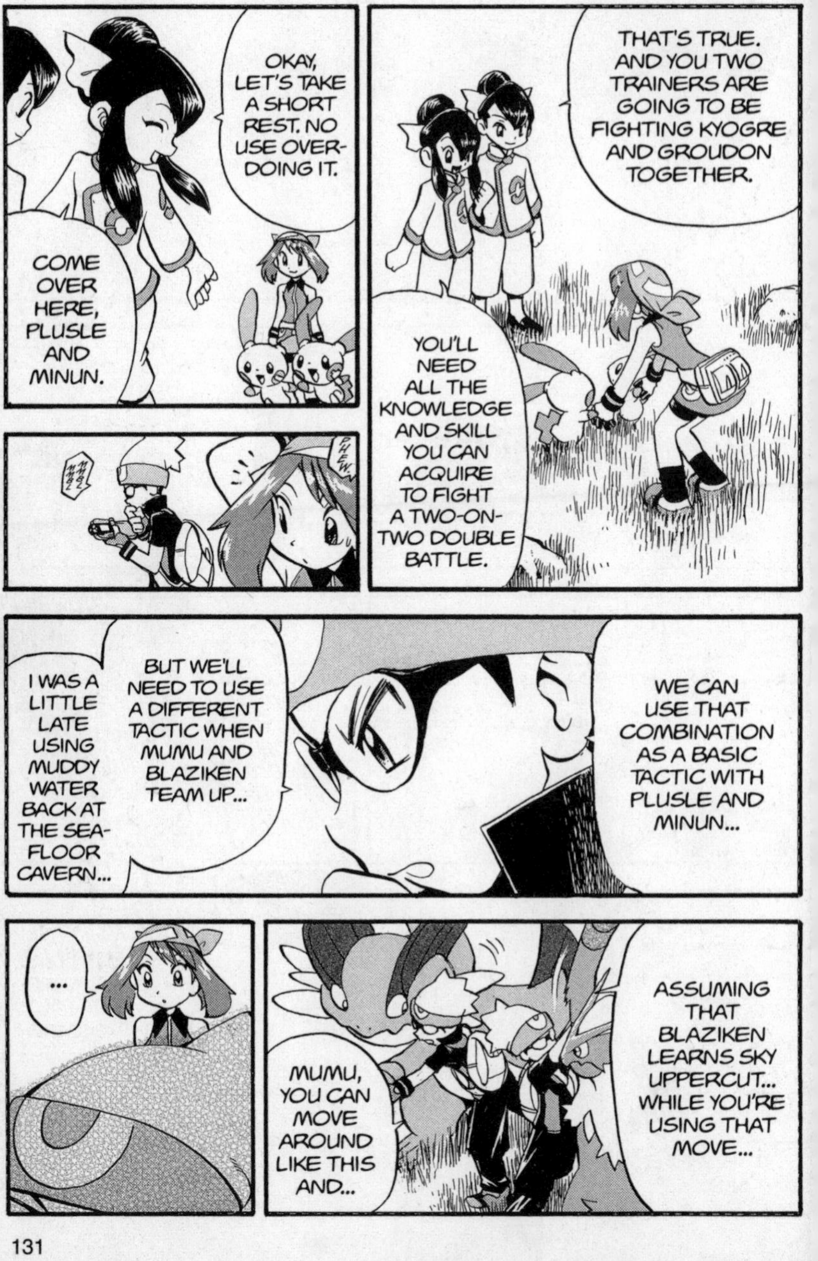
THAT'S TRUE. AND YOU TWO TRAINERS ARE GOING TO BE FIGHTING KYOGRE AND GROUDON TOGETHER.
YOU'LL NEED ALL THE KNOWLEDGE AND SKILL YOU CAN ACQUIRE TO FIGHT A TWO-ON-TWO DOUBLE BATTLE.
OKAY, LET'S TAKE A SHORT REST. NO USE OVER-DOING IT.
COME OVER HERE, PLUSLE AND MINUN.
PHEW.
WE CAN USE THAT COMBINATION AS A BASIC TACTIC WITH PLUSLE AND MINUN...
BUT WE'LL NEED TO USE A DIFFERENT TACTIC WHEN MUMU AND BLAZIKEN TEAM UP...
I WAS A LITTLE LATE USING MUDDY WATER BACK AT THE SEA-FLOOR CAVERN...
ASSUMING THAT BLAZIKEN LEARNS SKY UPPERCUT... WHILE YOU'RE USING THAT MOVE...
MUMU, YOU CAN MOVE AROUND LIKE THIS AND...
...

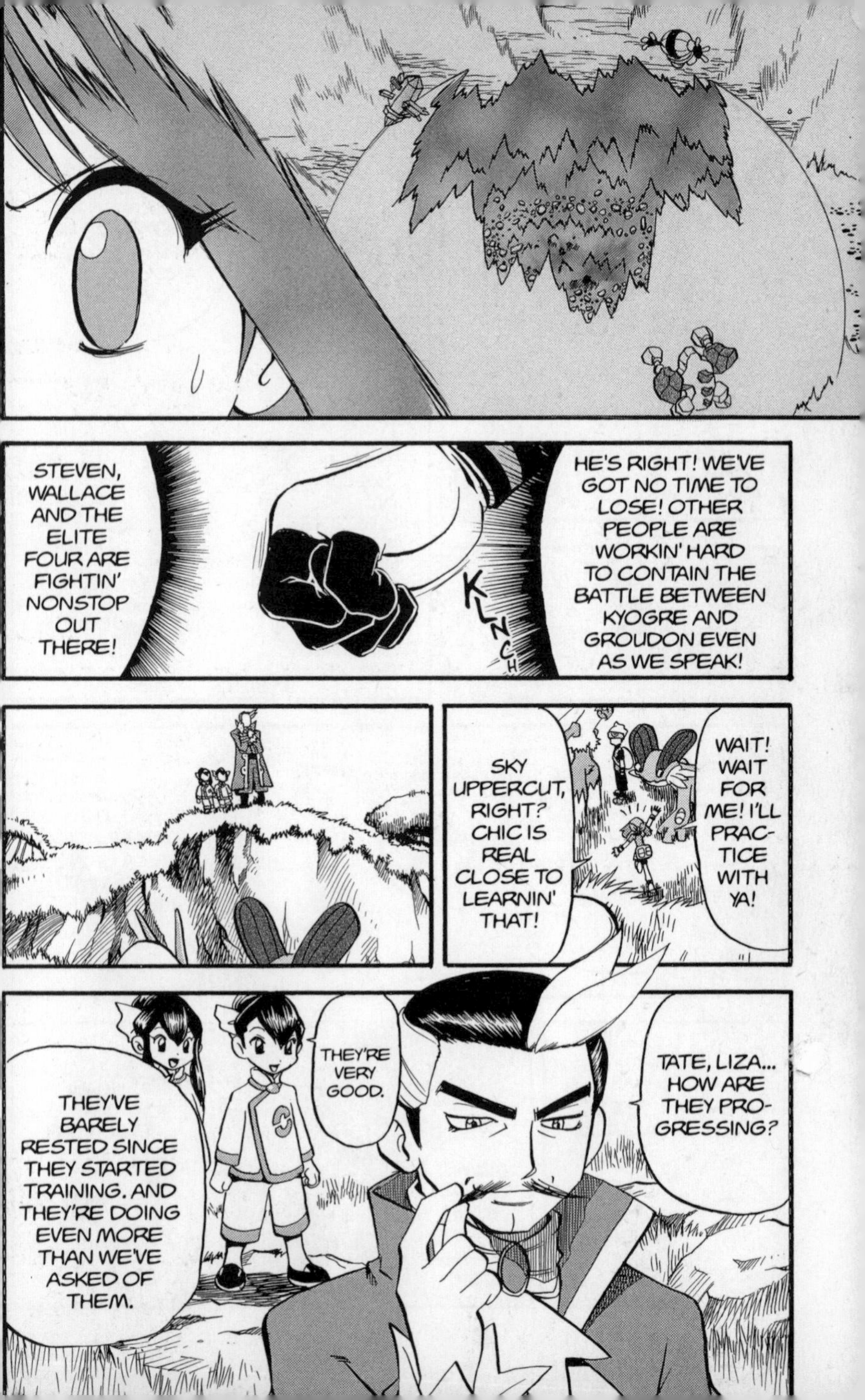
HE'S RIGHT! WE'VE GOT NO TIME TO LOSE! OTHER PEOPLE ARE WORKIN' HARD TO CONTAIN THE BATTLE BETWEEN KYOGRE AND GROUDON EVEN AS WE SPEAK!
KLNCH
STEVEN, WALLACE AND THE ELITE FOUR ARE FIGHTIN' NONSTOP OUT THERE!
WAIT! WAIT FOR ME! I'LL PRACTICE WITH YA!
SKY UPPERCUT, RIGHT? CHIC IS REAL CLOSE TO LEARNIN' THAT!
TATE, LIZA... HOW ARE THEY PROGRESSING?
THEY'RE VERY GOOD.
THEY'VE BARELY RESTED SINCE THEY STARTED TRAINING. AND THEY'RE DOING EVEN MORE THAN WE'VE ASKED OF THEM.

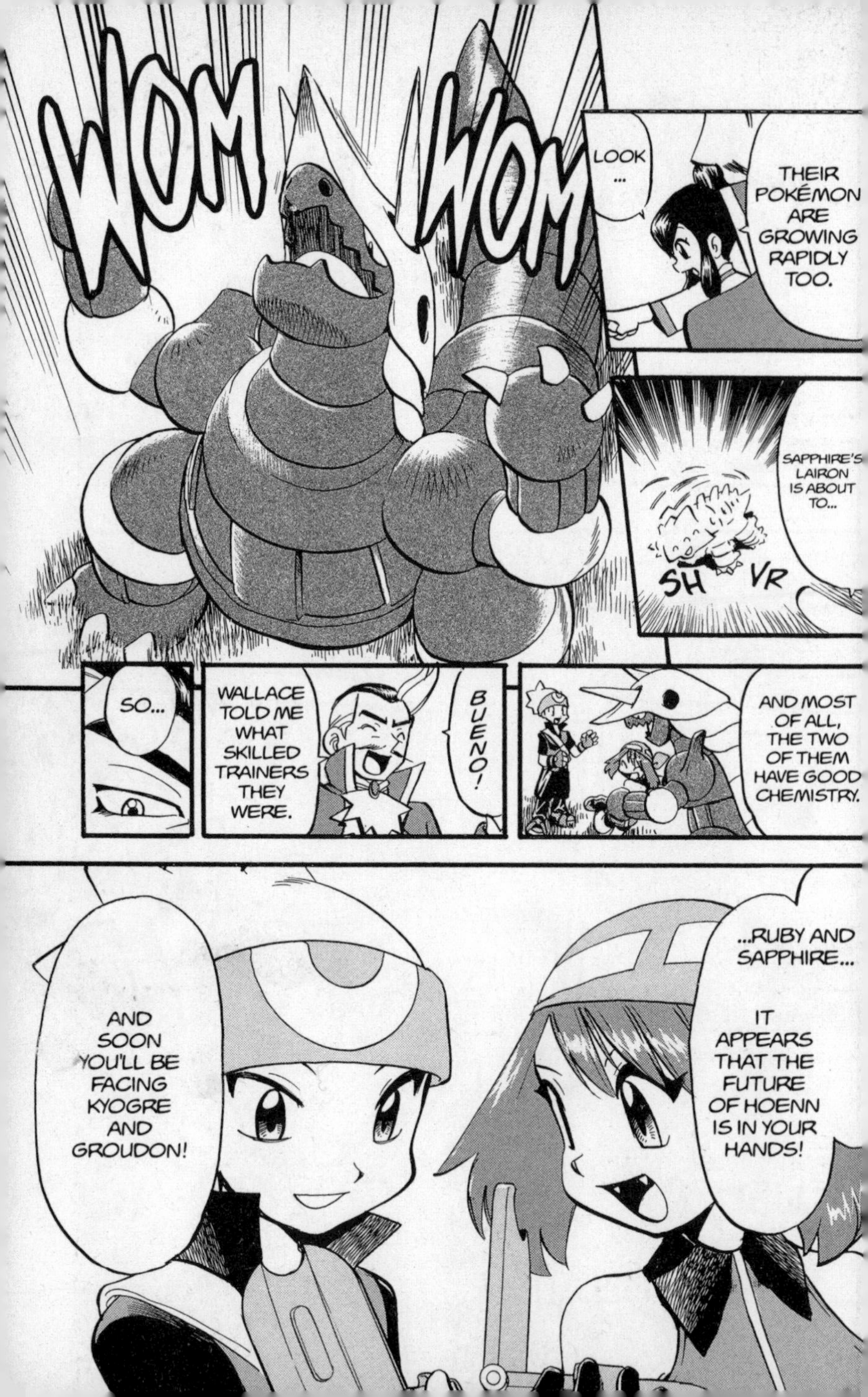
LOOK...
THEIR POKÉMON ARE GROWING RAPIDLY TOO.
SAPPHIRE'S LAIRON IS ABOUT TO...
SH VR
WOM WOM
AND MOST OF ALL, THE TWO OF THEM HAVE GOOD CHEMISTRY.
BUENO!
WALLACE TOLD ME WHAT SKILLED TRAINERS THEY WERE.
SO...
...RUBY AND SAPPHIRE...
IT APPEARS THAT THE FUTURE OF HOENN IS IN YOUR HANDS!
AND SOON YOU'LL BE FACING KYOGRE AND GROUDON!

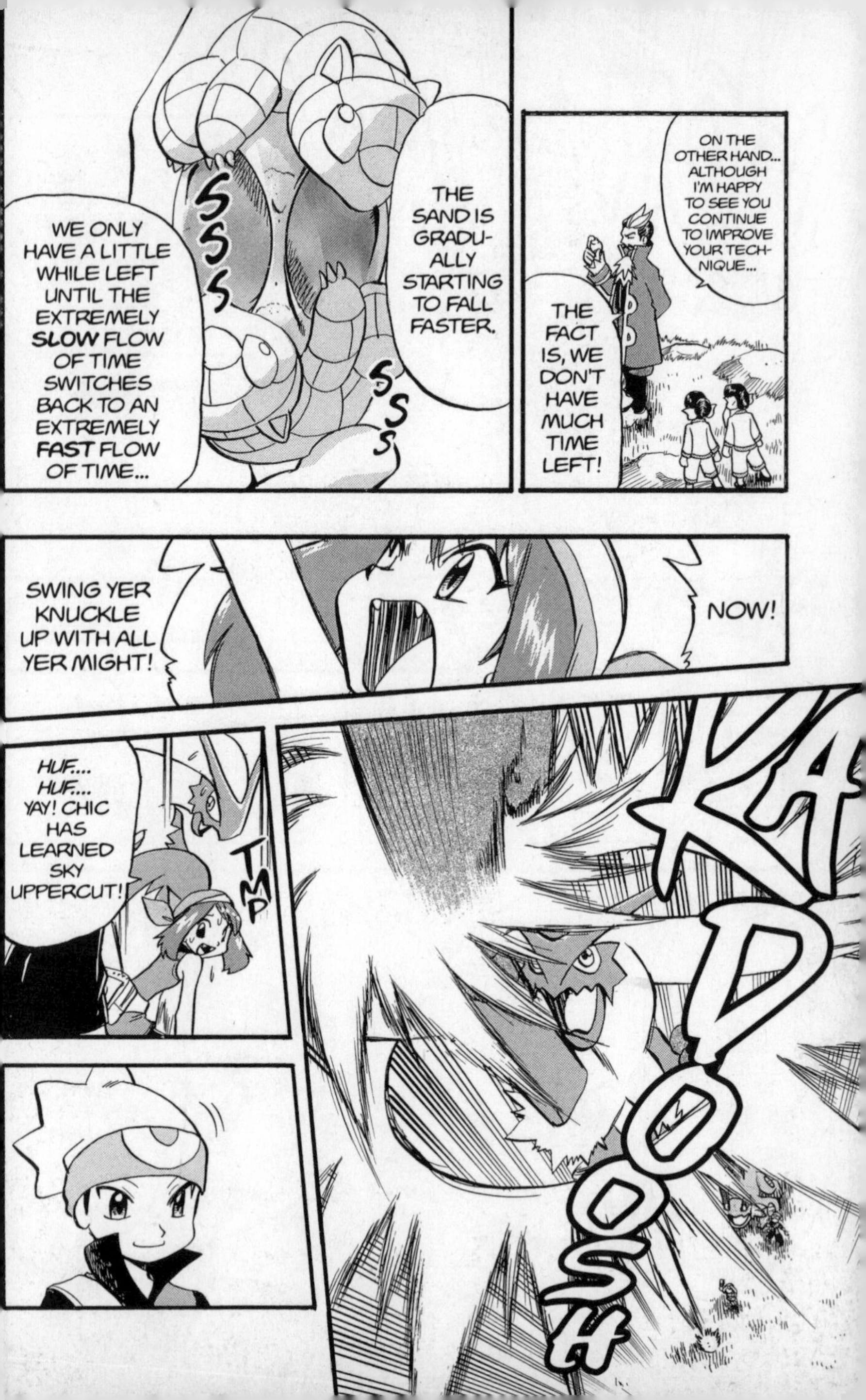
ON THE OTHER HAND... ALTHOUGH I'M HAPPY TO SEE YOU CONTINUE TO IMPROVE YOUR TECHNIQUE...
THE FACT IS, WE DON'T HAVE MUCH TIME LEFT!
THE SAND IS GRADUALLY STARTING TO FALL FASTER.
SSS
WE ONLY HAVE A LITTLE WHILE LEFT UNTIL THE EXTREMELY **SLOW** FLOW OF TIME SWITCHES BACK TO AN EXTREMELY **FAST** FLOW OF TIME...
SSS
NOW!
SWING YER KNUCKLE UP WITH ALL YER MIGHT!
KADOOSH
HUF.... HUF.... YAY! CHIC HAS LEARNED SKY UPPERCUT!
TMP

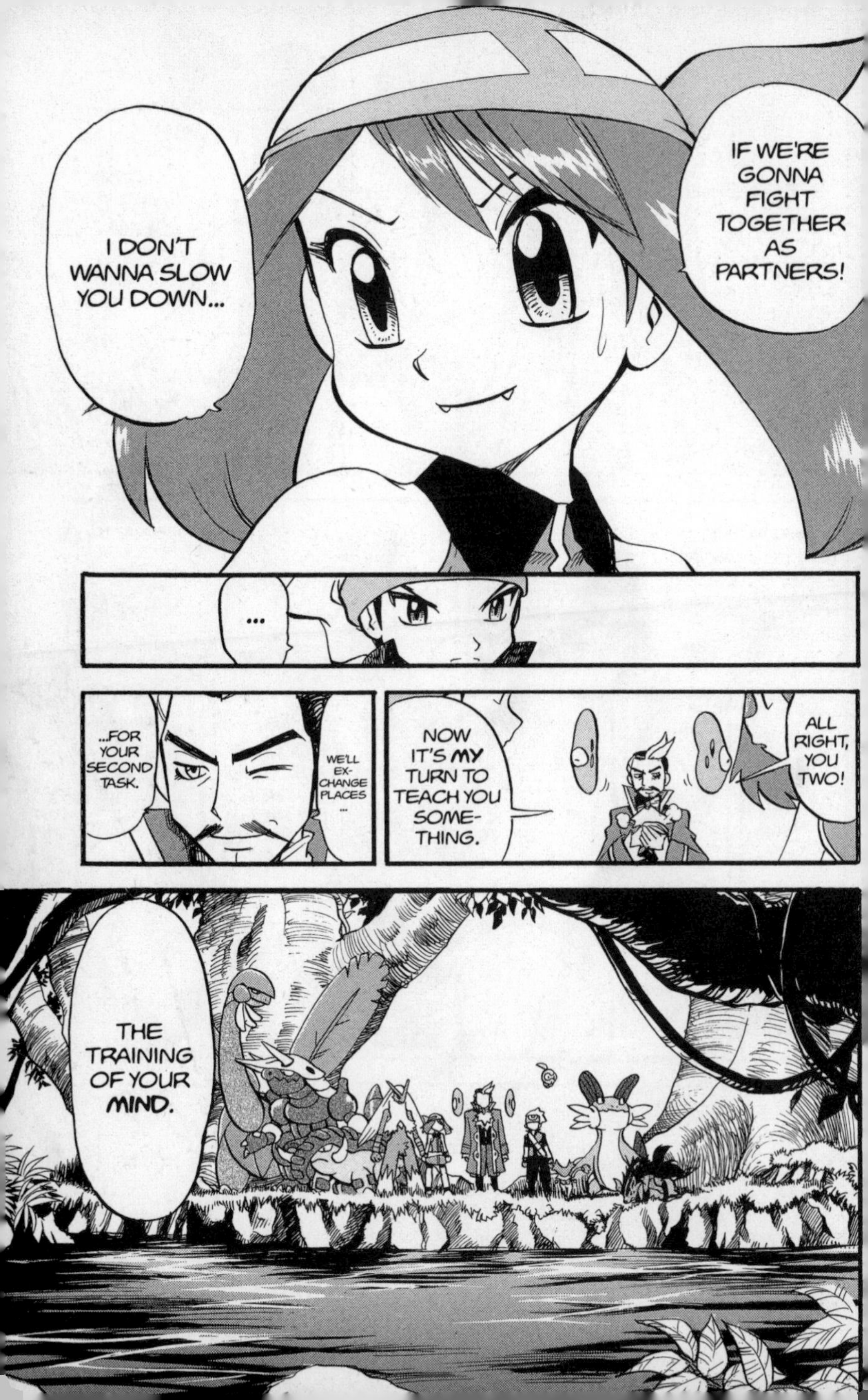
IF WE'RE GONNA FIGHT TOGETHER AS PARTNERS!
I DON'T WANNA SLOW YOU DOWN...
...
ALL RIGHT, YOU TWO!
NOW IT'S **MY** TURN TO TEACH YOU SOME-THING.
WE'LL EX-CHANGE PLACES...
...FOR YOUR SECOND TASK.
THE TRAINING OF YOUR **MIND**.

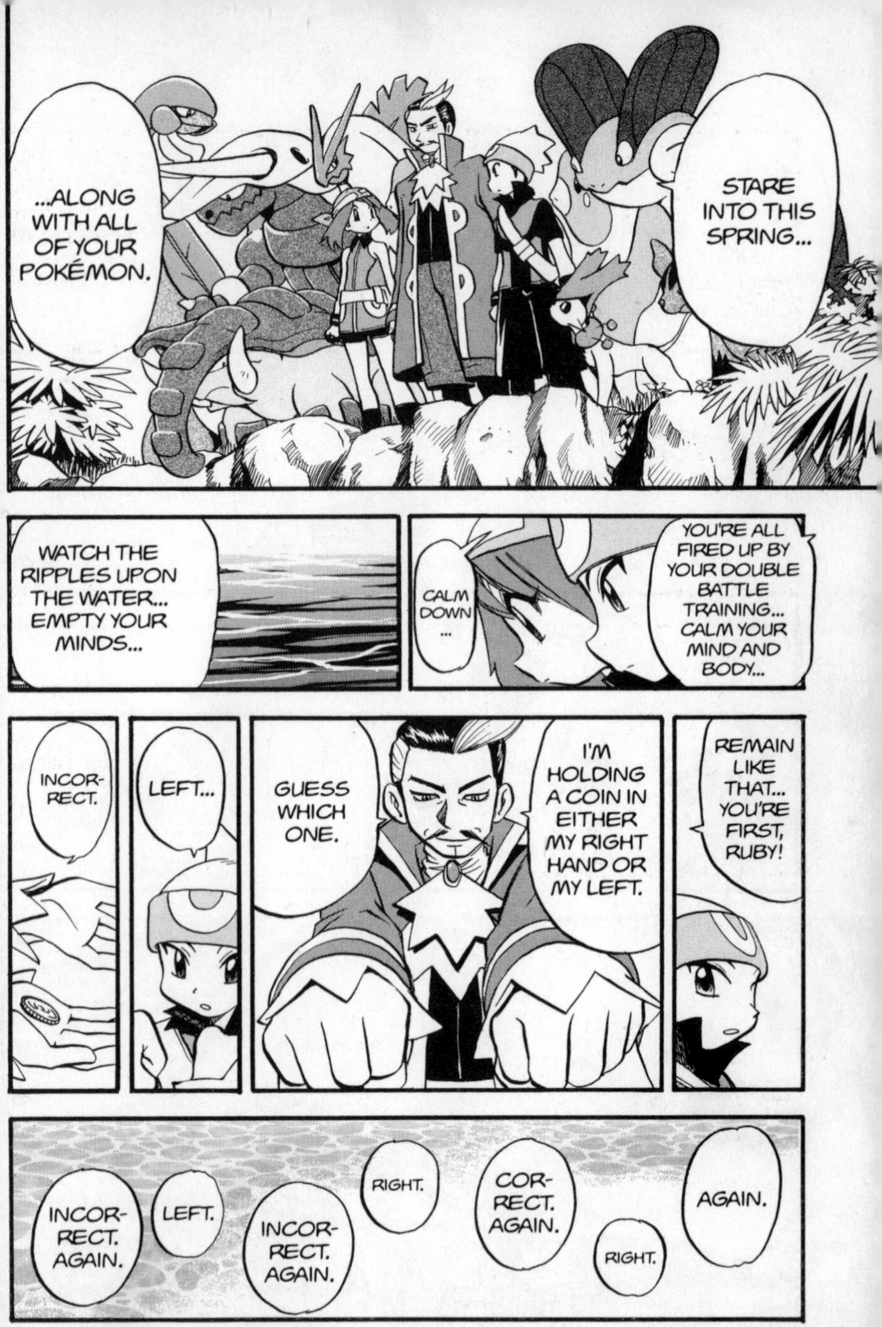
STARE INTO THIS SPRING...
...ALONG WITH ALL OF YOUR POKÉMON.
YOU'RE ALL FIRED UP BY YOUR DOUBLE BATTLE TRAINING... CALM YOUR MIND AND BODY...
CALM DOWN ...
WATCH THE RIPPLES UPON THE WATER... EMPTY YOUR MINDS...
REMAIN LIKE THAT... YOU'RE FIRST, RUBY!
I'M HOLDING A COIN IN EITHER MY RIGHT HAND OR MY LEFT.
GUESS WHICH ONE.
LEFT...
INCORRECT.
AGAIN.
RIGHT.
CORRECT. AGAIN.
RIGHT.
INCORRECT. AGAIN.
LEFT.
INCORRECT. AGAIN.

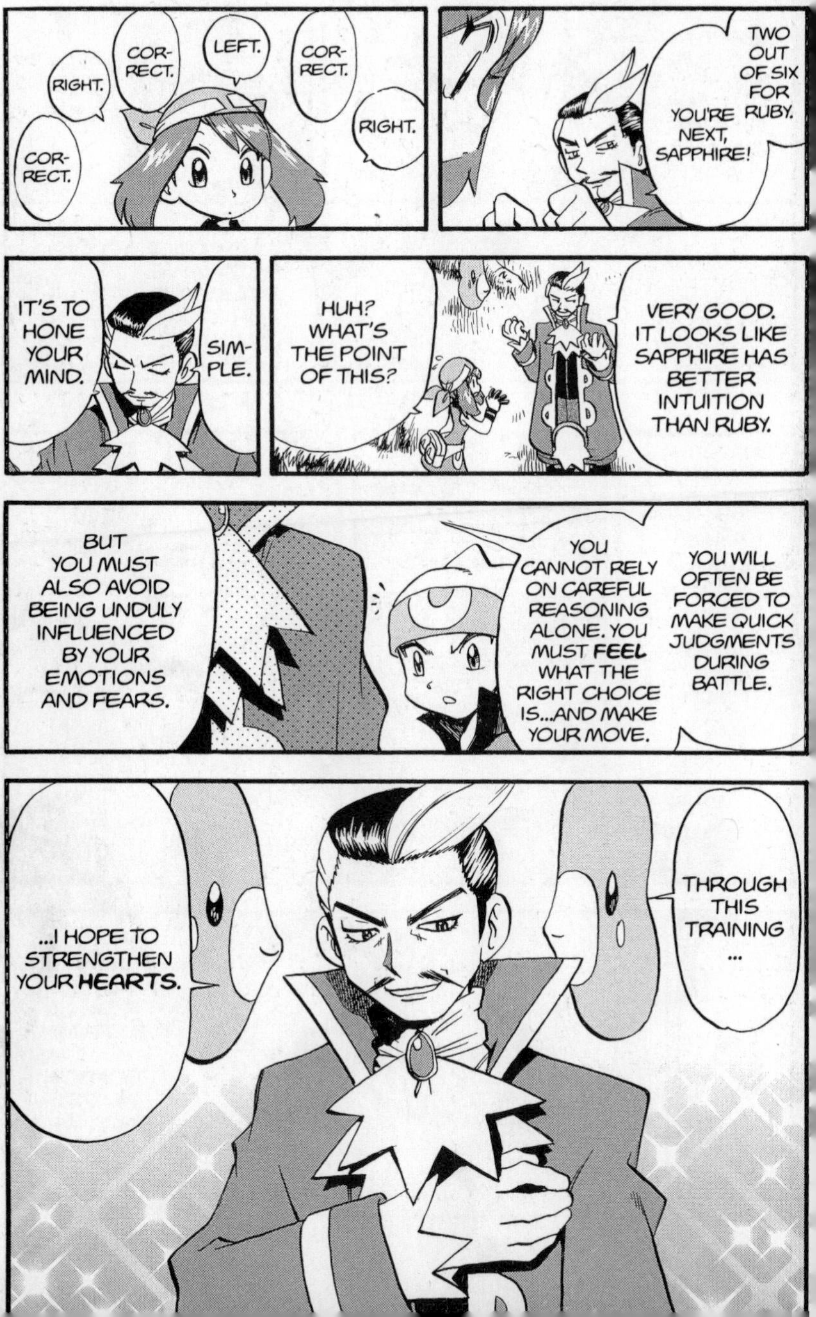
TWO OUT OF SIX FOR RUBY.
YOU'RE NEXT, SAPPHIRE!
RIGHT.
COR-RECT.
LEFT.
COR-RECT.
RIGHT.
COR-RECT.
VERY GOOD. IT LOOKS LIKE SAPPHIRE HAS BETTER INTUITION THAN RUBY.
HUH? WHAT'S THE POINT OF THIS?
SIM-PLE.
IT'S TO HONE YOUR MIND.
YOU WILL OFTEN BE FORCED TO MAKE QUICK JUDGMENTS DURING BATTLE.
YOU CANNOT RELY ON CAREFUL REASONING ALONE. YOU MUST **FEEL** WHAT THE RIGHT CHOICE IS...AND MAKE YOUR MOVE.
BUT YOU MUST ALSO AVOID BEING UNDULY INFLUENCED BY YOUR EMOTIONS AND FEARS.
THROUGH THIS TRAINING ...
...I HOPE TO STRENGTHEN YOUR **HEARTS**.

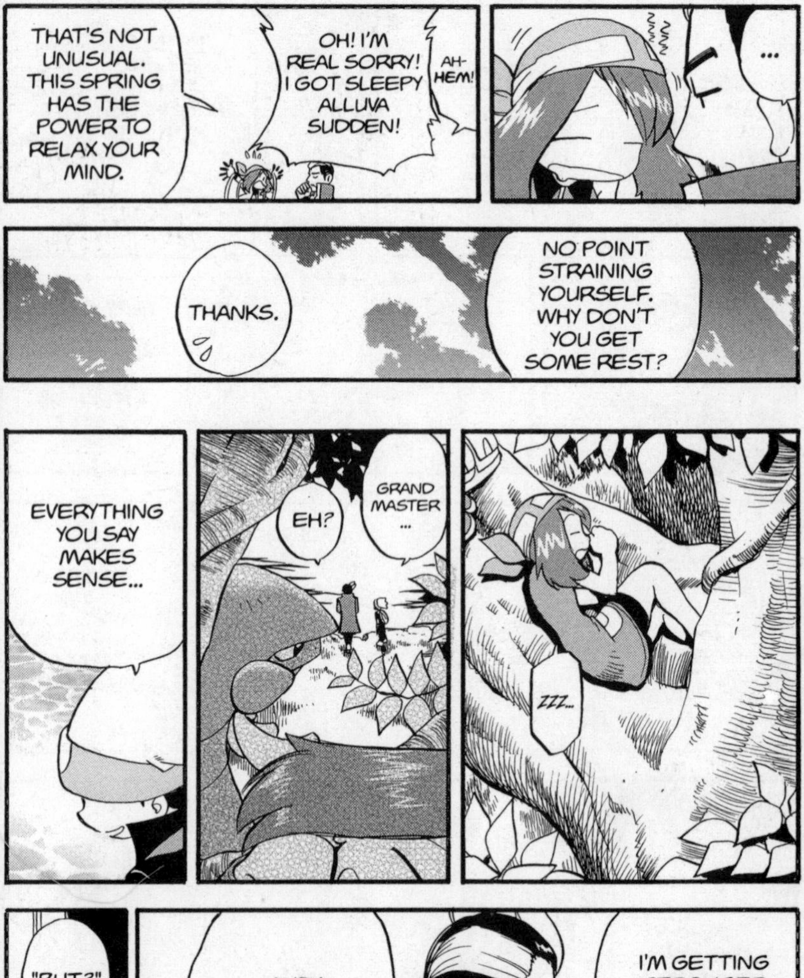
...
AH-HEM!
OH! I'M REAL SORRY! I GOT SLEEPY ALLUVA SUDDEN!
THAT'S NOT UNUSUAL. THIS SPRING HAS THE POWER TO RELAX YOUR MIND.
NO POINT STRAINING YOURSELF. WHY DON'T YOU GET SOME REST?
THANKS.
ZZZ...
GRAND MASTER ...
EH?
EVERYTHING YOU SAY MAKES SENSE...
I'M GETTING STRONGER FROM ALL THE TRAINING I'M GETTING FROM YOU AND TATE AND LIZA.
AND I RESPECT YOU BECAUSE YOU'RE MY MASTER'S MASTER.
BUT...
"BUT?"

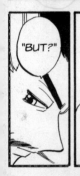

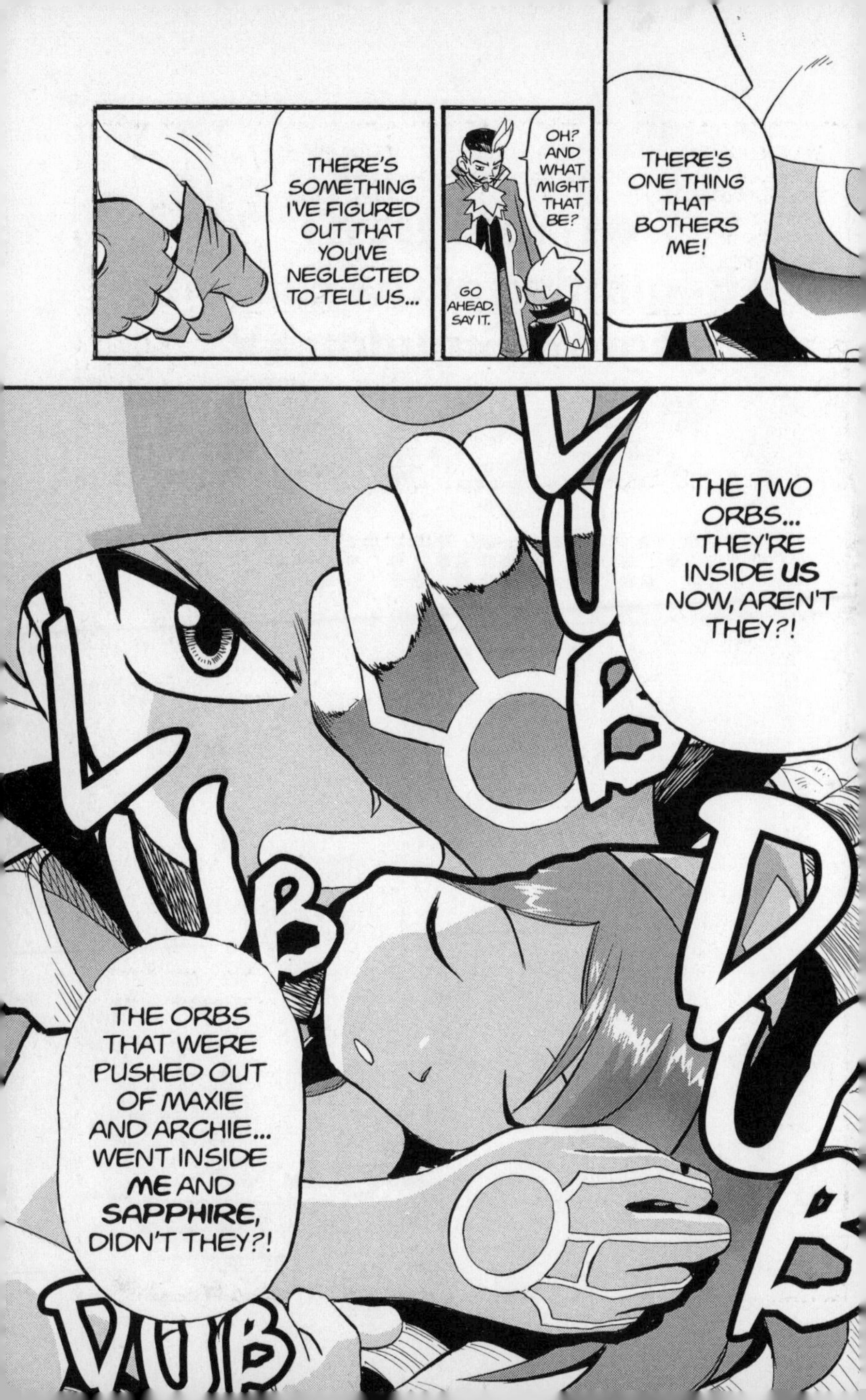
THERE'S ONE THING THAT BOTHERS ME!
OH? AND WHAT MIGHT THAT BE?
GO AHEAD. SAY IT.
THERE'S SOMETHING I'VE FIGURED OUT THAT YOU'VE NEGLECTED TO TELL US...
THE TWO ORBS... THEY'RE INSIDE US NOW, AREN'T THEY?!
LUB
DUB
LUB
THE ORBS THAT WERE PUSHED OUT OF MAXIE AND ARCHIE... WENT INSIDE ME AND SAPPHIRE, DIDN'T THEY?!
DUB

## ● Chapter 257 ●

# The Beginning of the End with Kyogre & Groudon XV

Pokémon™ Adventures Ruby & Sapphire

The Fourth Chapter

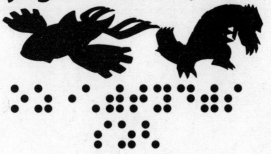

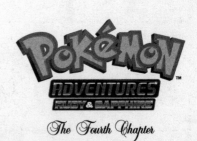

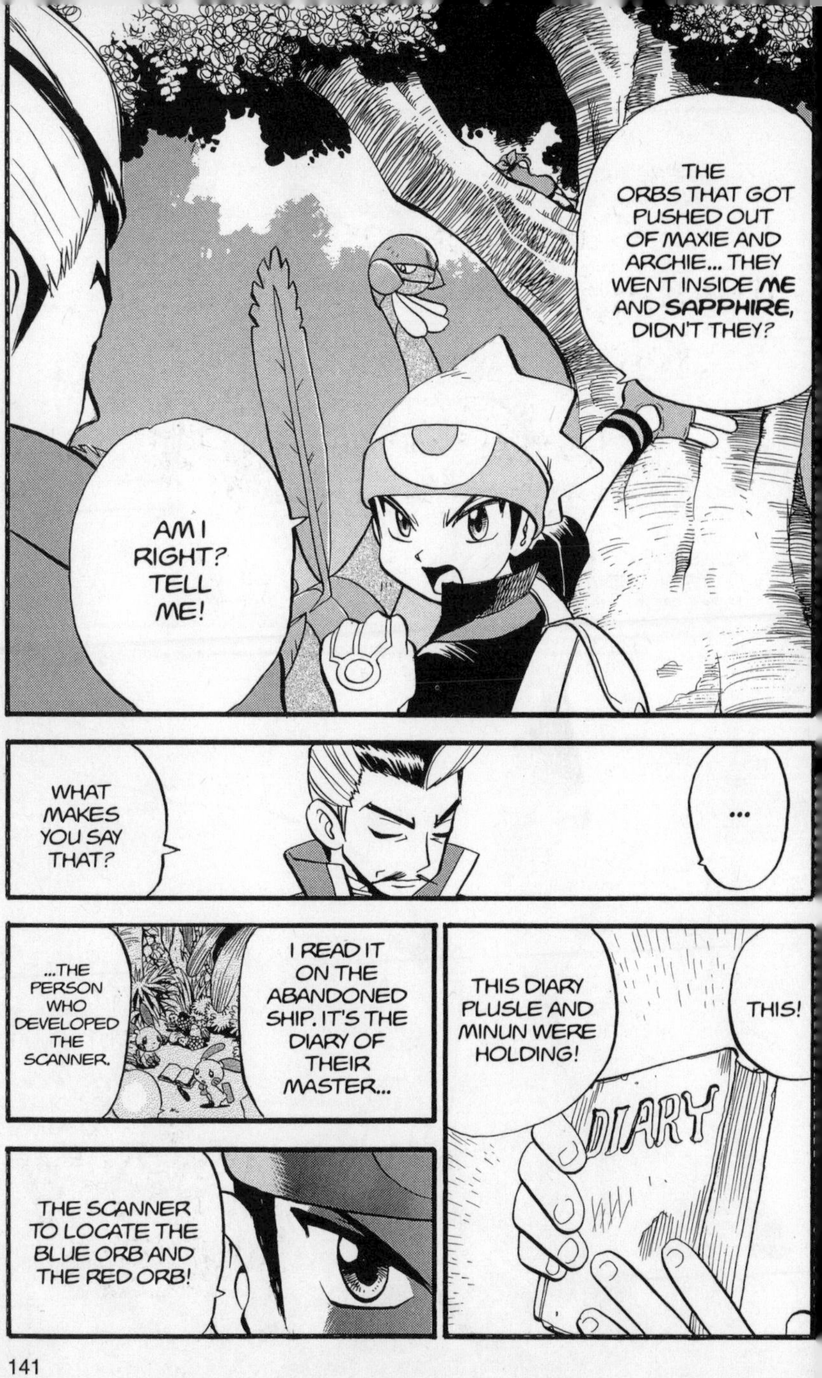
THE ORBS THAT GOT PUSHED OUT OF MAXIE AND ARCHIE... THEY WENT INSIDE **ME** AND **SAPPHIRE,** DIDN'T THEY?
AM I RIGHT? TELL ME!
...
WHAT MAKES YOU SAY THAT?
THIS!
THIS DIARY PLUSLE AND MINUN WERE HOLDING!
DIARY
I READ IT ON THE ABANDONED SHIP. IT'S THE DIARY OF THEIR MASTER...
...THE PERSON WHO DEVELOPED THE SCANNER.
THE SCANNER TO LOCATE THE BLUE ORB AND THE RED ORB!

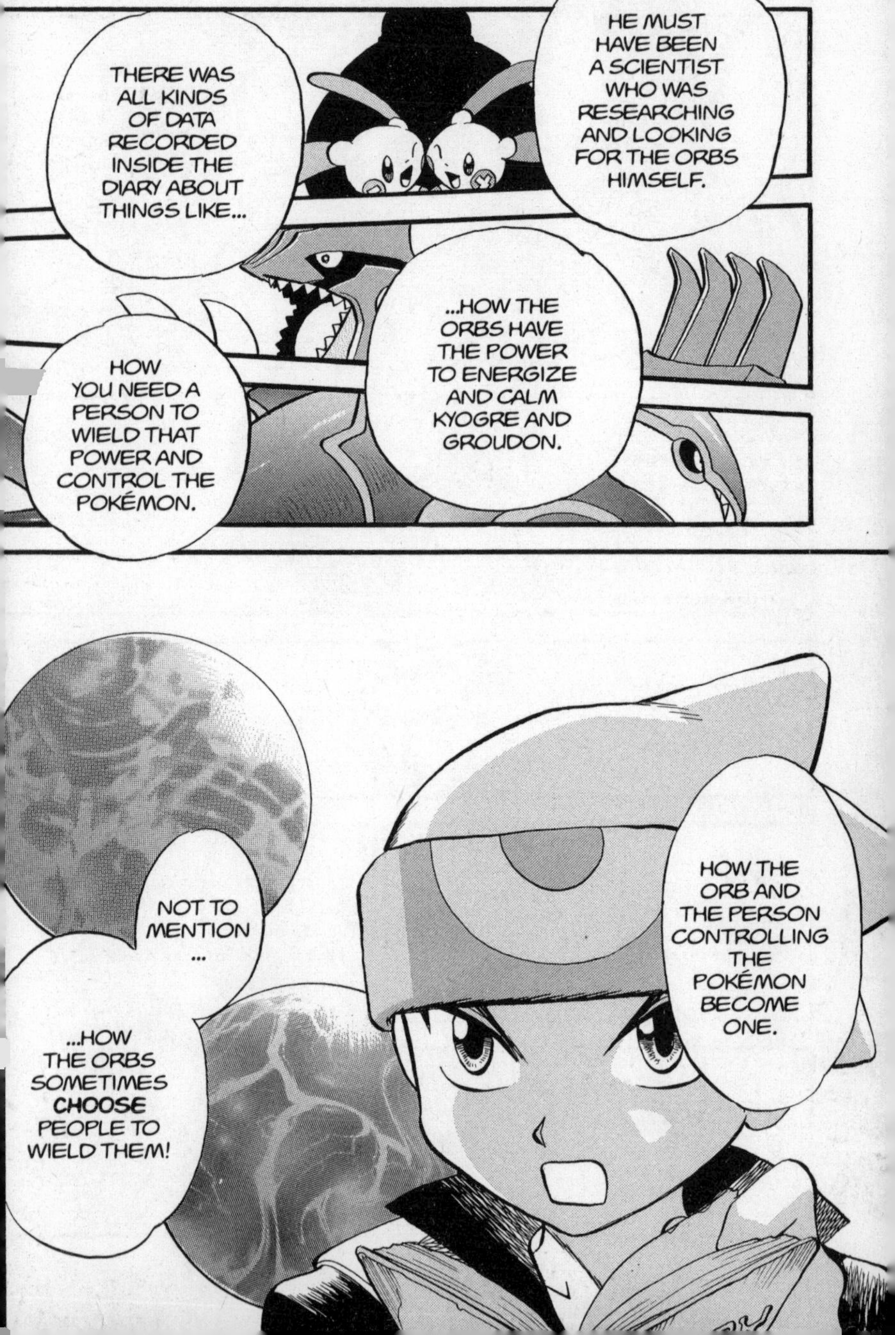
HE MUST HAVE BEEN A SCIENTIST WHO WAS RESEARCHING AND LOOKING FOR THE ORBS HIMSELF.
THERE WAS ALL KINDS OF DATA RECORDED INSIDE THE DIARY ABOUT THINGS LIKE...
...HOW THE ORBS HAVE THE POWER TO ENERGIZE AND CALM KYOGRE AND GROUDON.
HOW YOU NEED A PERSON TO WIELD THAT POWER AND CONTROL THE POKÉMON.
HOW THE ORB AND THE PERSON CONTROLLING THE POKÉMON BECOME ONE.
NOT TO MENTION ...
...HOW THE ORBS SOMETIMES **CHOOSE** PEOPLE TO WIELD THEM!

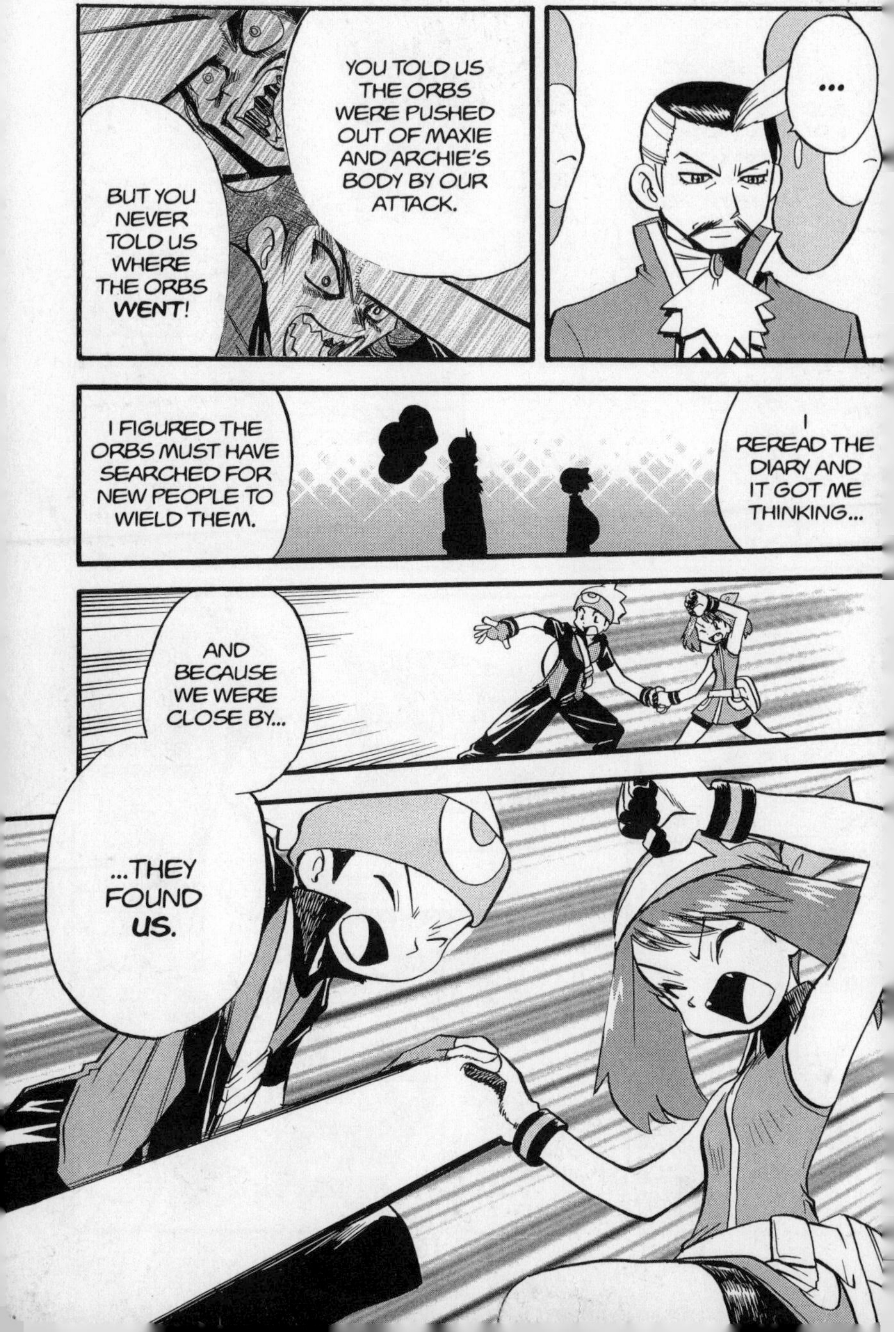
...
YOU TOLD US THE ORBS WERE PUSHED OUT OF MAXIE AND ARCHIE'S BODY BY OUR ATTACK.
BUT YOU NEVER TOLD US WHERE THE ORBS **WENT**!
I REREAD THE DIARY AND IT GOT ME THINKING...
I FIGURED THE ORBS MUST HAVE SEARCHED FOR NEW PEOPLE TO WIELD THEM.
AND BECAUSE WE WERE CLOSE BY...
...THEY FOUND **US**.

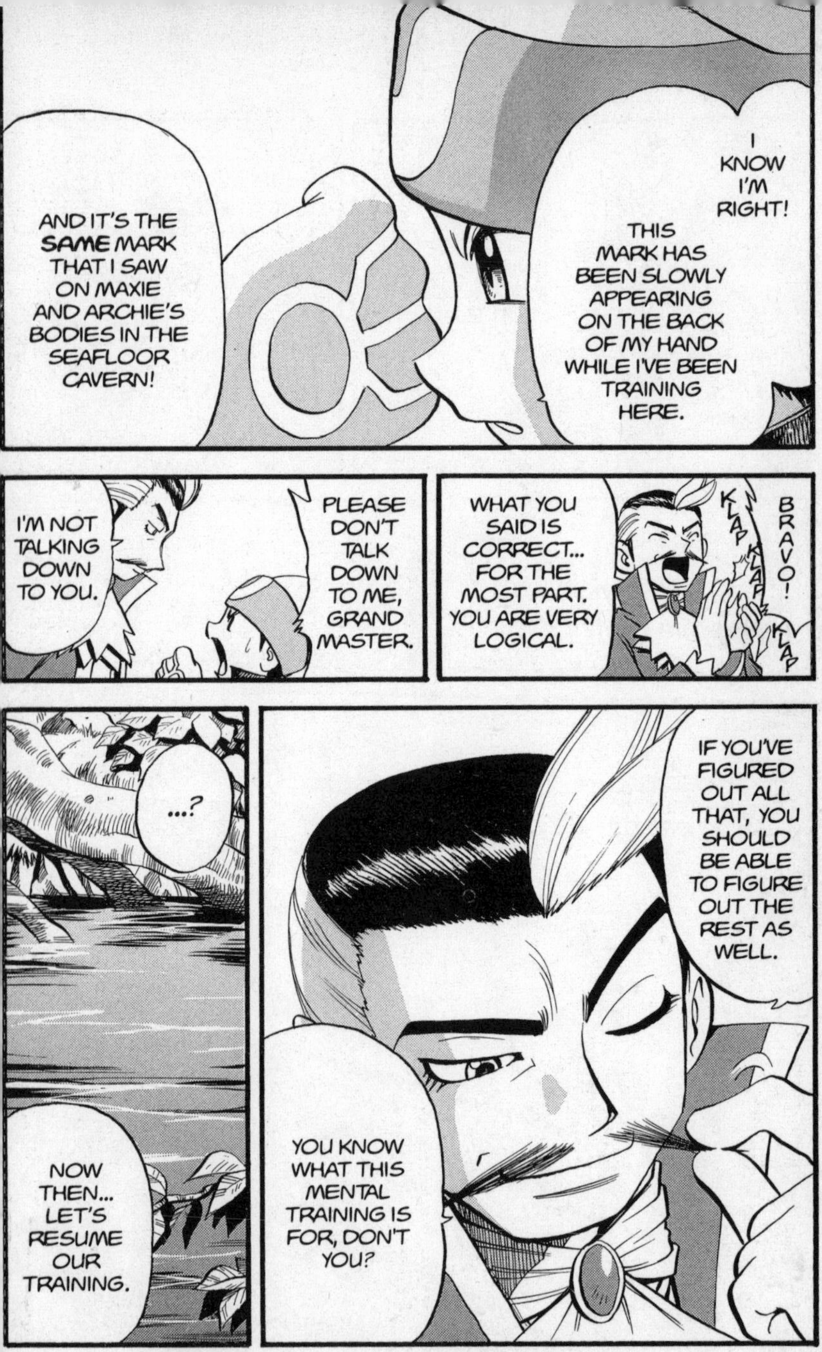
I KNOW I'M RIGHT!
THIS MARK HAS BEEN SLOWLY APPEARING ON THE BACK OF MY HAND WHILE I'VE BEEN TRAINING HERE.
AND IT'S THE **SAME** MARK THAT I SAW ON MAXIE AND ARCHIE'S BODIES IN THE SEAFLOOR CAVERN!
BRAVO!
KLAP KLAP KLAP KLAP
WHAT YOU SAID IS CORRECT... FOR THE MOST PART. YOU ARE VERY LOGICAL.
PLEASE DON'T TALK DOWN TO ME, GRAND MASTER.
I'M NOT TALKING DOWN TO YOU.
IF YOU'VE FIGURED OUT ALL THAT, YOU SHOULD BE ABLE TO FIGURE OUT THE REST AS WELL.
YOU KNOW WHAT THIS MENTAL TRAINING IS FOR, DON'T YOU?
...?
NOW THEN... LET'S RESUME OUR TRAINING.

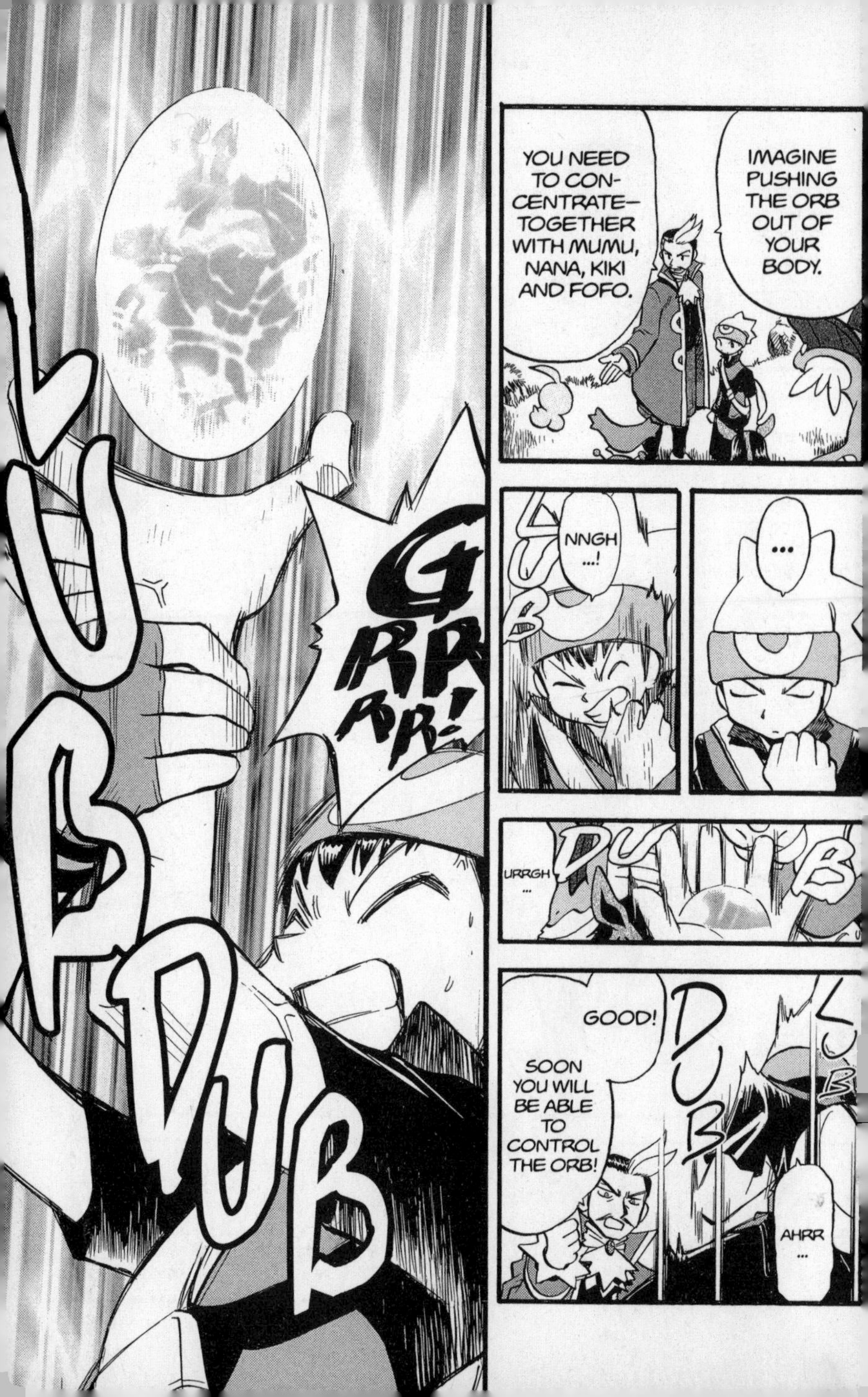
IMAGINE PUSHING THE ORB OUT OF YOUR BODY.
YOU NEED TO CON-CENTRATE— TOGETHER WITH MUMU, NANA, KIKI AND FOFO.
...
NNGH ...!
DUB
DUB
URRGH ...
GOOD!
SOON YOU WILL BE ABLE TO CONTROL THE ORB!
DUB
DUB
AHRR ...
GRRRRR!
DUB
DUB

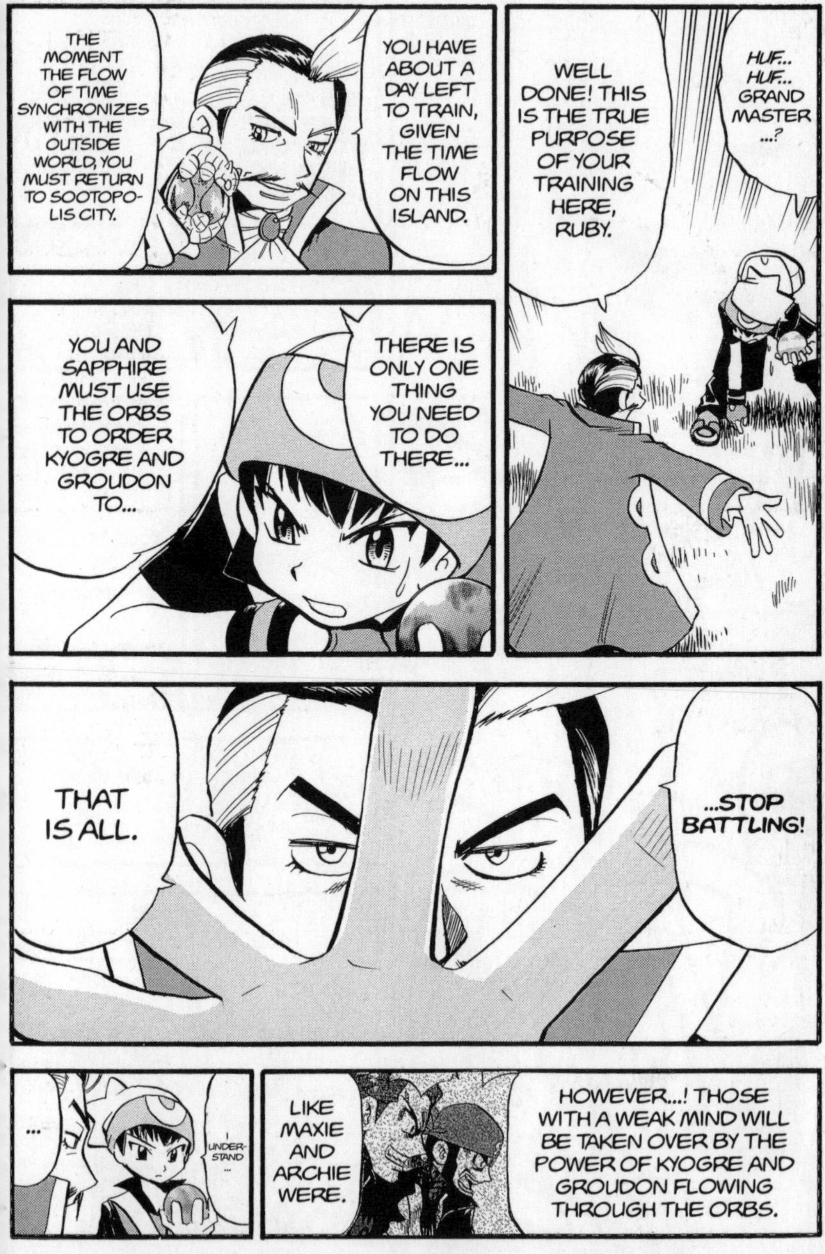
HUF... HUF... GRAND MASTER ...?
WELL DONE! THIS IS THE TRUE PURPOSE OF YOUR TRAINING HERE, RUBY.
YOU HAVE ABOUT A DAY LEFT TO TRAIN, GIVEN THE TIME FLOW ON THIS ISLAND.
THE MOMENT THE FLOW OF TIME SYNCHRONIZES WITH THE OUTSIDE WORLD, YOU MUST RETURN TO SOOTOPOLIS CITY.
THERE IS ONLY ONE THING YOU NEED TO DO THERE...
YOU AND SAPPHIRE MUST USE THE ORBS TO ORDER KYOGRE AND GROUDON TO...
...STOP BATTLING!
THAT IS ALL.
HOWEVER...! THOSE WITH A WEAK MIND WILL BE TAKEN OVER BY THE POWER OF KYOGRE AND GROUDON FLOWING THROUGH THE ORBS.
LIKE MAXIE AND ARCHIE WERE.
I UNDERSTAND ...
...

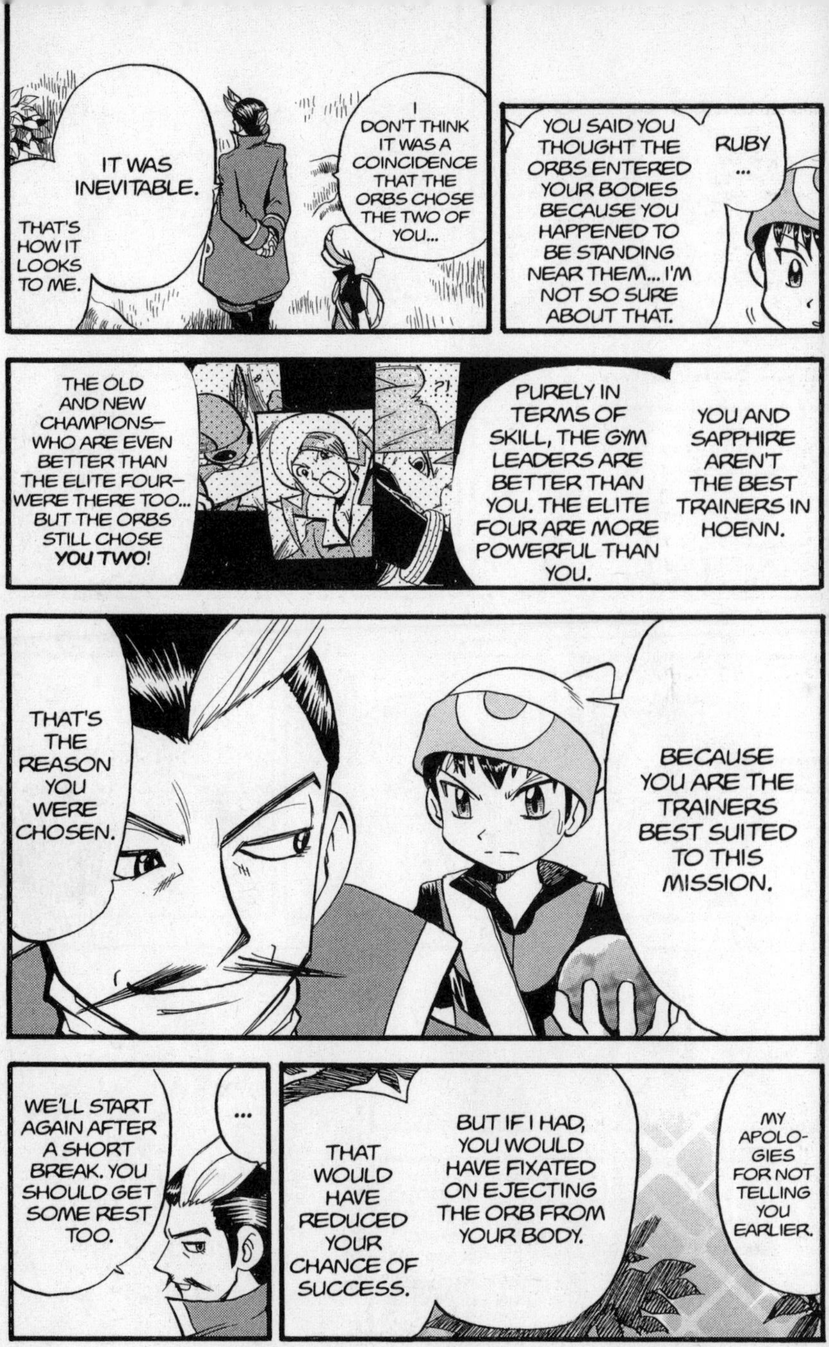
RUBY ...
YOU SAID YOU THOUGHT THE ORBS ENTERED YOUR BODIES BECAUSE YOU HAPPENED TO BE STANDING NEAR THEM... I'M NOT SO SURE ABOUT THAT.
I DON'T THINK IT WAS A COINCIDENCE THAT THE ORBS CHOSE THE TWO OF YOU...
IT WAS INEVITABLE.
THAT'S HOW IT LOOKS TO ME.
YOU AND SAPPHIRE AREN'T THE BEST TRAINERS IN HOENN.
PURELY IN TERMS OF SKILL, THE GYM LEADERS ARE BETTER THAN YOU. THE ELITE FOUR ARE MORE POWERFUL THAN YOU.
?!
THE OLD AND NEW CHAMPIONS—WHO ARE EVEN BETTER THAN THE ELITE FOUR—WERE THERE TOO... BUT THE ORBS STILL CHOSE **YOU TWO**!
BECAUSE YOU ARE THE TRAINERS BEST SUITED TO THIS MISSION.
THAT'S THE REASON YOU WERE CHOSEN.
MY APOLOGIES FOR NOT TELLING YOU EARLIER.
BUT IF I HAD, YOU WOULD HAVE FIXATED ON EJECTING THE ORB FROM YOUR BODY.
THAT WOULD HAVE REDUCED YOUR CHANCE OF SUCCESS.
...
WE'LL START AGAIN AFTER A SHORT BREAK. YOU SHOULD GET SOME REST TOO.

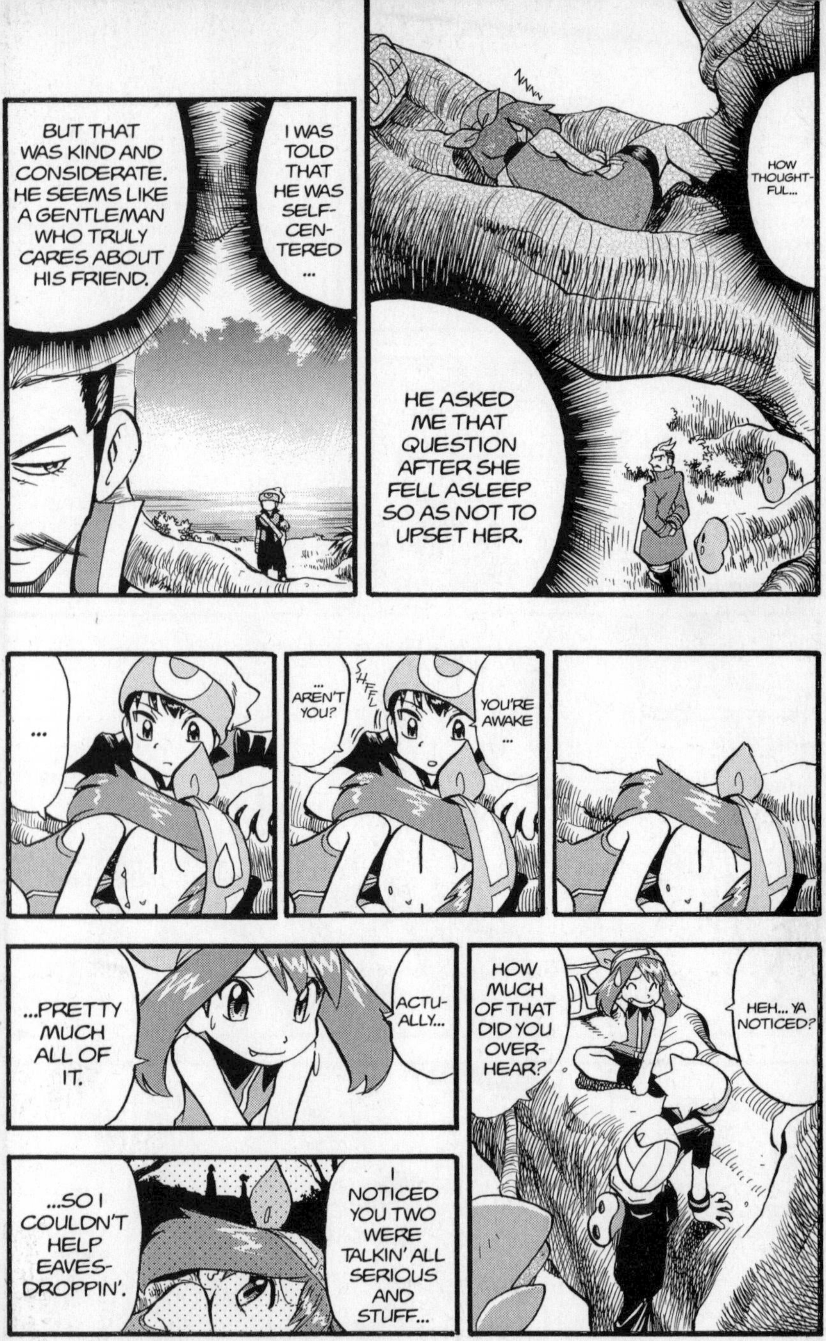
HOW THOUGHTFUL...
HE ASKED ME THAT QUESTION AFTER SHE FELL ASLEEP SO AS NOT TO UPSET HER.
I WAS TOLD THAT HE WAS SELF-CENTERED...
BUT THAT WAS KIND AND CONSIDERATE. HE SEEMS LIKE A GENTLEMAN WHO TRULY CARES ABOUT HIS FRIEND.
YOU'RE AWAKE...
SHFFL
... AREN'T YOU?
...
HEH... YA NOTICED?
HOW MUCH OF THAT DID YOU OVERHEAR?
ACTUALLY...
...PRETTY MUCH ALL OF IT.
I NOTICED YOU TWO WERE TALKIN' ALL SERIOUS AND STUFF...
...SO I COULDN'T HELP EAVESDROPPIN'.

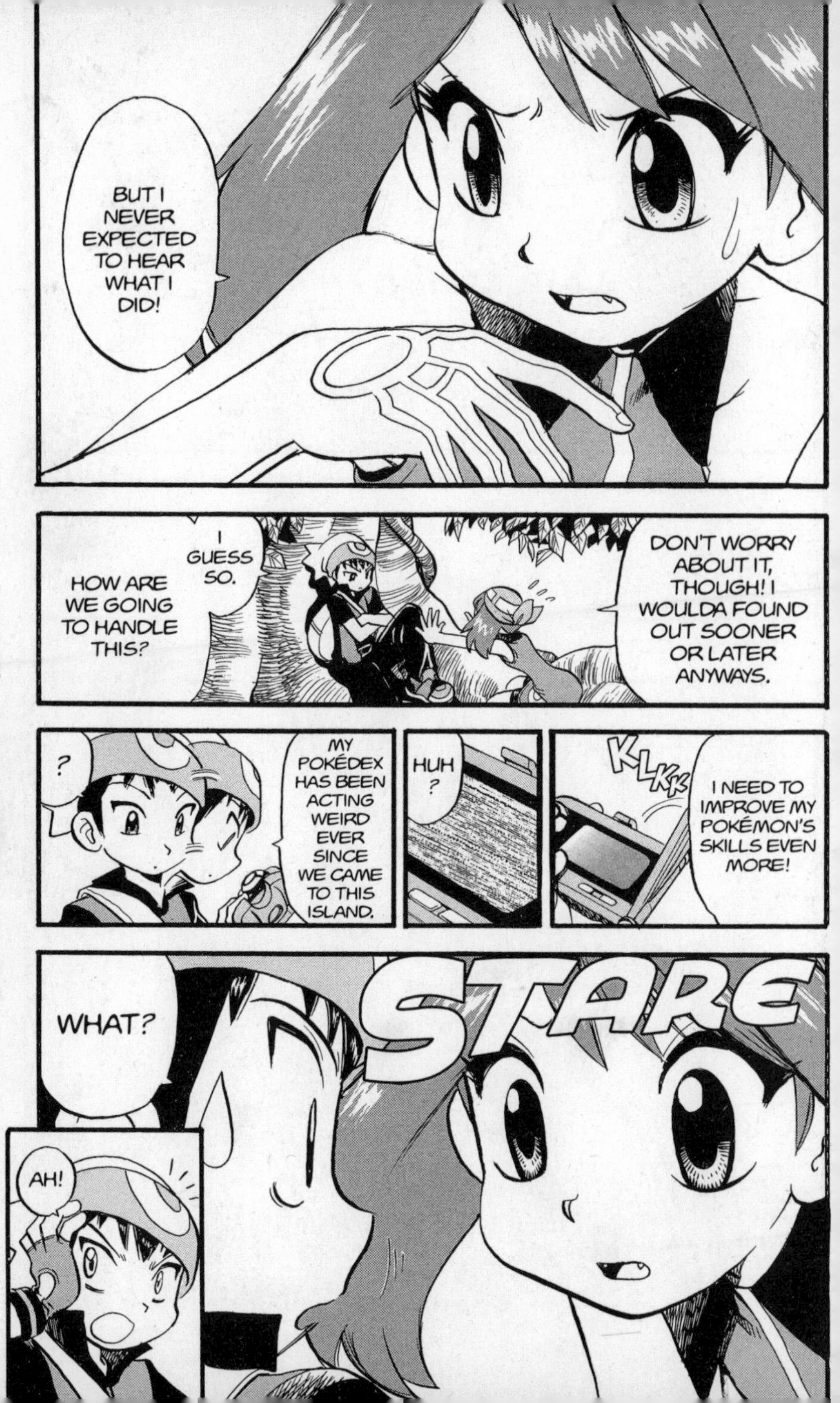
BUT I NEVER EXPECTED TO HEAR WHAT I DID!
DON'T WORRY ABOUT IT, THOUGH! I WOULDA FOUND OUT SOONER OR LATER ANYWAYS.
I GUESS SO.
HOW ARE WE GOING TO HANDLE THIS?
KLKK
I NEED TO IMPROVE MY POKÉMON'S SKILLS EVEN MORE!
HUH?
MY POKÉDEX HAS BEEN ACTING WEIRD EVER SINCE WE CAME TO THIS ISLAND.
?
STARE
WHAT?
AH!

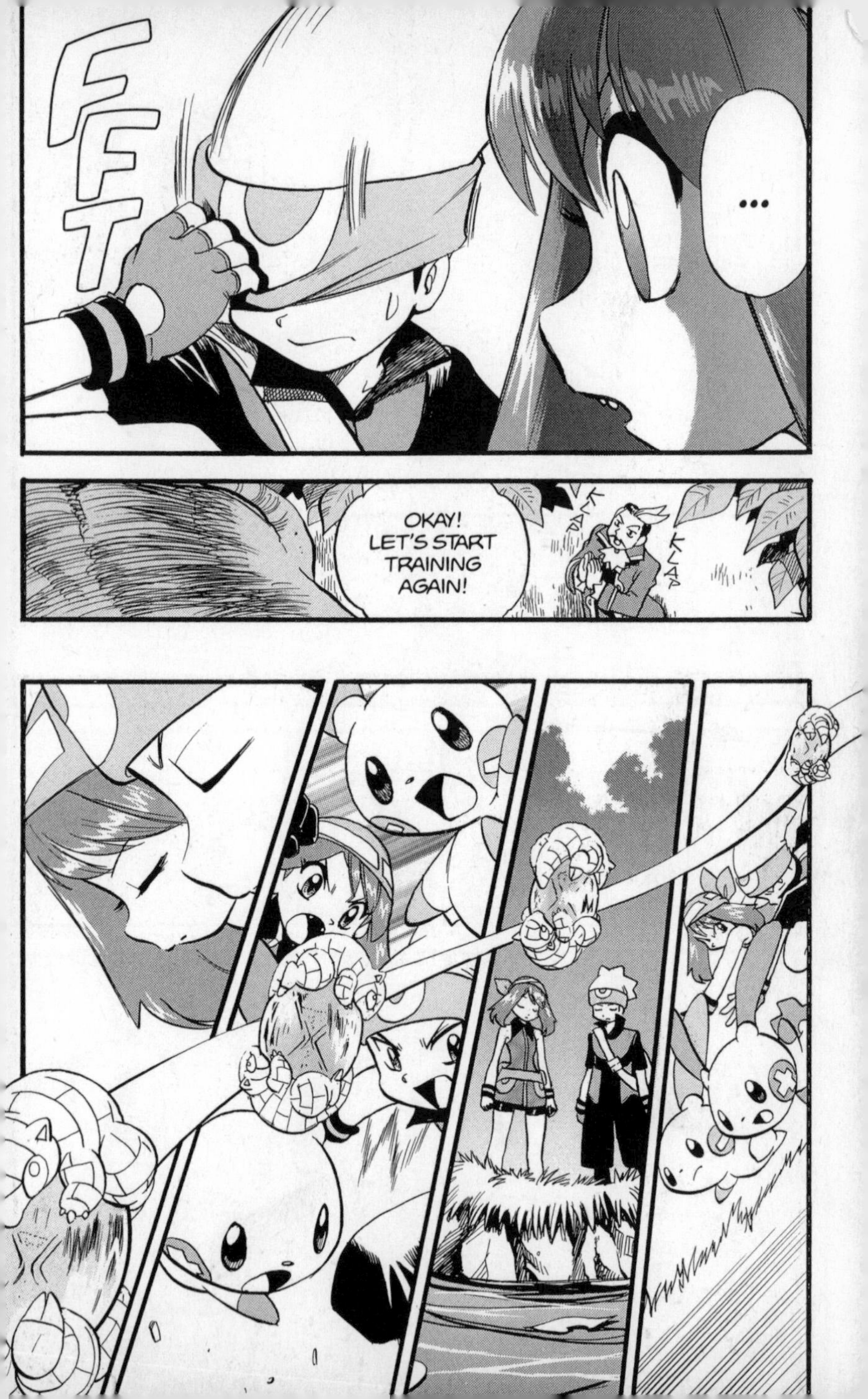
...
FFT
KLAP
KLAP
OKAY! LET'S START TRAINING AGAIN!

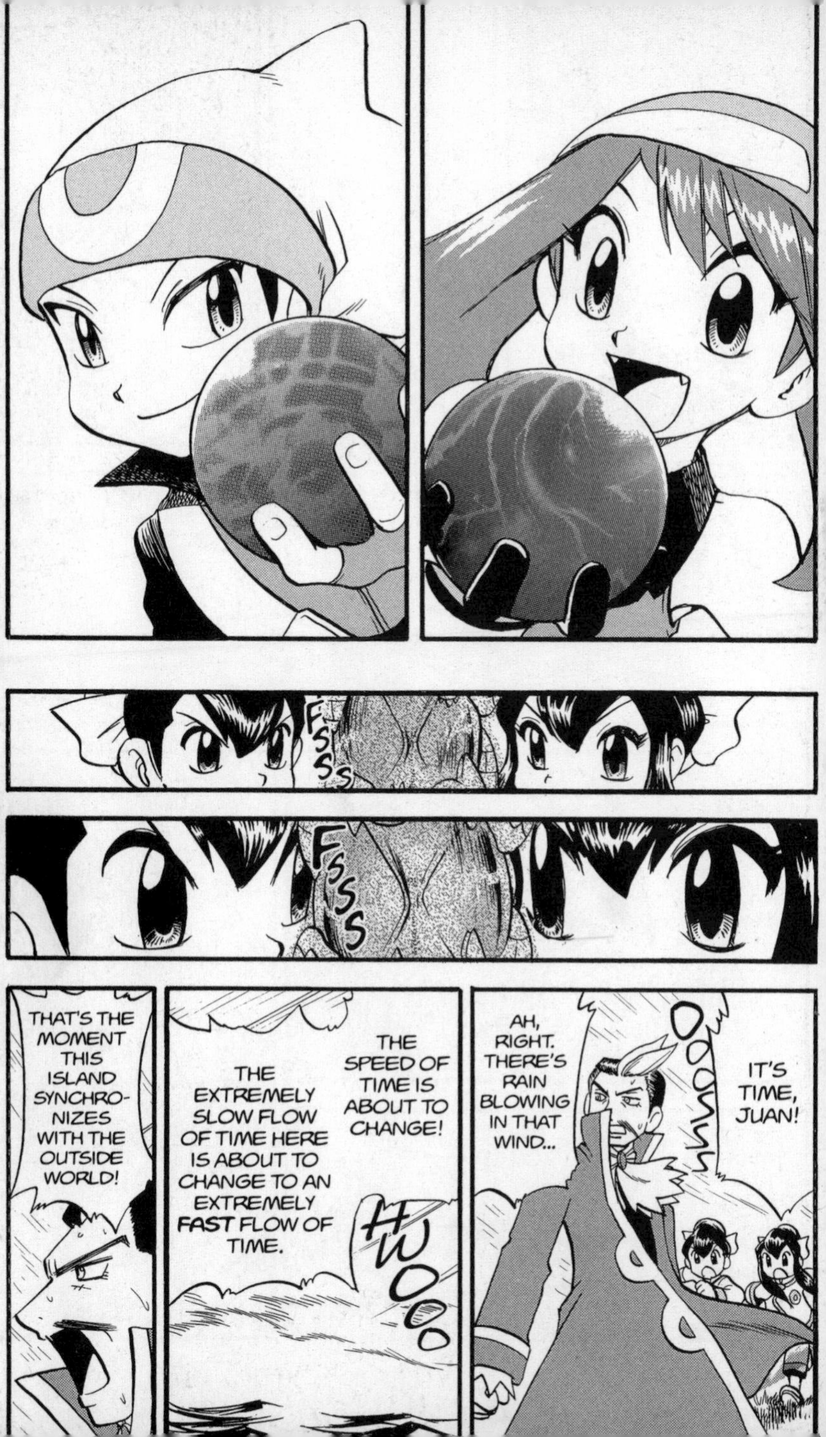
FSSS
FSSS
IT'S TIME, JUAN!
HWOOOO
AH, RIGHT. THERE'S RAIN BLOWING IN THAT WIND...
THE SPEED OF TIME IS ABOUT TO CHANGE!
THE EXTREMELY SLOW FLOW OF TIME HERE IS ABOUT TO CHANGE TO AN EXTREMELY **FAST** FLOW OF TIME.
HWOOOO
THAT'S THE MOMENT THIS ISLAND SYNCHRO-NIZES WITH THE OUTSIDE WORLD!

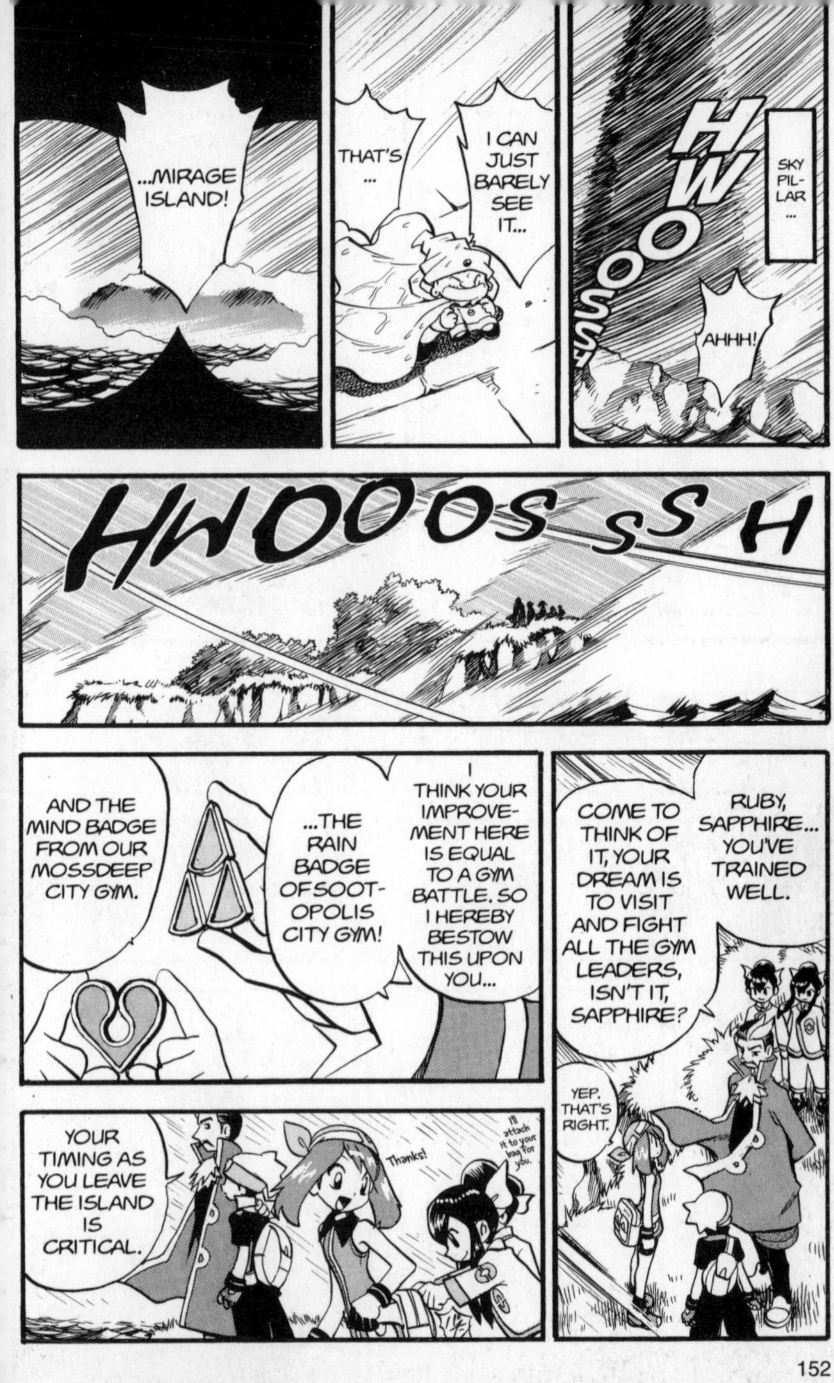
SKY PILLAR...
HWOOSSH
AHHH!
I CAN JUST BARELY SEE IT...
THAT'S...
...MIRAGE ISLAND!
HWOOOSSSH
RUBY, SAPPHIRE... YOU'VE TRAINED WELL.
COME TO THINK OF IT, YOUR DREAM IS TO VISIT AND FIGHT ALL THE GYM LEADERS, ISN'T IT, SAPPHIRE?
YEP. THAT'S RIGHT.
I THINK YOUR IMPROVEMENT HERE IS EQUAL TO A GYM BATTLE. SO I HEREBY BESTOW THIS UPON YOU...
...THE RAIN BADGE OF SOOTOPOLIS CITY GYM!
AND THE MIND BADGE FROM OUR MOSSDEEP CITY GYM.
I'll attach it to your bag for you.
Thanks!
YOUR TIMING AS YOU LEAVE THE ISLAND IS CRITICAL.

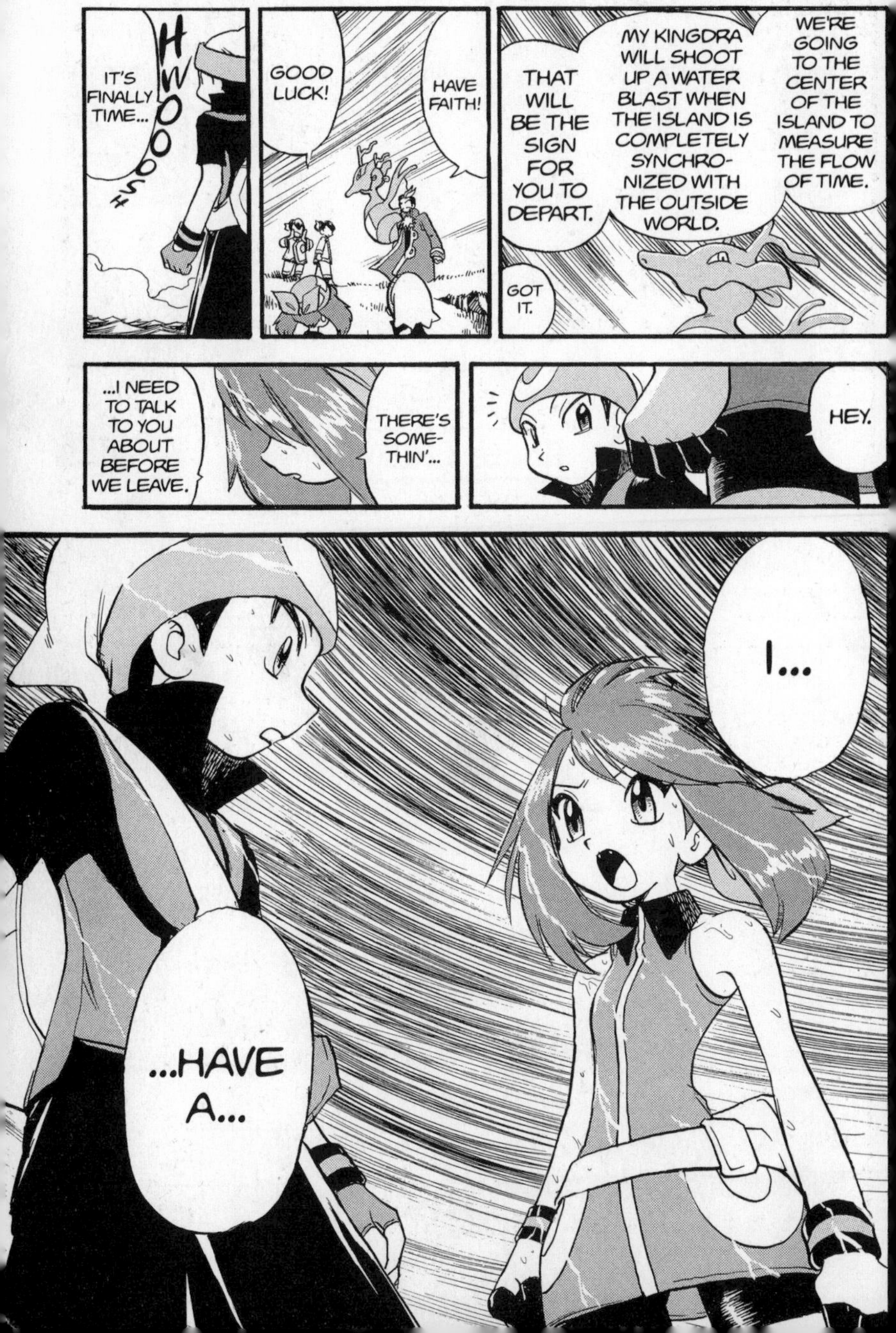
WE'RE GOING TO THE CENTER OF THE ISLAND TO MEASURE THE FLOW OF TIME.
MY KINGDRA WILL SHOOT UP A WATER BLAST WHEN THE ISLAND IS COMPLETELY SYNCHRO-NIZED WITH THE OUTSIDE WORLD.
THAT WILL BE THE SIGN FOR YOU TO DEPART.
GOT IT.
HAVE FAITH!
GOOD LUCK!
HWOOOSH
IT'S FINALLY TIME...
HEY.
THERE'S SOME-THIN'...
...I NEED TO TALK TO YOU ABOUT BEFORE WE LEAVE.
I...
...HAVE A...

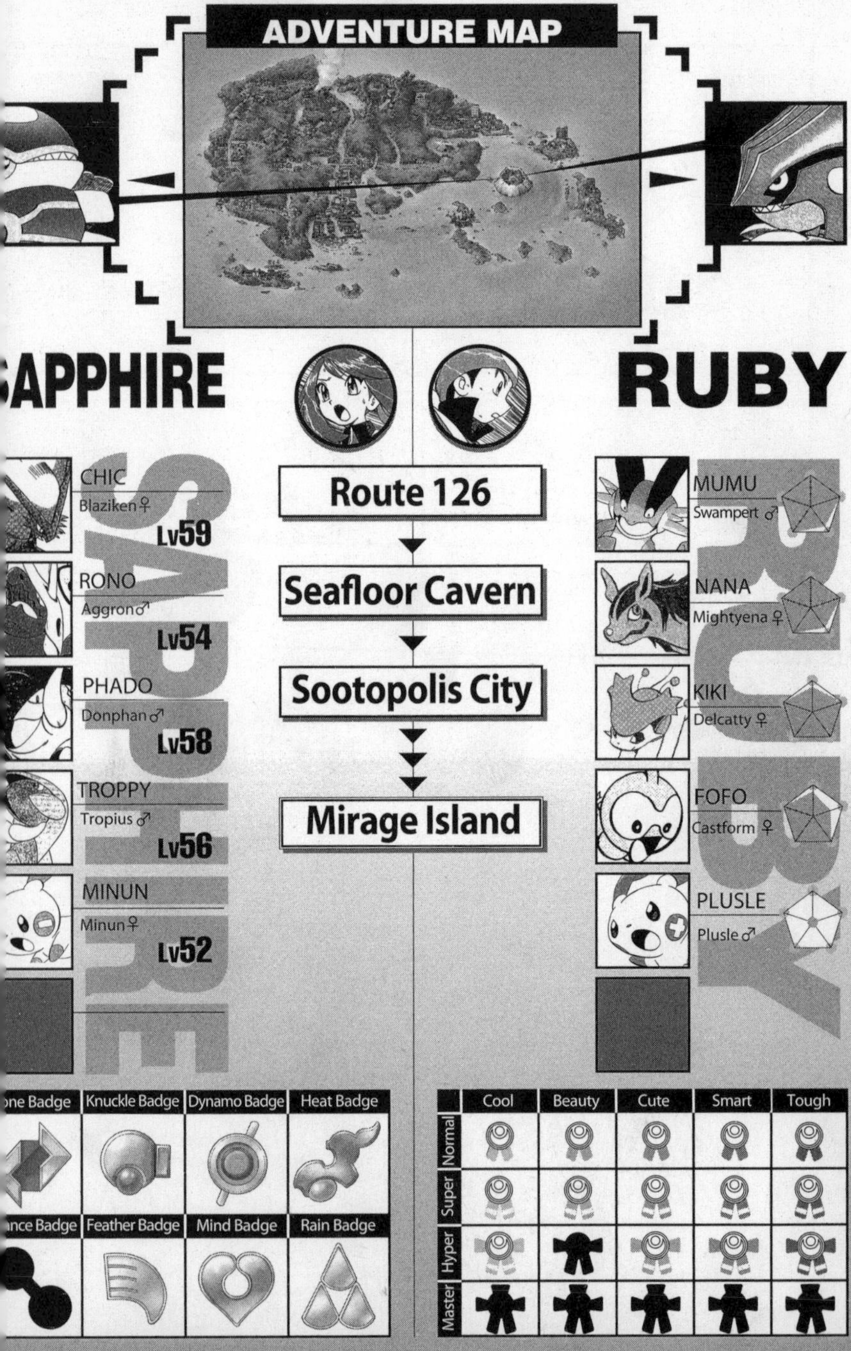

# ADVENTURE MAP

# SAPPHIRE

# RUBY

CHIC
Blaziken ♀
**Lv59**

RONO
Aggron ♂
**Lv54**

PHADO
Donphan ♂
**Lv58**

TROPPY
Tropius ♂
**Lv56**

MINUN
Minun ♀
**Lv52**

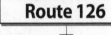

## Route 126
↓
## Seafloor Cavern
↓
## Sootopolis City
↓↓
## Mirage Island

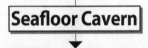
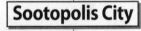

MUMU
Swampert ♂

NANA
Mightyena ♀

KIKI
Delcatty ♀

FOFO
Castform ♀

PLUSLE
Plusle ♂

| | ne Badge | Knuckle Badge | Dynamo Badge | Heat Badge |
|---|---|---|---|---|
|  |  |  |  |  |
| | nce Badge | Feather Badge | Mind Badge | Rain Badge |

| | | Cool | Beauty | Cute | Smart | Tough |
|---|---|---|---|---|---|---|
| | Normal | | | | | |
| Super | | | | | | |
| Hyper | | | | | | |
| Master | | | | | | |

# ● Chapter 258 ●
# Rayquaza Redemption I

The Fourth Chapter

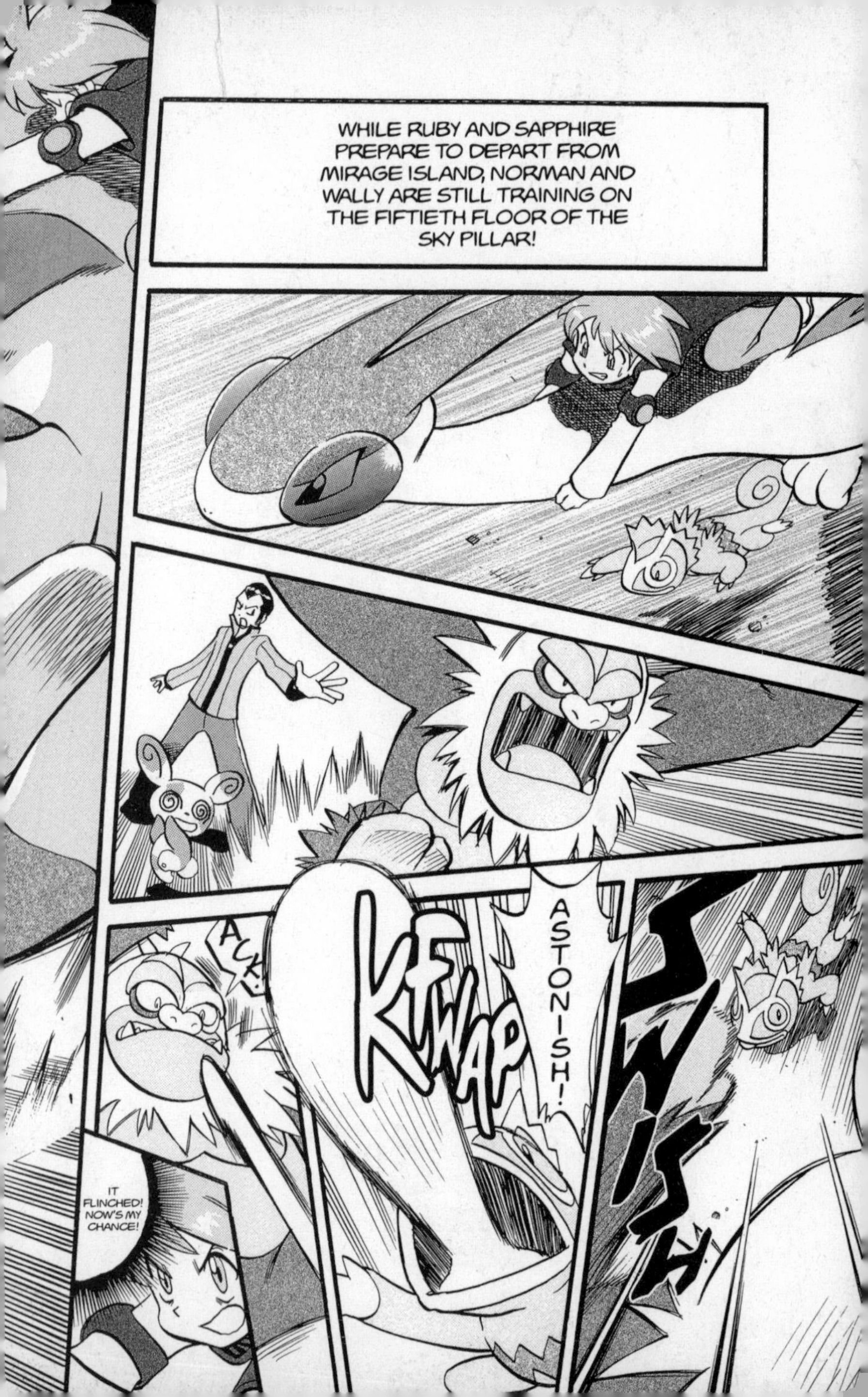
WHILE RUBY AND SAPPHIRE PREPARE TO DEPART FROM MIRAGE ISLAND, NORMAN AND WALLY ARE STILL TRAINING ON THE FIFTIETH FLOOR OF THE SKY PILLAR!
ASTONISH!
KFWAP
ACK!
IT FLINCHED! NOW'S MY CHANCE!

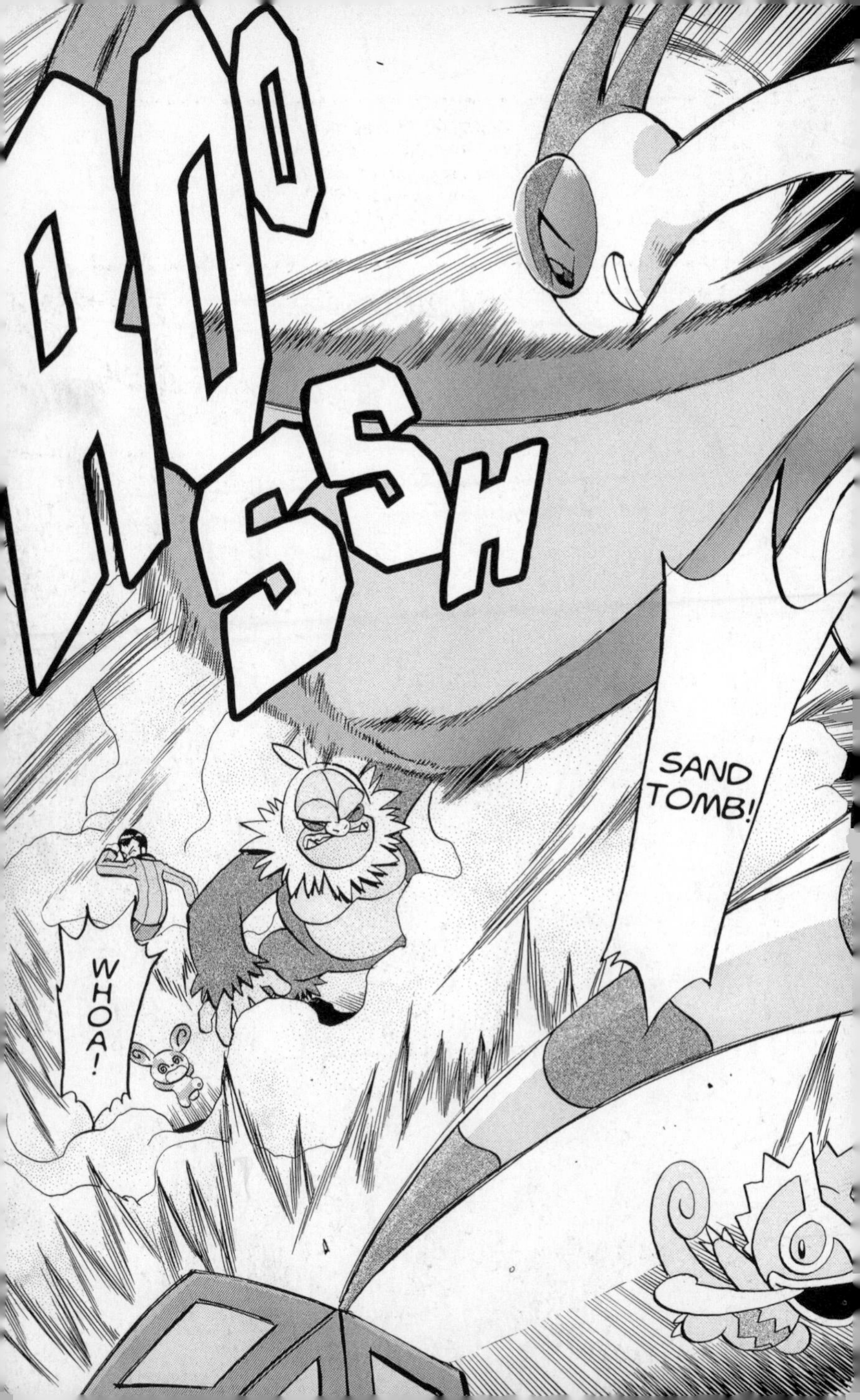
SAND TOMB!
WHOA!

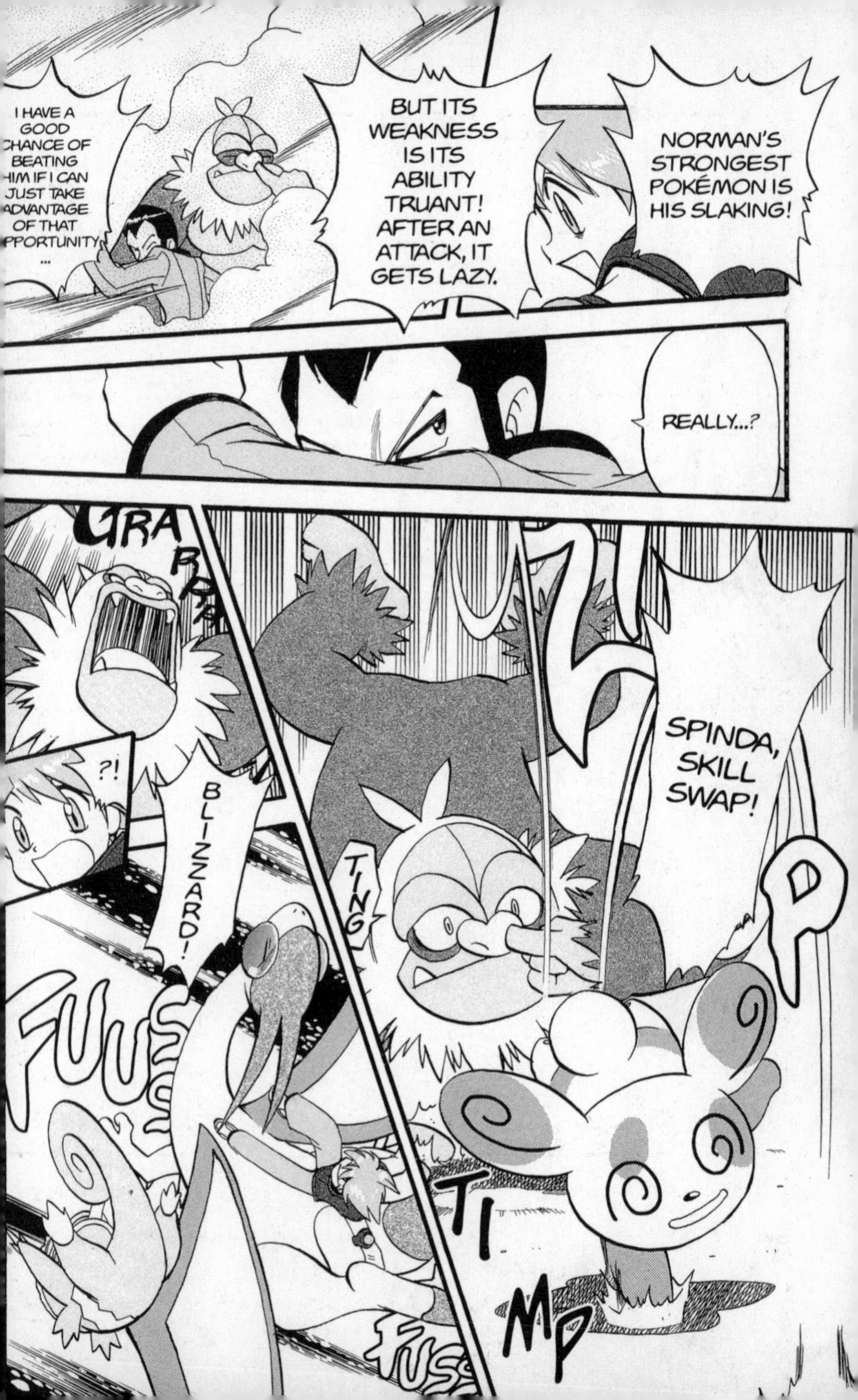
NORMAN'S STRONGEST POKÉMON IS HIS SLAKING!
BUT ITS WEAKNESS IS ITS ABILITY TRUANT! AFTER AN ATTACK, IT GETS LAZY.
I HAVE A GOOD CHANCE OF BEATING HIM IF I CAN JUST TAKE ADVANTAGE OF THAT OPPORTUNITY...
REALLY...?
GRARRR
SPINDA, SKILL SWAP!
?!
BLIZZARD!
TING
FUUSS
FUSS
P
TI
MP

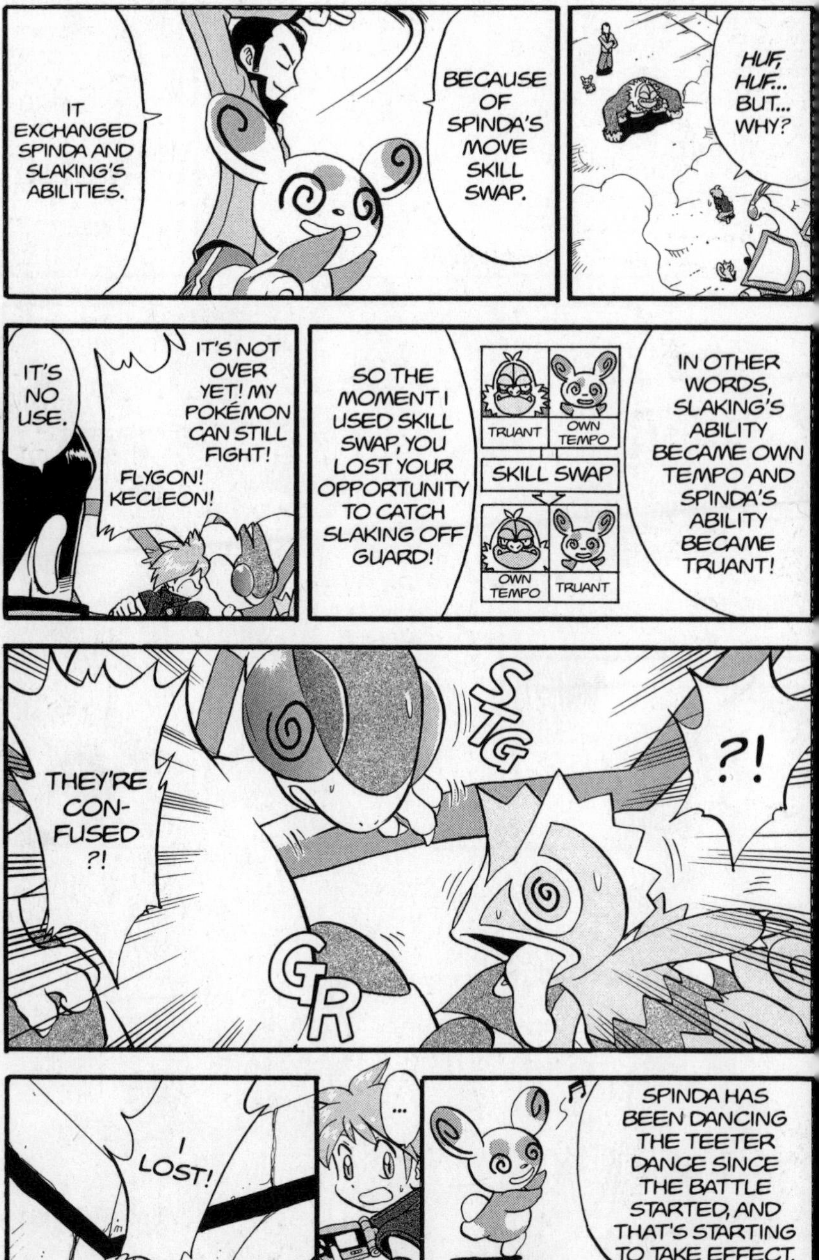
HUF, HUF... BUT... WHY?
BECAUSE OF SPINDA'S MOVE SKILL SWAP.
IT EXCHANGED SPINDA AND SLAKING'S ABILITIES.
IN OTHER WORDS, SLAKING'S ABILITY BECAME OWN TEMPO AND SPINDA'S ABILITY BECAME TRUANT!
TRUANT
OWN TEMPO
SKILL SWAP
OWN TEMPO
TRUANT
SO THE MOMENT I USED SKILL SWAP, YOU LOST YOUR OPPORTUNITY TO CATCH SLAKING OFF GUARD!
IT'S NOT OVER YET! MY POKÉMON CAN STILL FIGHT!
FLYGON! KECLEON!
IT'S NO USE.
?!
STG
THEY'RE CON-FUSED?!
GR
SPINDA HAS BEEN DANCING THE TEETER DANCE SINCE THE BATTLE STARTED, AND THAT'S STARTING TO TAKE EFFECT.
...
I LOST!

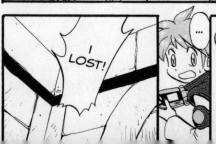

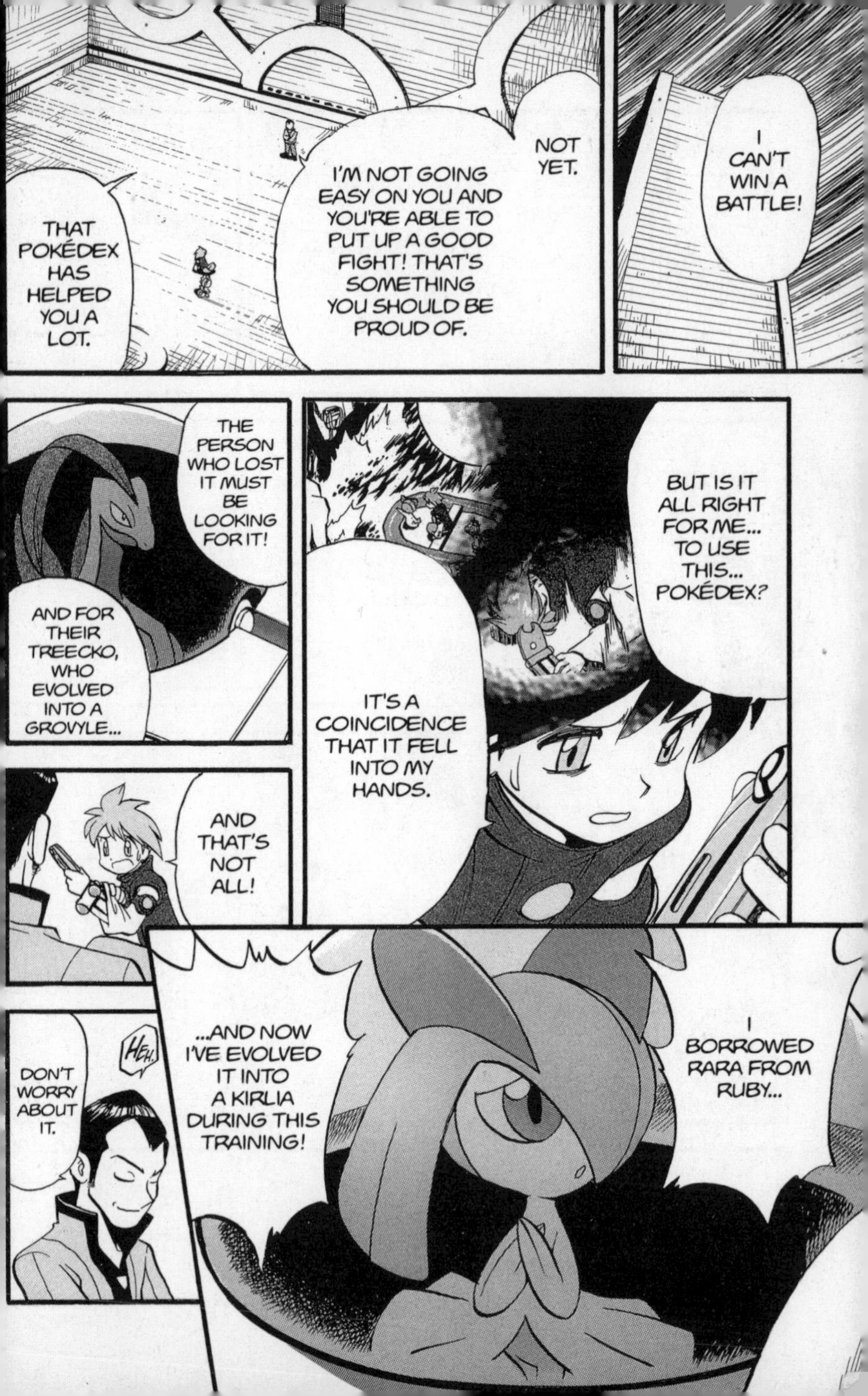
I CAN'T WIN A BATTLE!
NOT YET.
I'M NOT GOING EASY ON YOU AND YOU'RE ABLE TO PUT UP A GOOD FIGHT! THAT'S SOMETHING YOU SHOULD BE PROUD OF.
THAT POKÉDEX HAS HELPED YOU A LOT.
BUT IS IT ALL RIGHT FOR ME... TO USE THIS... POKÉDEX?
IT'S A COINCIDENCE THAT IT FELL INTO MY HANDS.
THE PERSON WHO LOST IT MUST BE LOOKING FOR IT!
AND FOR THEIR TREECKO, WHO EVOLVED INTO A GROVYLE...
AND THAT'S NOT ALL!
I BORROWED RARA FROM RUBY...
...AND NOW I'VE EVOLVED IT INTO A KIRLIA DURING THIS TRAINING!
HEH.
DON'T WORRY ABOUT IT.

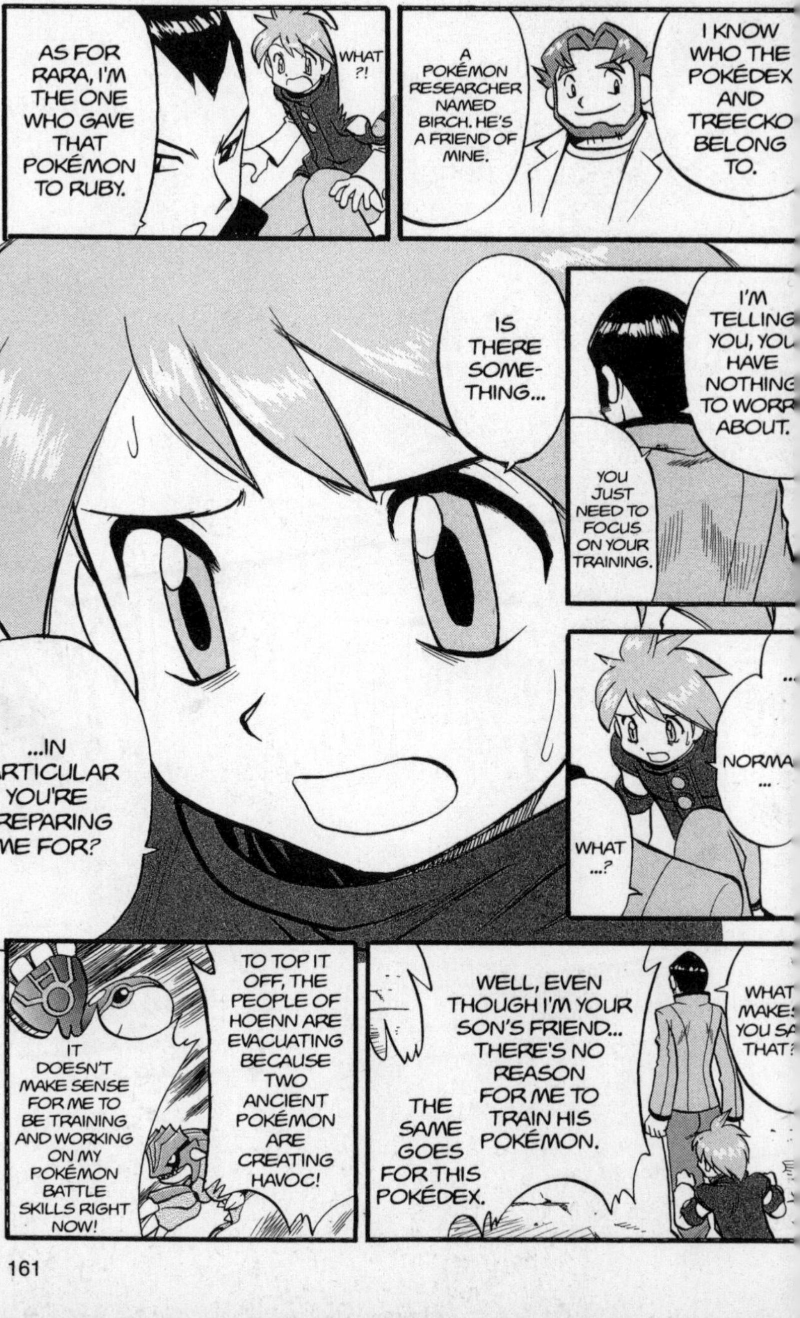
I KNOW WHO THE POKÉDEX AND TREECKO BELONG TO.
A POKÉMON RESEARCHER NAMED BIRCH. HE'S A FRIEND OF MINE.
AS FOR RARA, I'M THE ONE WHO GAVE THAT POKÉMON TO RUBY.
WHAT ?!
I'M TELLING YOU, YOU HAVE NOTHING TO WORR ABOUT.
YOU JUST NEED TO FOCUS ON YOUR TRAINING.
...
NORMA ...
WHAT ...?
IS THERE SOME-THING...
...IN PARTICULAR YOU'RE PREPARING ME FOR?
WHAT MAKES YOU SA THAT?
WELL, EVEN THOUGH I'M YOUR SON'S FRIEND... THERE'S NO REASON FOR ME TO TRAIN HIS POKÉMON.
THE SAME GOES FOR THIS POKÉDEX.
TO TOP IT OFF, THE PEOPLE OF HOENN ARE EVACUATING BECAUSE TWO ANCIENT POKÉMON ARE CREATING HAVOC!
IT DOESN'T MAKE SENSE FOR ME TO BE TRAINING AND WORKING ON MY POKÉMON BATTLE SKILLS RIGHT NOW!

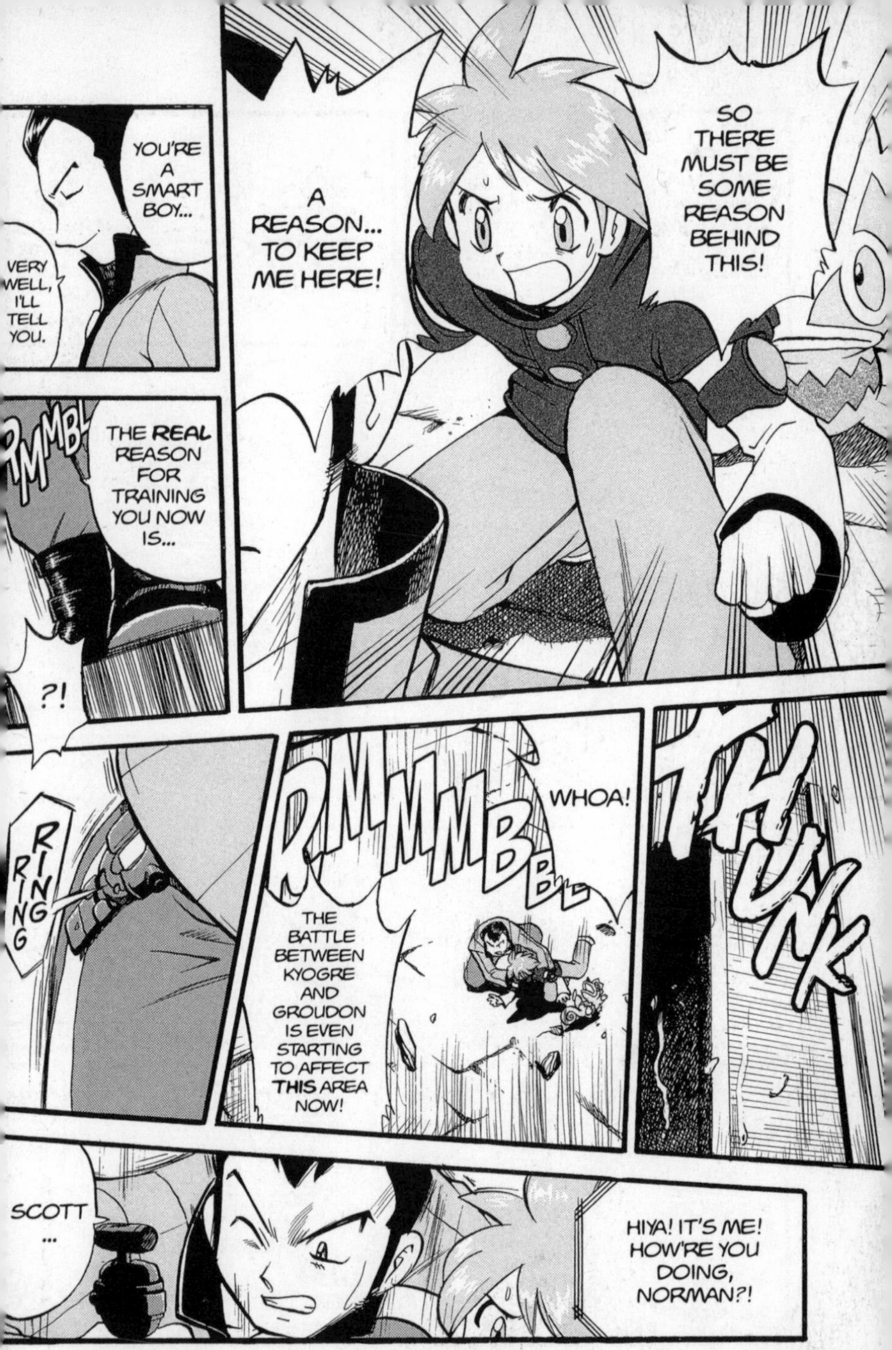
SO THERE MUST BE SOME REASON BEHIND THIS!
A REASON... TO KEEP ME HERE!
YOU'RE A SMART BOY...
VERY WELL, I'LL TELL YOU.
RMMBL
THE **REAL** REASON FOR TRAINING YOU NOW IS...
?!
THUNK
RMMMBBL
WHOA!
THE BATTLE BETWEEN KYOGRE AND GROUDON IS EVEN STARTING TO AFFECT **THIS** AREA NOW!
RING RING
HIYA! IT'S ME! HOW'RE YOU DOING, NORMAN?!
SCOTT ...

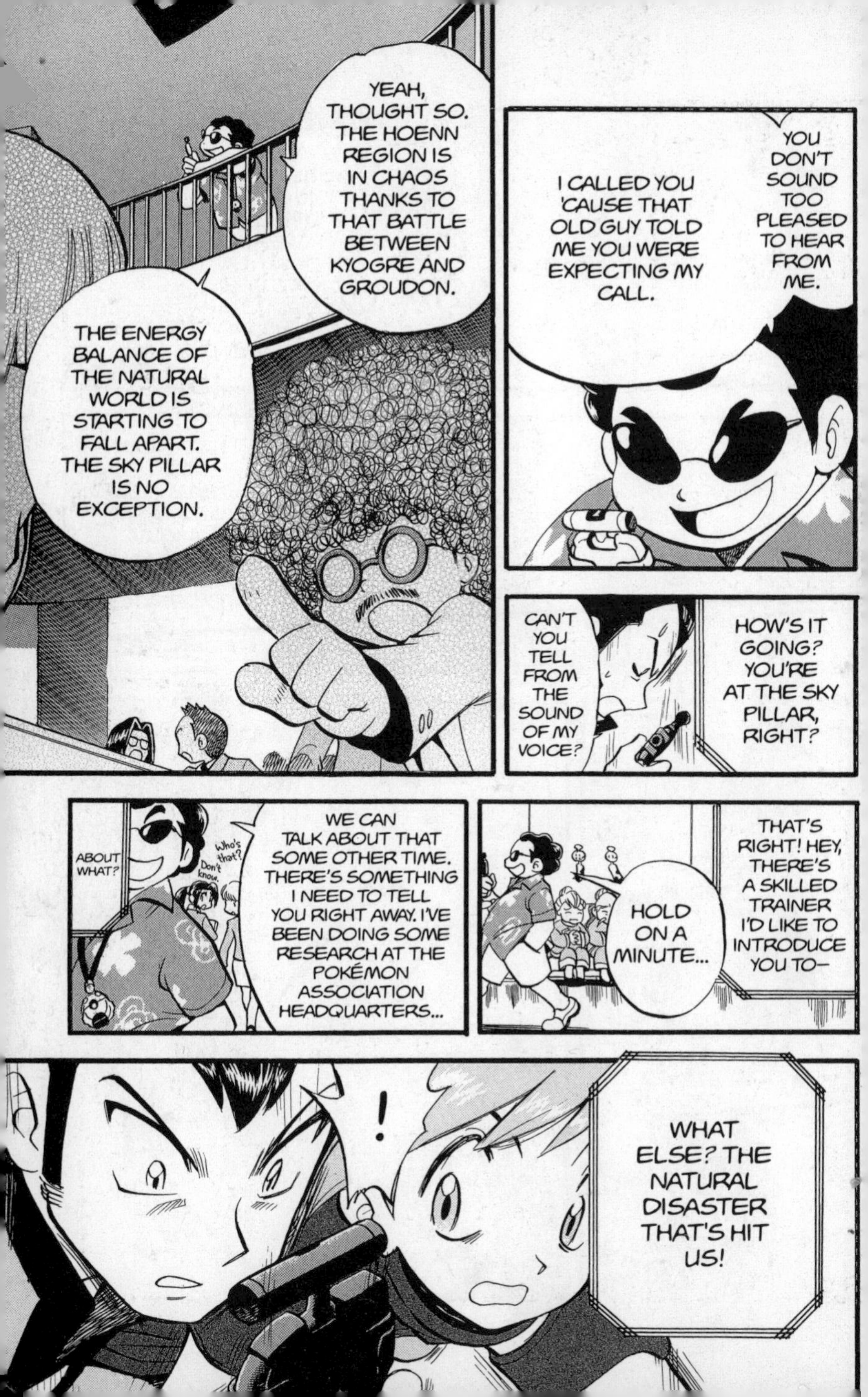
YOU DON'T SOUND TOO PLEASED TO HEAR FROM ME.
I CALLED YOU 'CAUSE THAT OLD GUY TOLD ME YOU WERE EXPECTING MY CALL.
HOW'S IT GOING? YOU'RE AT THE SKY PILLAR, RIGHT?
CAN'T YOU TELL FROM THE SOUND OF MY VOICE?
YEAH, THOUGHT SO. THE HOENN REGION IS IN CHAOS THANKS TO THAT BATTLE BETWEEN KYOGRE AND GROUDON.
THE ENERGY BALANCE OF THE NATURAL WORLD IS STARTING TO FALL APART. THE SKY PILLAR IS NO EXCEPTION.
THAT'S RIGHT! HEY, THERE'S A SKILLED TRAINER I'D LIKE TO INTRODUCE YOU TO—
HOLD ON A MINUTE...
WE CAN TALK ABOUT THAT SOME OTHER TIME. THERE'S SOMETHING I NEED TO TELL YOU RIGHT AWAY. I'VE BEEN DOING SOME RESEARCH AT THE POKÉMON ASSOCIATION HEADQUARTERS...
Who's that?
Don't know.
ABOUT WHAT?
WHAT ELSE? THE NATURAL DISASTER THAT'S HIT US!
!

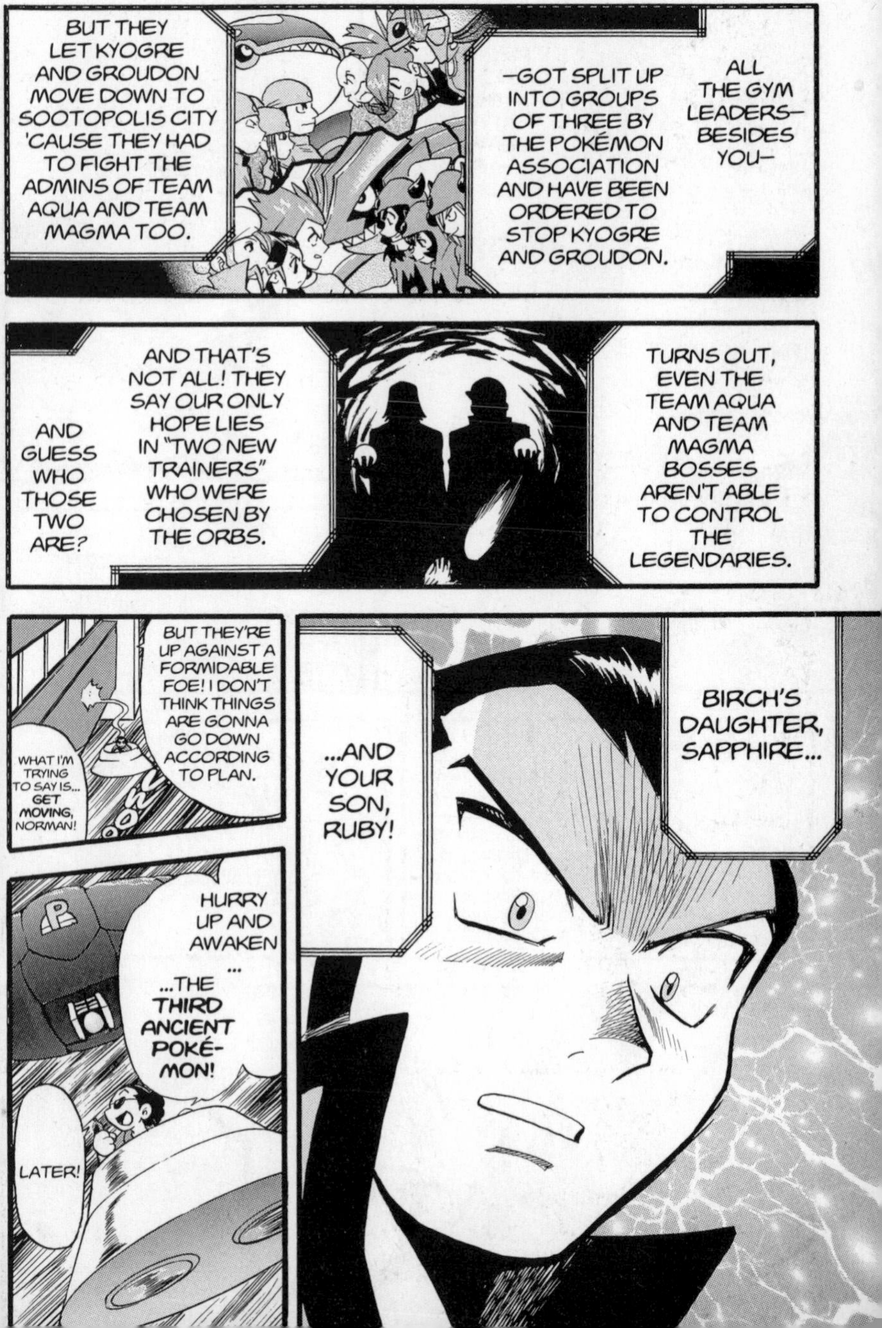
ALL THE GYM LEADERS—BESIDES YOU—
—GOT SPLIT UP INTO GROUPS OF THREE BY THE POKÉMON ASSOCIATION AND HAVE BEEN ORDERED TO STOP KYOGRE AND GROUDON.
BUT THEY LET KYOGRE AND GROUDON MOVE DOWN TO SOOTOPOLIS CITY 'CAUSE THEY HAD TO FIGHT THE ADMINS OF TEAM AQUA AND TEAM MAGMA TOO.
TURNS OUT, EVEN THE TEAM AQUA AND TEAM MAGMA BOSSES AREN'T ABLE TO CONTROL THE LEGENDARIES.
AND THAT'S NOT ALL! THEY SAY OUR ONLY HOPE LIES IN "TWO NEW TRAINERS" WHO WERE CHOSEN BY THE ORBS.
AND GUESS WHO THOSE TWO ARE?
BIRCH'S DAUGHTER, SAPPHIRE...
...AND YOUR SON, RUBY!
BUT THEY'RE UP AGAINST A FORMIDABLE FOE! I DON'T THINK THINGS ARE GONNA GO DOWN ACCORDING TO PLAN.
WHAT I'M TRYING TO SAY IS... GET MOVING, NORMAN!
HURRY UP AND AWAKEN ...
...THE **THIRD ANCIENT** POKÉMON!
LATER!

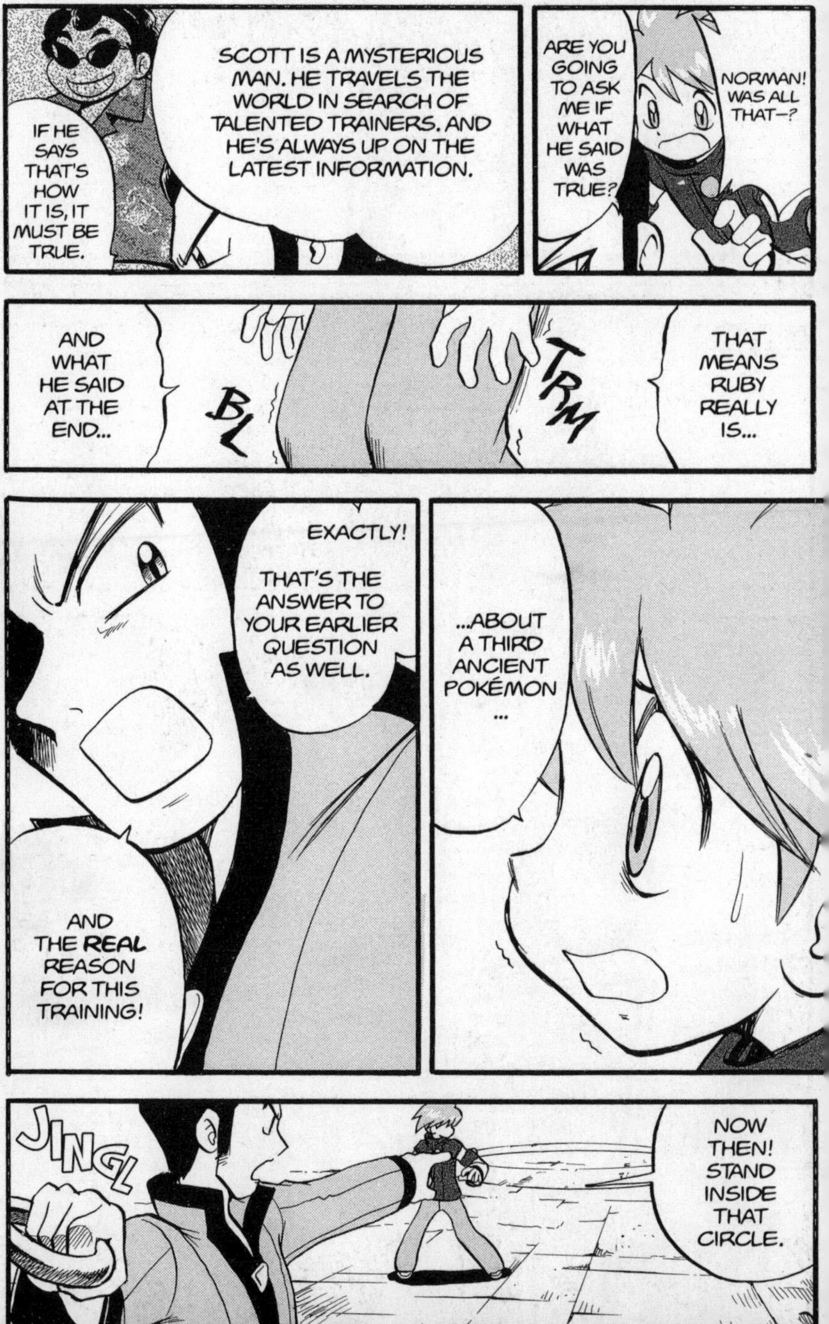
NORMAN! WAS ALL THAT—?
ARE YOU GOING TO ASK ME IF WHAT HE SAID WAS TRUE?
SCOTT IS A MYSTERIOUS MAN. HE TRAVELS THE WORLD IN SEARCH OF TALENTED TRAINERS. AND HE'S ALWAYS UP ON THE LATEST INFORMATION.
IF HE SAYS THAT'S HOW IT IS, IT MUST BE TRUE.
THAT MEANS RUBY REALLY IS...
TRM
BL
AND WHAT HE SAID AT THE END...
...ABOUT A THIRD ANCIENT POKÉMON ...
EXACTLY!
THAT'S THE ANSWER TO YOUR EARLIER QUESTION AS WELL.
AND THE **REAL** REASON FOR THIS TRAINING!
NOW THEN! STAND INSIDE THAT CIRCLE.
JINGL

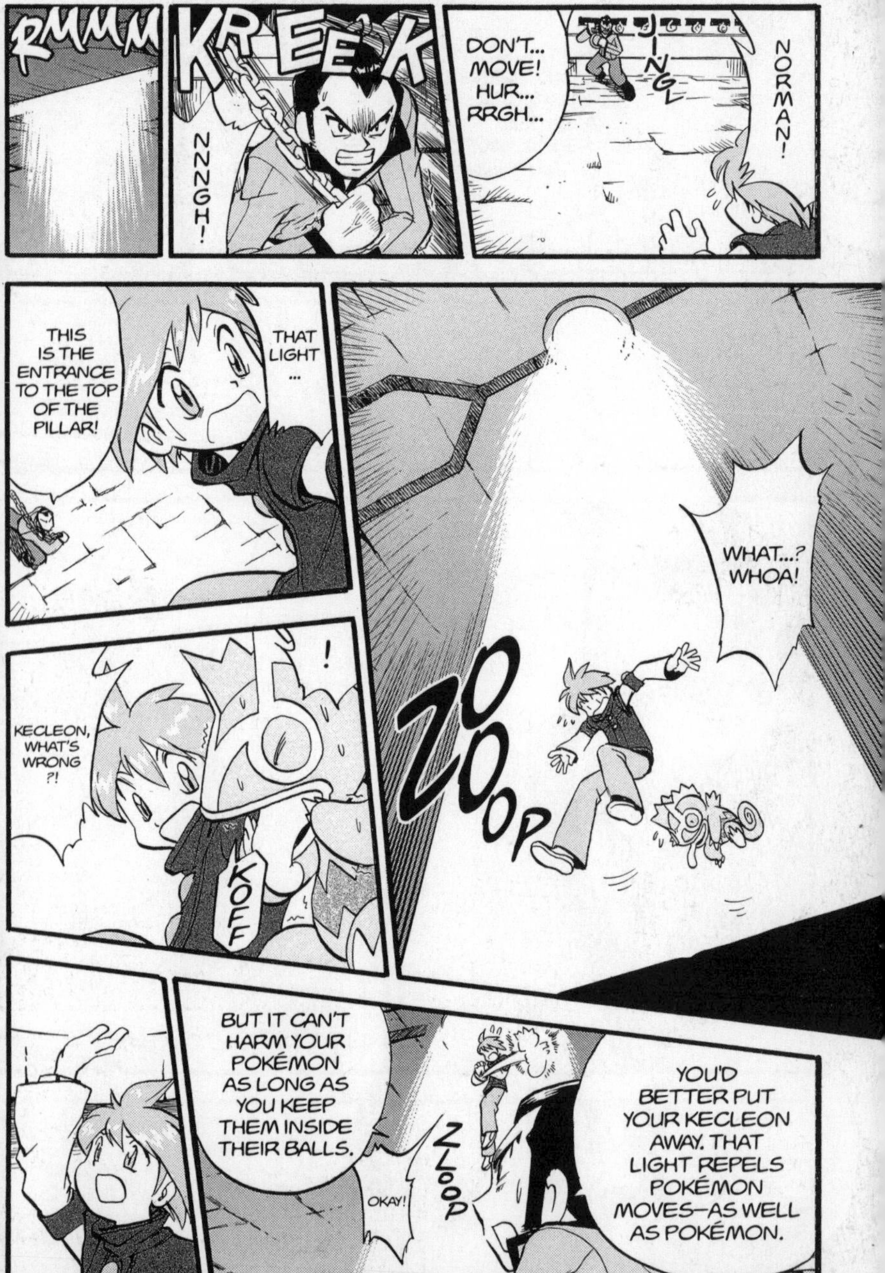
NORMAN!
JINGL
DON'T... MOVE! HUR... RRGH...
KREEEK
NNNGH!
RMMM
WHAT...? WHOA!
ZOOOP
THAT LIGHT ...
THIS IS THE ENTRANCE TO THE TOP OF THE PILLAR!
!
KECLEON, WHAT'S WRONG ?!
KOFF
YOU'D BETTER PUT YOUR KECLEON AWAY. THAT LIGHT REPELS POKÉMON MOVES—AS WELL AS POKÉMON.
BUT IT CAN'T HARM YOUR POKÉMON AS LONG AS YOU KEEP THEM INSIDE THEIR BALLS.
ZLOOP
OKAY!

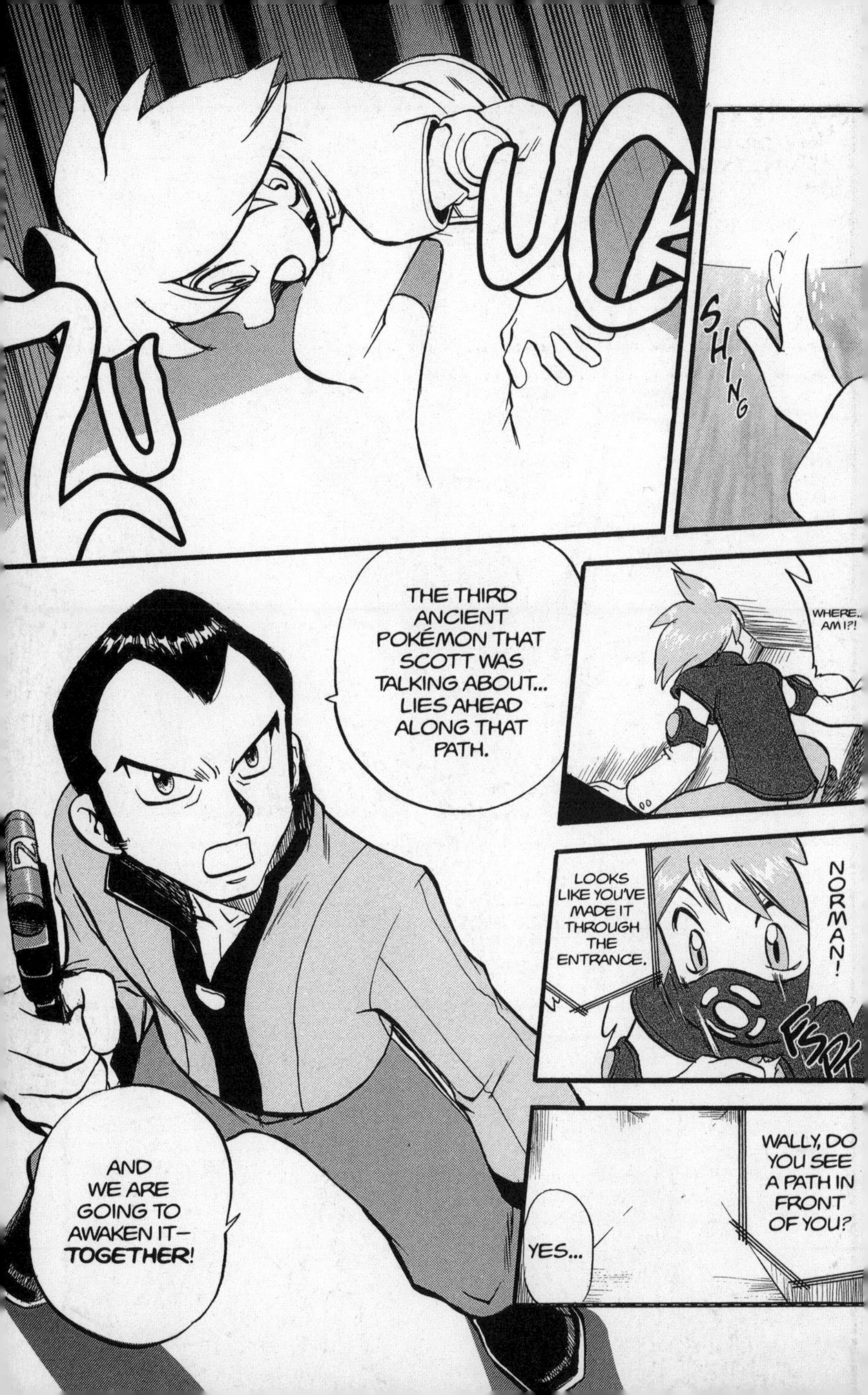
SHING
ZU
UCK
WHERE... AM I?!
NORMAN!
LOOKS LIKE YOU'VE MADE IT THROUGH THE ENTRANCE.
FSPK
WALLY, DO YOU SEE A PATH IN FRONT OF YOU?
YES...
THE THIRD ANCIENT POKÉMON THAT SCOTT WAS TALKING ABOUT... LIES AHEAD ALONG THAT PATH.
AND WE ARE GOING TO AWAKEN IT— **TOGETHER!**

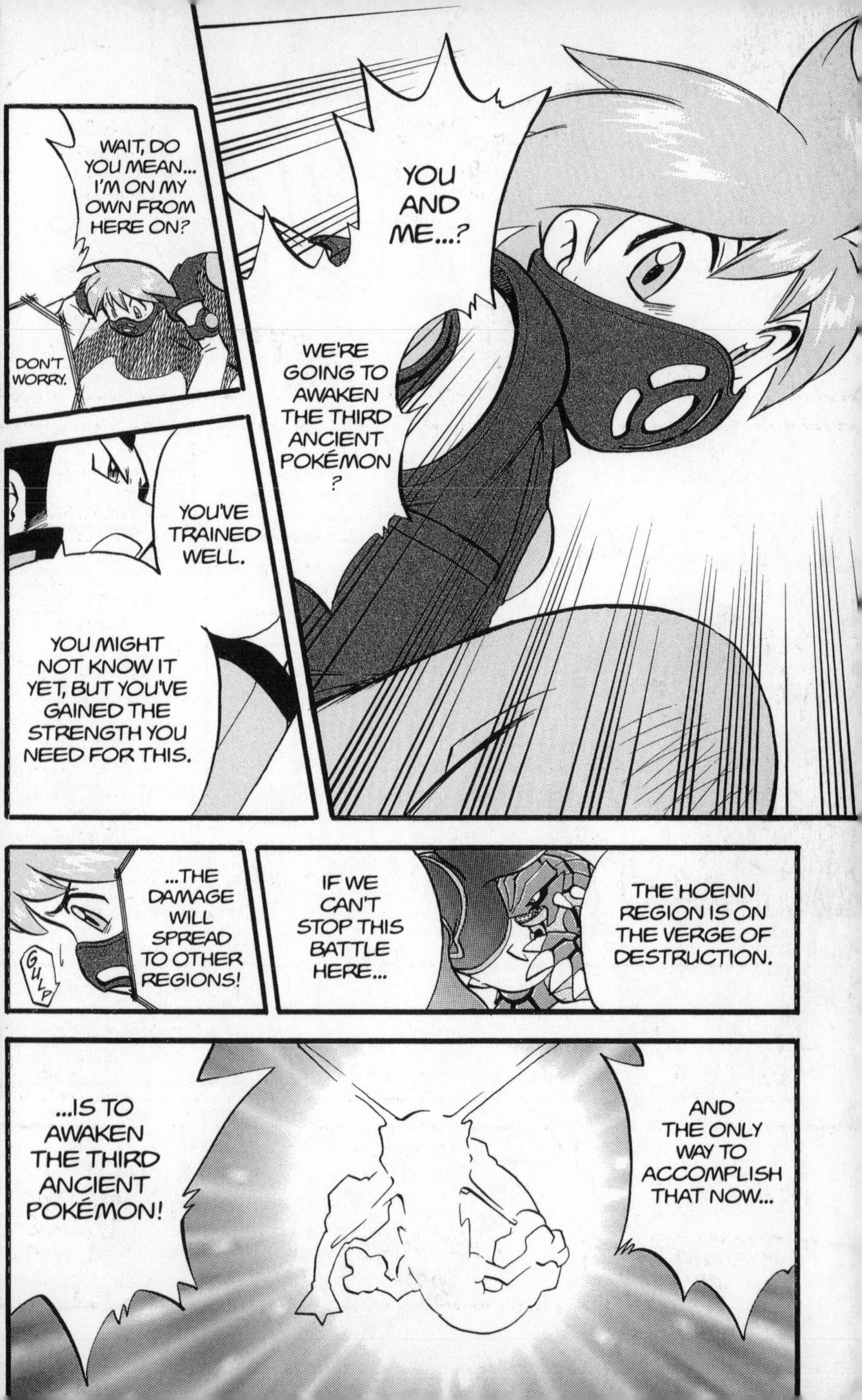
YOU AND ME...?
WE'RE GOING TO AWAKEN THE THIRD ANCIENT POKÉMON?
WAIT, DO YOU MEAN... I'M ON MY OWN FROM HERE ON?
DON'T WORRY.
YOU'VE TRAINED WELL.
YOU MIGHT NOT KNOW IT YET, BUT YOU'VE GAINED THE STRENGTH YOU NEED FOR THIS.
THE HOENN REGION IS ON THE VERGE OF DESTRUCTION.
IF WE CAN'T STOP THIS BATTLE HERE...
...THE DAMAGE WILL SPREAD TO OTHER REGIONS!
GULP
AND THE ONLY WAY TO ACCOMPLISH THAT NOW...
...IS TO AWAKEN THE THIRD ANCIENT POKÉMON!

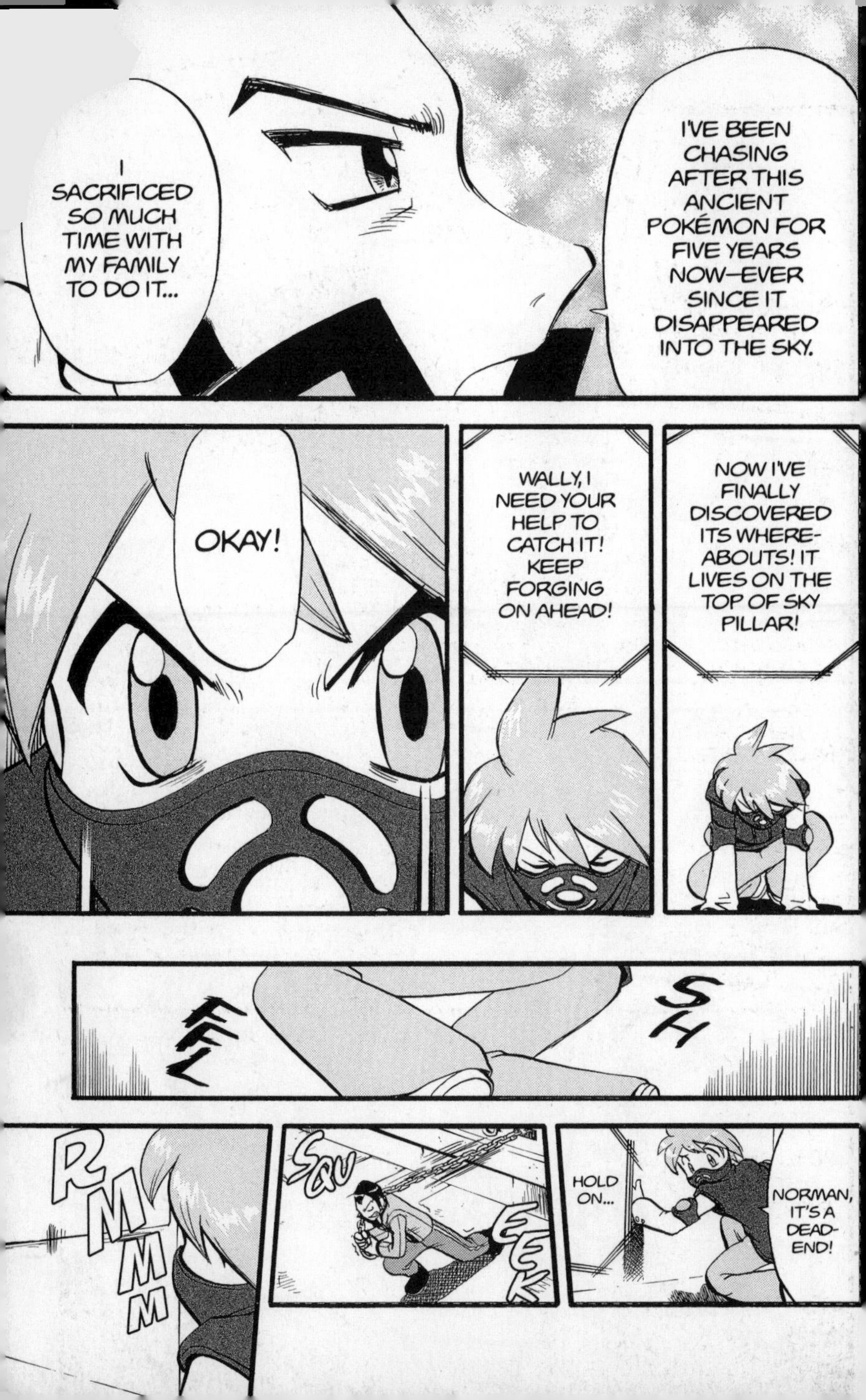
I'VE BEEN CHASING AFTER THIS ANCIENT POKÉMON FOR FIVE YEARS NOW—EVER SINCE IT DISAPPEARED INTO THE SKY.
I SACRIFICED SO MUCH TIME WITH MY FAMILY TO DO IT...
NOW I'VE FINALLY DISCOVERED ITS WHERE-ABOUTS! IT LIVES ON THE TOP OF SKY PILLAR!
WALLY, I NEED YOUR HELP TO CATCH IT! KEEP FORGING ON AHEAD!
OKAY!
SH
FFL
NORMAN, IT'S A DEAD-END!
HOLD ON...
SQU
EEK
RMMMM

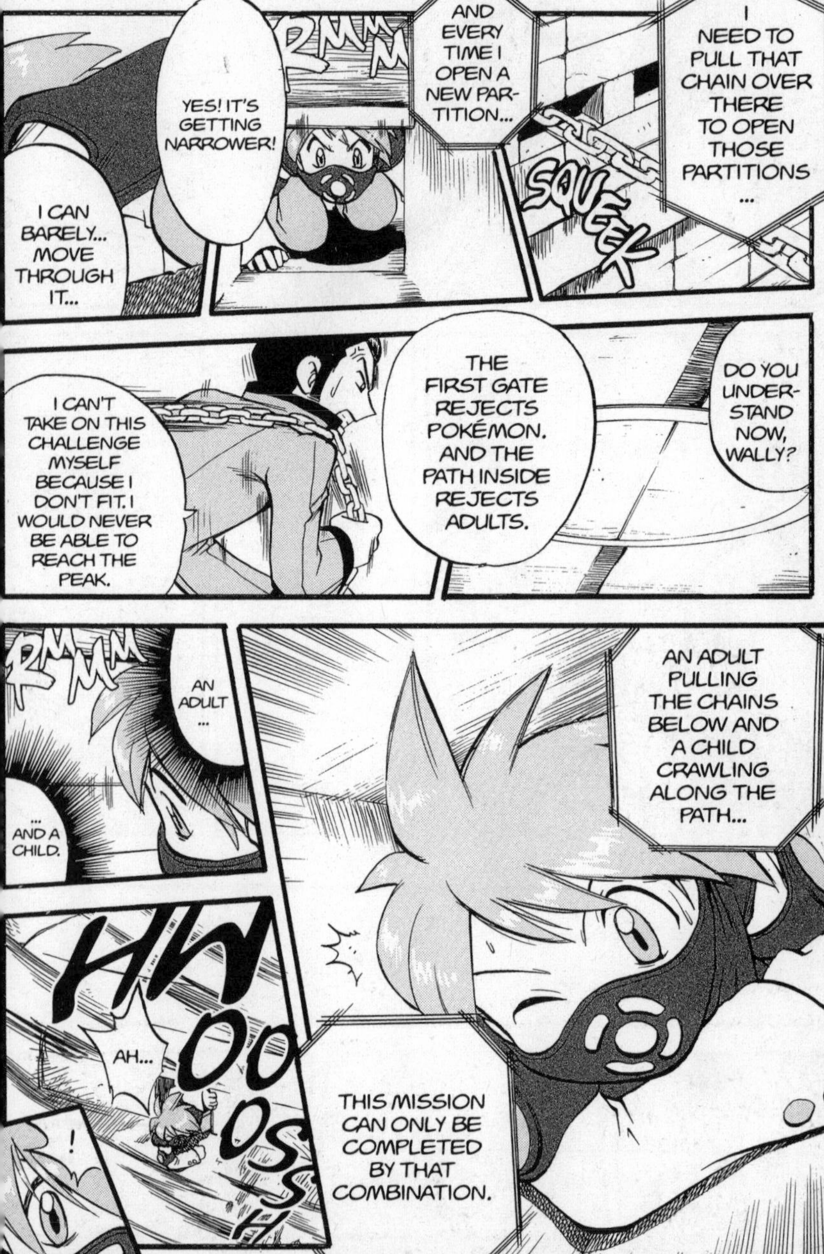
I NEED TO PULL THAT CHAIN OVER THERE TO OPEN THOSE PARTITIONS ...
SQUEEK
AND EVERY TIME I OPEN A NEW PARTITION...
RMMM
YES! IT'S GETTING NARROWER!
I CAN BARELY... MOVE THROUGH IT...
DO YOU UNDERSTAND NOW, WALLY?
THE FIRST GATE REJECTS POKÉMON. AND THE PATH INSIDE REJECTS ADULTS.
I CAN'T TAKE ON THIS CHALLENGE MYSELF BECAUSE I DON'T FIT. I WOULD NEVER BE ABLE TO REACH THE PEAK.
AN ADULT PULLING THE CHAINS BELOW AND A CHILD CRAWLING ALONG THE PATH...
THIS MISSION CAN ONLY BE COMPLETED BY THAT COMBINATION.
RMMM
AN ADULT ...
... AND A CHILD.
HWOOSH
AH...
!

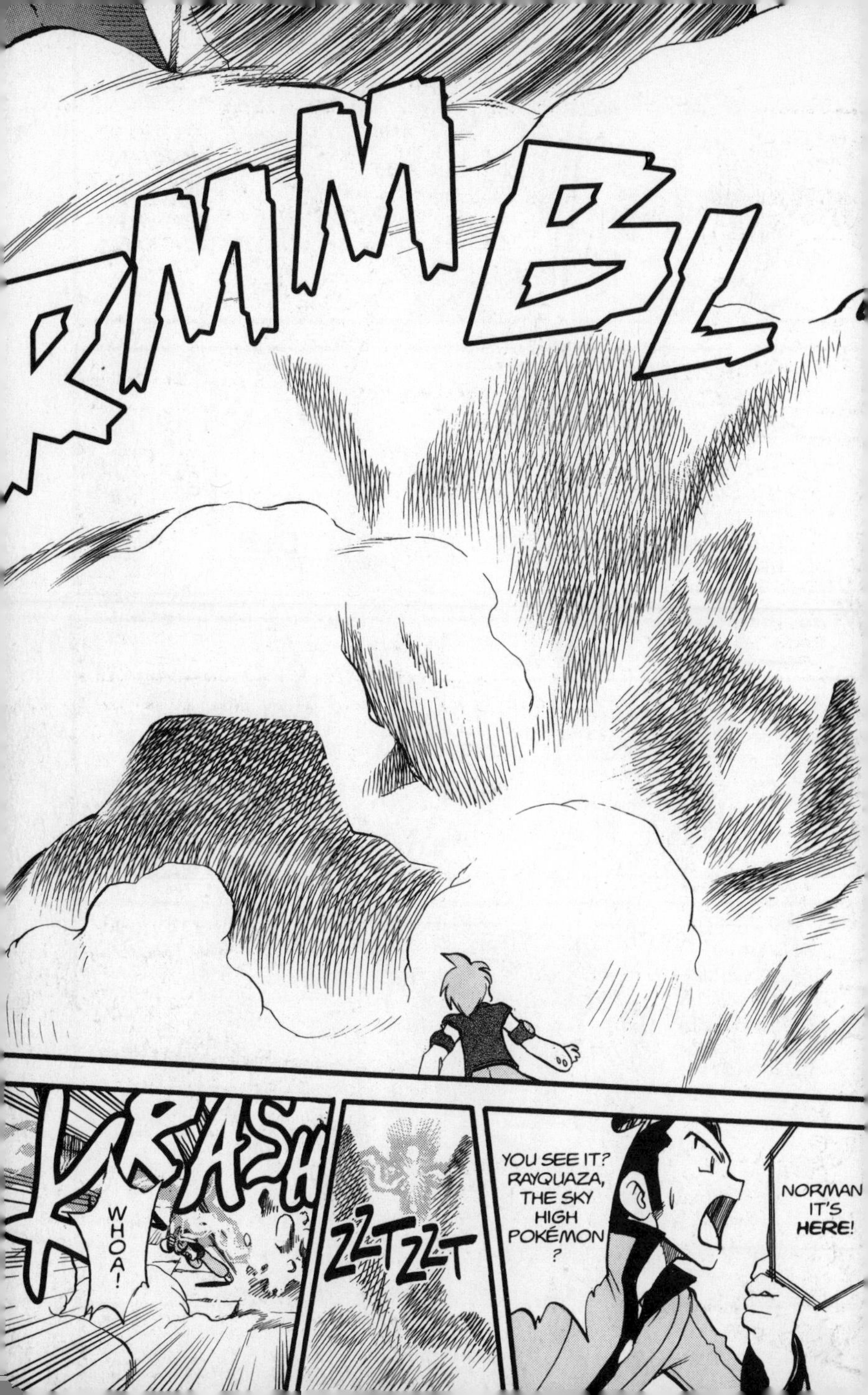
RMMBL
NORMAN IT'S HERE!
YOU SEE IT? RAYQUAZA, THE SKY HIGH POKÉMON?
ZZTZZT
KRASH
WHOA!

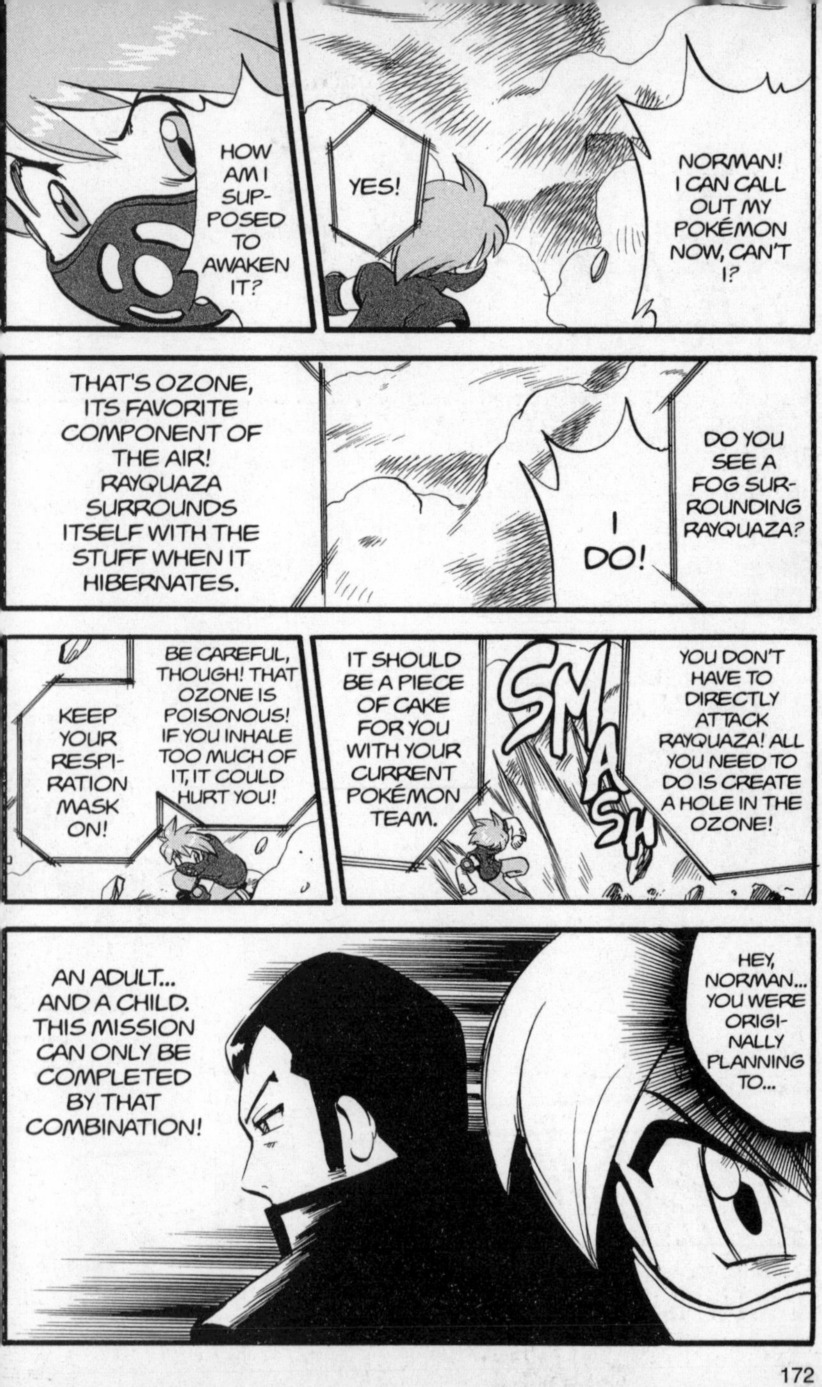
NORMAN! I CAN CALL OUT MY POKÉMON NOW, CAN'T I?
YES!
HOW AM I SUP-POSED TO AWAKEN IT?
DO YOU SEE A FOG SUR-ROUNDING RAYQUAZA?
I DO!
THAT'S OZONE, ITS FAVORITE COMPONENT OF THE AIR! RAYQUAZA SURROUNDS ITSELF WITH THE STUFF WHEN IT HIBERNATES.
YOU DON'T HAVE TO DIRECTLY ATTACK RAYQUAZA! ALL YOU NEED TO DO IS CREATE A HOLE IN THE OZONE!
SMASH
IT SHOULD BE A PIECE OF CAKE FOR YOU WITH YOUR CURRENT POKÉMON TEAM.
BE CAREFUL, THOUGH! THAT OZONE IS POISONOUS! IF YOU INHALE TOO MUCH OF IT, IT COULD HURT YOU!
KEEP YOUR RESPI-RATION MASK ON!
HEY, NORMAN... YOU WERE ORIGI-NALLY PLANNING TO...
AN ADULT... AND A CHILD. THIS MISSION CAN ONLY BE COMPLETED BY THAT COMBINATION!

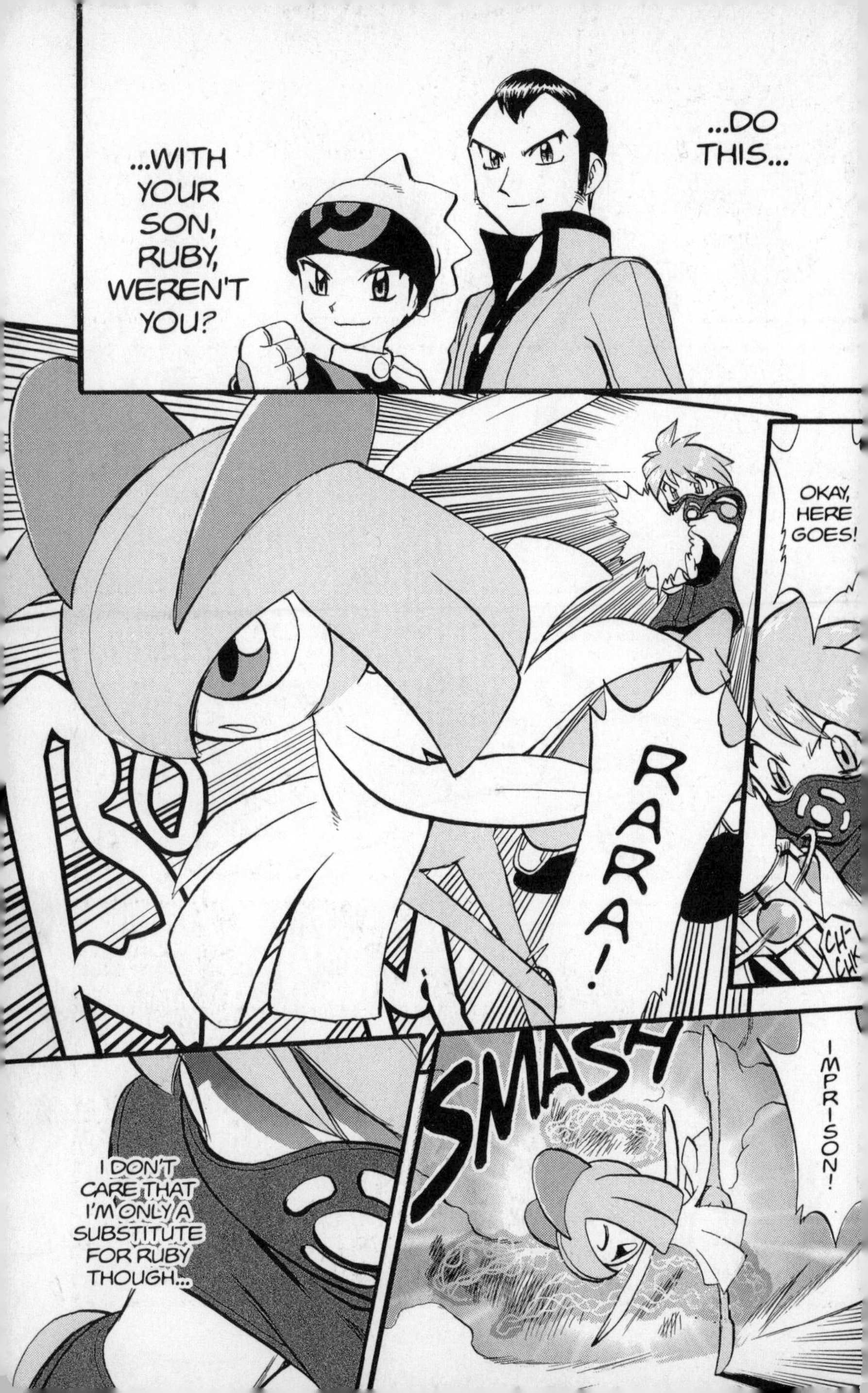
...DO THIS...
...WITH YOUR SON, RUBY, WEREN'T YOU?
OKAY, HERE GOES!
CH-CHK
RARA!
IMPRISON!
SMASH
I DON'T CARE THAT I'M ONLY A SUBSTITUTE FOR RUBY THOUGH...

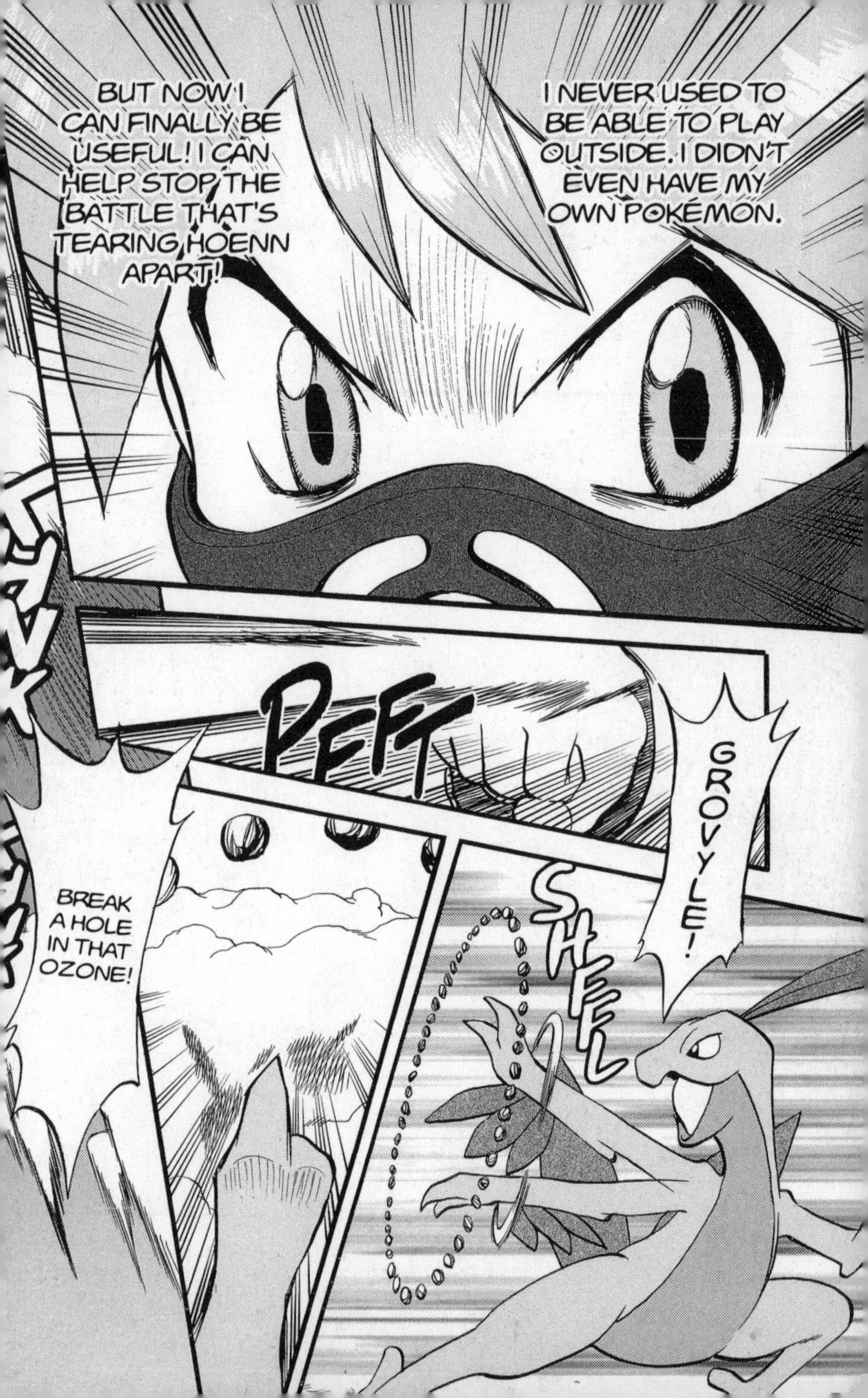
I NEVER USED TO BE ABLE TO PLAY OUTSIDE. I DIDN'T EVEN HAVE MY OWN POKÉMON.
BUT NOW I CAN FINALLY BE USEFUL! I CAN HELP STOP THE BATTLE THAT'S TEARING HOENN APART!
PFFT
GROVYLE!
SHFFL
BREAK A HOLE IN THAT OZONE!

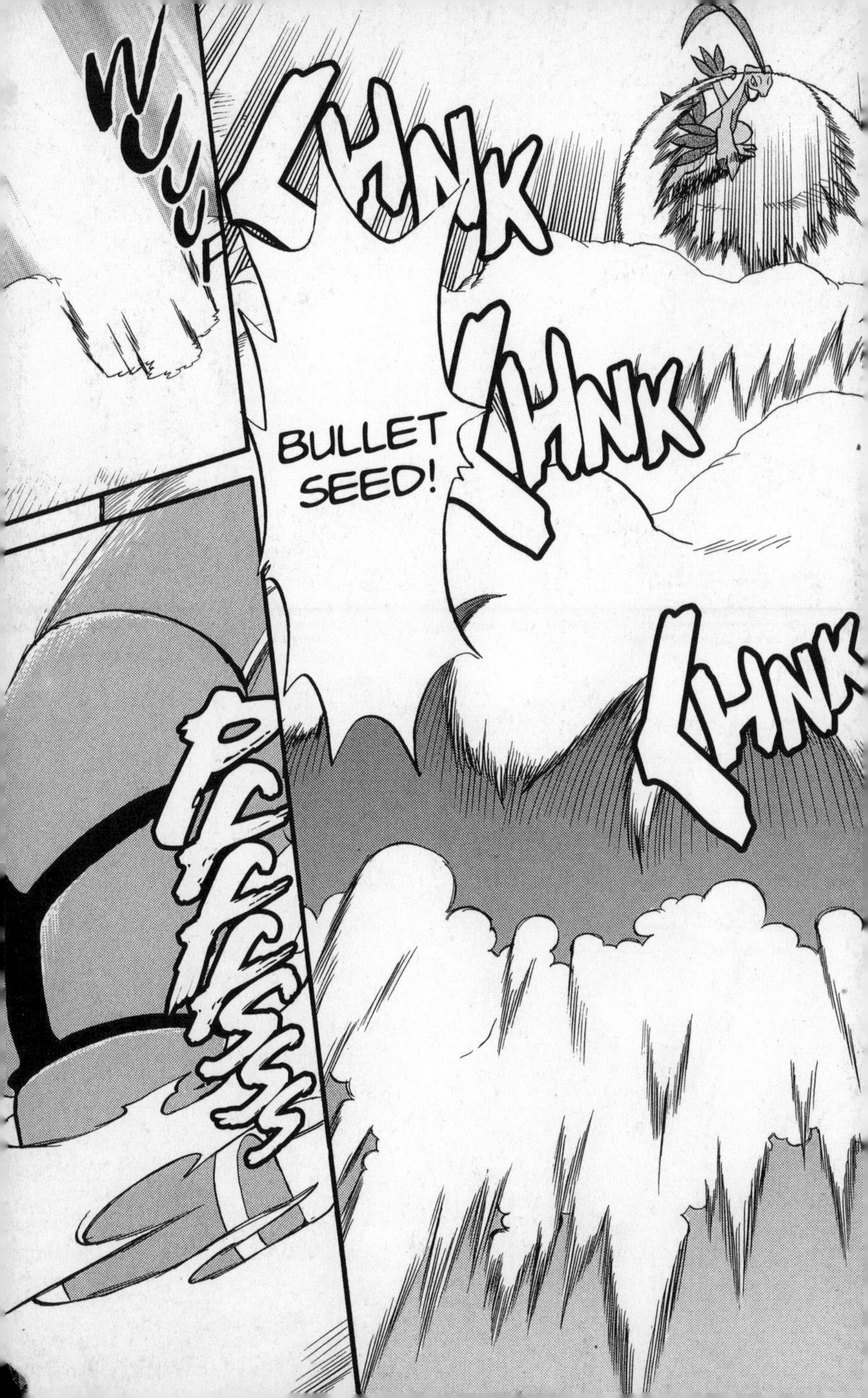
BULLET SEED!

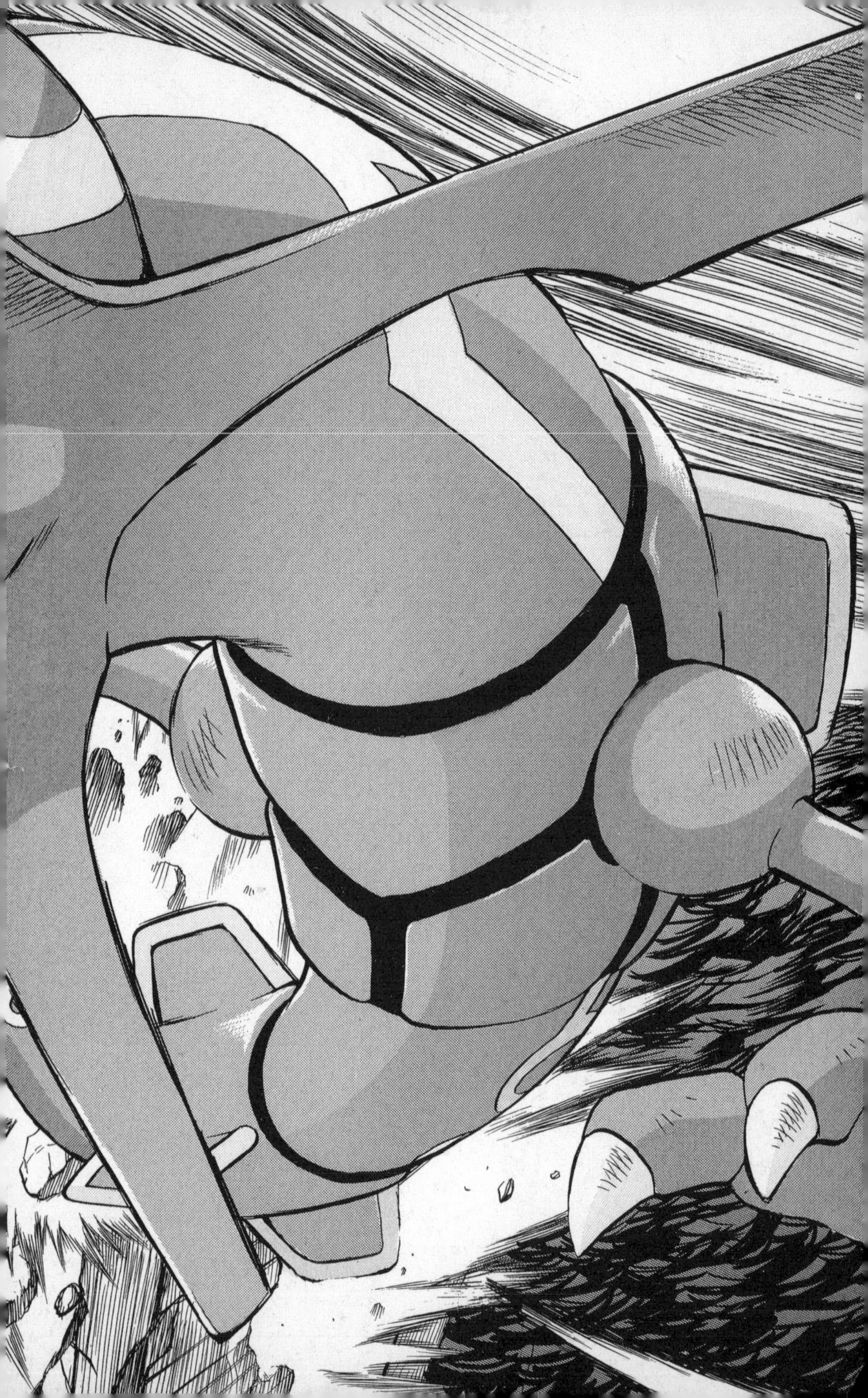

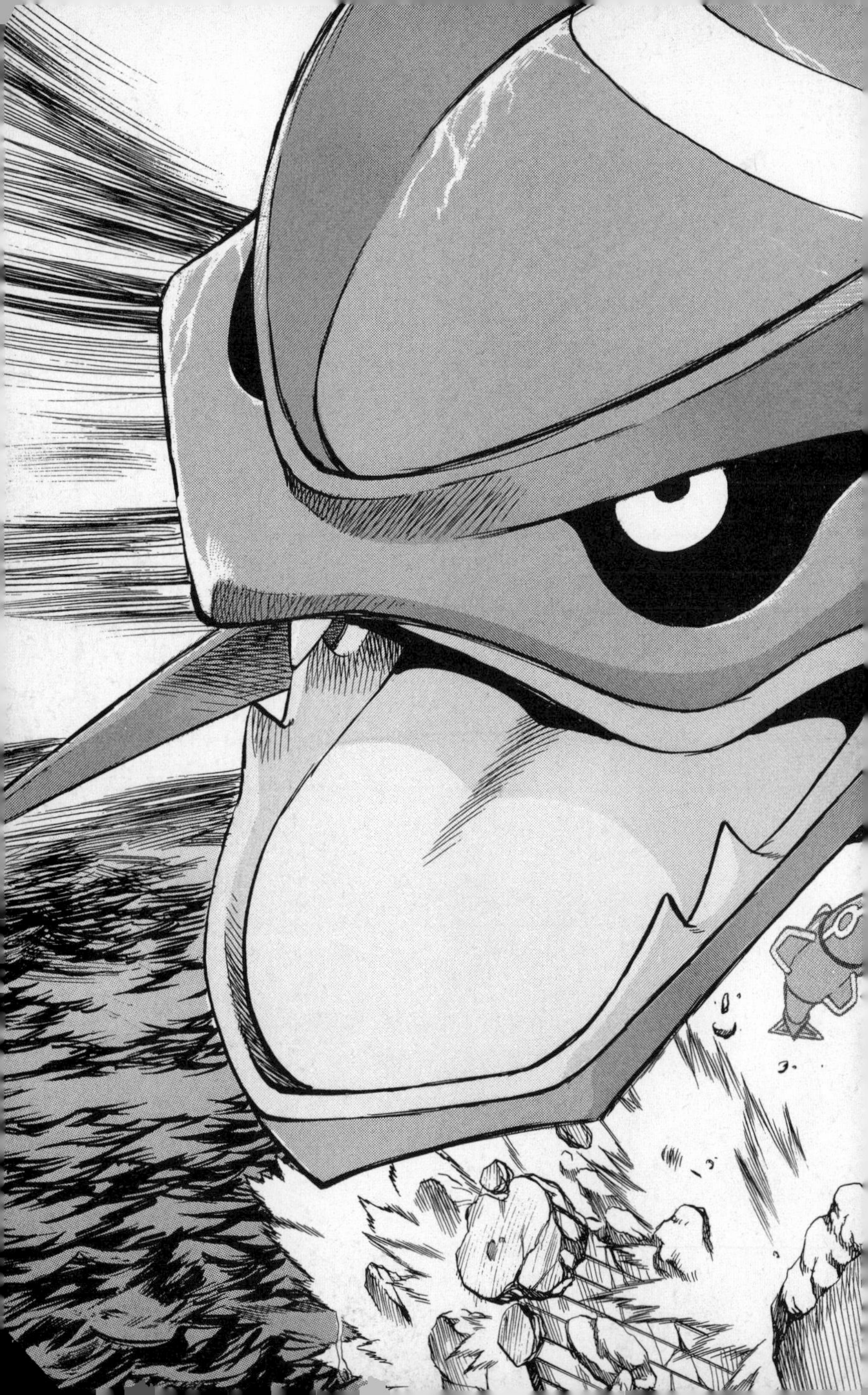

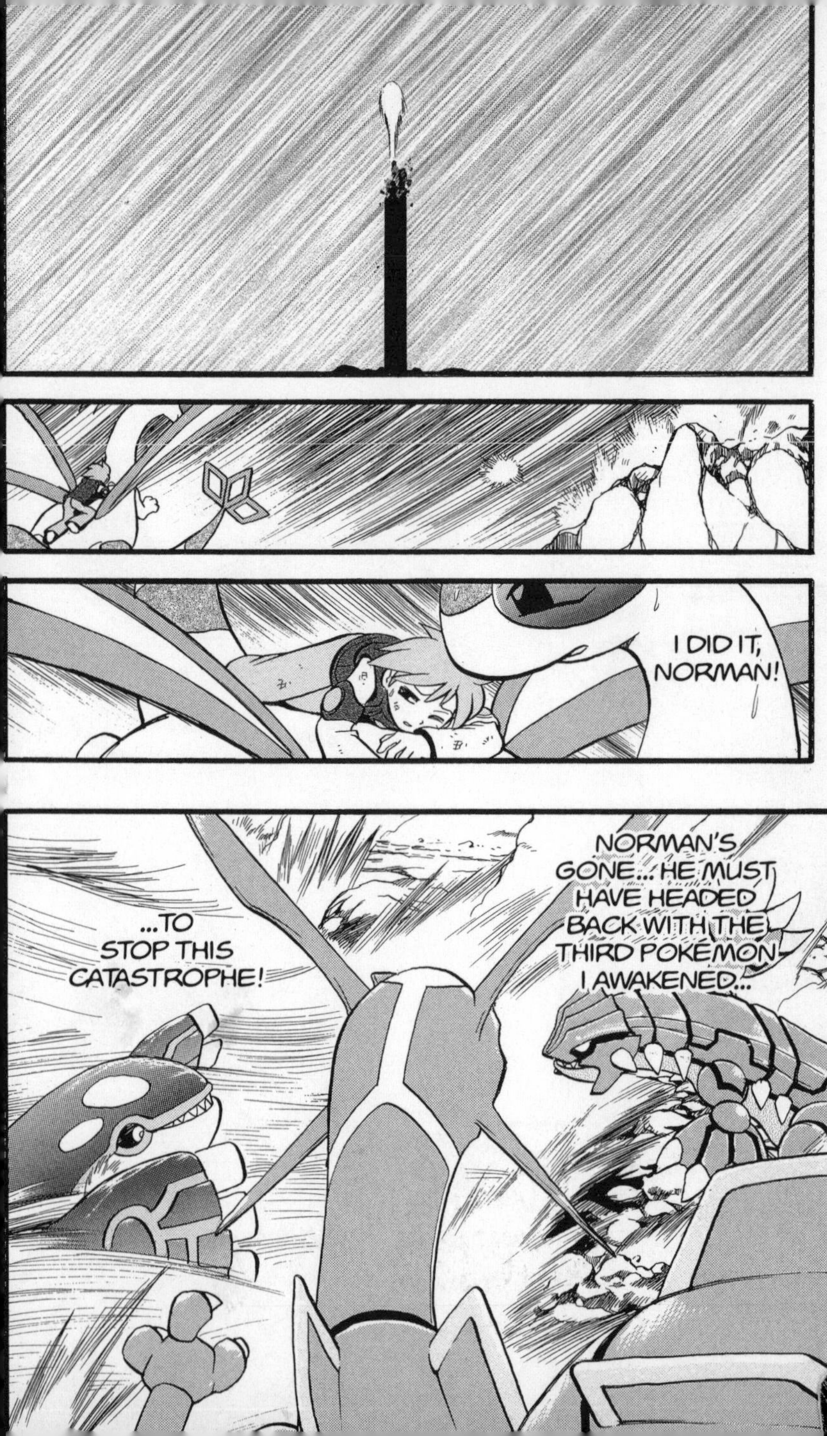
I DID IT, NORMAN!
NORMAN'S GONE... HE MUST HAVE HEADED BACK WITH THE THIRD POKÉMON I AWAKENED...
...TO STOP THIS CATASTROPHE!

# ● Chapter 259 ●
# Rayquaza Redemption II

Pokémon™ Adventures
Ruby & Sapphire
The Fourth Chapter

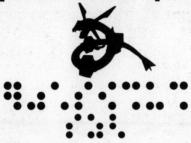

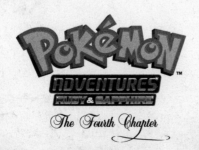

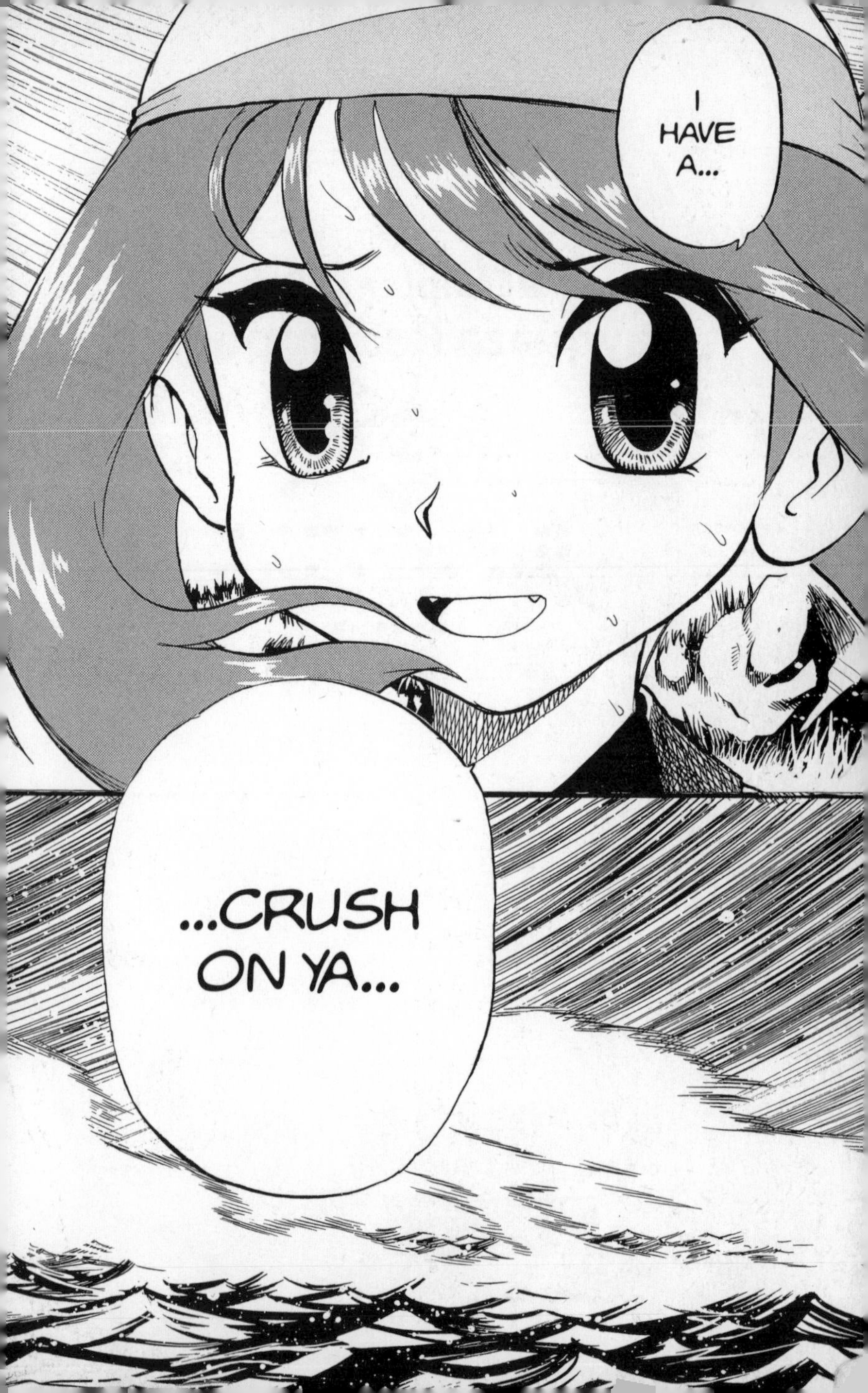
I HAVE A...
...CRUSH ON YA...

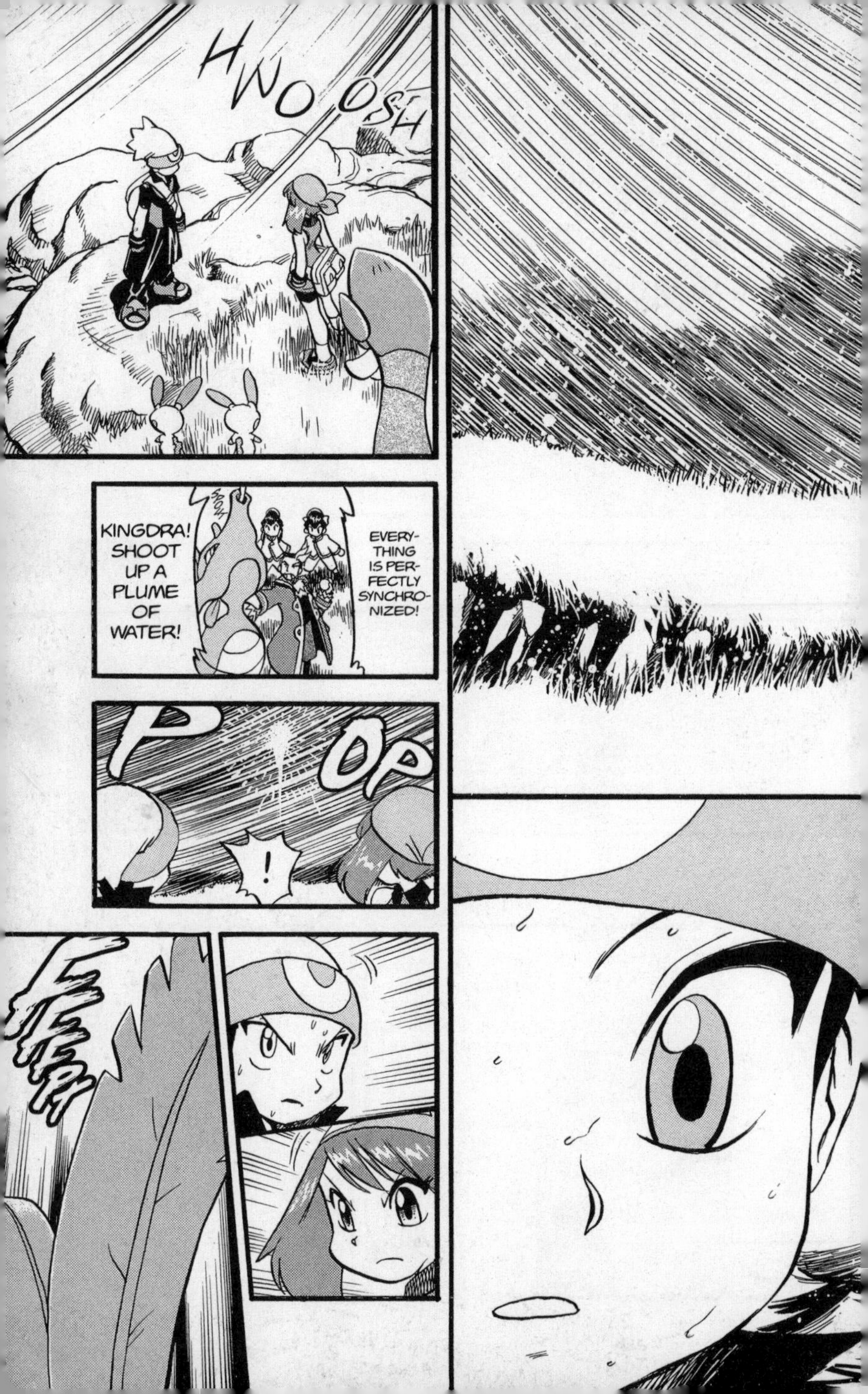
HWOOSH
EVERY-THING IS PER-FECTLY SYNCHRO-NIZED!
KINGDRA! SHOOT UP A PLUME OF WATER!
POP
!

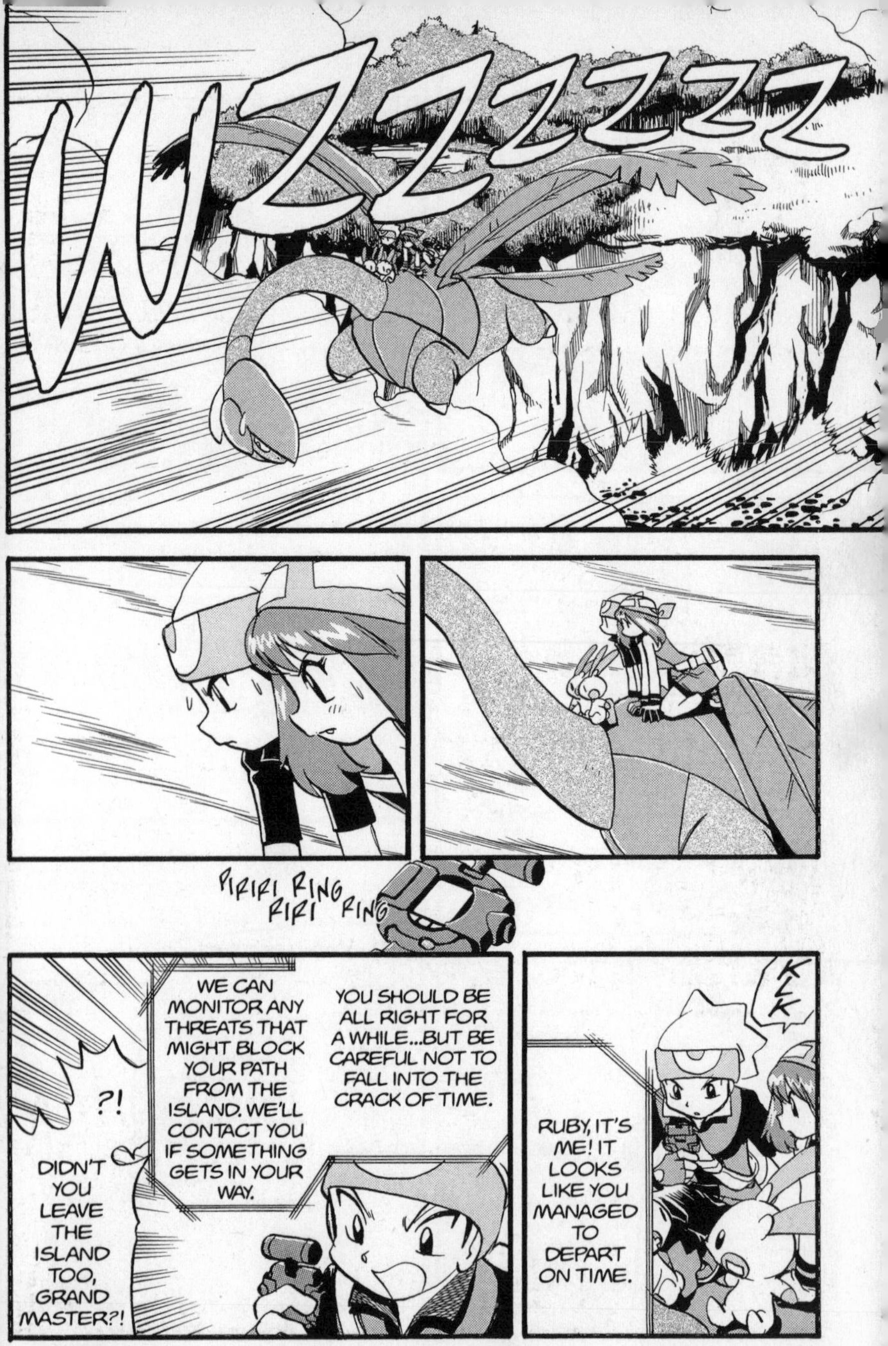
WZZZZZZZ
PIRIRI RING RIRI RING
KLK
RUBY, IT'S ME! IT LOOKS LIKE YOU MANAGED TO DEPART ON TIME.
YOU SHOULD BE ALL RIGHT FOR A WHILE...BUT BE CAREFUL NOT TO FALL INTO THE CRACK OF TIME.
WE CAN MONITOR ANY THREATS THAT MIGHT BLOCK YOUR PATH FROM THE ISLAND. WE'LL CONTACT YOU IF SOMETHING GETS IN YOUR WAY.
?!
DIDN'T YOU LEAVE THE ISLAND TOO, GRAND MASTER?!

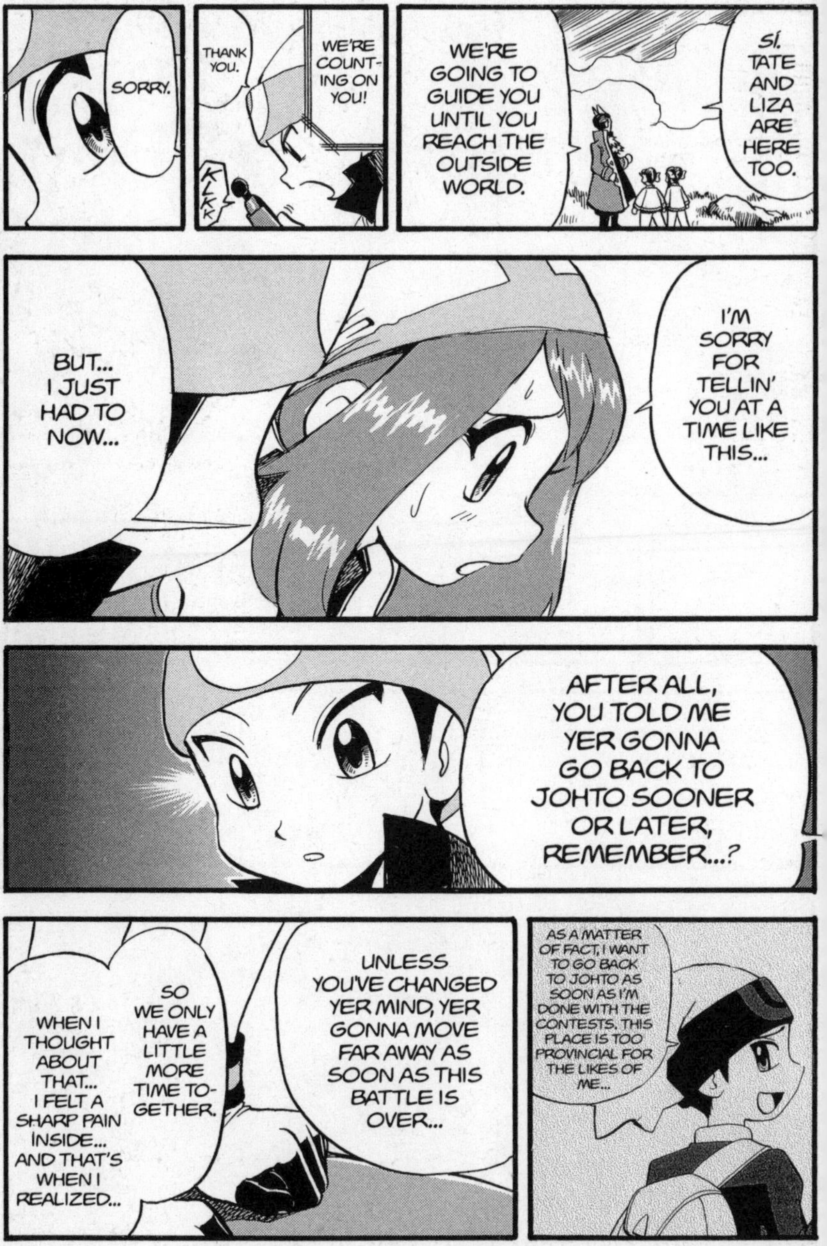
SÍ. TATE AND LIZA ARE HERE TOO.
WE'RE GOING TO GUIDE YOU UNTIL YOU REACH THE OUTSIDE WORLD.
WE'RE COUNTING ON YOU!
THANK YOU.
KLKK
SORRY.
I'M SORRY FOR TELLIN' YOU AT A TIME LIKE THIS...
BUT... I JUST HAD TO NOW...
AFTER ALL, YOU TOLD ME YER GONNA GO BACK TO JOHTO SOONER OR LATER, REMEMBER...?
AS A MATTER OF FACT, I WANT TO GO BACK TO JOHTO AS SOON AS I'M DONE WITH THE CONTESTS. THIS PLACE IS TOO PROVINCIAL FOR THE LIKES OF ME...
UNLESS YOU'VE CHANGED YER MIND, YER GONNA MOVE FAR AWAY AS SOON AS THIS BATTLE IS OVER...
SO WE ONLY HAVE A LITTLE MORE TIME TO-GETHER.
WHEN I THOUGHT ABOUT THAT... I FELT A SHARP PAIN INSIDE... AND THAT'S WHEN I REALIZED...

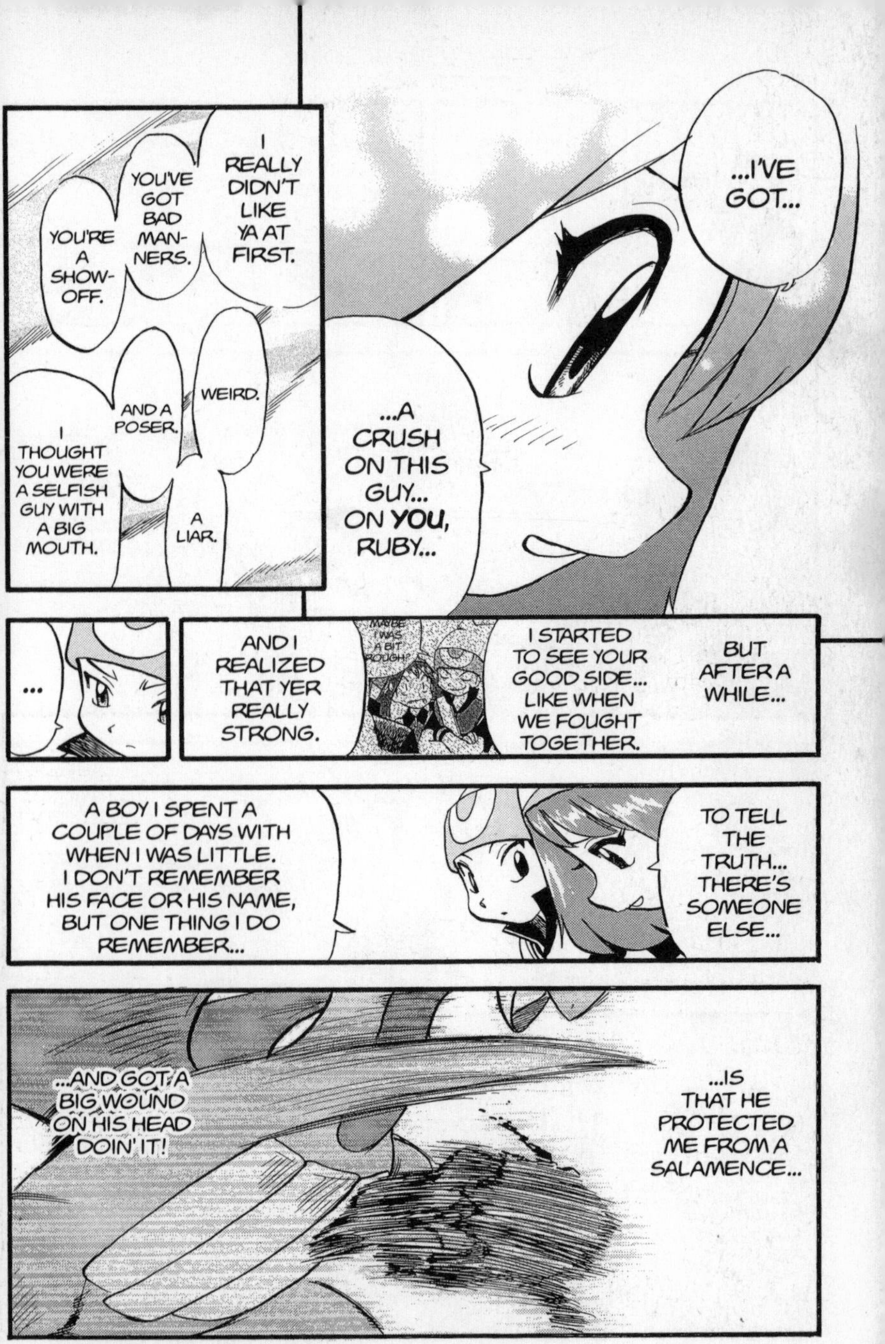
...I'VE GOT...
...A CRUSH ON THIS GUY... ON **YOU**, RUBY...
I REALLY DIDN'T LIKE YA AT FIRST.
YOU'VE GOT BAD MAN-NERS.
YOU'RE A SHOW-OFF.
WEIRD.
AND A POSER.
A LIAR.
I THOUGHT YOU WERE A SELFISH GUY WITH A BIG MOUTH.
BUT AFTER A WHILE...
I STARTED TO SEE YOUR GOOD SIDE... LIKE WHEN WE FOUGHT TOGETHER.
MAYBE I WAS A BIT ROUGH?
AND I REALIZED THAT YER REALLY STRONG.
...
TO TELL THE TRUTH... THERE'S SOMEONE ELSE...
A BOY I SPENT A COUPLE OF DAYS WITH WHEN I WAS LITTLE. I DON'T REMEMBER HIS FACE OR HIS NAME, BUT ONE THING I DO REMEMBER...
...IS THAT HE PROTECTED ME FROM A SALAMENCE...
...AND GOT A BIG WOUND ON HIS HEAD DOIN' IT!

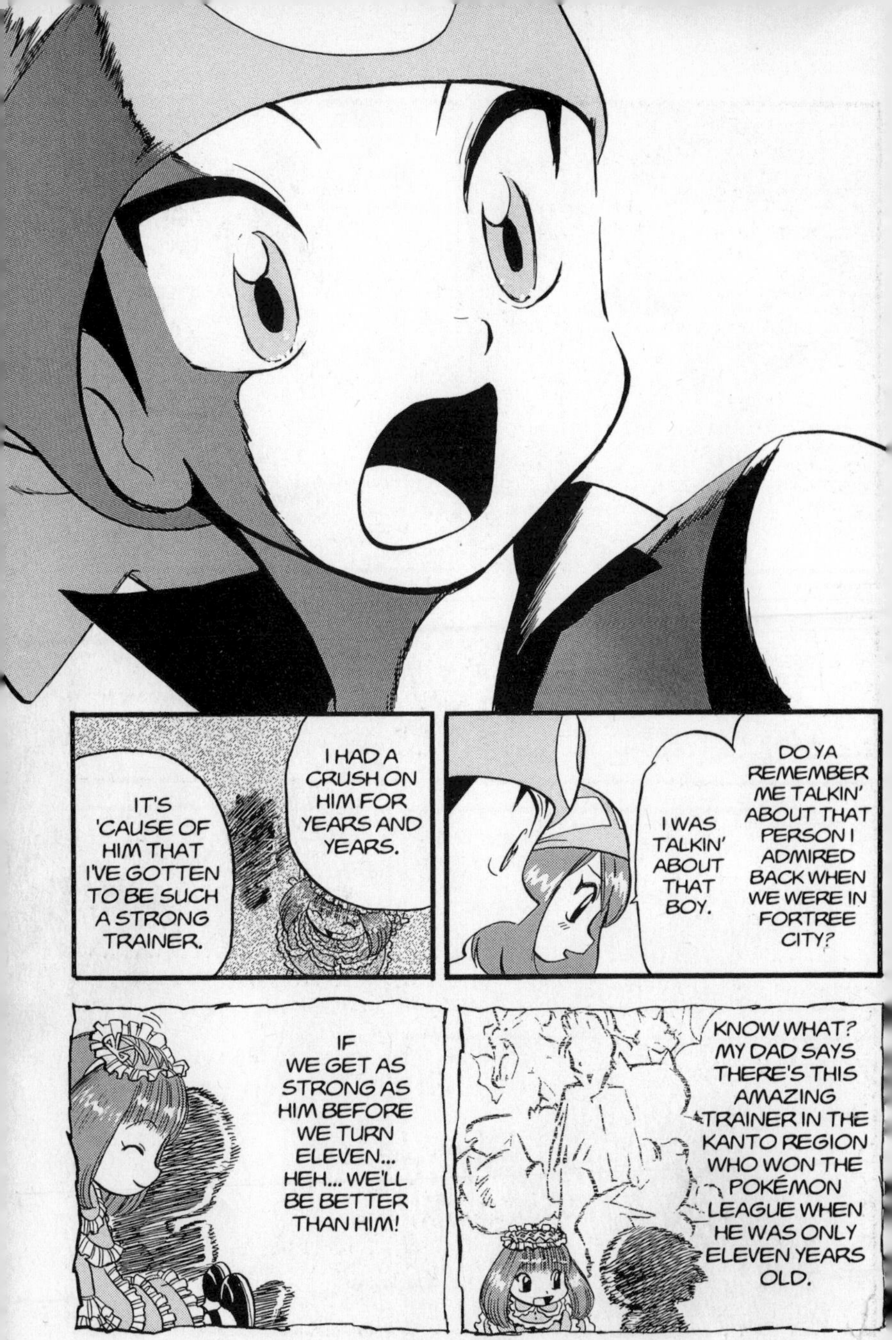
DO YA REMEMBER ME TALKIN' ABOUT THAT PERSON I ADMIRED BACK WHEN WE WERE IN FORTREE CITY?
I WAS TALKIN' ABOUT THAT BOY.
I HAD A CRUSH ON HIM FOR YEARS AND YEARS.
IT'S 'CAUSE OF HIM THAT I'VE GOTTEN TO BE SUCH A STRONG TRAINER.
KNOW WHAT? MY DAD SAYS THERE'S THIS AMAZING TRAINER IN THE KANTO REGION WHO WON THE POKÉMON LEAGUE WHEN HE WAS ONLY ELEVEN YEARS OLD.
IF WE GET AS STRONG AS HIM BEFORE WE TURN ELEVEN... HEH... WE'LL BE BETTER THAN HIM!

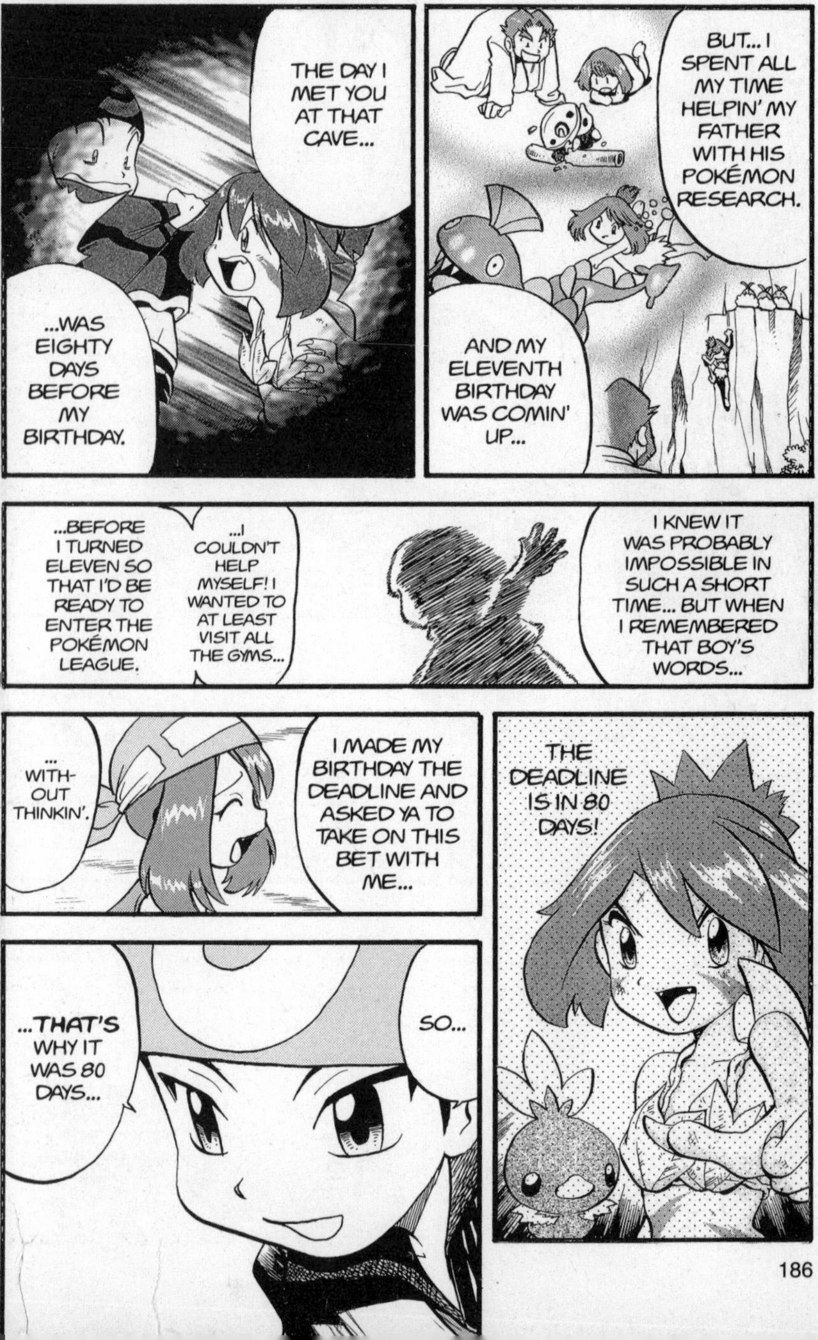
BUT... I SPENT ALL MY TIME HELPIN' MY FATHER WITH HIS POKÉMON RESEARCH.
AND MY ELEVENTH BIRTHDAY WAS COMIN' UP...
THE DAY I MET YOU AT THAT CAVE...
...WAS EIGHTY DAYS BEFORE MY BIRTHDAY.
I KNEW IT WAS PROBABLY IMPOSSIBLE IN SUCH A SHORT TIME... BUT WHEN I REMEMBERED THAT BOY'S WORDS...
...I COULDN'T HELP MYSELF! I WANTED TO AT LEAST VISIT ALL THE GYMS...
...BEFORE I TURNED ELEVEN SO THAT I'D BE READY TO ENTER THE POKÉMON LEAGUE.
THE DEADLINE IS IN 80 DAYS!
I MADE MY BIRTHDAY THE DEADLINE AND ASKED YA TO TAKE ON THIS BET WITH ME...
...WITH-OUT THINKIN'.
SO...
...THAT'S WHY IT WAS 80 DAYS...

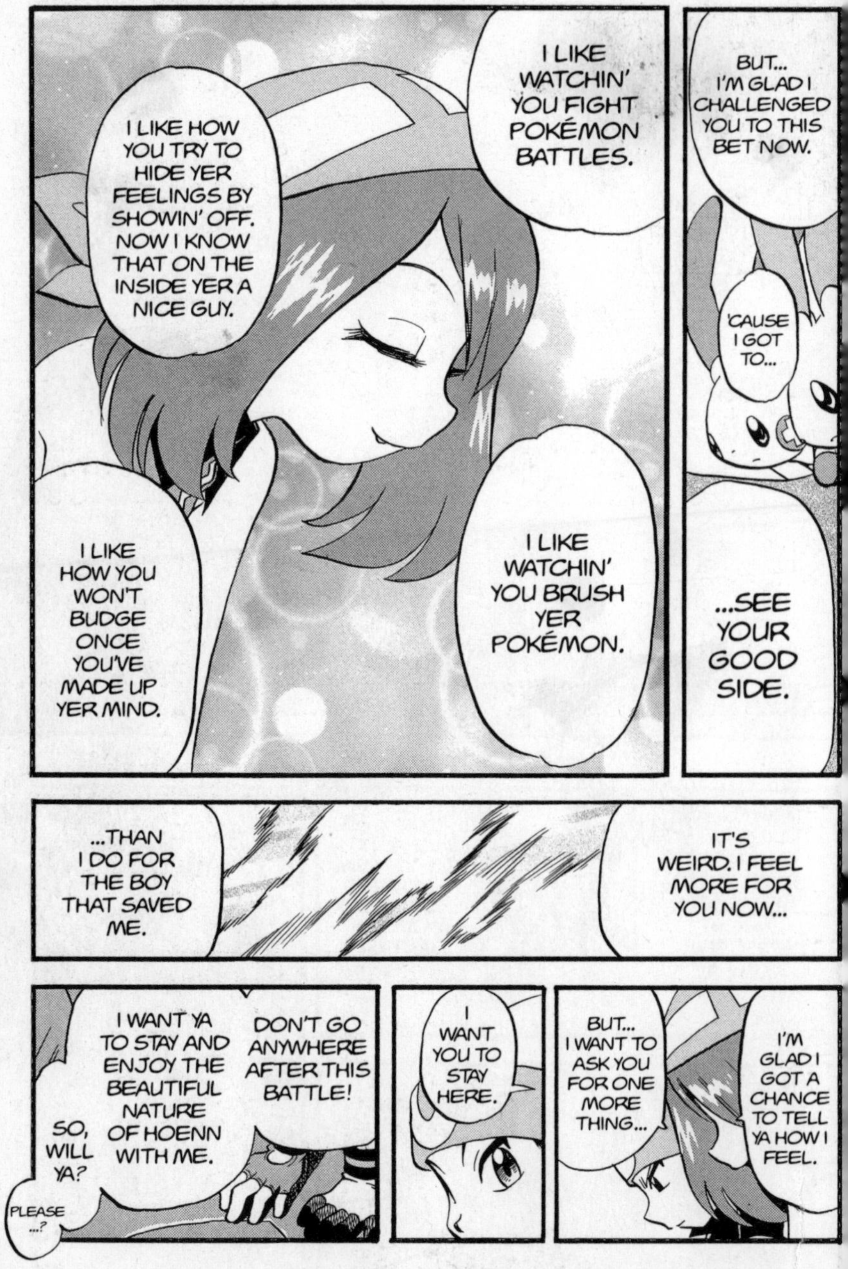
BUT... I'M GLAD I CHALLENGED YOU TO THIS BET NOW.
'CAUSE I GOT TO...
...SEE YOUR GOOD SIDE.
I LIKE WATCHIN' YOU FIGHT POKÉMON BATTLES.
I LIKE HOW YOU TRY TO HIDE YER FEELINGS BY SHOWIN' OFF. NOW I KNOW THAT ON THE INSIDE YER A NICE GUY.
I LIKE WATCHIN' YOU BRUSH YER POKÉMON.
I LIKE HOW YOU WON'T BUDGE ONCE YOU'VE MADE UP YER MIND.
IT'S WEIRD. I FEEL MORE FOR YOU NOW...
...THAN I DO FOR THE BOY THAT SAVED ME.
I'M GLAD I GOT A CHANCE TO TELL YA HOW I FEEL.
BUT... I WANT TO ASK YOU FOR ONE MORE THING...
I WANT YOU TO STAY HERE.
DON'T GO ANYWHERE AFTER THIS BATTLE!
I WANT YA TO STAY AND ENJOY THE BEAUTIFUL NATURE OF HOENN WITH ME.
SO, WILL YA?
PLEASE ...?

LET'S...

...GO BACK TO LITTLEROOT TOWN TOGETHER.

HOW ODD. THE SYNCHRONIZATION OF TIME WITH THE OUTSIDE WORLD IS RATHER UNSTABLE.

RIGHT... TO TELL YOU THE TRUTH, THE SAME THING HAPPENED WHEN I BROUGHT RUBY TO MIRAGE ISLAND.

THAT'S WHY I DECIDED TO STAY BEHIND AND NAVIGATE ...

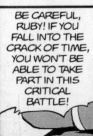

BE CAREFUL, RUBY! IF YOU FALL INTO THE CRACK OF TIME, YOU WON'T BE ABLE TO TAKE PART IN THIS CRITICAL BATTLE!

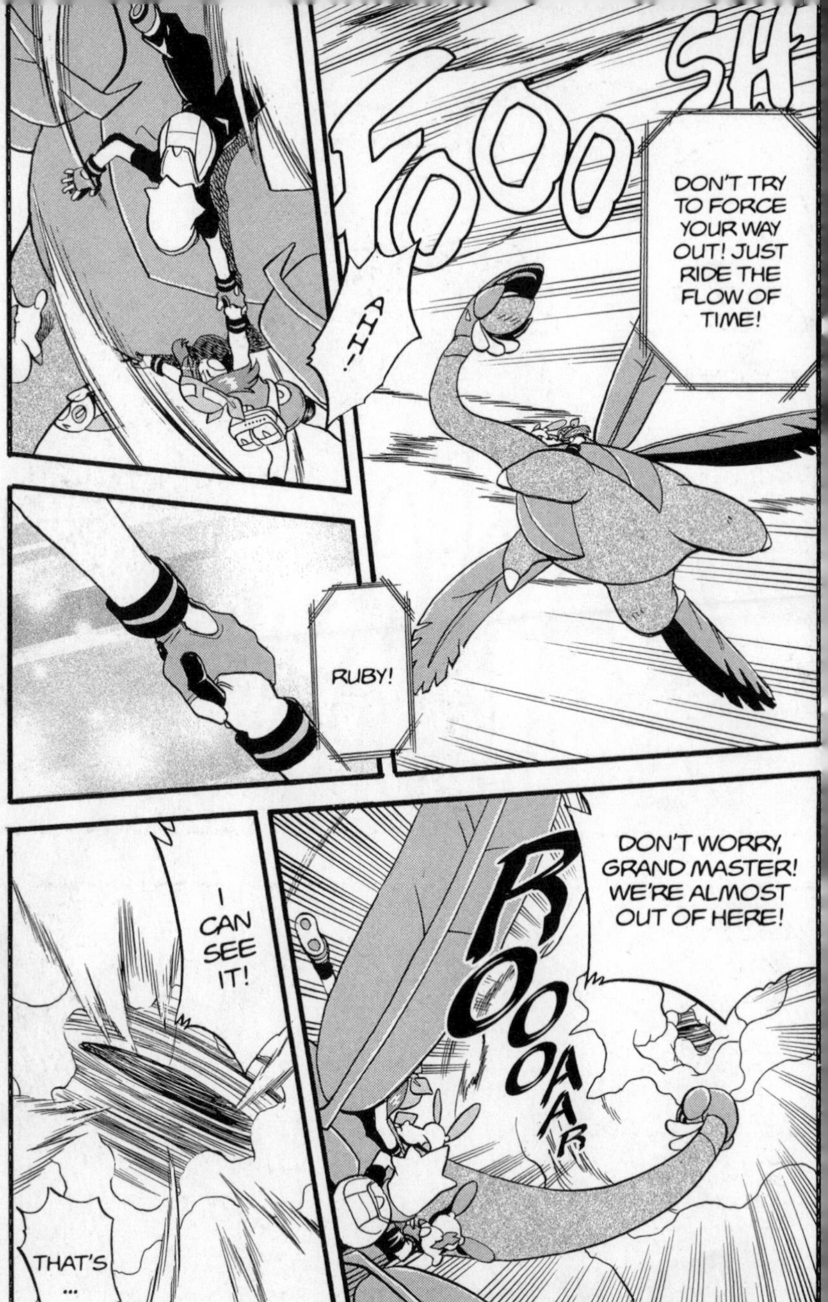
SHOOO
DON'T TRY TO FORCE YOUR WAY OUT! JUST RIDE THE FLOW OF TIME!
AHH!
RUBY!
ROOOAR
DON'T WORRY, GRAND MASTER! WE'RE ALMOST OUT OF HERE!
I CAN SEE IT!
THAT'S ...

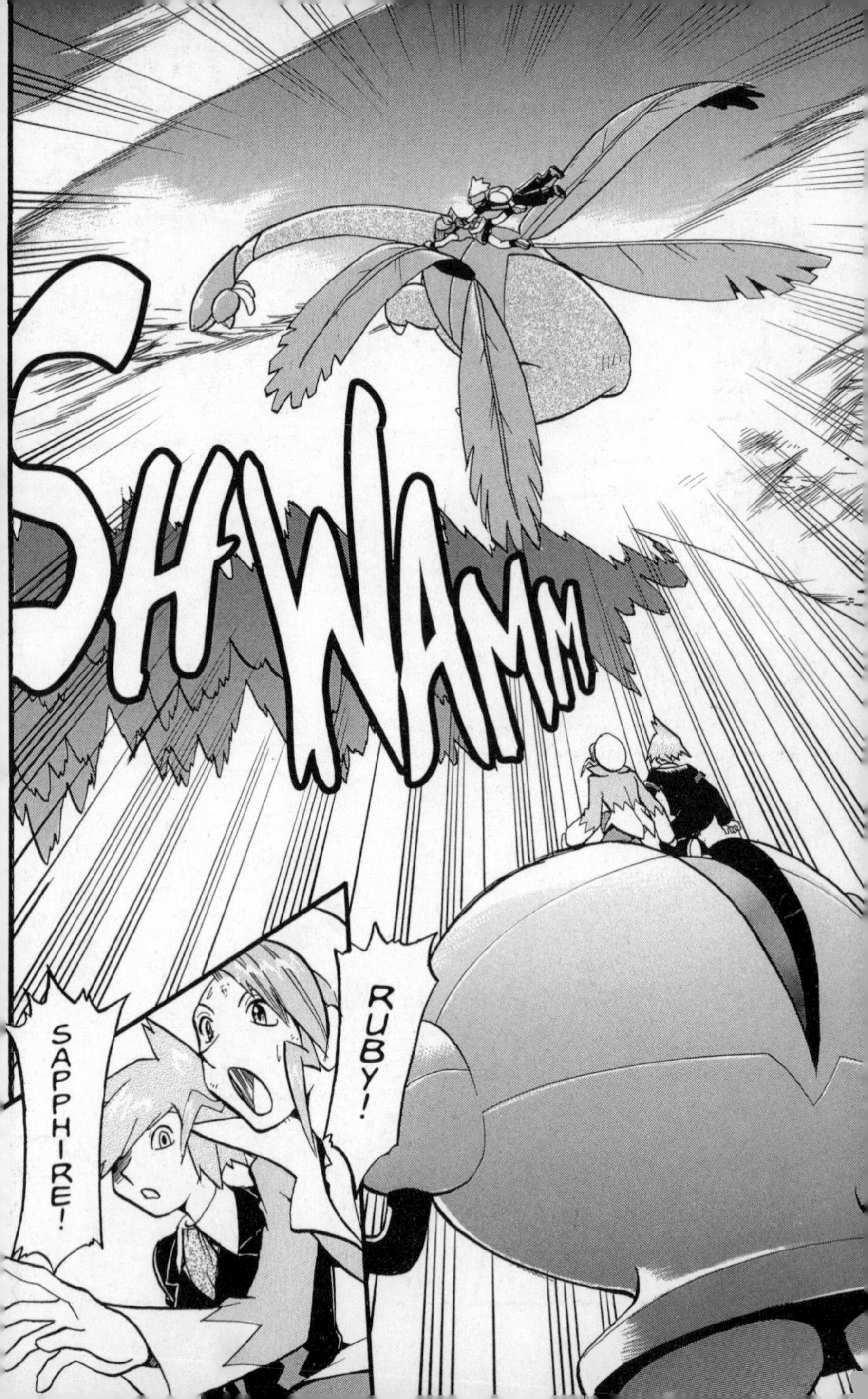
SHWAMM
RUBY!
SAPPHIRE!

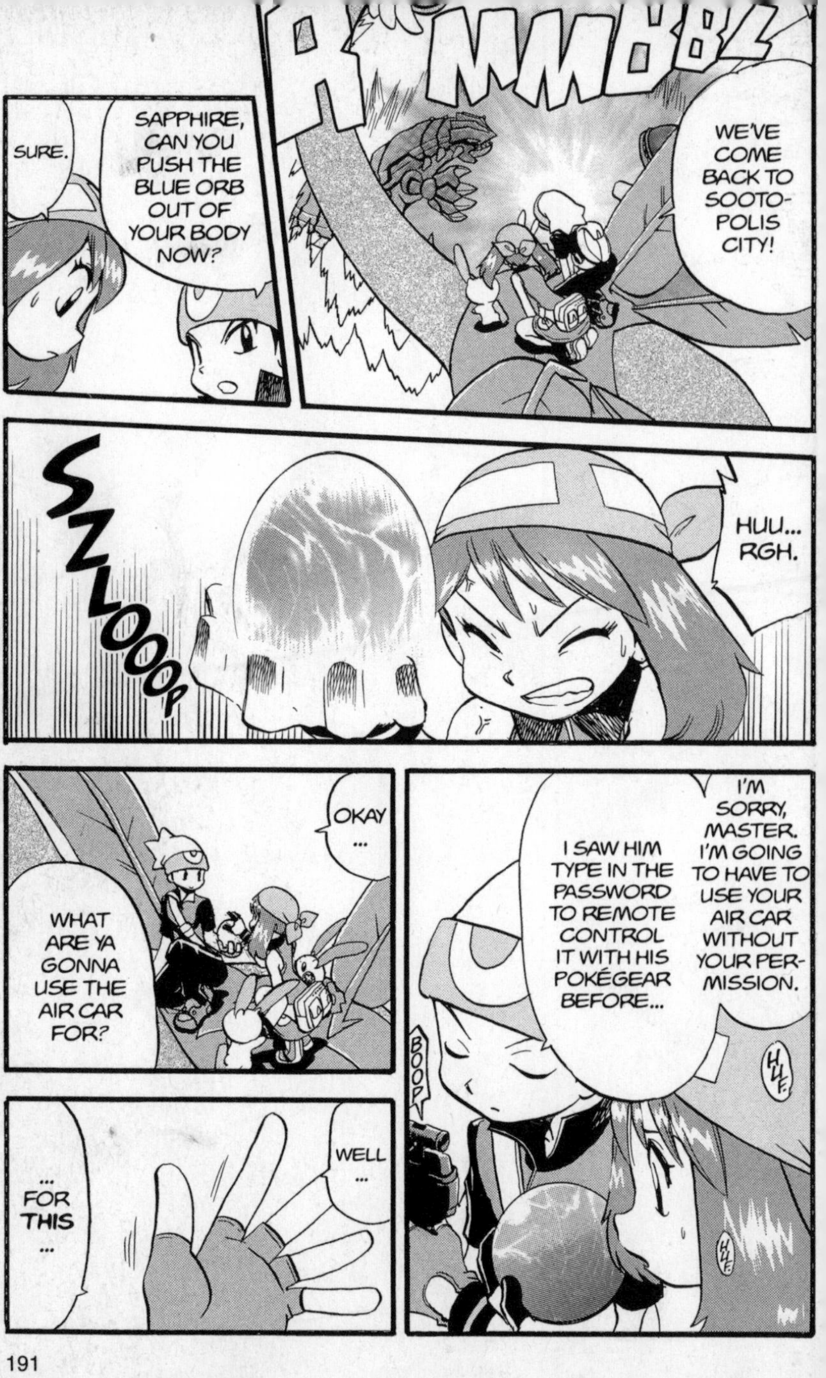
RMMBBZ
WE'VE COME BACK TO SOOTOPOLIS CITY!
SAPPHIRE, CAN YOU PUSH THE BLUE ORB OUT OF YOUR BODY NOW?
SURE.
HUU... RGH.
SZLOOOP
I'M SORRY, MASTER. I'M GOING TO HAVE TO USE YOUR AIR CAR WITHOUT YOUR PERMISSION.
I SAW HIM TYPE IN THE PASSWORD TO REMOTE CONTROL IT WITH HIS POKÉGEAR BEFORE...
BOOP
HUF
HUF
OKAY ...
WHAT ARE YA GONNA USE THE AIR CAR FOR?
WELL ...
... FOR THIS ...

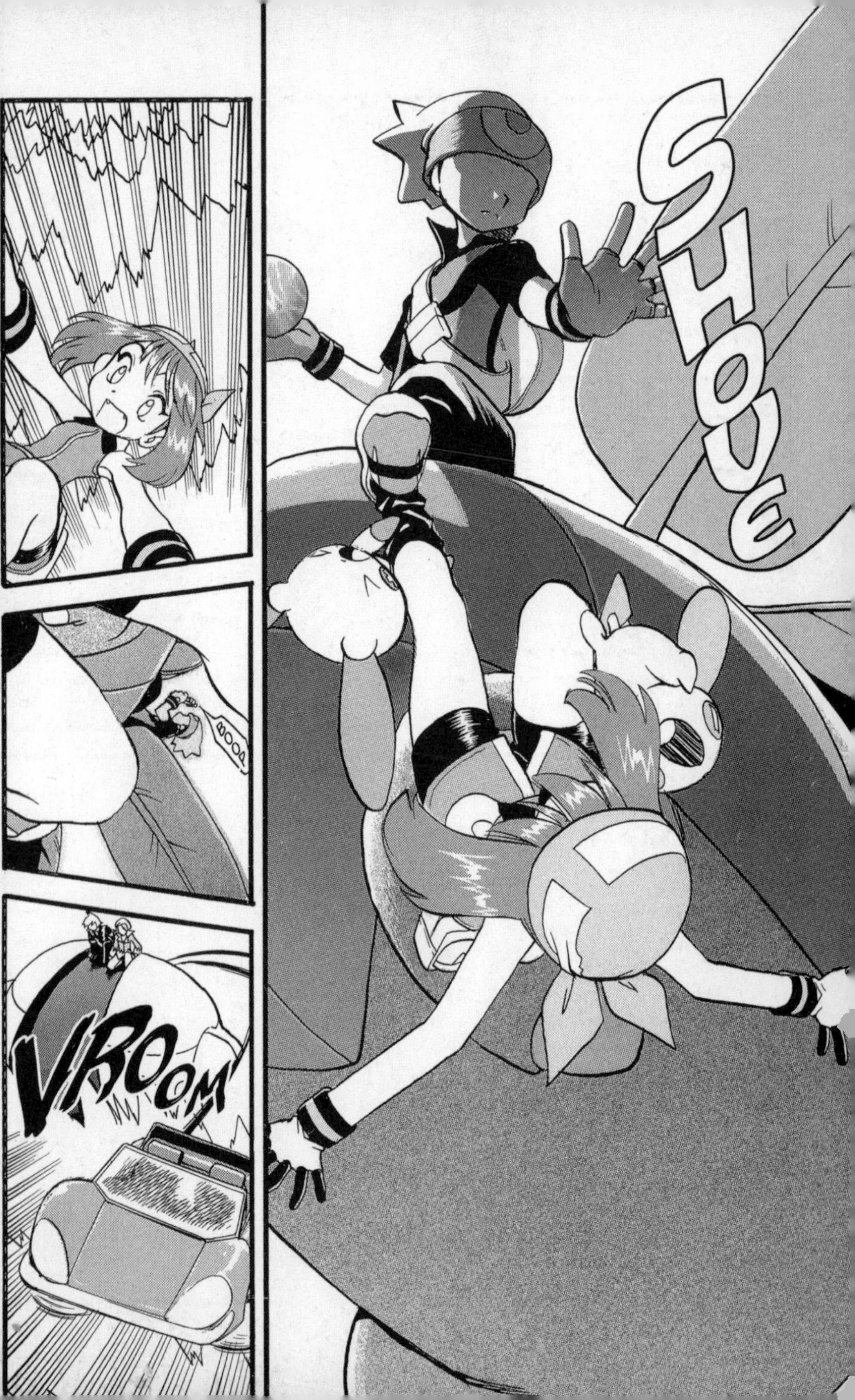
SHOVE
BOOA
VROOM

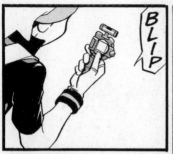

BLIP

FSSSt

WHY?!

WHY ARE YA DOIN' THIS?!

SMAK

SMAK

SMAK

SMAK

I WANT TO THANK YOU. I'M GLAD I ACCEPTED THIS BET.

I REALLY AM.

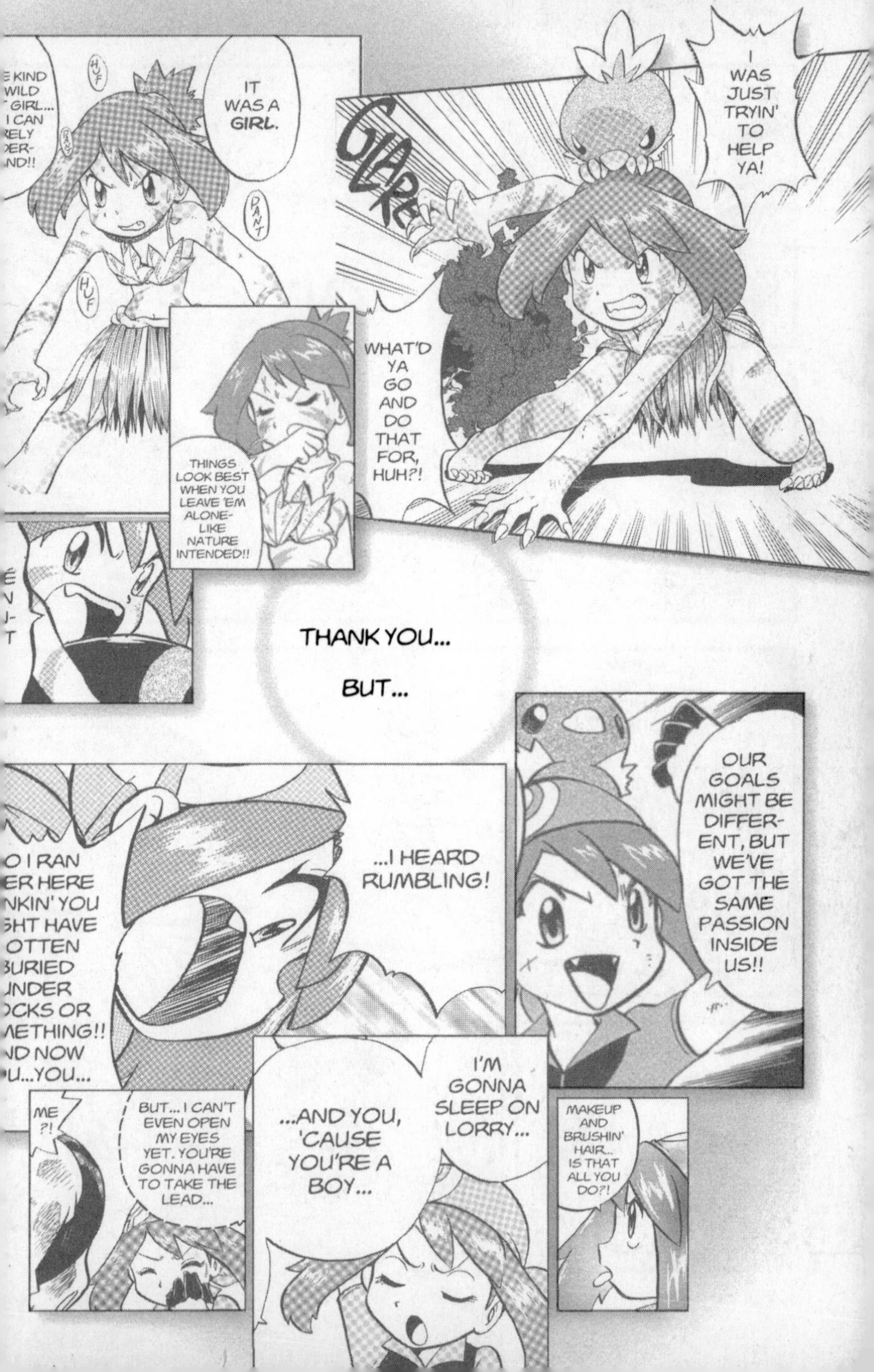
I WAS JUST TRYIN' TO HELP YA!
GLARE
WHAT'D YA GO AND DO THAT FOR, HUH?!
THINGS LOOK BEST WHEN YOU LEAVE 'EM ALONE-LIKE NATURE INTENDED!!
IT WAS A GIRL.
HUF
PANT
HUF
THANK YOU...
BUT...
OUR GOALS MIGHT BE DIFFERENT, BUT WE'VE GOT THE SAME PASSION INSIDE US!!
...I HEARD RUMBLING!
MAKEUP AND BRUSHIN' HAIR... IS THAT ALL YOU DO?!
I'M GONNA SLEEP ON LORRY...
...AND YOU, 'CAUSE YOU'RE A BOY...
BUT... I CAN'T EVEN OPEN MY EYES YET. YOU'RE GONNA HAVE TO TAKE THE LEAD...
ME?!

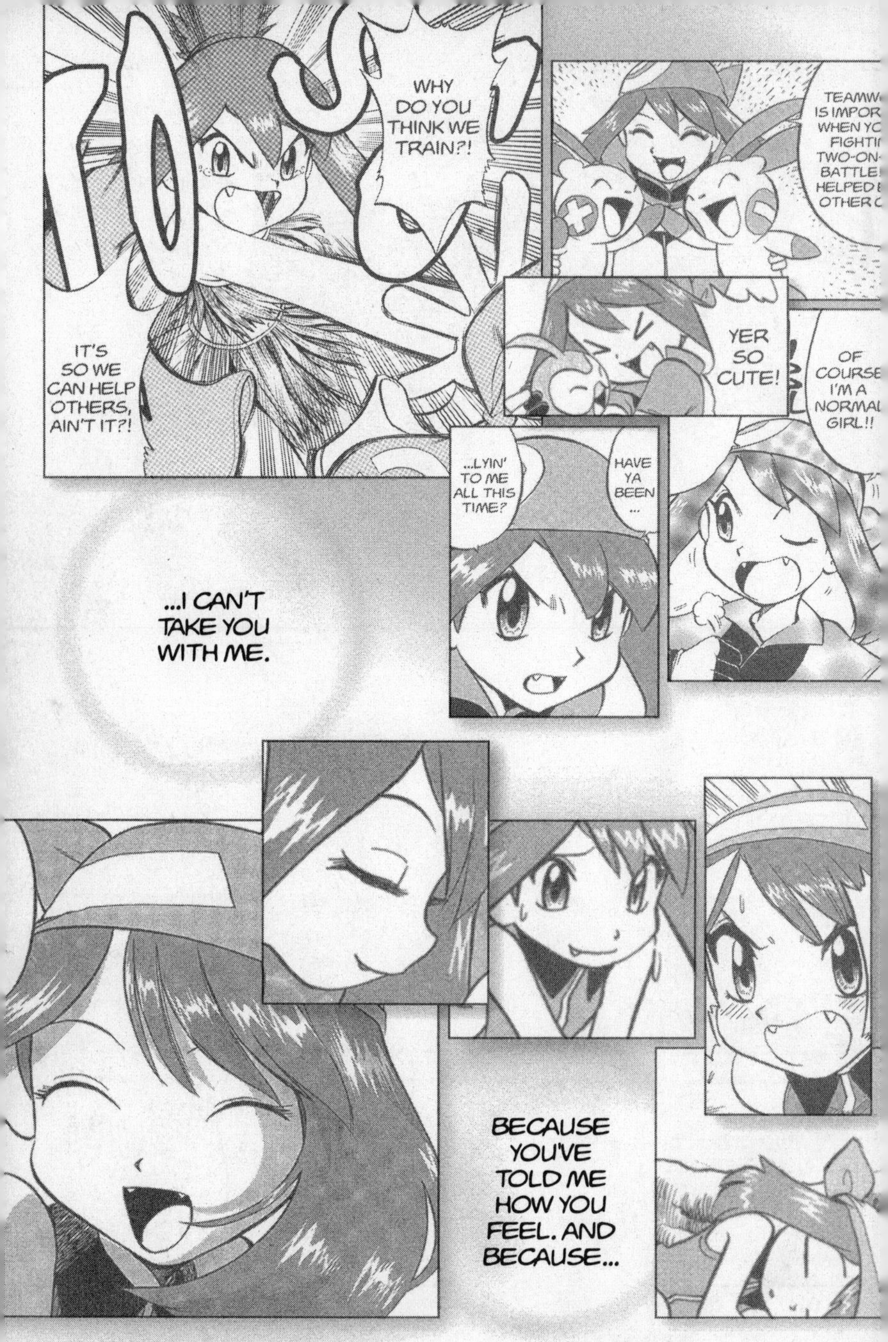
TEAMW IS IMPOR WHEN YO FIGHTI TWO-ON- BATTLE HELPED OTHER C
YER SO CUTE!
OF COURSE I'M A NORMAL GIRL!!
HAVE YA BEEN ...
...LYIN' TO ME ALL THIS TIME?
WHY DO YOU THINK WE TRAIN?!
IT'S SO WE CAN HELP OTHERS, AIN'T IT?!
...I CAN'T TAKE YOU WITH ME.
BECAUSE YOU'VE TOLD ME HOW YOU FEEL. AND BECAUSE...

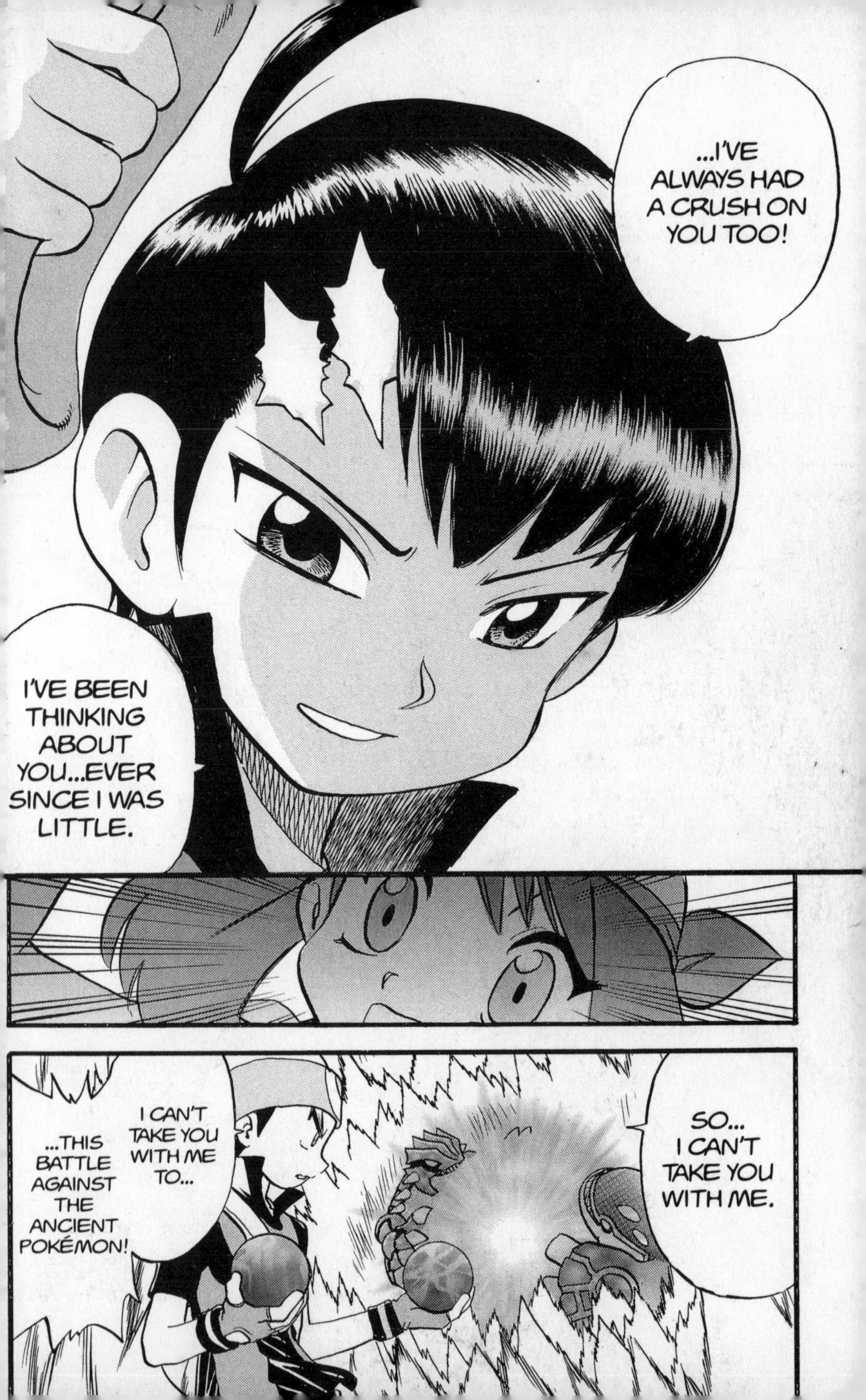
...I'VE ALWAYS HAD A CRUSH ON YOU TOO!
I'VE BEEN THINKING ABOUT YOU...EVER SINCE I WAS LITTLE.
SO... I CAN'T TAKE YOU WITH ME.
I CAN'T TAKE YOU WITH ME TO...
...THIS BATTLE AGAINST THE ANCIENT POKÉMON!

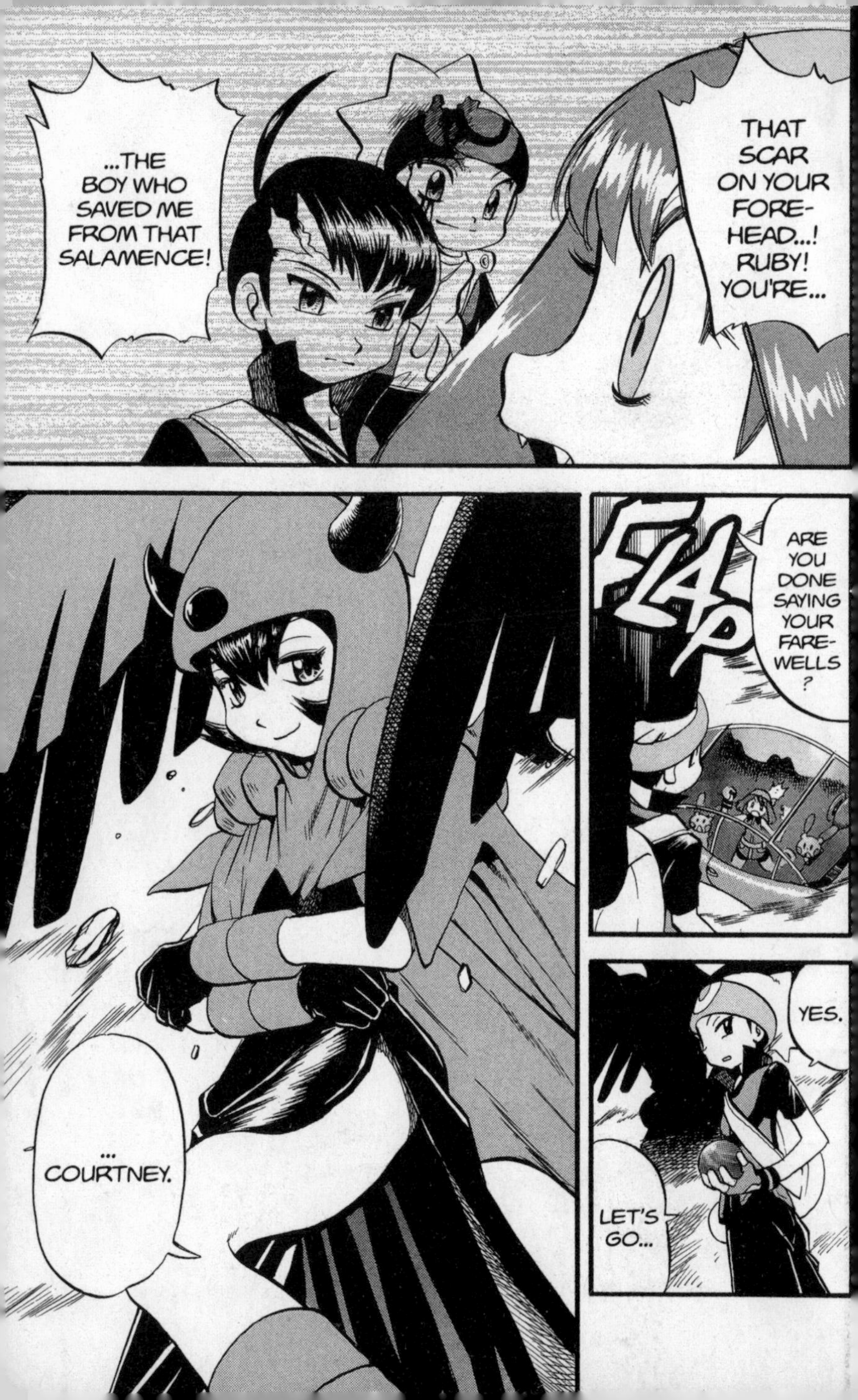
THAT SCAR ON YOUR FORE-HEAD...! RUBY! YOU'RE...
...THE BOY WHO SAVED ME FROM THAT SALAMENCE!
FLAP
ARE YOU DONE SAYING YOUR FARE-WELLS?
YES.
LET'S GO...
...COURTNEY.

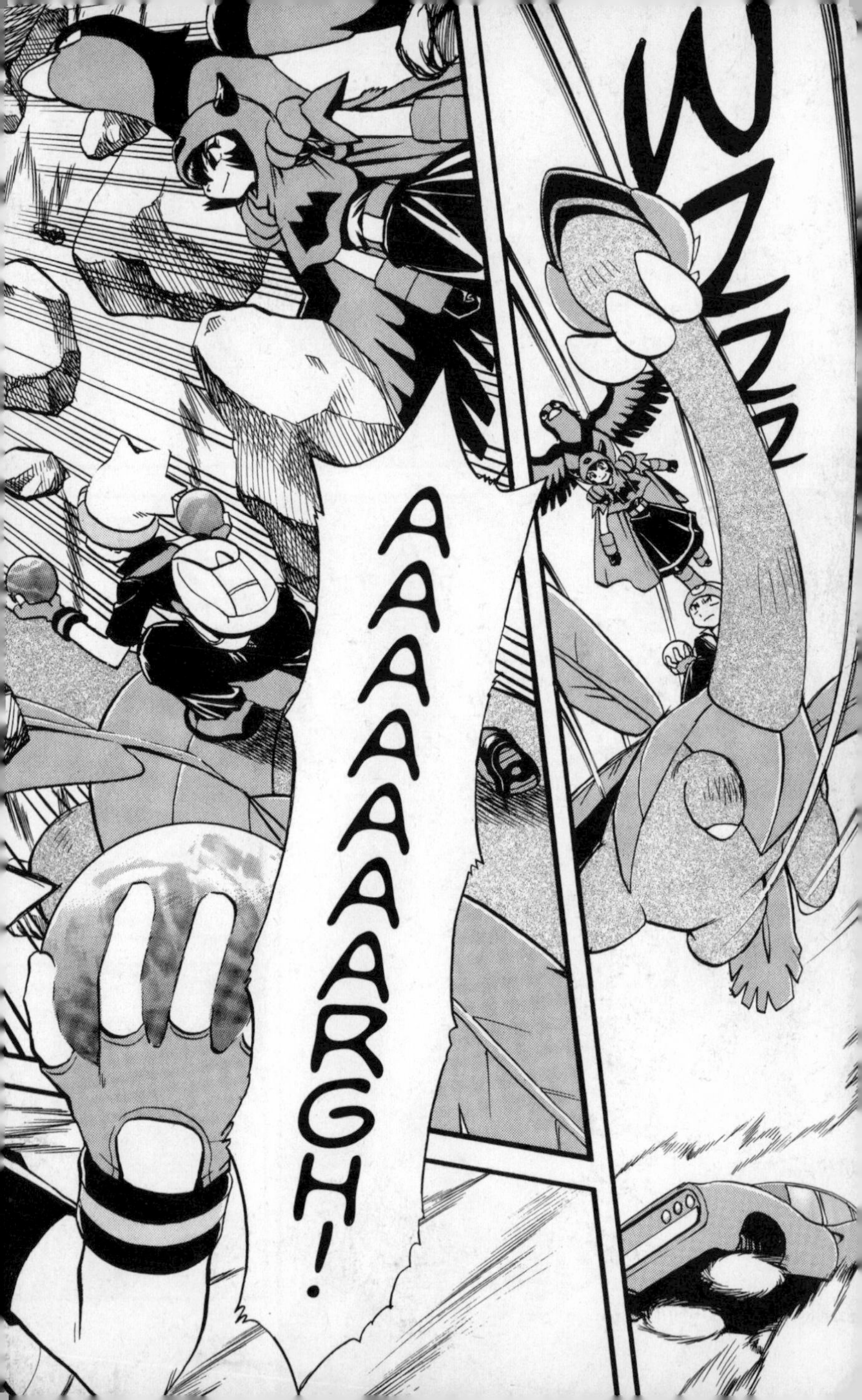
WAAAA
AAAAAAARRGH!

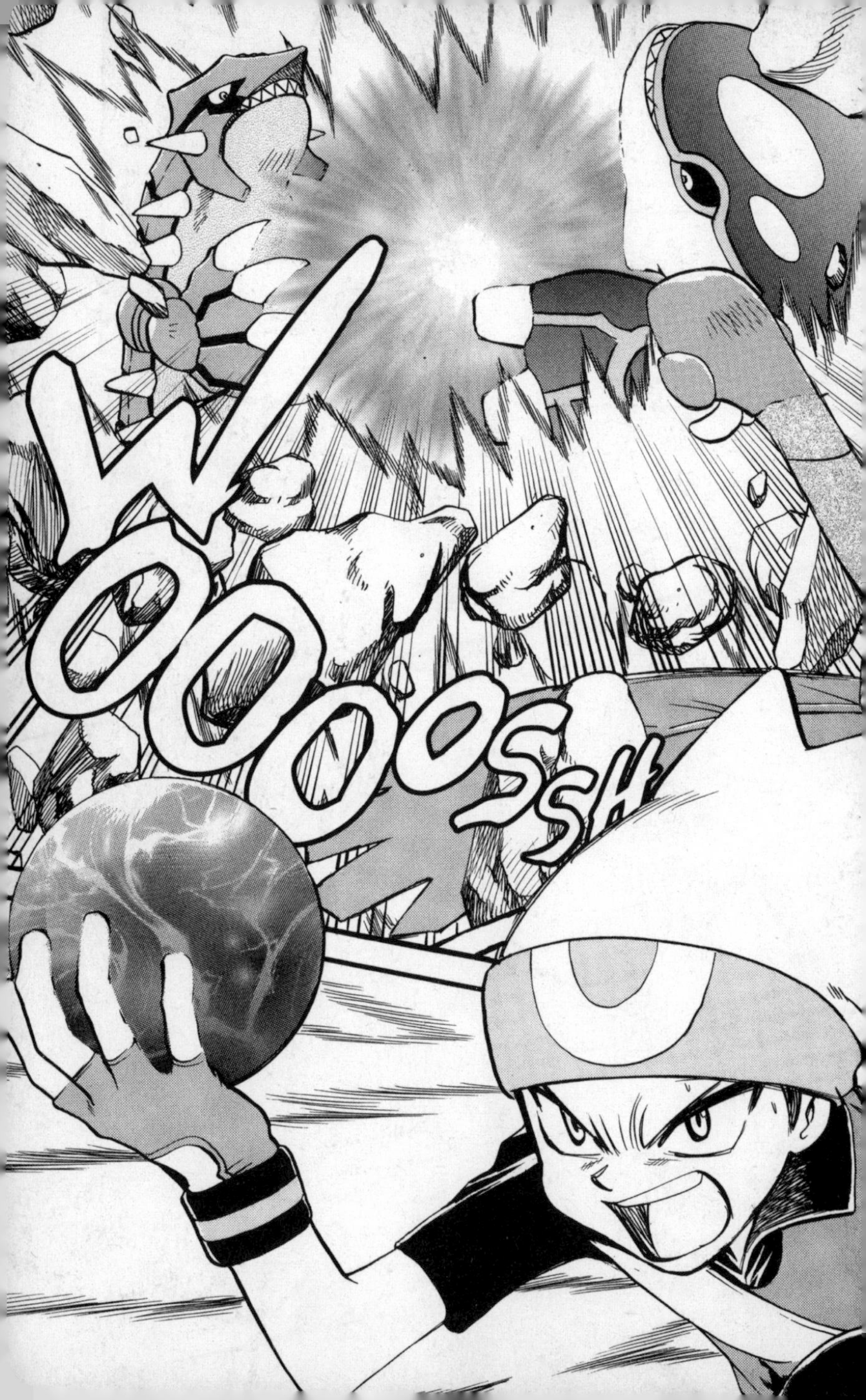
WOOOOOSSH

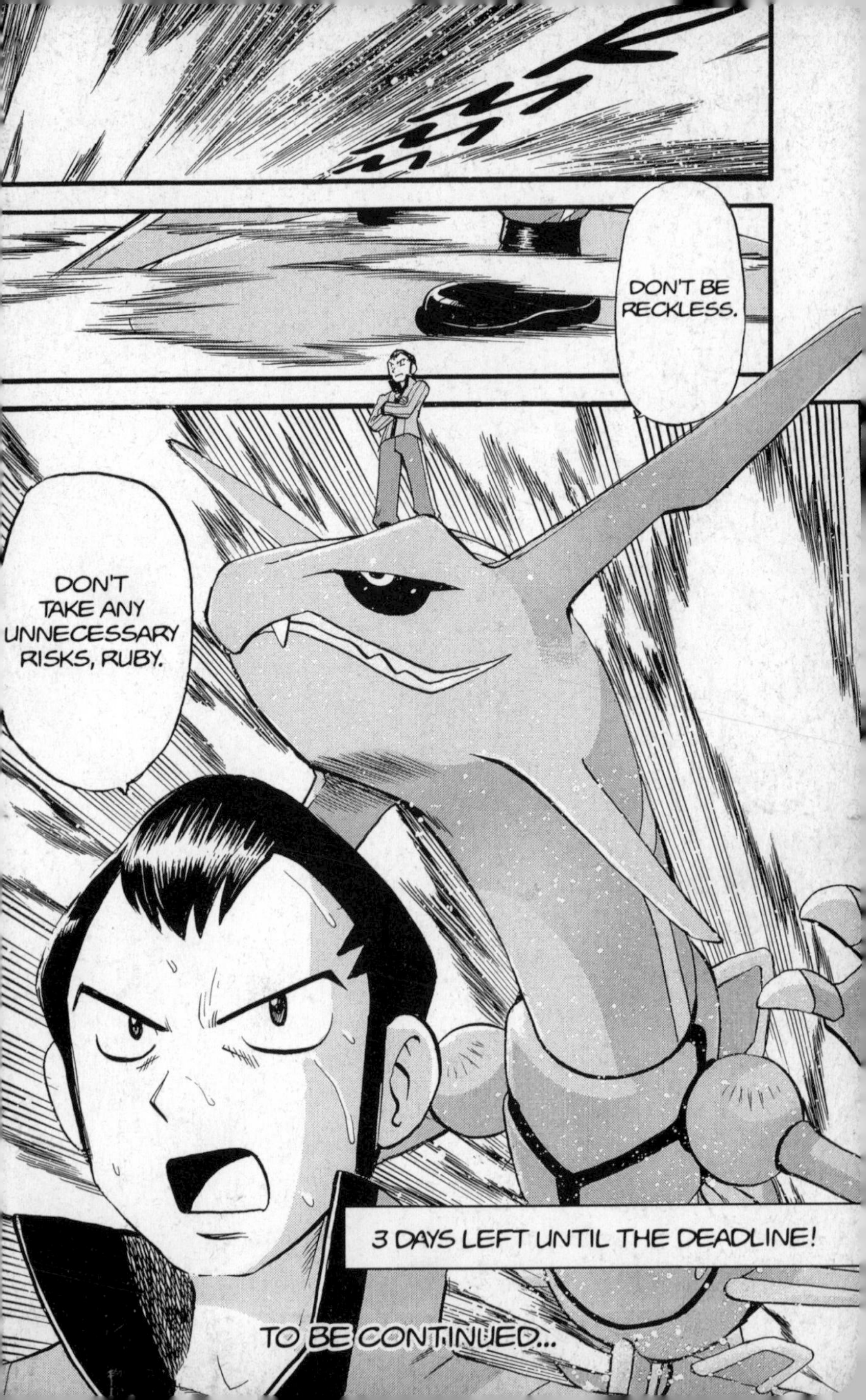
DON'T BE RECKLESS.
DON'T TAKE ANY UNNECESSARY RISKS, RUBY.
3 DAYS LEFT UNTIL THE DEADLINE!
TO BE CONTINUED...

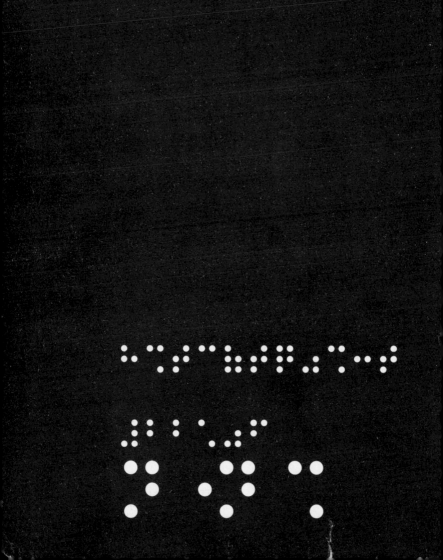

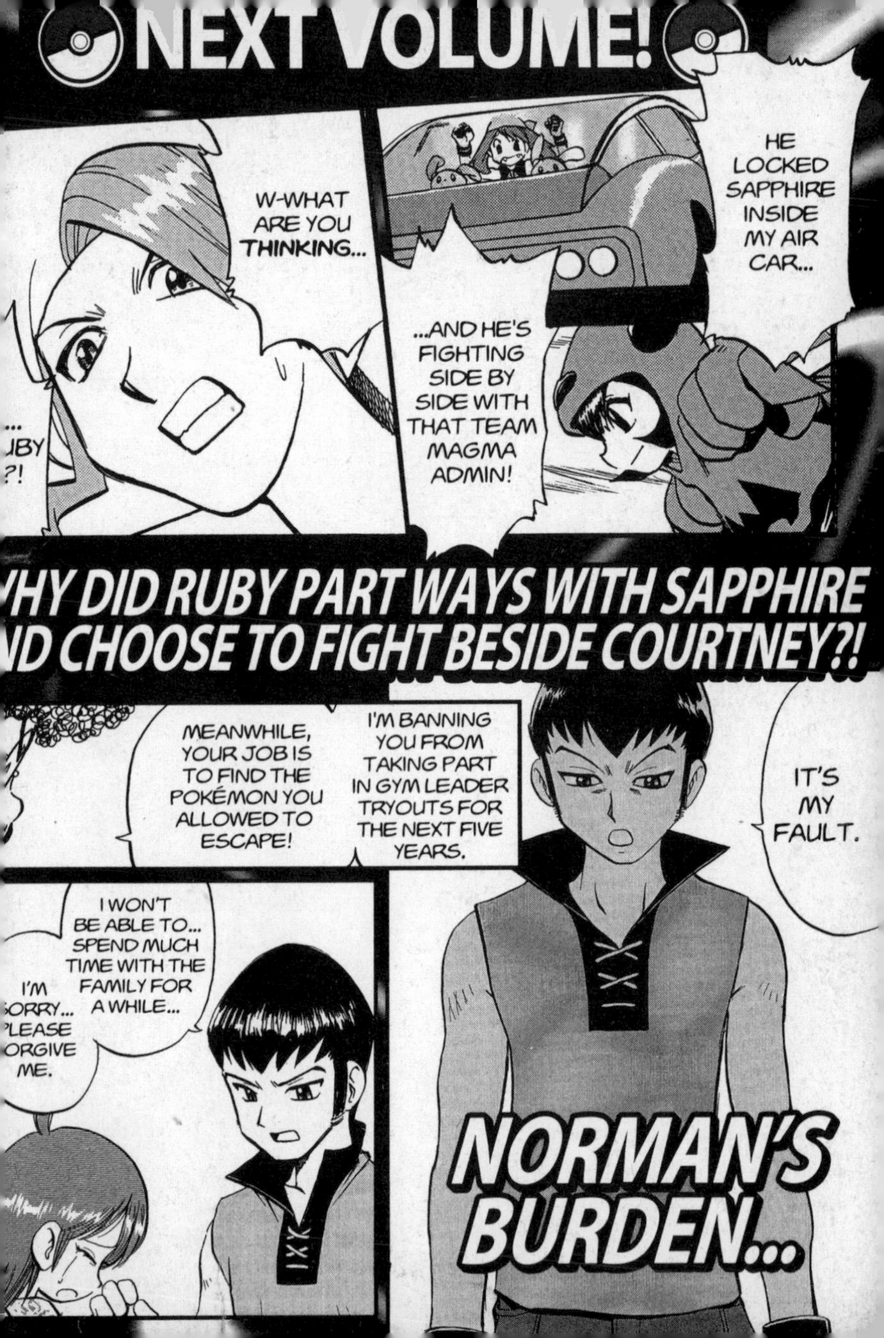
NEXT VOLUME!
HE LOCKED SAPPHIRE INSIDE MY AIR CAR...
...AND HE'S FIGHTING SIDE BY SIDE WITH THAT TEAM MAGMA ADMIN!
W-WHAT ARE YOU THINKING...
... UBY ?!
HY DID RUBY PART WAYS WITH SAPPHIRE
D CHOOSE TO FIGHT BESIDE COURTNEY?!
IT'S MY FAULT.
I'M BANNING YOU FROM TAKING PART IN GYM LEADER TRYOUTS FOR THE NEXT FIVE YEARS.
MEANWHILE, YOUR JOB IS TO FIND THE POKÉMON YOU ALLOWED TO ESCAPE!
NORMAN'S BURDEN...
I WON'T BE ABLE TO... SPEND MUCH TIME WITH THE FAMILY FOR A WHILE...
I'M ORRY... LEASE ORGIVE ME.

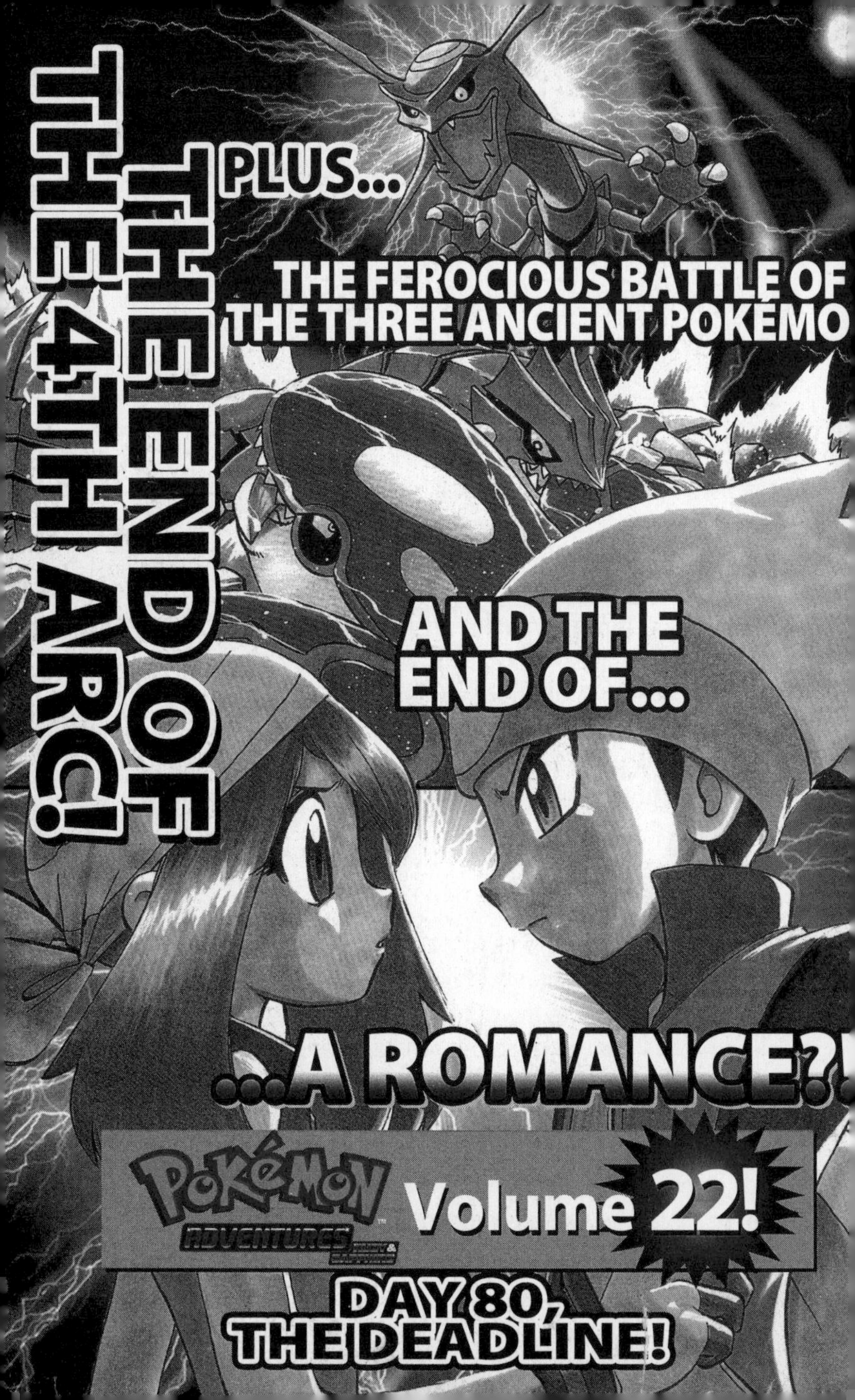
THE END OF THE 4TH ARC!
PLUS...
THE FEROCIOUS BATTLE OF THE THREE ANCIENT POKÉMO
AND THE END OF...
...A ROMANCE?!
POKÉMON ADVENTURES
Volume 22!
DAY 80, THE DEADLINE!

# Message from
## Hidenori Kusaka

The Ruby/Sapphire story arc will be completed in the next two volumes, vols. 21 and 22. Since it's the end of this story, I had Satoshi Yamamoto draw an illustration of Sapphire's complete team for the cover of vol. 21 and Ruby's complete team for the cover of vol. 22. Also, these two illustrations are drawn as a pair and connect at the top! Put the covers of the two volumes together and see for yourselves. This is the climax of the adventure set in the Hoenn region... I hope you enjoy finding out how our heroes fulfill their destiny!

# Message from
## Satoshi Yamamoto

Sorry to keep you waiting!! I now bring you...vol. 21! The story is building up to the climax. This volume is filled with all sorts of major events, such as the appearance of the Elite Four and the Legendary Pokémon. It's packed with even more excitement than the last volume! Also, you'll learn about Ruby and Sapphire's past. I drew the scenes with passion in hopes of knocking your socks off, so please be careful not to get motion sickness as you read the scenes. (LOL)

# More Adventures Coming Soon...

As the battle between Legendary Pokémon Groudon and Kyogre rages on, so does the battle to control the orbs that control them. Then, when tragedy strikes, long hidden secrets are revealed... and Ruby comes to a profound realization.

Now, what role will Ruby's secret sixth Pokémon play in turning things around...?!

**AVAILABLE MAY 2014!**

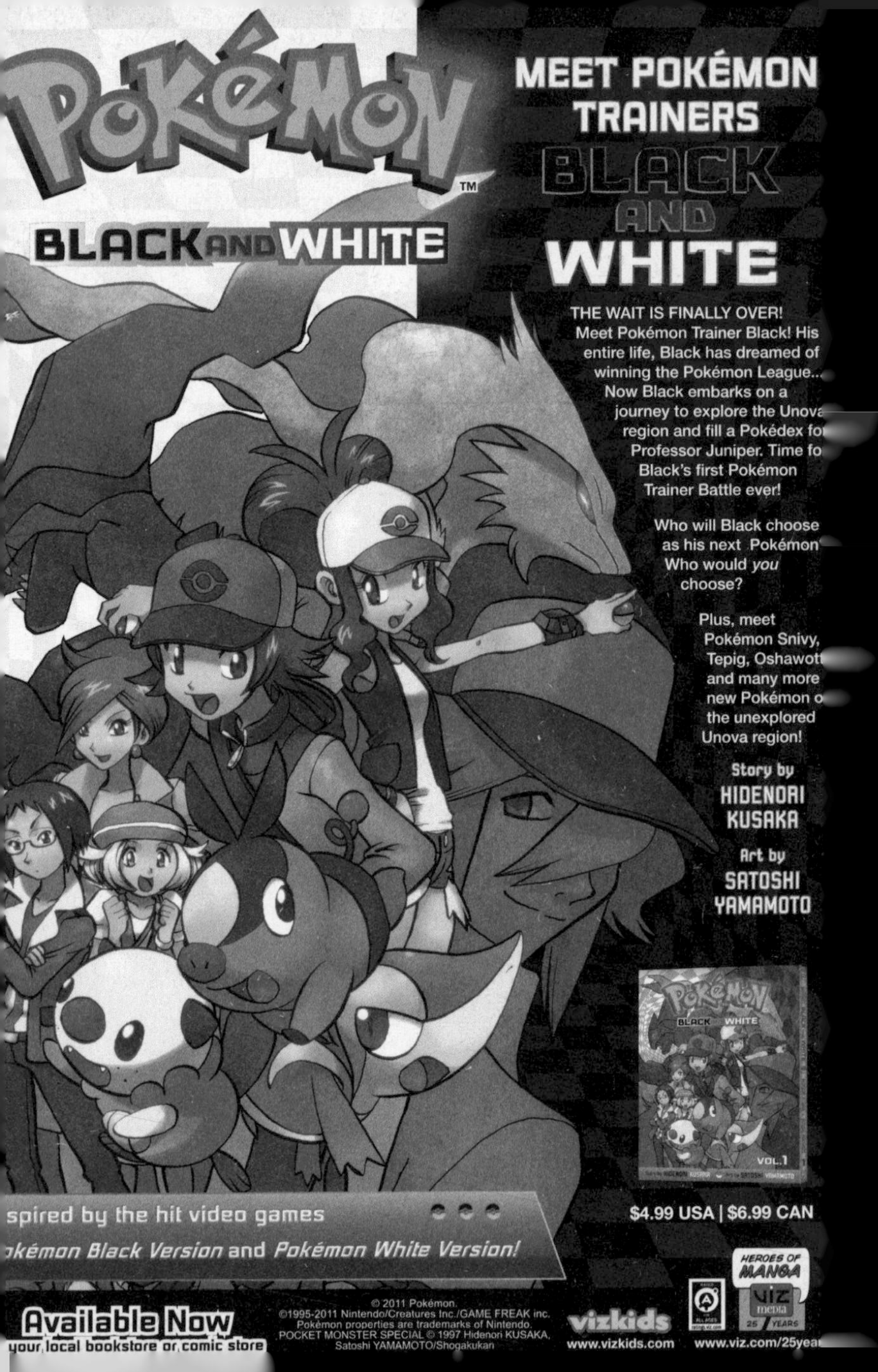

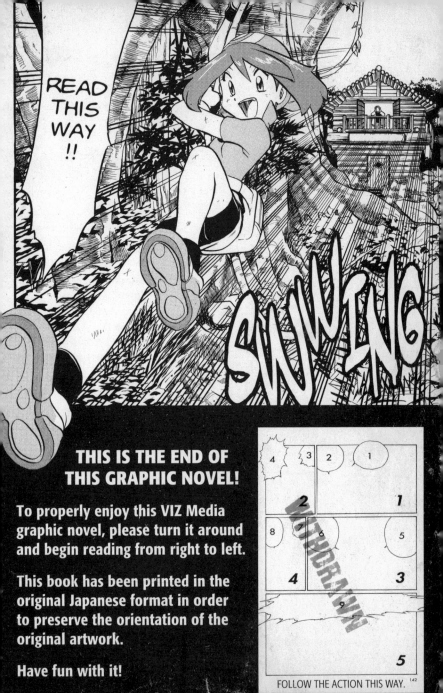

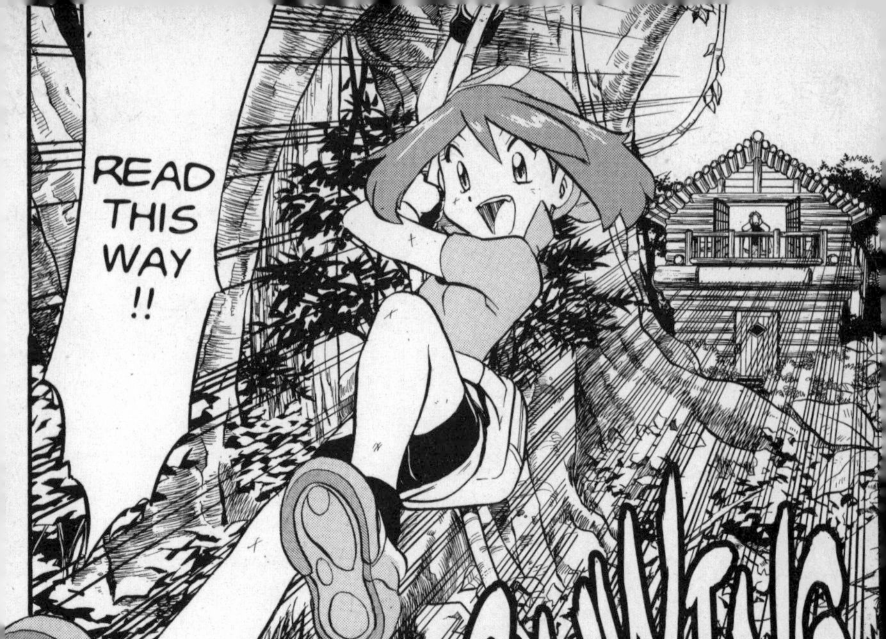
READ THIS WAY !!
SWWING

## THIS IS THE END OF THIS GRAPHIC NOVEL!

To properly enjoy this VIZ Media graphic novel, please turn it around and begin reading from right to left.

This book has been printed in the original Japanese format in order to preserve the orientation of the original artwork.

Have fun with it!

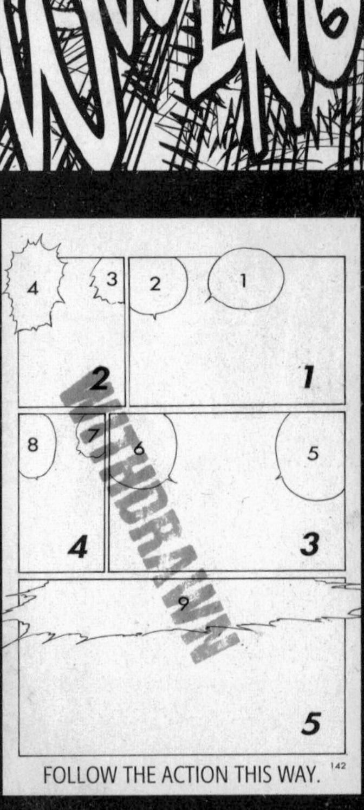
1
2
3
4
5
6
7
8
9
1
2
3
4
5


FOLLOW THE ACTION THIS WAY.